Philip Spires, born in 1............orkshire, spent his first ten years in Sharlst............ining village, followed by eight in Crofton, a mile nearer Wakefield. He went to London University, where he obtained a BSc from Imperial College and a PGCE from King's. After two years as a VSO in Kenya, he taught in London for 16 years and devoted much of his spare time to assisting an NGO concerned with development and human rights. In 1992, after completing an MA, he worked in Brunei technical education. From 1999 he worked in Zayed University in the United Arab Emirates. Since 2003, he has lived in Spain, and has completed a PhD in education's role in Philippine development and his first published novel, **Mission**.

www.philipspires.co.uk

The right of Philip Spires to be identified as the Author of this Work has been asserted by him in accordance with the Copyright, Designs and Patents Act 1998.

Copyright © Philip Spires 2007

All characters in this publication are fictitious and resemblance to real persons, living or dead, is purely coincidental.

All rights reserved. No part of this publication may be reproduced, stored in a retrieval system, or transmitted, in any form or by any means without the prior written permission of the publisher, nor be otherwise circulated in any form of binding or cover other than that in which it is published and without a similar condition being imposed on the subsequent purchaser. Any person who does so may be liable to criminal prosecution and civil claims for damages.

ISBN 1-905988-07-9   978-1-905988-07-5

Book Cover: adapted from an original oil painting by Kaizala

Published by Libros International

www.librosinternational.com

Mission

Philip Spires

Libros International

Acknowledgements

With thanks to all involved with Libros International and, in particular, to Carol Griffith for her careful editing.

*In human works, tho' labour'd on with pain,
A thousand movements scarce one purpose gain;
In God's, one single can its end produce;
Yet serves to second too some other use.
So man, who here seems principal alone,
Perhaps acts second to some sphere unknown,
Touches some wheel, or verges to some goal;
'Tis but part we see, and not a whole.*

**Alexander Pope (1688 – 1744)
'Essay on Man'**

Contents

Michael	13
Mulonzya	99
Janet	183
Boniface	263
Munyasya	341

For Caroline

Michael

Enter Michael, dishevelled and panting. His movements are hurried, agitated and anxious. The kitchen door creaks on its hinges after his disinterested push. It does not close and it swings ajar behind him. In an instant, Michael has crossed the room as if out of a desire to distance himself from some pursuer, but now he is cornered. He stops, thinks for a moment and, realising the futility of trying to run away, returns to the door. He pauses there and, with his head cocked on one side, listens intently, trying to discern the frantic sounds of a shouted argument taking place outside. The sounds are dulled and muffled by echoes, but he stays where he is, afraid to approach them. There are several voices: at least five are shouting in apparent opposition without any one gaining the ascendancy. Thus all blend to form a single, incoherent and meaningless noise. Trying to listen is pointless and so, with a rueful shake of the head, he advances into the room again, but this time he moves more slowly, with greater resignation, beneath some weight.

He decides to sit but cannot relax. Perched on the very edge of the settee, he leans forward with his head bowed and his hands resting on his knees. He seems poised to act but is powerless. He can do nothing, now. It is too late. Still without success he tries again to make sense of the garbled noise from outside. Although he knows what is being said, he is still curious to hear, to eavesdrop on this mêlée which is surely about him and him alone. He becomes so engrossed in what he thinks he can hear in the waves of sound, that he remains quite oblivious to his own discomfort. He is sweating profusely and his tanned face is flushed red. He remains totally engrossed until a drop of perspiration runs down the side of his nose. It tickles. A facial muscle twitches and his hand involuntarily rises to scratch.

Partly out of tiredness, partly out of frustration, he continues to rub hard at his cheek long after the discomfort has waned and then he wipes his brow. For a moment he studies the beads of sweat which now glisten on his fingers and then, sighing resignedly through pursed lips, he finally removes his camouflage hat and uses it to fan himself. All thoughts of immediate discomfort are dispelled by the sound of an animated crescendo in the argument outside. Again he listens intently, but still only deciphers an odd expected word. Apparently without knowing, he twists his hat into a tight ball and does not let go. He is powerless in his frustration.

Gradually he becomes aware of his tiredness. Sitting back on the settee, he rests his head. For a few brief moments he sifts through his recollections of the day behind closed eyes. As if to confirm this unfortunate reality, he tries to reorder his memories, to analyse them, perhaps understand them, but even the most recent are clouded in doubt and all paths lead inexorably toward the same unfortunate end.

Tension again refuses him any relaxation. His eyes open and glance toward the sideboard beneath the iron-framed window. He stands, impatiently discards his crumpled hat without bothering to look where it lands and crosses the room. From within the sideboard he selects a small dainty glass - a sherry schooner, which happened to be the nearest - and proceeds to examine the labels of the numerous bottles. Just as he had expected, tucked away at the back of the cupboard for safety's sake, he finds John O'Hara's private store of poteen. The harsh liquor seems to clear his mind. The act of drinking, itself, seems to demand his total concentration; demands it so completely that he seems to be lost in some judgment of the quality of the brew as he savours every remnant of its taste. For a while he can ignore the complications of the moment as his thoughts follow the inch-by-inch progress of the liquid in his dust-dried throat. Slowly, thoughtfully, he wanders back to the settee, taking the glass and bottle with him, apparently only partly conscious of what he is doing, as if he might just have forgotten to let go of them. He seems to be consciously trying to exclude the here and now. His eyes are blank, as if his thoughts are removed to another time or place. But the voices are impossible to ignore. They will not go away.

This time he is determined to relax, to ignore the noise before it destroys him. Having poured another whiskey and lit a cigarette, he begins to feel at least a little easier through the exhaustion. So, lying spread-eagled across the settee with one foot resting on the Bishop's coffee table, he begins to doze. Consequently, he does not notice, after only a few moments, that the argument subsides. For him, it merely continues, apparently as it has done already for so long. The oft-repeated words and familiar pictures continue to fill his head and render him oblivious to all else. He is not even conscious that the kitchen door is opening.

Enter John O'Hara, Bishop of Kitui. Like Michael's, his movements too are hurried, but unlike Michael's, their impatience is clearly born of great anger. His face too is flushed red, but his expression testifies to the frustration that reels inside him without release. His gaze darts about the room like that of a cornered animal, but then fixes with an intensifying glare on Michael. Carefully, O'Hara moves away from the door and faces the settee, moving silently save for the light rustling of his white nylon robe. Even his usual wheezy breathing is suppressed and inaudible. He stands by the low table staring at Michael for some time and, though he grows visibly more impatient with the passing of every second, he makes no attempt to rouse the priest from his apparent comfort.

Eventually Michael opens his eyes and sees O'Hara standing before him, hands on his hips and face set in condemnation. Michael hurriedly tries to stand but O'Hara's cold and calculated words pre-empt any movement.

"Oh no, don't get up, Michael," he says, sarcastically. "Don't let me disturb you. Sleep on. Sleep as long as you like. I'll pick up the pieces." As Michael stands, O'Hara turns aside offering a dismissive gesture of the hand.

"What happened out there?" Michael's manner is again nervous and hurried. His face is tense as he looks across to O'Hara who is now staring through the French windows into the garden, with his back squarely offered to the room. A number of near-explosive ripe passion fruit frame the view.

O'Hara does not answer immediately. He is obviously trying hard not to over-react, which under the circumstances would be his normal reaction. But he loses his battle with himself and turns in anger to face Michael. "Didn't you just look the perfect picture?" O'Hara casts a long and condemnatory stare, but now Michael simply turns away. Both men know they are now following a script, which has been enacted before in less exacting circumstances.

As O'Hara continues, Michael turns his back and slowly walks around the back of the settee. Though he is obviously trying to ignore the criticism, every word bites deep and causes much pain. "You have just murdered some poor wretch out there. You leave me to carry the can and then wander in here, help yourself to my whiskey and calmly go to sleep on the sofa... as if nothing had happened!" O'Hara's voice begins to break with emotion.

Michael too seems ready to explode with anger. He turns to face O'Hara and, counting out each point on his fingers for added emphasis, shouts his reply. "One: I have murdered no one. Two: you ordered me in here because you said I was getting in your way. Three: if you had any idea what I have been through recently, and today in particular, you would begrudge me nothing!"

O'Hara displays a complete lack of respect for Michael's point of view. Shaking his head, he turns away impatiently and says, "Michael, a dozen people or more witnessed what happened. If what they say is true, you're in deep trouble. Don't you see that?" O'Hara's pleading eyes demand that Michael should accept reason.

"And what about my version? Aren't you interested in that? Don't you believe me?"

"It's not a question of what I believe. All I want to know is what happened so I can decide what we ought or ought not to do." His fists are now clenched in despair. He wants to help, but all Michael's actions seem to reject every offer. Perhaps he is not worth the trouble. O'Hara cannot begin to understand why his priest seems to resent any help or advice he is offered.

During the strained silence that follows, both men appear to grow calmer. It is possibly fatigue that has silenced them. For an hour or more they have stood in the sun to argue with a shouting and hostile crowd. Pure shock has taxed Michael's strength. Self-pity, a product of the frustration at being cornered, has sapped most of O'Hara's strength. He slumps in the chair beside the French windows and buries his face in his hands. Michael stares at him at first. This is perhaps the first time he has ever seen the man admit any limitation. But then, as if through guilt, his gaze drops. He runs his fingers through his hair and bows his head. His hand grasps the back of his neck almost aggressively. He is powerless now.

After some minutes of silence, O'Hara sits up in his chair, takes a deep wheezing breath and then speaks in a changed voice. Clearly he has used the pause to discipline his emotions. "Sit down, Michael. Sit down. Let's go through the whole story. No one can interrupt you now." As Michael returns to his place on the settee, O'Hara lights a cigarette. His voice is suddenly ever so slightly paternalistic and falsely reassuring, which suggests to Michael that his mind is already made up. "Let's start right from the beginning." O'Hara leans forward with his palms outstretched, preaching.

Michael vacillates for a moment, but then resignedly decides that whatever the outcome, he is trapped. In the current debacle, O'Hara is his one and only potential ally. He tries to cast his mind back several hours to that morning, but finds it difficult to remember anything with clarity. "My mind's gone completely blank." O'Hara watches him reach for the bottle to refill his glass.

"You've been drinking far too much of late."

Michael glances across at him. Conflicting emotions force two instinctive replies to the forefront of his mind. He wants to tell O'Hara in no uncertain terms to mind his own business, to counter threat with threat, but his conscience knows that the Bishop is right. In silence, he continues to fill his glass with whiskey, but his internally acknowledged guilt shows through as attempted defiance.

"I thought you would have realised long ago, Michael, that you have no secrets here. Reports about you have been reaching me for some time now and, as you know, if it has reached me..."

"... Every other muckraker in the district knows already. I seem to have heard that somewhere before," says Michael with deep and angry sarcasm.

O'Hara is much calmer now and does not accept the obvious invitation to argument. Again he tries to defuse the tension that still threatens to break Michael's voice. "You're not doing yourself any good at all, Michael." The older man's words seem to be weighted with wisdom. He takes his chance. "We've got to start somewhere. Why don't you start by telling me why you drove into town today?"

Michael barely hesitates here. It is clear that, though there is a gulf between them, he retains an ultimate trust of the Bishop's intentions. "All right, John -" his voice is suddenly and unpredictably animated, " - but I've explained all this once when I made my statement to that whore of a policeman." O'Hara remains vigilant. His silence tells Michael not only that this makes no difference to his desire to hear it again, but also that this time there will be more space. Inwardly, Michael is deeply grateful for this.

"All right. First of all, you will remember that about a year ago my

Thitani catechist's wife had a baby?" Michael looks up and sees O'Hara nod. "Well there were complications. It finished up with me rushing the two of them, Boniface and his wife to Muthale. It turned out to be a breech birth and Sister Mary had to do a Caesarean. She needed some blood so I gave it. Anyway the result of it all was both mother and child survived. Now as you will know I have always had a very good relationship with Boniface..."

"Yes I know him. He's a fine, fine man." For just a moment, O'Hara is trying to picture Boniface Mutisya. He sieves through recollections of the numerous reports relayed by Michael, which have spoken consistently of the young catechist's devoted and conscientious work in Thitani.

Michael then continues. "Well the fact that his child would have died without my help - without my blood - has made me in his eyes almost a member of the family." He pauses for a moment. His frustration begins to return as he realises that all this is nothing more than irrelevant. It is mere background, no more than the mechanics of how he came to be in the wrong place at the wrong time. He looks up toward John O'Hara with an expression of almost complete hopelessness.

"Go on Michael. It's all important."

With his eyes momentarily closed, he continues, but now more slowly, less impetuously. "I suppose you know that the child has been sick for some time. I was over in Thitani last week and even then the poor thing looked all but finished. I told Boniface that if things were to get any worse he should come to see me straight away and I would take them all to the hospital. Well, he came to me this morning."

At first John O'Hara nods, but his expression quickly changes to one of confusion. "I'm sorry, Michael," he says, holding up his hand to enforce a pause in the story, "but why didn't you go to Muthale? Why come all the way to Kitui?"

An ironic smile spreads across Michael's face as he stares pensively at the floor by his feet. He shakes his head as he frantically searches for a simple answer to the question. He can see a clear and tangible motive for his decision, but how can he possibly communicate it? Frustration tightens his grip on a handful of his own hair and his face apparently grimaces in pain; but, for all his efforts, all he can muster in reply is "Oh shit, where the hell do I start?" He looks up, apparently in search of help, though quite obviously without expecting to receive any. He is stunned by O'Hara's calculated prompt.

"It has something to do with Miss Rowlandson, I think?"

With both surprise and contempt, Michael bursts out into a histrionic, sighing laugh. "You really do keep your eyes and ears propped open, don't you?"

"Eyes, Michael, not ears. I'm not, and never have been, interested in idle gossip, but I know that Miss Rowlandson has been in some kind of trouble. You've been expecting a letter from her for some time."

Sheer astonishment brings an involuntary smile to Michael's face, but as O'Hara continues it fades to be replaced by an expression closer to hopelessness.

"Whether or not you realise it, you've been going around in a dream for weeks. Privately I have been very worried about you." A slight scoff from Michael causes O'Hara to speak more sternly. "Should I say then that I have felt a lot of sympathy for you. I know what it's like to be in a position like that..."

"I doubt it." Michael is mumbling sarcastically.

"Well let me tell you, I do know. And let me tell you something else. Your letter came to my post-box by mistake. I don't know why it happened, because it was correctly addressed, but you know as well as I do that things often go astray across the road in the post office. Anyway, after I'd put it in the Migwani pigeonhole down at the mission, I came back here to find Pat waiting for me with his parish accounts. I asked him to call in at the mission, pick up the letter and then to drop it in to you on his way up north. He obviously forgot. He left here in a hurry, you see, to collect his messages from Hassan before he closed the shop for siesta. It must just have slipped his mind."

"Well it did and it didn't, it seems. He forgot the letter, all right, and then, when he called in on me late last night, he suddenly remembered he'd left it behind. Typical fucking Irishman. 'Now I remember', he says. 'I've forgotten your letter. It's in the mission in your box. I was supposed to bring it'. I almost set off for town there and then, but it was really late and I'd been out on the bike all day. I was just too tired... and Pat and I had finished the whole bottle." The last phrase was delivered silently.

"All right, Michael, never mind the ifs and buts. So you decided to leave it until this morning. Now carry on..."

"I got up especially early. I just couldn't wait to get into town. I was ready to set off at seven. It was then that Boniface arrived looking very flustered, the poor sod."

***

'Wednesday
My dear Michael
I shouldn't really be trying to write this - I'm in no fit state. If it all sounds a bit strange, then put it down to the Valium. I've been on them for a week - but I thought I'd better write to keep you in the picture. I know you'll be worrying, but really there's no need.

Funny, I can hardly remember where I got to in the last letter. Oh yes, I need to explain all that first. I tried to finish that letter dozens of times, but I never really succeeded. I kept having to add bits as things developed. It must have given you quite a shock. In all, that letter covered over a month - about five weeks, I think, between the first and the last tests. I really was in a terrible state when I first got those results. I knew I was pregnant all along. That's why I couldn't bring myself to believe the negative results of the others. My periods always have been irregular, but somehow I knew it was different this time. But even then, when I'd seen it written down in black and white, I still couldn't accept it was going to happen. I suppose I wasn't quite with it anyway. Pete, bless him, got me some Valium, because my nerves were just so on edge. I can remember sitting in front of the doctor's desk and him handing me a slip of paper with my results on it. I remember that he asked me about Pete and I somehow managed in a few sentences to tell him virtually everything I have ever told you in two years' worth of letters. God knows how I did it. I can't remember a word of what I said. Things are just the same, by the way. As usual he has been a godsend as far as helping me to get by is concerned but, again as always, on his own terms. He just refuses to talk about the baby in any way whatsoever. It's as if it didn't exist. In fact, you know, you're the only other person who knows about it apart from him and myself and my doctor. I certainly can't tell my mother. I just couldn't face her. I've been so stupid. You know I can't help laughing at times. It's nearly two years since I saw you but yet I feel I am still closer to you than to any other person on earth.

Now Thursday. Couldn't write any more last night. I was falling asleep *with the pen in my hand and anyway Pete had to get up early this morning so he wanted the light off. I got your letter this morning - but more about that later. I've got some important news. I met Pete for lunch today and we had a really good talk. That's the annoying thing about him. When I want to discuss something with him, I can hardly prise a word out of him. Any other time he won't shut up. Anyway the result of it all was that I made my mind up. Whatever happens I can't envisage myself being tied to him in the future. I don't trust him. We still get on all right, don't misunderstand me. It's just that he's so immature. Anyway as a result of our talk I've made my mind up to have an abortion. The stupid thing is that he now seems to want me to have the baby. He won't marry me. (Which is good because I won't marry him). He seems to think that we could carry on just as we are now and the presence of a child would make our relationship stronger. See what I mean about being immature? I'd booked to see the doctor this afternoon and by the time I'd got there my mind was made up. So, it seems, was his. Basically, he produced a couple of forms. I signed them and that was it. It didn't really hit me until I got home. I simply burst into tears and cried for an hour or more. I feel a little bit silly at the moment, a bit like a little girl crying for her mummy. I really don't want to have an abortion, but it's the only practical solution. I just don't trust Pete so if I keep the baby I'll have to be prepared to bring it up myself, and I don't feel strong enough to do that. Adoption? If I went through with it and had the baby, I'm sure I wouldn't be able to give it away. So you see it's the only choice left. Must go. Pete's home.*

Oh shit, Michael. Some hours later. What have I done? Pete was furious when I told him. Suddenly he wants to talk about it. He says he wants to marry me for the sake of the baby. I was so surprised I could hardly answer. What came out, almost without my thinking about it, was that I had written to you saying that I didn't trust him because he was too immature. And then what does he do? He storms off saying that he's going off to spend the evening with Jenny. I know we decided from the start that living together didn't mean owning one another, but to offer to marry me in one breath and then to say you've got a date in the next is a bit thick. I'm sure he only does it to convince me how lucky I am that he gives me any attention at all.

I haven't told you the full story yet. The doctor said he would get me into the clinic some time next week. He's put me down as an urgent case because he reckons I'm over twelve weeks pregnant. Sounds horrible, doesn't it? He told me it would all be over within twenty-four hours - that I'd only have to stay in one night. I may even be able to get away without having to tell my mother. I'll write to you as soon as it's over. Don't worry.

Later in bed. I must try to finish this. It's about four o'clock and Pete hasn't come home yet. I've been waiting up for him drinking coffee by the gallon and smoking cigarettes two at a time. He must have stayed the night with Jenny. I've decided to carry on writing because I want to be awake when he comes in. He'll have to come home before he goes to work in the morning because all his stuff is here. I've got to do something to stay awake because I've taken some more Valium. Now where was I? Oh yes. Your letter. I've just read it again. Oh Michael, how could you have written that? I wrote to you before because I just didn't know what to do next. I wanted advice, not a proposal. I was dallying with the idea of having an abortion even then. I wanted you to give me some support by telling me that I had to do what I thought was best, which at that time was to go through with it and have it adopted. You can imagine the shock I got when I opened your reply and realised you were telling me in one breath to have the baby and then in the next asking to marry me! If only it were possible - what am I saying? You are and always will be the closest of friends, but marriage? I thought you were joking at first, but then I realised just how serious you were. I must admit that it made me get very emotional. But surely you know I could never ever accept. I know how much your work means to you - I know how much you love Africa - and how little is your desire ever to come back here for good. Thinking about you has certainly brought back very sweet memories of my time in Migwani. I'll never forget it ... or you ... Oh I don't know. I'm so mixed up I don't know what I want. I wish you were here. I'm sure it would all seem so much clearer with you around. Here's Pete.

Am going to sign off now or I'll never get this letter sent. Pete asked me if he could read both your letter and this one. He was really upset about what I was writing to you. I think it may have shocked him a little. Maybe he'll realise now just how little help he's been of late. By the way, just as an example of how silly he can be, when he read your letter, he just laughed. The fact that you, a priest, were proposing to me for the sake of his baby amused him, but I'm afraid the joke was lost on me. If he finds the idea so silly, then maybe that's a sign that I should think *about it more seriously! Anyway, Michael, please don't worry about me. I'll write again as soon as I've got anything definite to report.*

Love, Janet'

With a deep sigh, Michael laid the letter aside and leaned back in his chair. He had read it so many times that now he seemed to read almost exclusively between the lines. In his own mind, he had invented so many things that were not said, that they had begun to cloud and obscure those things that were there. Above all other thoughts, however, were those provoked again by the last line, "... as soon as I've got anything definite to report..." The letter had been posted almost two months ago. He had heard nothing more from Janet. He himself had written three times asking for more news. At last a letter was waiting for him in his post-box in Kitui.

After drinking the last of his breakfast coffee, he carefully folded the letter and replaced it in its envelope, tucking it into the breast pocket of his shirt. He then went into the kitchen, where he rocked in turn each of three blue gas bottles stowed away beneath the sink. Two were obviously empty, so he carried these, one in each hand, out of the back door of the mission house and set them down on the baked earth of the driveway next to the car. Back inside the house, he picked up his cook's shopping list from the kitchen windowsill and then returned to the living room. For a moment he simply stared blankly around the room to make sure he had not forgotten anything. There was nothing more to remember. After a visit to the toilet he would be on the road.

On returning to the living room, he again looked around pensively. He was convinced he had forgotten something. It was one of those occasions when senses tell you one thing, but something else, much wiser, seems to know better.

Surveying the confused state of the mission house, he racked his brains for some clue to the source of his indecision. The building site that lay before him offered no help, only more confusion. The place had been in hiatus ever since the fire and, though the debris had all been cleared and even the new roof had been completed, there were still numerous finishing jobs to be done, such as panel fixing, a new ceiling to complete, painting and general decoration. As a result, there were still piles of used paint tins, tools, off-cuts and fixings lying around the edges of the room, some half-covered by dirty sheeting. There was a smell of fresh wood shavings in the air, remarkably strong, even alongside the pungency of paint stripper and putty. The place was in a complete mess, nothing less. The lack of ceiling boards actually also made it rather a noisy place to be, as gusts of Migwani's incessant dust-laden wind regularly blasted the new and shining sheets of corrugated iron with grit. And even louder, when the metal sheets changed temperature, they would expand or contract and pull against the fixing nails. These were, of course, all so new that the structure had not yet found its own tolerance, and occasionally there would be a sudden and quite immense, unexpected crash when a particular sheet tore a little as its vast internal forces strained against one of the toughened nails. Amidst all this, he was frantically trying to remember some detail he was sure he had forgotten. A minute later he gave up. There was nothing else to remember. It was then that Boniface rushed into the room, panting.

"Boniface. I didn't expect to see you today. I'm just on my way to town."

He did not wait for Michael to finish. "Father, it is very serious," he gasped. "I have rushed here on my bicycle to ask you for a very great favour. Muthuu is much worse since last night. This morning he is still very sick. We are very afraid for him. I have come to ask you if you can take him to hospital?"

Though Boniface was obviously suffering great distress, Michael's first reaction was one of impatience. This did not seem to cause any surprise. After a quick glance at his watch, he turned to face the young man and said, "Look, I have to get to Kitui this morning. I don't want to stop on the way."

"That will be all right, Father," said Boniface. "We can go with you and go to the government hospital."

"But you ought to go to Muthale. Sister Mary knows the baby. If you go to Kitui you'll have to stand in queues all day. I'll drop you in at Muthale on the way into town." There was a hint of frustrated resignation about these last words. It caused Boniface to feel very defensive.

"But my wife is in Thitani..." This was a problem. Muthale Hospital would be on the way from Migwani to Kitui, but Thitani was in another direction, and it was near inaccessible by car from Migwani.

"Oh Jaysus," said Michael, turning aside and waving his arms in a gesture of despair. "All right. Let's go. You can leave your bike here."

There was no point driving to Thitani and then back to Muthale. That would take about as long as going straight to Kitui on the main road.

Within a couple of minutes they were under way, the car trailing a swirl of red dust from the dirt road. The noise of the road, the bangs of the bottoming suspension in the potholes and the rattling shudder of corrugations precluded any further conversation. Michael's mind began to wander through the memories of that night, almost a year before, when Boniface and his heavily pregnant wife had arrived at the mission house together. Momentarily, he remembered the two forgotten blue gas bottles that he presumed were still standing by the kitchen door.

***

"Good evening, Father. My wife, she is ready. You promised you would take her to Muthale." Boniface stood proudly upright to make his announcement. He smiled broadly as he spoke.

Having his child born in hospital was a kind of ambition for Boniface. It had become part of his way of proving that he was the epitome of the modern Kenyan. Owning a bicycle was another part of the same phenomenon. The fact that he, himself, had been born in his father's homestead, dropped by his mother onto bare earth cushioned by banana leaves, was enough to convince him that his own children must expect something different. This image had become merely the progress to which he was now entitled. Besides, his wife, Josephine, had already lost one child, which he believed would have survived in hospital. He was determined not to leave anything to chance this time. The fact that the accomplishment of this ambition would necessitate his already labouring wife walking six or seven miles just to get a lift from Father Michael to the hospital did not seem to worry him. As Michael looked out along the cone of light which spread from the open mission door, she stared pleadingly back at him, her breathing heavy, yet her breath light, her back rounded as she stooped with pain.

The twenty-minute drive to Muthale she bore with great discomfort. While Boniface sat proudly upright alongside Michael in the front, his wife lay on the back seat, uttering a low groan every time the car lurched over a bump. Michael drove as quickly as he dare. If he jolted her too violently, or, on the other hand, took too long over the journey, she would probably give birth on the back seat of the car and Michael possessed no confidence whatsoever in his midwifery skills. Boniface, however, seemed little worried by anything. His gaze, throughout, remained fixed on the road ahead, a hint of a smile displaying his pride.

Michael drove straight up to the main entrance of the hospital. When a nurse came out to greet them, he told Boniface to help his wife out of the car while he went to find Sister Mary.

"Father Michael, what brings you here? Come in, come in." Sister Benedict began to withdraw back into the sitting room.

"I've got an urgent case for Sister Mary." He was panting heavily. "My catechist's wife is about to give birth."

With no more than a business-like nod, Sister Benedict acknowledged Michael's words and then quietly, efficiently, disappeared into the rear of the convent to find Sister Mary. It seemed that even before Michael had time to regain his breath, the doctor and her assistant were already prepared for action and despatched. Benedict returned to find Michael lying on the settee.

"A cup of tea, Father?"

He nodded.

Some minutes later he was aroused from his dozing by the clinking of china. With a tired groan, Michael sat upright on the settee.

"That's marvellous, Sister. Just the job."

"And how are you, Father? Keeping well?"

"All right," he replied, "but I'm having a fierce crisis with my celibacy."

Sister Benedict eyed him with a disciplined air, tantamount to gentle maternal distrust. Shaking her head, she said, "What are we going to do with you?" Michael smiled. "Now don't you laugh," she continued sternly. "I know your game. You and Father Patrick must have got together over a beer at some point and said 'Now next time Sister asks "How are you?" tell her that you're having trouble with your blasted celibacy'. You're like a pair of children at times."

Michael smiled and raised his eyebrows in surprise as he reached across the low table for a biscuit.

"Don't come over all innocent with me. I know your game." She remained serious, but still smiled broadly as she spoke.

Still Michael said nothing. With a hint of a smile creasing his face, he took a bite from his biscuit and a mouthful of tea. The slight slurp seemed almost deliberate.

"And don't go trying to change the subject. Father Patrick came here yesterday on his way home from Kitui. He came through the door," she said, gesturing vaguely across the room, "and sat down exactly where you are now. 'How are you, Father', says I and, just like you, he comes out with, 'OK, but I'm having a fierce crisis with my celibacy'. It's just too much of a coincidence."

Michael now burst out laughing.

"Go on with you. You've had your joke. Sister Benedict is always good for a bit of crack. I know."

"And what if it really were true?" Michael was still playing the game and Sister Benedict knew it.

"Go on with you."

They both laughed.

"Seriously, Sister, what if it were true?"

"What on earth would make you want to confide in me? Surely I'd be the last person to go to?"

"You're the right sex."

"Nuns don't have a sex! Go on with you. You'd get nowhere with me, so you might as well get that idea out of your head."

Their banter was noisily interrupted by the return of a breathless Sister Mary.

"What's your blood, Michael?"

"Red, Sister."

"I'll strangle you one day. What's your blood group?"

"O-positive. Why?"

"You'll do. The poor madam is fit to burst and your man Boniface is no help at all. Come on. Follow me." And she was gone. "Come on Michael," she shouted from outside. She was already half way across the compound back towards the hospital. Suddenly ashen-faced, Michael rose, thanked Sister Benedict for the tea and followed.

In the end, Boniface had been proved right. Without the hospital, his wife would have lost her second child. Whether he himself had brought about the complications by dragging her across country from Thitani was a question he never seriously considered. All he saw was that without the doctor and, above all, without Michael's blood, his child and, perhaps, his wife would not have survived. Not only was the immediate significance of this act gratefully acknowledged by Boniface, but also its future consequences were already being mapped out. In his eyes, it endowed Michael with special and permanent responsibilities toward the child. Michael accepted this without question and so promised that if ever the young Muthuu needed help, Boniface should tell him straight away and he would do all he could.

**

Michael seems to have run out of words. For some time he is silent, lost in thought as if he is finding it hard to locate the right memory. At first John O'Hara does not try to push him, since his perception of his own fairness demands that he should hear Michael's version uncomplicated by any strictures he himself might impose. Eventually, however, he reluctantly tries to help Michael along. "So this morning you drove to Thitani?" Michael nods in agreement. "And from there straight to Kitui?" Again Michael nods. O'Hara says no more to try to encourage Michael to continue, but still he seems lost for words. "What is it, Michael?" he asks at last. "What happened next?"

Michael answers by shrugging his shoulders. "It's all wrong, John. If all I can do is go on reporting events blandly one after the other, you'll only hear the same as what was said by that crowd outside." He nods vaguely towards their memory of the argument outside. O'Hara's only reply to this is a rather confused frown.

"Don't misunderstand me," Michael says hastily. "I'm not saying that I agree with their interpretation, just that I have to explain why I was feeling the way I was for you to be able to understand why I reacted in the way that I did."

O'Hara's accommodating gesture invites him to continue, effectively inviting him to accept complete freedom of expression thenceforth.

After a few moments to collect his thoughts, Michael continues, beginning as if embarking upon an epic. "It goes back a long way, this feeling. Probably the best way to start is to forget about today for the moment. That will certainly help me to get closer to it again rather than just run away from it. You know, for quite some time I've meant to come here and bare my soul to you, so to speak. Obviously I never got round to doing it and so all the frustrations I needed to get off my chest have only been getting worse." Michael pauses here to reach for a match and then light a cigarette. As he inhales the smoke, he feels his thoughts begin to focus. "John, what I want to do is just talk things out. Please let me do that. Let me start by going right back - a long way back, to Nigeria."

"Ah..." O'Hara's reaction is instinctive. In all the years he has known Michael, he has never heard him speak of his time in Nigeria. Unlike the several other priests in the diocese who have spent time in that country, Michael has throughout remained deeply reticent about his experiences there. "You were deported in the end?"

Michael smiles. "Indeed I was," he says sardonically. "Yes. I was. I was adjudged as having collaborated with the state of Biafra."

"But your station wasn't inside Biafra..."

"That's right, but if you remember, just after war was declared, the Biafrans had the government forces on the run and they quickly gained a lot of territory. So in fact, for the majority of the war, my parish was inside Biafra ... and in the front line for a while later on. When the Government forces started pushing the Ibos back with the help of their new weapons, they made ground only very slowly. Until quite close to the end, they had pushed the Biafrans back only twenty miles or so on that part of the front. Then, of course, came the collapse."

***

There had been no hint that the war would reach them that day. There had not even been the sound of distant firing during the night. Though from the beginning there had been no way of escaping the conflict, people here had come to terms with it and learned to live with its existence. The community accepted that its sons, husbands and fathers would go to fight because their common belief was that the war would start and that they would win through to secure their aim. Even when casualties began to mount, this common determination did not waver. News of victories in the early days of the war had served to strengthen this resolve to such a degree that later, even when eventual defeat had become inevitable, it effectively spurred men to suicide. Perhaps before any war can even begin, it is necessary that people should start to believe their own propaganda. When self-belief suffers from that degree of myopia, even death's absolute reality becomes a dream.

But at this late stage no one knew the real story. For some days the villagers had heard nothing from relatives nearer the front and so they lived their unchanged life ignorant of the fact that the war was all but lost. Anyway why should they worry? Wars, after all, are fought by armies and not by farmers. They wore no uniforms, held no guns and obeyed no orders. Whoever might win the war, they would still need to eat and so they would still need the yams the village grew.

Content in this ultimate security, village life had continued largely unchanged. The market, with its trade and gossip, remained its focus. Food shortages were a growing cause of concern, however, but it was still not serious, certainly not serious enough to deserve much more than passing comment. Market day remained a day of meeting, reunion and conversation. It remained the day when deals were struck, plans made and arguments revisited. It was the day, also, even more so than Sunday, when Father Michael's church was filled to capacity for afternoon mass and this day was no exception.

There was no panic. It was not because people quickly realised their fate and calmly accepted it, but merely because they had no understanding of what was about to happen. Gunshots would have set everyone running for cover. Approaching government forces would have sent them fleeing. But on that day, like goats that will run from a man but not from a car, they simply stood and watched. Thus, like goats mowed down in the road, they suffered a fate they could not comprehend.

Initially the dull drone from the north went quite unnoticed. As it grew in intensity, however, conversations and trading stopped. Even Father Michael paused in the middle of his sermon to listen. He had never known a congregation fall so suddenly silent. From inside the church it sounded like the approach of a storm. The roar echoed in the building and caused the tin roof to rattle on its nails and the interior to reverberate in sympathy. Like people everywhere when confronted with dangers they cannot comprehend, these people reacted immediately and in entirely the wrong way. Consequently they were the first to suffer. As if with one mind the entire congregation rushed to the exit. Everyone knew that the walls had been built very cheaply and then Father Michael had come along and, in his wisdom in such matters, had finished the building off with a heavy iron roof complete with unsupported overhangs to provide verandas. Michael had never bothered to strengthen the structure. In his eyes its obvious frailty endowed new meaning to his oft-said words, "Let us lift up our eyes and pray..." So it was with some amusement and some experience that people rushed towards the exit, for all approaching storms were greeted with this practice.

For a few seconds a steady stream of people spewed from the doorway into the dull light of the overcast afternoon, each immediately turning towards those behind to offer a smile or a few words to comment on just how close to collapse the roof appeared to be. Michael, of course, had grown used to this and reacted in the same way as everyone else, since the heavens were prone to open almost every afternoon. For the duration of the storm, a half hour or so, people would shelter under the veranda outside - under the same dubious roof! - and then, when the wind had abated would file back into the church to resume their service.

That day, however, was to see no usual storm. The first people pushed outside by the rush turned to face those inside, but before they could speak or even offer a smile, the expected rumble of thunder grew to an unknown roar which drew their eyes skyward. Those still pushing to get out saw in the same instant the earth outside begin to explode in a thousand puffs of dust. The roar rose to a deafening intensity and then swept away with a speed greater than any storm. And now there were a number of people lying motionless on the ground, their blood seeping into the dirt. Amid gasps of fear, the entire congregation left the church and ran to the prostrate bodies. Some were dead or dying. Then, while a collective shock numbed the senses and prevented all action save for the wailing of a few women, the roar of engines again filled the sky. The helicopter flew low, hugging the contours of the gently undulating land, almost clipping the top of the surrounding forest. No one knew how to react. All hesitated, stared at the dark shape in the sky as it loomed ever larger. When they decided to run, it was too late. The shadow flashed overhead and again the earth boiled in plumes of dust. A handful of people who had remained in the church covered their eyes and shrieked with pain as the searing noise reached its crescendo. A second later, they looked outside and could not believe what they saw. Surely only by magic could so many people be hit so quickly. Not a second before fifty or sixty people had stood in the wide clearing before the church. Now half of them were prostrate on the earth.

"Come on! Follow me quickly," Michael shouted. Immediately he took another by the arm and almost dragged him from the church, their fear of being left alone now greater than any other. Together they ran across the clearing, stepping over bodies on the way until they reached the edge of the forest. There they stopped, panting for the breath their fear denied them. Only a moment remained to survey the scene before the helicopter again returned. This time the aircraft flashed across the village and more shots were fired.

The helicopter did not return, its roar fading slowly to a distant moan, revealing a silence of shock and disbelief. Then, without daring to move for many minutes, they stood motionless and still silent, surveying what was before them. It felt as if they had been transported to a different world. When they tentatively left their hiding place, they were all in tears, crying like helpless children, because it was all they could do. A total silence seemed to pervade all. Punctuated only by their own voices and an occasional groan from the wounded, it oppressed them, frightened them. It was the silence of death and it was all around them.

So, at first as a group and then singly, they went in search of the living. There had been a crowd of people in the small market, the church full and a dozen shops overflowing. The bullets had strafed the whole clearing, and, of the hundreds who had come to market many had been hit. There were no more tears to cry. The survivors, now sure of their own safety, moved from one corpse to another with their eyes now dry. No emotion could penetrate the wall of shock, which now protected them. Some, it seemed, had died of fright. They lay with their flesh and clothes apparently unblemished but with expressions of terror tearing their faces. For how long the living wandered apparently aimlessly through the village they would never remember. Probably they expected help to arrive. A government lorry with doctors, maybe? Or a Land Rover from the mission hospital down the road. But no one came. Thus the survivors waited in vain.

Under the large tree near the church was Michael's car. He inspected it for damage and, though the body was riddled with bullet holes, and one of the tyres had been holed, it seemed at least to be in one piece. He tried the engine and it started. He offered a silent prayer of thanks. He was obviously useless here. Elsewhere he might find someone who could tend the few who stood a chance of surviving. There was a mission hospital run by nuns a few miles to the west. Surely they could do something. If the hospital were still under Biafran control, he would need Nelson to negotiate the help they needed.

He could not go alone, however. If the war was close he might meet soldiers and he was not sufficiently skilled in the different languages to be sure he could explain himself. Nelson should go with him. He had been one of the lucky ones who had followed Michael from the church to safety. He was an Ibo, the local representative of the General's government who had come to the area to assess the harvest and obtain supplies of food for their now hard-pressed army.

Michael looked around but could not see him. A blast on the car horn produced the desired result. Michael beckoned to Nelson who appeared from a nearby shop where frightened people had crowded to seek shelter. Whilst he crossed the clearing to the car, Michael shouted to a nearby group that he was going for help, but they seemed strangely disinterested. After all, what could anyone do now? When Michael pointed out the possibility of meeting soldiers on the road, Nelson, an educated man, who also spoke good English, agreed that he should come along, since Michael spoke no Ibo. As the car slithered off along the only road, those left in the town stood silently and watched until it and its wheel-rim clanking disappeared into the all-enveloping forest.

The ride was distinctly uncomfortable. The flat tyre flapped noisily as the wheel cut deep furrows in the soft soil of the road and the car frequently veered from side to side. Michael constantly had to fight with the steering to maintain a mere twenty miles per hour and caused him to rue his decision some weeks before to give away his spare to a friend when he knew full well that the war meant he would not find a replacement. Nevertheless, they made progress, but Nelson held onto his seat and the dashboard as if in fear of his life. As the narrow track wound its devious way through the forest, Michael fought to keep the car straight, but apparently to no avail. It seemed that they made progress sideways, as the wheel constantly lost traction in the soft dust. The consequent skids, first one way and then the other as Michael corrected and over-corrected, caused Nelson to think that they might even be bouncing from tree to tree. So quickly did their trunks seem to pass by that after only a few minutes he simply held on, closed his eyes and prayed. Michael was working hard to maintain a semblance of control, but, in his own inimitable style, he showed none of it, with his head lolling to one side and his eyes looking quite vacant.

On reaching the river they were surprised to find the ferry unattended. Luckily, the boatman had left the pontoon on their bank. It took only a few minutes for Michael and Nelson to work the car across the river. The ferry had certainly not been abandoned for long. Numerous puddles of fresh oil on the platform suggested that it had been used that day and, though neither Michael nor Nelson made any comment, both were privately troubled by the fact that they had passed no other vehicle on their side of the river. Something felt very wrong. First the boatman was nowhere to be seen. Even after they had loaded the car onto the pontoon and begun to work it across the river, he had not appeared. Why had he not come to them? Why had they not seen vehicles on the road? And still there was not a sign of war. They had not seen a single person.

Michael drove the car off the pontoon whilst Nelson held the guide rope to make sure it could not slip. Here the road rose steeply up the bank to disappear again into the darkness of the forest and so, rather than risk stopping and thus having to restart on the slippery mud of the river bank, he drove on up to the top and waited there for Nelson. Michael reached for a cigarette and lit it. As he exhaled the smoke and sighed, his eyes closed momentarily and with great deliberation he moved his head from side to side to try to relieve the stiffness, which his confinement in the car had produced. The engine still ticked over. Where was Nelson? He opened his eyes with a start, suddenly realising he had waited for his companion for a minute or more. He turned round and saw that Nelson was still only half way up the riverbank. He was surrounded by a group of armed men. Some of them wore camouflage, but most wore tattered vests and shorts.

Michael did not know whether they were government forces, Biafran forces or merely locals bent on self-preservation. When he moved to get out of the car, however, he was left in no doubt. His hand had hardly reached the door handle when a voice to his left spoke firmly in a language he did not know. Obviously he was being told to sit still. This he did. The passenger door opened. Someone reached into the car, switched off the engine and carefully removed the keys from the dashboard. Immediately Michael could smell palm wine. The man reeked of it. Someone then prodded Michael on the shoulder through the open window in the driver's door. He turned. A man stood beside the car pointing a rifle into his eyes. He was told to get out.

A few seconds later, Michael was standing by the car, his hands flat on the roof, the tip of a rifle pressed into his back. He, it seemed, deserved the attentions of only one man. Nelson, however, was surrounded by a dozen or more. There was a lot of noise, a lot of shouting, but Nelson was quiet, not uttering a single word. Michael tried to move, but a short nervous prod in his back returned him to submission.

The shouting continued. Nelson said nothing. They pushed him, hit him, but he still remained silent. At last Michael shouted, "Does any of you speak English? Can I help?"

At first nothing happened, but then one of those dressed in army fatigues spoke above the rest, apparently ordering them to stop what they were doing and wait for him. He approached Michael and gestured to the man at his back to step aside. Michael turned to face him.

"Hello, Father," he said. "This man is refusing to speak."

"What do you want to know?"

"We want to know who he is, where he comes from and where he is going." He punctuated his demands by tapping emphatically on his rifle stock.

"He is travelling with me. We're going to the hospital." He gestured vaguely into the distance. "This morning our village was attacked and..."

"I know," interrupted the other. "We merely want to know who he is. You can tell us."

Before Michael could offer any reply, everyone's attention was demanded by the arrival of a white vehicle, driving towards the river on their side. The road, of course, was blocked by Michael's car, so it had to stop. Four doors immediately opened and only minutes later the proceedings were being filmed. Four Europeans and their local driver had burst from the car and to the utter astonishment of everyone on the riverbank, the white men assembled cameras and sound recording equipment. It was a television crew.

With attentions diverted, Nelson saw his chance and made a dash for the forest. He had taken barely four steps before he was caught and tripped by one of the armed men. He fell against tree roots, hit his head and screamed with pain before rolling into the mud of the riverbank.

"Who is this man, Father?" The man in the camouflage shouted, playing a little to the camera and thus not sounding quite angry enough as he approached Michael. He allowed the muzzle of his rifle to dangle above Michael's face.

"Look, I told you. We're going to get doctors to help the wounded in our village..." His voice was beginning to break with fear. The man smiled.

"He is an Ibo. Yes?"

A few yards away Nelson slithered to his feet in the mud.

A member of the television crew then intervened. He approached the man who was giving all the orders and asked him what was happening. The corporal introduced himself and then explained that their task that day was to guard this river crossing, effectively to close it. This car and these two men had used the ferry illegally and were being interrogated. The presenter asked if he could speak to the driver and, after the corporal's clearly reluctant nod, he approached Michael, whose guard lowered his rifle as the microphone was presented. Michael began to speak, saying that the village on the other side had been attacked and that he and Nelson were on their way to get help for the wounded, but he did not have time to finish his answer.

A sudden commotion arose from within the group surrounding Nelson, thus dissolving the complete absurdity, which had arrived with the film crew. The camera, microphone and presenter all turned to capture the moment. The corporal explained willingly, and perhaps a little too proudly for an anticipated European television audience that one of his men had recognised their prisoner and claimed that he had been the commander of a Biafran unit that had murdered many people in his village at the start of the war. They approached Nelson, who sat in the mud by the river with his knees drawn up to his chest, watched over by four rifle-pointing guards.

"So what will happen to him now?" asked the television presenter.

"We will interrogate," answered the corporal and, as he spoke, a rifle muzzle was pushed against Nelson's cheek. Neither the presenter nor the crew could understand anything of what followed, as the five men all seemed to want to shout at Nelson, so they turned to Michael, asking him if he knew this man.

"Of course I know him. He's been in my village for months. He's some sort of official... Look, we need medical help in our village. There are wounded people there...."

A noise from the group again attracted the television crew's attention. Nelson was being beaten around the face, but in an almost ceremonial and perfunctory way and he now bore an expression of complete, undiluted terror. Without waiting to be asked a question, the corporal turned to face the camera pointed towards him and said that they were now convinced that this man was the one who had led a group of Biafran soldiers into a nearby village a year before and ordered the killing of a dozen people. He was thus a criminal and an enemy officer. Again, the television man asked what would happen next, but before his sentence was even complete, the corporal had turned to face Nelson and removed the revolver from his hip. In a single movement, he raised the gun to Nelson's temple and shot, and thus a European television audience was later able to experience war at first hand.

***

"They presumed you were trying to smuggle an official out of the war zone?"

"That's about it. They took the car and put me behind bars until a bishop from the North came down and vouched for me. I didn't know at the time, but all hell broke loose when the television footage was shown in Britain. It cause such a stir that the Nigerian authorities a few days later claimed to have identified the corporal, court-martialled him and executed him by firing squad. They seemed to think that it might help their tarnished image, but it merely confirmed their barbarity. Nobody seemed to be the slightest bit interested in my safety, so I was told when I got to London. I was held for a few days in jail and then they deported me. I never saw the village again."

John O'Hara now feels much more at ease. It occurs to him that during the years he has known Michael Doherty he has never once spoken to him merely as another person. All communication - for want of a better word - between them has relied, even hinged upon their functional roles of priest and bishop. This reminds him that in the present circumstances he is not merely passing the time of day with conversation, and so, unwillingly, he is forced to revert to type. He is trying to find out why Michael behaved so apparently irresponsibly, so much out of character, that morning. "Now listen, Michael. I know all this already and none of it has anything to do with what happened this morning. What I want to know..."

Michael does not allow him to finish. "You don't understand, John, do you?" There is a touch of anger, a hardened edge to his voice, which cuts through O'Hara's calculatedly soft tone. "I was on the way to Kitui to do two things. One, as you know, was to pick up the letter from Janet, but that was not the prime reason for my trip to town today. I was coming here to see you: to see you personally -" Michael is almost pleading with him. His wide stare openly invites O'Hara to glean the intended meaning. O'Hara, however, does not appear to grasp what Michael is trying to convey. There are still questions in his eyes.

"Do you expect me to read your mind?"

Michael ignores the question and continues. His tone of voice suggests he is ready to take the offensive. "If I were to ask you about the standard of my work of late, what would you say? Compare my achievements over the last few months with what you would have normally expected of me." He is now leaning forward on the settee, eager to hear the Bishop's reply.

Initially, John O'Hara is visibly uncomfortable with Michael's new assertiveness. He is not used to being questioned so directly on his opinions and is not sufficiently confident of his relationship with Michael to speak his mind. Of course, if this were a meeting of his own Diocesan Council, when discussion of such matters would be normal, but in a highly structured and impersonal form, he would not hesitate and would speak his mind: but here, face to face with Michael, and requested by him to reveal his own still only partially-formed opinions, the confrontation serves only to distress him. He stumbles on his words until Michael interjects to offer him a starting point.

"Lax? Lacking in commitment?"

"Your words, not mine."

"But nevertheless true?"

"Undoubtedly. I'm afraid that reports about you have been reaching me for some weeks. If we ignore the usual ones - about your drinking, womanising, et cetera - although I must say that you have been drinking very heavily and very openly recently. I have to point that out to you. It's not good for us, you know, Michael. I've spoken to you before about this and I know your opinion..." John O'Hara, now very much reincarnated Bishop O'Hara, raises his hand and turns aside as Michael attempts to interrupt, "but it seems that whatever I say you will carry on in your own way. Now I'm prepared to accept that, or should I say that I have been prepared to accept that when, in the past - and I stress that - in the past your occasional unacceptable behaviour has been counterbalanced by your quite exceptional work - and I say that to you with complete sincerity. I have - I used to have - great respect, even admiration for your work. On many occasions, I have cited Migwani, and your work in it, as a model of our aims. You have managed to succeed in every way - apart from one - you might say small - I would say important way. On the Church side you have established new stations, worked to provide them with new churches. You've doubled the number of people on parish registers -"

Michael's expression at this point conveys a hint of an impatient scoff.

"It might be unfashionable to measure a priest's success by the number of baptisms he makes -" John O'Hara's voice is growing sterner now, "- but in the absence of any other tangible pointer, I happen to view it still with a great deal of respect and I would encourage you to do the same. But let me finish what I started. This spiritual side of your work, though never exemplary, has been more than adequate, but it is in the pastoral side of the work where you - where you *used to* excel. My goodness, Michael, you were the first person in the District to set up literacy schemes, agricultural and health work - the list is so long, so impressive that quite honestly it makes me feel quite humble even to think of it."

"High praise indeed." Michael is trying hard to be sincere, but circumstance injects a cynical bite to his words. "But then who ever heard of a humble bishop?"

O'Hara eyes him quizzically for a moment, still not really knowing how to broach his criticisms. "I mentioned one important duty which, for some reason, you seem quite incapable of fulfilling." O'Hara speaks slowly, deliberately forcing Michael to register every word. For some moments both he and Michael stay silent. O'Hara is at a loss for words. Michael is brooding on a random jumble of thoughts. A grimace spreads over O'Hara's face as he searches for the words he needs. "Tell me, Michael. Why is it that you always manage to offend - nay to alienate - those people whose influence we need?"

"I don't." Michael's reply was quick, spoken in a flat calculated tone. He offers no more than this and continues to stare at the floor.

O'Hara smiles a little, paternalistically. "Come on Michael. If I had a pound for every time you'd insulted James Mulonzya, for instance, I'd have been a rich man long ago." He finishes with a hard, almost mocking laugh.

"Mulonzya? That whore?" There is a broad smile across Michael's face when he continues. "As I said, John, I never offend the important people."

O'Hara's calculated smile communicates that he has covered this same ground innumerable times with Michael. Through it he is saying, "Will he never learn?" without words. "Mulonzya is a member of parliament, whether you like it or not. He is one of the most important, most influential people in your area -" He raises his hands to quash Michael's intended interruption. " - So as far as I'm concerned it would be stupid not to court his attention. But to insult the poor beggar in public like you do is to invite problems." O'Hara finishes on a critical, declamatory tone. After a short emphatic pause, he continues, still in control. "You might think that these things don't get back to me but..."

"I'm not the least bit surprised, John. You seem to be the eyes and ears of the entire District."

"Well there's no need to feign ignorance, is there?"

***

They ought to have left the bar at least two hours earlier, by which time everyone who had a home to go to had already departed. Michael and Mulonzya, however, had stayed, Michael because he was getting free beer and Mulonzya because he was being given ample opportunity to indulge in his one great weakness, that of listening to the sound of his own voice. Though they were not alone, they both behaved as if they were. The barman sat on a high stool behind the counter. Leaning forward to rest his arms and head on the bar, he dozed, neglecting his duty though confident that two people as well known and well respected as Michael and Mulonzya would not try to leave without paying.

Michael had assumed the role of barman, having humbly explained to Mulonzya that since he was a guest in Migwani he should not be expected to fetch his own beer. This arrangement suited Michael admirably, since he had systematically been adding the beers for every new round to Mulonzya's tally, never his own. The only other person in the stark, grey concrete box of a room was the madman, Munyasya, whose wizened old body had long before succumbed to sleep. He lay in a heap in a corner, half in and half out of the shadow cast by the bar's only table, his hand still clutching at a half-full bottle of beer. Neither Michael nor Mulonzya had paid him, or anyone else for that matter, the slightest attention for some time, so engrossed had they become in the meandering of their own conversation. Even at this late hour, though, an occasional customer had appeared in the doorway and greeted those inside, before buying a single beer, to be drunk quickly, in near silence, standing at the bar.

By that late hour they had already crossed the same ground many times. Both had run out of new ideas and more than just an occasional word was slurred, or punctuated by a belch or a hiccough, but still the veracity with which they spoke was undiminished.

"I agree with you, Mister Michael," said Mulonzya, shaking his head and slapping the bar with the palm of his hand. His words pleaded with the other. "I have said before that a man should have a philosophy of life and that he should live by it. My goodness, life would be impossible if it had no meaning - and it is only belief that gives it meaning. What I just said was that sometimes, when a man has to make a decision, he sees that what he ideally would like is not always possible. Then he must be satisfied with what he can achieve. He must be practical."

"What is your philosophy, then?" Michael smiled through his question.

Mulonzya threw up his hands in frustration. "How can I say? There are as many different philosophies as there are men." After a pause, during which he was obviously as deep in thought as he could manage at that hour, he continued, at first merely thinking aloud. "Who was that man?...Ah yes. Descartes." After another pause, designed to prepare Michael's attention for the pearl of wisdom to follow, he said with pride, "I think, - THEREFORE! - I think!"

Both Mulonzya and Michael smile. "I am," said Michael.

"What?"

"I am. I think therefore I am."

"I just said that." Mulonzya looked confused for a moment, but then went on. "Do you see what I mean? We could quote hundreds, thousands, even millions of ideas. How can anyone say which is right and which is wrong? Sometimes some of those ideas will be correct, will be relevant. Sometimes they will not. We must learn to pick and choose in an informed manner depending on the circumstances." His expression implored Michael to agree. "Anyway, Mister Michael, if you think a man should be able to quote his own beliefs, what are yours?"

"I am a Christian," replied Michael without hesitation, but in a voice that seemed to be tinged with embarrassment.

Mulonzya scoffed and then laughed. "No. You haven't understood the question. We are all Christians, Mister Michael. I was talking about - "

"I know quite a few people who aren't Christian," interrupted Michael, deliberately trying to disrupt the well-lubricated flow of his adversary.

Mulonzya again thought for a moment before answering. "No, you still haven't understood. Look, you know and I know that there is only one God and that He is a Christian God." Here Mulonzya began to laugh. "I hope that I don't have to try to convince you, a priest, of that! What you are saying, I think, is that there are still people in the world who do not believe in God - but that is only to be expected because not everyone in the world is civilised yet. When they become civilised - or developed, that's it, developed - they will then be able to understand Christianity."

"How do you explain then that there are - and always have been - highly civilised people who do not believe in God and are not Christians?"

"Because there are communists and they are evil!" Mulonzya very nearly spat this self-evident truth. "As I was about to say..."

"No, wait," interrupted Michael again. "I think it is you who does not understand. I am speaking about Europeans, British or Irish people. They will all say that they believe in God, but I would call very few of them Christian."

Mulonzya laughed knowingly. "That is because your society has many problems. Crime, violence ...er ...sex." The word came like a flash of inspiration. "We have been hearing for some time about the decay of your country, Mister Michael, and not only your own country, but the whole of the developed world. It is a sad thing, but what can people expect when they turn away from their own beliefs? After all, Christianity was the very foundation of their success. That is what I was saying to you earlier, Mister Michael. We in Africa will not make the same mistakes. As our countries develop we will make sure that no decay can grow."

Michael has still not explained himself fully. "But what if all these people, these decadent people, say and believe that they are Christians? There are many people here who are just the same. They might say they are Christian, but in their actions they are not."

"Ah there are always some people who are liars," said Mulonzya, with a dismissive wave of the hand. "I know many people who say they are Christian because they think it makes them seem civilised and educated, and yet I know for a fact that they never go to church." The last words he emphasised with a slap on the counter.

In reply Michael smiled, shook his head and said, "Mulonzya, there are many people who go to church - they probably never miss a service, and yet in my opinion they are not and never will be Christians."

"How can that be? They worship God, don't they? Ah, you are playing with me!"

"Being a Christian is not about going to church..."

Mulonzya's eyes widened with a mixture of surprise and shock.

"Being a Christian is about living in a Christian manner, about accepting the philosophy -" Michael laid great stress on the word, "- of Christ. It doesn't matter to me which God people worship - or even if they worship no God at all."

Mulonzya's eyes have opened even wider.

"If they live their lives by Christian principles then they have the right to call themselves Christian. It may well be that even those who do not wish to call themselves Christian in any shape or form still have the right to do so, because of the quality of their actions. Those who do not accept the responsibility of Christ's example - note, not necessarily his verbal teaching - those people simply are not Christians, and it doesn't matter how many times they go to church in a week."

Mulonzya was by now almost speechless with disbelief. "But... but... a Christian is a man who worships a Christian God. Your own Church teaches that as gospel." Mulonzya again pats the bar top, though less vehemently this time. It is as if the power of the slap is proportional to his confidence of the truth of his statement. "What you are saying is that an uncivilised pagan, like some old man from the bush who has never been to church, never been baptised, you are saying that he is a Christian?"

"Not necessarily," answered Michael, "but he could be. It would depend on how he lives his life. If he lives in the image of Christ, it doesn't matter why he thinks he is doing it. In Christ's eyes, he is a believer."

Mulonzya scoffed in disbelief. "Never. If that is so then why do you - and others like you - come here? What need is there for you to build your churches, to drive your flock inside like sheep to teach them how to worship Christ, when they might even be closer to Christ than you are yourselves? Why shouldn't we all just stay as we are?"

As Michael began to answer, Mulonzya mumbled on for a moment in a disapproving tone. "I have said that there are many people who do not live by Christian principles. Most people in fact. The Church is Christ's school, where people go to learn his teaching. Not everyone, of course, manages to learn the message, no matter how many times they attend the classes! As a Christian, myself, my aim is not just to fill my church - that is only the beginning. When a person first comes to church to worship, I accept that person like a teacher admitting a pupil to a standard one class. The act of worship is but the first step towards learning the teaching of Christ that might take years of study and practice. The person might never learn. Not everyone who wants to be a Christian is capable of living a Christian life. After all, we are only human. We are all imperfect. Christ learned this when he walked the earth as a man and so, in our teaching, we recognise this. We accept the fact that even when people try to live up to Christ's principles, they will sometimes fail to satisfy what he expects of them. Therefore every human being is a sinner and only redeems that sin through worship. That is the important thing about going to church. It is not simply a place to pray to God, to keep on the right side of the all-powerful. It is a place where one might ask for forgiveness for one's failure to live up to the most essential human standards of Christ's teaching."

Though somewhat confused by Michael's position, Mulonzya thought he had seen a giant flaw in the argument. "But Mister Michael, do you not see what you are saying? You have just said that there are no Christians." Mulonzya's finger wagged in emphasis. "To be a Christian, a man must live by Christian principles. Correct? But because he is a man, you say, he is incapable of doing this. There are no Christians and there never can be."

"No. As long as a man continues to live by those principles and remains conscious and repentant of his failure to live up to them, he remains a Christian. He might not be perfect, but he is at least part of the way. It is those people who choose to ignore those principles, which they are taught through the Church who are not real Christians. People are not saved by their proximity to Christ's Church, as your faith teaches. It is not the act of worship which is our salvation, but the way that we live our lives."

Mulonzya's expression was impatient and dismissive as he answered quickly. "Now, there, Mister Michael, I agree with you. The emphasis of the Protestants is wrong. They play too much on people's superstitions." Michael nodded in agreement. Mulonzya gave a quick laugh before continuing. "Look at what they are doing. They don't even bother to build proper churches. Years ago, when I was young, they built their churches strong and permanent, made them from concrete, but what do they do now? They build them out of sticks and mud like cattle sheds. How do they expect our people to learn to develop from such an example?"

In reply to this, Michael offered only a broad, knowing smile and total silence. He was confident that his trap was finally ready to spring.

When the expected comment did not materialise, Mulonzya continued. "You know, Mister Michael, let me tell you what I and many of my colleagues are thinking these days." Instinctively, he glanced about the bar as if to check that even in this small bush place there were no 'official' eyes or ears to witness the secret he was about to divulge. He then felt able to continue, but in a lower, more confidential, less self-promotional style. "Many of us believe that the Protestants' time is up. There was a time when they positively helped our nation's development, but now it is becoming clear that they are hindering it. For example, they used to aid our country actively with real hard currency. They used to finance the building of their churches and schools from overseas, by collections from the rich in rich countries. But nowadays? They tell us that it is good for our souls to make sacrifices for God, that we should learn to provide everything for ourselves. Self-reliance is good for the self, Mister Michael. Now you know at first hand that most people are poor. How can they be expected to provide thousands of shillings to build adequate churches? They cannot, obviously, and so what happens? All they are able to provide these days are cattle sheds. Now how is that helping development? Why should they expect people here to be satisfied with second best when anyone can see the magnificence of the cathedral in Kitui town? Confidentially ..." Though it was unlikely that either of the others in the bar was listening, Mulonzya leaned across the bar towards Michael and spoke in a whisper. "... there is a fast growing belief in the government that unless they change their ways they will have to go. We will send their missionaries home and withdraw our support for their church." As Mulonzya straightened from his sincere position, offering a serious, emphatic nod of the head in affirmation, Michael burst out laughing.

It was a harsh mocking laugh, and Mulonzya's overtly serious expression soon changed, first to confusion and then to a frown of mistrust. "And why is that funny, Mister Michael?" he asked, stressing the Mister.

"Ah Mulonzya," Michael began, "you astound me." He thinks for a moment before continuing. "Now where was it? Ah yes, I remember. It was at Ndau, just before the election. Now you know as well as I do that Ndau is a solidly Protestant area. The speech you gave there told people exactly what you thought they wanted to hear."

"And what was that?" asked Mulonzya defiantly. He was beginning to be offended by Michael's laughter.

"At Ndau you told your audience that it was widely believed in the government that unless the Catholic Church began to ordain more African priests in this area then it would be kicked out. You would send its missionaries home."

"A quite valid criticism in my opinion," snapped Mulonzya, changing his tack with effortless ease.

"I suppose that is an example of your being practical, of judging what is possible depending on the circumstances?" Mulonzya began to eye Michael with suspicion and some anger. "I call it convenient and calculated to win votes like everything else you do. Your sole end is to reinforce your position so that you can continue to line your own nest. You even called yourself a Christian in the same speech."

Mulonzya took hold of his bottle of beer and slammed it hard onto the counter. "Then why is it, Mister Michael," he shouted angrily, "that I have so much support in the District? Do you think that people would vote for me if they did not believe what I said? Do you think I would have such support if I were not telling the truth? Do you not think that it shows that people are satisfied with what I am doing on their behalf?"

"People vote for you because you are a chameleon, Mulonzya." Michael's voice hardened as he continued. "Out here in the bush you tell people how hard you work for them. You tell them exactly what you think they want to hear, but as soon as you get through the barrier and on your way to Nairobi, you completely forget them. Everything you do from then on is calculated to achieve your only true aim which is nothing other than lining your own pocket and increasing your power - your potential for further earning. If people knew that you and other politicians are actively working against their interests, you'd probably have a revolution on your hands."

After a tense silence, Mulonzya spoke with uncharacteristic reticence, in a slow cynical tone. "And what, Mister Michael, is going to convince people that what you say is true?"

"I would have thought that was obvious. As they grow poorer you grow richer. It's plain for all to see. While their crops fail, forcing them to sell their animals and land just so they can eat, it's people like you who come along and do the buying. You're getting people's hard-earned assets for a song, just because times are difficult. And then what do you do with the land? You sink boreholes and then plant cash crops like coffee or sisal for sale out of the area and then you pocket the profit to build a new house in Nairobi!"

Mulonzya reacted dismissively, waving his hand and scoffing. "What rubbish you are saying! People are happy to see their location developed by those who have the resources to do it in just the same way that they are proud when they see fine buildings like schools and churches being erected. They are all signs of our nation's increasing prosperity. It makes people happy to see such progress."

"Well I suppose they all need something to keep them going while they starve because less and less land is being used to grow food. They need some consolation when they eventually find that their men folk have to go to the city to live in the shanties of Mathare valley to find whatever work they can, just so that the family can eat."

"People are starving because of drought. Whom do you blame for that? Me or your God?"

"Neither, of course, but I do blame you for making the effects of the drought much worse than they need be. If you and others like you were to use your fine tracts of land to grow food, there would be no famine. You have the best land, boreholes to irrigate it and often tractors to plough it - and yet the people of this area gain absolutely no benefit from the end product. You don't even provide people with jobs."

"So this is what you preach in your church?"

"Yes." Though Michael was clearly trying to antagonise, the reply took Mulonzya by surprise and shocked him. "I tell my congregation," Michael continued, "that they should live by Christian teaching and seek to work for the benefit of their fellow men - and that they should not respect those people who flout Christ's ideals - whatever their standing in the community."

"You say that as if you believe I do not live by those principles."

Michael's laughter angered Mulonzya further. "After what you have done to the Mwangangis at Kamandiu, that is what everyone believes, not just me. Look at what you have done to that family!" Michael implored Mulonzya to listen, but by this time the other was growing ever more disaffected by what he heard and had taken to staring proudly into space, feigning deafness. "After the complete tragedy of Musyoka killing John, the family picks itself up from the floor and sets about trying to make a life for itself again. They understandably assume that John Mwangangi's land will stay in the family and that it is theirs to farm. No one challenges them. They work hard to till the land and plant their crops. Meanwhile, in Nairobi, you have been doing your homework. You know that John left everything to his wife so you can bribe her to marry your son and so become a member of your family. And then of course, tradition demands that she change the deed on the land to favour the husband's family - which ultimately turns out to be you. You offer no compensation whatsoever to the family, despite the fact that the profit on the sale of old Musyoka's stock helped John to buy the farm in the first place. And to cap it all you claim half of the produce from the crops the family have planted, leaving them as good as destitute. You get a big farm, complete with borehole, ready-made to plant a cash crop, tilled for you by unpaid labour, maize and beans to sell, to which you had no right in the first place - and all for nothing!"

Mulonzya's patience ran out. He reached across the counter and shook the barman, who somehow had managed to sleep right through the crescendo of argument. When he awoke with a start, he found Mulonzya almost shouting at him. "I want my bill. It's time I was going." Turning to Michael again, he emphatically stated his case. "What I did was perfectly legal, so beware of what you say, Mister Michael!"

As the young man behind the bar lethargically eased himself off his stool and began to count the biro tally marks along the edges of the drinkers' beer mats to calculate their bills, Mulonzya again spoke, but this time in a patronising, admonitory tone which was tinged with threat. "For your own good, Mister Michael, I would like to remind you that you are a guest here - a guest of the Kenyan people and the Kenyan government. You have no God-given right to stay here, as you will soon discover if you continue to concern yourself with things that are none of your business. Furthermore, should you break the law here - and I will remind you that slander is a crime, even if it is delivered from a pulpit - I will personally see that you are expelled from our country."

"Well then let me point out to you, Right Honourable James Mulonzya MP," said Michael defiantly, "that if you believe it is part of your job to denounce publicly the work of my Church and my fellow priests within it, then I have the right, as a man of the Church, to explain why you have no right to express such opinions."

"Why do I have no right? What makes me so special?"

"Because, Mulonzya, your actions prove you are no Christian and not a practising member of any Church worthy of the name, and yet you court the votes of the young by quoting scripture in your speeches and by saying that you follow its principles in public life. In my view you do the exact opposite. You are no Christian. If people ask me to explain to them what I think, then it is my duty to do so. Mulonzya, all I do is allow your deeds to speak for themselves."

At this point, two completely unexpected events intervened and thus averted the danger of Michael and Mulonzya setting about one another in a full-blown row. First, the barman who had completed his sums presented the two of them with their bills. Michael gave his a quick glance, extracted a crumpled ten-shilling note from his pocket and said diffidently, "Keep the change," as he placed it on the bar with the receipt. Meanwhile Mulonzya had been rendered uncharacteristically speechless by what he had read. His jaw sagged and then he issued a few short words of Kikamba to the barman who replied instantly, nodding towards Michael, obviously saying that the priest had been keeping a tally of the beers whilst he, himself, had been asleep.

As Michael looked on innocently, feigning incomprehension, the old man who had been dozing in the corner began to rise to his feet, uttering loud grunts of discomfort at the exertion. With a hint of a wry smile on his lips, Michael looked on as Mulonzya begrudgingly counted out from his fat wallet a total of forty-five shillings and fifty cents to settle his bill. So absorbed were these three, Michael, Mulonzya and the barman, in counting money, that none of them paid any attention to the wizened form of old Munyasya slowly shuffling across the bar towards them, his stick punctuating the sand-scraping of his feet with light staccato taps.

With all dues paid and checked, Mulonzya finally turned towards Michael with the intention of asking how he had managed to amass a bill almost five times as large as Michael's. He was angry, but the encounter would also clearly have been carried through with a good deal of humour. After all, what was fifty shillings to a member of parliament like him? But his question was cut short by Munyasya, who pushed himself between the two of them.

Munyasya lifted his head to look Michael straight in the eye. He was smiling, as ever, and stood so close that the priest winced and drew away as the smell of the old man's hot and fetid breath hit him full in the face. Then, without any warning, without any hint of a growl in his throat to raise the mucus and phlegm, Munyasya spat directly into Michael's face. The priest jerked to avoid it but did not succeed and was left with a heavy streak of slime on his cheek.

Mulonzya began to snigger as an embarrassed Michael wiped his face with his handkerchief and glared back at the old man who simply carried on staring and smiling. Then, as if activated by the flick of a switch, Munyasya's entire body stiffened. He threw his head back until almost horizontal and shouted at the ceiling. But his words were so garbled, so slurred that only he, himself, knew what he had said. Both Mulonzya and the barman began to snigger again, but Mulonzya soon stopped when the old man turned to face him.

"Well I'll be going then." "Goodnight and thank you." Michael and Mulonzya thus announced their departures at the same moment, as if sharing the same breath and, as they left the bar and walked out into the night, the only sound that rose above the rattle of the wind was the continued laughter of the barman as he bolted the door behind them. The old man, grinning still, settled down for the night in his usual place, along the concrete veranda of the bar, just to the left of the closing door.

***

John O'Hara has refrained from interrupting, allowing Michael to tell the story as he, himself, remembered it. As the story has progressed, the initial expression of interested concern on the Bishop's face has hardened to obvious worry. When Michael finishes, he remains silent, pensively turning over his own recollections of the argument he has just had outside with Mulonzya and the others. Michael does not break the silence now. He seems content to lean back on the settee and blow long curling swirls of smoke at the ceiling. Eventually, it is O'Hara who is first to break the silence. He speaks slowly, in a low heavy voice, which seems to communicate more meaning than the words themselves. "That explains quite a lot."

Michael jerks his head forward in a silent question. "When I was outside earlier, it was Mulonzya who was doing all the talking. To be honest I couldn't make much of sense of it. He went ranting on about...

this and that ... as if I ought to know the whole story, which of course - I now know - I didn't. What you have just told me has filled in some of the gaps and now I can see what he was getting at."

"Well? Enlighten me."

"No. Not yet. I want to hear the rest of your story first. This fellow Munyasya, the old man. He keeps on cropping up, doesn't he? Wasn't it him who was hanging around outside the mission when I came up to see you the morning after the fire?"

Michael gives a short resigned grunt of a laugh. "It was indeed. I'd quite forgotten about that." During a short pause he is obviously searching for words to express an idea, which has become suddenly clear in his mind but which also has remained perennially difficult to relate. "It's ironic, you know." In answer to O'Hara's glance he continues. "It's a hell of a coincidence when I think back on it. I remember that evening..." He seems momentarily to have forgotten the tragic events of that morning. He seems suddenly absorbed by his memories of a day some weeks earlier. "It was the day we opened the new church in Thitani. I got back just after dark feeling particularly low for a number of reasons. It's quite funny, really, but I decided that night to commit my frustrations to paper and present them to you. I never managed it of course, but I was ready that night to resign from the priesthood and actually tried to write a letter to you to explain my reasons." O'Hara shows no visible surprise at this. "Anyway, as is usual with me, when it came to the crunch I just couldn't find the words so I gave it up as a bad job. I decided to write to Janet instead. Why is it, John, that I can express with such ease to her things which I find impossible to describe to anyone else?" O'Hara privately hopes that this is a rhetorical question. "Anyway, old Munyasya was hanging around then as well, as well as the following morning. I didn't give it a second thought because for some months now he's been coming to the mission for food and water. I haven't seen him much but Mutua tells me that he calls at least twice a week. Mutua usually sees him, not me."

"You said you were feeling depressed that night, Michael. Why? Just things in general or..."

"Oh everything, John. Things in general, things in particular. I'd just got Janet's letter telling me she was pregnant - and then there was Thitani - and all the other frustrations I've been talking about just seemed to pile up before my eyes. It made everything seem so hopeless."

***

Three scorpions in a week. The compound would have to be cleared. In his heart of hearts, Michael knew how much he had been neglecting the day-to-day running of the mission, but for some weeks both his energy and his willingness to devote time to such tasks had deserted him. Certainly the mission compound would have to be cleared. After the recent rain, it had become overgrown with long grass and weeds and he was now beginning to pay for not clearing it straight away. Scorpions and, more likely than not, snakes as well had moved in with him as unwelcome guests. As he stooped to clear the mess on the floor, he mumbled out loud to himself that he would have to get Boniface and the other catechists to help him to cut down the grass the following morning.

Only a minute before he had inhabited only his own mind and had been totally engrossed in the task he had set himself that evening. He had lost all awareness of the physical world around him and of his own presence in it. He had deliberated over words, reliving through memory the feelings which had prompted him to begin the letter and trying to imagine a new future which, he was convinced, its writing would unfold. Thus he had ceased to notice the silent room. Not even the flickering shadows of the candle-light by which he wrote disturbed this private world, which still would not quite reveal itself completely either in his mind or on paper.

The table was littered with sheets of writing paper. Some were almost blank, save for an odd word or two. Others had only crossings out which could in no way testify to the amount of time and thought Michael had invested in them.

Then, by the sound of scaly scratching across the floor, he was suddenly, abruptly, prodded back into the tangible world. Only a split second later, it was clear that the source of this sound had become everything, overriding both thought and sense. It was as if he, himself, had done nothing, as if a separate being inside his body had taken control and ordered complete subservience. This sound of scratching on concrete had triggered the reaction, a reaction which was now a part of him, unthought and unconscious, used but rarely felt, like walking, standing or thinking.

Immediately he drew up his feet from the floor. His eyes raced with the sound and its echoes until they had fixed on their target. In an instant he had taken off his shoe and set off across the room with it in his hand. With one giant lunge forward, he struck the blow apparently without thought or planning. The slap of the heel on the concrete floor and the crack of the scorpion's skeleton were simultaneous, but nevertheless distinct sounds, experienced together, but perceived separately. The slap without the crack would have prompted another immediate strike. There would have been no time to think, no time to ponder, just the need to act. Only when he withdrew to sit on the floor a yard from his prey with his shoe still in his hand still ready to strike, only then did he become conscious of having done anything at all. Only then did he see that he had caught the animal but a glancing blow with the very edge of the heel, a blow which had cracked an oozing furrow diagonally across the carapace just above the tail. It had been enough, though, to weld the carcase to the floor, to leave the claws open and outstretched, to bring the sting high for the last time. In the same amnesia of instinct, he inspected the shoe for debris and, finding nothing sticking to the sole, put it back on his foot.

An inquisitive head rose above the arm of the chair by the bookcase and surveyed the scene for a moment. Then, with languorous disinterest, Michael's cat, Ikuli, silently crossed the room and stopped a yard from the dead scorpion. Ikuli's eyes fixed on the animal and then turned to stare wide and questioning towards Michael. With continued glances for reassurance, the cat tentatively reached forward and gently flicked the dead scorpion with an outstretched paw. The front of the body rose and fell, whist the rest remained still, the whole hinging along the impact line of Michael's blow. With growing confidence the cat then lunged forward and a paw sent the carcase slithering and spinning across the floor. As it hit the far wall, Ikuli's eyes again turned to seek Michael's reassurance. Was this really no more than a plaything now? Then with a mad dash across the room, Ikuli regained his prize and immediately bit the dead animal through the middle of its body, neatly avoiding the claws, bringing another loud crack from the carapace. Again Ikuli looked up as he stood proudly over his prize, but a moment later his interest faded. His face stretched and then shrank in a yawn before returning to his chair to lick his lips and sleep.

"I feed you too much porridge," said Michael out loud as he rose to his feet.

A couple of minutes later the corpse was in the dustbin and Michael was back at the table, trying to recreate the sentient inner world of his own mind, which would again shut out all reality. He soon realised, however, that the disturbance caused by the scorpion had broken his concentration. Instinct - or was it a lack of commitment? - immediately told him that his desire to express what he believed were his true feelings in a letter of resignation to John O'Hara had yet again been thwarted. How many times in the last few months had he tried to write that letter? He had tried as many times as he had failed. On every occasion, and this was to be no exception, he had been prevented by his inability to make his grievances sound sufficiently important or credible to warrant the unquestionably drastic action of leaving the priesthood. After all, were not the frustrations he was currently experiencing neither more nor less serious than those he had encountered and, for the most part, learned to accept at any time during more than ten years as a missionary priest? Could it be that the merely over-zealous activities of an eager-to-impress catechist in Thitani that day had focused his conscience on what was never more than a collection of isolated trivia and magnified it out of all proportion?

The day was to have been one of joyous celebration. For some years the people of Thitani had clamoured for their own church. Though Michael had tried to convince them that the primary school classroom that they had always used for mass was perfectly sufficient, they remained adamant. Ever since John O'Hara, during his time as parish priest in Migwani, had deigned to create this small market centre as one of his stations, the Catholics of Thitani had consistently demanded their own church. Their demands were understandable for numerous reasons, paramount among which was the fact that this small town could already boast of two small but purpose-built Protestant churches.

It had taken the Catholic minority several years to amass enough money even to lay the mere foundation of their dream. The final designs, accepted by both the diocese and the parishioners were very ambitious. The church would be large to cater for the equally large number of expected converts who would be attracted to the faith by the magnificence of the new building. It would be built from cement blocks, not the much cheaper earth bricks which people used to build their homes. Its stature would be worthy of respect and its solidity and air of permanence would inspire the confidence of its congregation.

The scheme had, of course, suffered its ups and downs over the years. They had run out of money several times. They had been forced to rely at one stage on money collected by Michael during a tour of American dioceses. He had been sent on a fund raising tour by John O'Hara and his photographs of the unfinished church in Thitani had created more interest and thus raised more money than any of the other - and in his opinion more deserving - aspects of the diocese's work. It was therefore slowly, sometimes almost brick by brick, that he and his Thitani parishioners had seen the project through to its conclusion and that day was to see the first service under its resplendent, shining tin roof.

The daylong celebration was proudly enjoyed by all who attended. The mass was solemn and uplifting, both joyous and sad, quite different in feeling from any other the Thitani congregation had ever known in their primary school classroom. It was perhaps the sense of weight and permanence that the new building gave to the ceremony which muted people's usual exuberance. Whereas, on a normal day, the entire congregation would have belted out their contributions in full voice, on this day they had behaved rather like the English at evensong.

And then there was a meal laid on by the parish council for the numerous guests. Surely cow peas and stewed goat had never tasted so sweet. In the heat of the afternoon, over two hundred people, including an uninvited but welcome few who had sneaked in for a free meal, sat on the ground in the church compound. A deep contentment, even a sense of fulfilment pervaded all conversation. Everyone confessed that they had felt that day a true feeling of community. Individually, every person who had lived through the duration of the project from idea to completion greeted Michael with great affection, shook his hand for minutes on end and thanked him sincerely. Though he often complained that he was not getting a chance to eat his food, he could not deter the seemingly endless queue of people who waited their turn to express personal, heart-felt thanks for his help and encouragement over the years. By the time the sun began to sink towards the horizon, tiredness had begun to take its toll on the celebrant and some of those who had shared the day had already set off home. Most, however, remained to stand in small groups discussing their lives in the spirit of hopefulness, reconciliation and brotherhood that the day had sought, apparently successfully, to engender.

When Michael began to announce his departure by explaining that he wanted to reach Migwani before darkness fell, it was Boniface who stepped forward to interrupt. He told Michael and the attentive crowd, though it was obvious they already knew what he was about to say, that there was one more thing they wanted Michael to see before the day could be brought to an official close.

Having offered no more information than this, he invited everyone to follow him across to his own homestead a few minutes away on the other side of the main road. Michael assumed - even hoped! - this extra unexpected event would probably be a beer, or a bottle of soda or some memento, a carving possibly to commemorate the occasion. Though by then he felt thoroughly exhausted, he made no excuses and accepted the invitation with sincere enthusiasm. As the large group made its way over the road and on through a wide gap in the thorn-bush thicket which surrounded Boniface's homestead, it occurred to Michael that he seemed to be the only person present who did not know what was about to happen.

All the invited guests, the Bishop, the District Officer, the Members of Parliament, the Chiefs and the like had all left some time before. It was obviously something laid on especially for him and, though he tried not to show it, he began to feel both touched and embarrassed at the same time.

As the hundred-strong party approached the admixture of round earth-walled huts and part-built concrete structures that made up Boniface's homestead, these feelings were heightened by the mood of those around him. Everyone seemed to have grown strangely serious, solemn, in fact. Boniface led them all to a granary made from split sisal poles and set on sturdy legs to stand a foot above the ground. It was obviously very new. The roofing thatch had been left untrimmed and in places strands of green showed clearly that grass freshly cut after the recent rain had been used to complete the covering.

People took up positions around the structure as if they had rehearsed the entire affair. There was suddenly no talking, no joking, just a sea of serious and now determined faces which seemed to Michael to express more a sense of duty than celebration. Boniface beckoned to Michael to come forward and then invited him to look inside the granary. As he peered into the darkness, Boniface began to speak in a low voice.

He addressed only Michael, saying that this was designed to show him how much people wanted to thank him for having transformed their town from a small bush market place to one worthy of a fine grand church. It would also display to Michael just how much the members of his church truly wished to follow the teaching of Christ. Boniface said several other things, but by this time Michael had ceased to listen.

Inside the granary, piled from floor to ceiling was a collection of objects the like of which he had never before seen in Kenya. The interior of the hut was packed so tightly he could hardly make out what most of the objects were. Certainly there were carvings, both large and small, painted shields and spears, clothes, headdresses, knives, skins and much, much more. Michael was transfixed by the sight, rendered utterly speechless by the wealth of beauty he saw.

Boniface was still speaking, saying something about now wanting to publicly prove their desire to be true Christians. By the time Michael shifted his gaze from the interior of the granary back to Boniface and then to the faces of the crowd, a number of appointed children had already pushed armfuls of dried grass between the legs of the structure. Boniface took Michael's arm and led him aside. All drew back away from the hut except Boniface, who again came forward, pausing on the way to take a corked bottle from an old man. Then, after quickly sprinkling the contents of the bottle inside the hut, he stood back and lit the dry grass below. "For you, Father," he said as the grass smoked white and flames began to lick the base of the granary.

Michael wept, just a little, not enough for anyone to see. Surely this had never been his intention. This hut was obviously filled with these people's most treasured possessions, many of them family heirlooms passed down from long-forgotten generations who had never even heard of a white man, let alone his God. Obviously everything which was about to fuel this bonfire was of great religious or ceremonial significance and hence the need to destroy it in order to confirm the strength of their conviction to Christ. Or could it be that they were merely symbols, artefacts of the 'old life' being destroyed to demonstrate that Thitani and its people had entered a new age and with it the state of 'development'? Whatever the explanation, whatever the significance of these beautiful things, the seriousness of this gesture was plain to see. The crowd looked on in silence as first the grass burned and then, with an almost foreboding thud, the kerosene inside lit to engulf the entire structure in flames. No, this had never been Michael's intention, but he had no means of communicating this now without adding insult to obvious injury.

This single event had soured his entire day. In his eyes it nullified, even outweighed, all the good that a new church in Thitani could ever hope to realise. In the long run this act could surely alienate people from the Church or turn people against Christ in whose name it was being perpetuated. Thus it was with great sadness and a sense of failure that Michael rode home. No external sound penetrated the cocoon of noise from the motorbike's engine. His thoughts turned inward as his body instinctively and efficiently kept the motorcycle upright and moving through the sandy dry river beds and the loose scree of the narrow, scrub-lined track. By the time he reached the mission in Migwani, his resolve to write to the Bishop was set. It seemed that every potential step forward was necessarily accompanied by an immediate and tangible step back. Every plus had its inevitable and greater minus.

And yet the conviction remained that if only he were qualified - or even just allowed - to attack what he considered to be the root causes of suffering, then his work, both in and out of the church, would see real progress. What could he ever achieve with his hands tied? He could see himself as a child plugging the dyke with his fingers to hold back the inevitable flood. His handicap in the task appeared to be that forces out of his control were driving bulldozers by the dozen into the other side of the dam.

Why was it that he could not write such things to the Bishop, but only to Janet? Having failed to express a single relevant feeling in his letter to O'Hara, and having been disturbed by his encounter with the scorpion, he decided to shelve the project and write a short note to Janet instead. First, however, he re-read her last letter which had told so much, as ever, of her clearly non-relationship with Pete. As he read on, the thin yellow sheets told of her fears that she might be pregnant. A hurried postscript said simply, "Oh hell, Michael, I've just got a positive result. What can I do? I'll write soon."

Could it be that all these frustrations with his work were merely by-products of an unattainable desire to be with Janet? Every time he re-read her letter the feeling grew that he could be of more help to her in London than ever he could be to anyone in Kenya. Was he imagining this bond of friendship between them? Is it possible to imagine love? Is it possible to do anything other than imagine it! How else could he explain this tendency of his to allow petty frustrations to come between him and his work? And was the feeling so great that he should lose the motivation to continue? Surely there was only one possible conclusion. His one desire was to be with Janet, to try to help her through her difficulties, not out of vague ideas of Christian charity, but because he loved her! To admit to himself that above all else in life he would choose Janet and marriage was a revelation of the most powerful kind. For some minutes he was nervous with happiness, unable to suppress the smile that eventually gave rise to tears of relief. The mere thought, the committing of it to paper thus confirming its existence released knots of unacknowledged inner tension.

Emotions pent up by months or even years of suppression flooded to the forefront of his mind. Surely the fact that he could so easily communicate these things to her whilst their expression to John O'Hara had been impossible, surely this proved that she was something very special to him. Every time he had tried to write that letter to O'Hara he had failed. Every time he had written to Janet instead and he suddenly would find that he could express everything he wanted with ease. He could communicate with her. He could express his ideas simply and be sure she would understand. Why could he not write about the same things to O'Hara and have done with it, once and for all? John O'Hara would demand that every argument, every point raised should be neatly worked out and wrapped up in watertight logic. Michael could never hope to do that. To Janet he simply said what he felt and that was enough. His frustrations were not born of any reasoned analysis of his position; they were instinctive, gut reactions to obvious contradictions. Or could it be that the source of all this discontent was his as yet unacknowledged desire to be with Janet? How could he ever hope to explain that to someone like O'Hara?

Surely in this letter he had uncovered the truth. It was his love for her that was changing his attitude to life. She had to realise this. Once stated, it seemed so obvious, even trivial. Would she take the revelation seriously? Would she agree that the best thing for everyone concerned was what he had suggested? He undoubtedly loved her enough to marry her. He undoubtedly loved her enough to be a father for her child. Without re-reading what he had written to her, he folded the letter, placed it in an envelope and added the address.

It was a sharp tap of a stick on the kitchen door that cracked open his inner world this time. He glanced at his watch before rising from his seat at the table. It was very late indeed. Taking the storm lamp, his only light, with him, he went to answer the call. As the door swung open it revealed a sorry sight. Standing, hunched and shivering in a puddle of water which had dripped from the tap on the rain-water tank was Munyasya, a vague smile still showing through the contortions which the cold night had set his face. "Oh Christ," muttered Michael beneath his breath, expressing both pity and anger.

The old man made no sound. Neither did he move as Michael withdrew into the kitchen. A moment later, Michael reappeared in the open doorway to hand over first a cup of water and then a piece of bread that the old man's grip holed and tore. He took one sip of water and then emptied the rest onto the ground. Much of it splashed over his feet. Without a discernible word coming from his lips, he mumbled to himself, handed back the cup and walked slowly away with his thin fingers clutching the bread like blades. After locking the kitchen door, Michael yawned. The day's exertions had at last caught up with him. On his way through to the bedroom, he paused to pick up the letter to Janet, knowing full well that unless he placed it now in his jacket pocket, he was bound to leave it behind when he set off for Kitui in the morning.

He awoke in a smoke-filled room. When he gasped for air the acrid fumes stung his throat. He rushed to the door, opened it and peered down the hallway. He saw through the open door at the end of the corridor what appeared to be a wall of flame. He was trapped and began to panic. All the mission windows were iron-framed and barred against thieves. They would certainly keep him in. As he left his room, another glance confirmed that the fire in the living room really was there. He crossed the hall into the bathroom. He was relieved to find that he had not flushed the toilet that day. The bucket of dirty water reserved for that purpose was still there and it was full.

He took a blanket from his bed and soaked it in the bucket. He then draped it around himself and moved quickly along the hall. The fumes were almost overpowering. With his hand over his mouth, he ran across the blazing living room to the front door, turned the key and stepped outside. After several hacking coughs and a moment to regain his senses, he rushed to the window to look inside. From this safe viewpoint, the fire seemed nowhere near as bad as it had looked from inside. The table was burning and all the softboard ceiling above it. The books and bookcase were just beginning to catch fire. As yet, however, only the kitchen end of the living room was alight. He felt sure he could put it out.

Luckily all three of his water tanks were full after the recent rain. He had three thousand gallons of water in the compound if he needed it. If only he could get the back door open... Deciding that now, while his blanket and clothes were still wet, was as good a time as any, he went back inside the house. In one headlong dash he reached the far end of the room. He seemed to be surrounded by flames. Then, with a staggered turn to the right he was there, in the kitchen. He had the door open in a flash. He had forgotten to lock it. But now he could get at the tank that was right next to the door.

The first bucket of water he threw did no good at all. He had filled it to the top and then found that he was not strong enough to throw its contents anywhere near the still high flames. All he managed to put out were a few embers on the concrete floor. He felt more confident, though, that he could put out the fire with each subsequent trip to the tank. It was only the ceiling that was properly alight and only the ceiling that was likely to burn quickly. The more the fire was doused, the less oppressive became the fumes, enabling him to get closer to what flames still burnt.

He became completely lost to time and maintained the frenzied pace with which he began right to the very end. Within twenty minutes he had doused most of the flames, but the fire had continued and in fact rekindled in a score of nooks and crannies that his cascading buckets of water had not penetrated. Not until some three hours later, after making a complete inspection of the ceiling from above did he finally consider the job finished. Then, after climbing down from the rafters, he surveyed the remains of the living room by the light of the torch he kept in his bedroom, which had remained untouched by the fire throughout.

The entire ceiling had gone and his torch beam shone straight onto the underside of the tin roof. The metal sheets had become so hot that they had pulled off their securing nails. A whole sheet was flapping in the wind, the noise echoing right through the house. The table was badly charred but amazingly still in one piece. The fridge had melted. His chairs were destroyed, as were the bookshelves and all the books they had contained. The kitchen door had burnt through and the living room curtains had completely disappeared. The other rooms had been largely untouched. Most of the ceilings had burnt through at least in part, but the only real damage below them was occasional scorches caused by hot embers that had flaked off the ceiling boards.

In fact the damage cause by the fire seemed negligible when compared to the mess produced by trying to put it out. Everything was dripping with soot-blackened water. The floor was covered with an ankle-deep layer of semi-solid black sludge of water, charred paper, wood, and ash. For an hour or more Michael simply sat on the metal frame of an armchair from which the cushions had been burned and listened through the constant drips of water for a telltale hiss of renewed burning. But he heard none. He could obviously do no more. After a wash to get some of the smell of smoke from his hair, he changed into dry clothes and set off for Kitui to tell John O'Hara of his mishap. He remembered, however, to take the jacket with Janet's letter in it. After deciding to drive to town immediately, rather than wait until the morning, it had been the first thing that came to mind.

Dawn came during the return journey. By the time Michael and John reached Migwani - the Bishop had insisted on coming in person to inspect the damage - it was fully light. In daylight the damage looked much worse than Michael thought it would. During his absence the central part of the roof had collapsed, pulling more down with it. As the two men stood silently surveying the charred, sludge-covered remains of the living room, loose sheets of roofing metal swung in the wind, clanking against the rafters, occasionally hitting the charred ceiling and knocking down pieces of half-burned softboard and flakes of ash.

"What a mess," said O'Hara. "Any idea what caused it?"

"The only thing I can think of is the fridge." Michael set off across the room and beckoned O'Hara to follow. The tangle of fallen timbers had created an obstacle course. On the wall behind the fridge, previously unnoticed by Michael were several long black streaks of soot, too solid and even and certainly at the wrong angle to have been deposited by dripping water.

"That's your culprit."

"The flame did have a tendency to go out sometimes," said Michael. He gave a short laugh and continued, "I even filled the tin with fresh kerosene last night. I suppose that's what they call the luck of the Irish. One day we might even get electricity here so then we won't have to use these stupid kerosene machines. They're dangerous."

A knock on the door behind them demanded their attention. Framed in the doorway, clearly reluctant to venture any further was Munyasya, smiling.

"Not you again! I've got no drinking water. I threw it all on the fire."

The old man smiled and put his finger to his lips. "I think he wants a cigarette," said John. "Here, give him one of mine." Michael made the tortuous crossing of the room and offered Munyasya a cigarette from the packet of Sportsman O'Hara had given him. The old man took it with a mumble. When Michael lit it, he inhaled deeply and then blew a long column of smoke high into the air. Michael watched pensively as then he turned and left without a word.

"Well Michael you've got a lot to do. Don't worry yourself about money. I'll see to that. Get started right away. Try to get Daniel to come over from Kanyaa to have a look. He's a very dependable fellow and the best carpenter I know. It's not as bad as it looks. Once you get all the materials here it will be presentable again in a fortnight." O'Hara was soon ready to leave. "Don't bother coming back with me for the car. The lads from Mwingi will be in town later today. I'll get one of them to drive it back for you." With that O'Hara turned and left the room. Michael suddenly remembered the letter to Janet, which he had managed to take into town and then bring straight back home again. He called after O'Hara.

"John, will you post this letter in Kitui? I forgot about it earlier. It's quite important."

As the Bishop took the airmail envelope, Michael felt the irony of the situation. He might not be able to communicate his difficulties to the man, but at least he could get him to post his proposal of marriage. As the car disappeared over the hill to the south, however, Michael realised he had again missed an opportunity to have a real talk with O'Hara. Was the Bishop really so unapproachable, or was it Michael that simply could not face up to his dilemma except in his own imagination where his motives and reactions were safe from scrutiny? "Ah well," he said to himself. "One step forward and two steps back."

***

O'Hara is smiling whimsically as Michael finishes. "I don't believe it. Any of it. To think that I posted the letter in which one of my own priests proposed marriage to a girl half his age on the other side of the world. And it's quite laughable that the old fellow should come to the house after it's burned down and ask for a smoke!"

Michael was thoughtful and silent for a moment. "You don't think there could be more to him than we've allowed up to now?" he asked.

"In what way?"

Michael utters a short laugh and then stretches his neck. "I must be suffering from a persecution complex or something. It's just that he keeps on cropping up doesn't he? He was in the bar when I had the argument with Mulonzya. He was around both before and after the fire... and now this morning..." He pauses for a moment to seek a change of tack. In that moment, the lighter tone that had grown during his description of the fire disappeared suddenly, to be replaced by a return of the earlier gloom. "I've had run-ins with him before as well."

"Didn't he attack Janet a couple of years ago?"

"He did. She was in one of the *dukas* near the market, I think, and he came along and did one of his spitting acts. I don't think he meant any harm. He seemed to want to confront every *mzungu* he saw. He was a strange man." Here Michael's speech tapers to an inconclusive silence.

Both remain silent for some time, each lost in his own thoughts. Michael is considering how he might proceed with his case, but now there seems to be nothing left to relate except the events of that morning. He is surprised that O'Hara has made no reference to the content of his letter to Janet. He had hoped, by seeking a perspective in which to place the events of the day, to offer an explanation for his apparent carelessness. He had hoped also to promote an understanding of his current state of mind, which he believed, had been responsible for his thoughtless behaviour, but now he begins to see that nothing could possibly temper John O'Hara's judgment. However he tries to change the reality, the conclusion remains the same. Old Munyasya is dead and he, Michael, is responsible. There can be no escape.

Considerations of how or why begin to seem insignificant when weighed against the indisputable, tangible evidence of the old man's corpse at the roadside. Michael finds that there is no way forward, no path along which he can continue to explore his own motives. The inevitable is still as unacceptable now as it was when he began, except that now there appears to be no refuge in the past, no further reminiscence which could shed more light on his actions or endeavour to provide an excuse for his crime.

O'Hara on the other hand finds that two considerations have come between him and the matter in hand, relegating it, for the moment at least, to a position of relative insignificance. First he is struck by a realisation that during the eight years or so that Michael has worked under him, he has never really talked to him before simply as one person to another. All contact between them seems to have revolved around their respective functions of bishop and priest, of leader and disciple, whilst all conversation has been directed whether explicitly or obliquely towards the further accomplishment of the task to which they have both devoted their lives. As their conversation this morning has progressed, however, Michael has revealed ever more openly his personal feelings and motivations and has thus become steadily less recognisable as the priest O'Hara knows. Paradoxically, the more they have talked, the more like a stranger Michael has become.

This saddens O'Hara deeply, for it reminds him that his position as a figurehead often precludes him from such simple human contact. If he has never before found either the time or the opportunity to talk like this with one of his own priests, how far must he now be from the desires, hopes and needs of the common folk he has pledged his life to serve? It was after all for their benefit that he originally chose this life. He thus begins to feel that he has become parted from his mission, enwrapped in a cocoon of tasks and functions which prevent him from doing what ought to be his real work. Furthermore, he sees no refuge in the stance that all the good work of his priests is made possible by virtue of his direction and guidance. All too often it seems that he is the one who tries to dampen the enthusiasm of the priests. It is they who approach him with their schemes, their ideas and projects; most of them with truly laudable aims and then it falls to him, and him alone, to point out possible difficulties or undesired repercussions. He is always the one saying "no".

Rarely does he criticise his priests' ideas or ideals on grounds of their motivation or desired ends. Far from it, he has often found himself filled with admiration for their achievements. The strictures he has imposed could loosely be described only as 'practical considerations'. Sometimes a shortage of money has caused him to use his veto to block some of their ideas, but for the most part his reasons for appearing to thwart his priests' sincere desires to attack the root causes of the area's poverty have been purely political in the widest sense, born of a desire to retain some support from those with the influence to assist the Church's continued work.

Secondly, memories of his own time in Migwani begin to flood into his mind. The frustrations with the work of which Michael has spoken have served to remind him of the days when he dealt with those same problems, those same contradictions every day. Though he is convinced that the difficulties he encountered and had to overcome in those early days were greater, more deep-rooted than now, his self-admission that he had probably lost touch with the day-to-day practicalities of parish work cause him to withhold the opinion. He does, however, have sympathy for Michael's point of view, but doubts that Michael realises this. Thus he decides to offer Michael a respite from the tension of his self-analysis by relating some of his own experiences. It is an attempt to show solidarity.

As O'Hara begins to speak, Michael seems to be lost in hopelessness. He expects to have the final, inevitable details of the morning's events prised from his unwilling memory. He is therefore surprised, pleasantly, when it becomes clear that for once this man he has always had to make an appointment to see, wishes to talk openly of himself, to discuss common experience without imposing conditions upon the dialogue.

"Michael, I understand everything - all the frustrations, the joys - I know them well. I think you have a tendency to assume those years ago in my time it was different, that someone like me did not experience the same things. Well that's not true, because the problems then were just as difficult, just as unsolvable, just as frustrating."

"But it was different, John. The Church was different and you saw your role in a fundamentally different way in those days." Michael's is the voice of a mind already made up.

O'Hara shakes his head. "No. It was just the same," he says quietly.

Michael again is apparently unable to express the obvious truth he perceives. "But surely the whole emphasis was different. From my experience I can say that my greatest pressure, the greatest shortfall between desire and achievement, comes in the pastoral side of the work. In the furtherance of Christianity with a small 'c'."

"Oh come on, Michael, stop being trendy. There's no such thing and you know that. Christianity means Christ. Let's at least be clear about that."

"I'm sorry. I'm not expressing myself very well." He pauses to allow his ideas to re-form. "You see it's not the Church itself or my place within it or the preaching or even the spiritual lives of myself or my parishioners... Somehow all these things seem to take care of themselves and what's more they aren't really measurable in any meaningful sense. Now there are some... no! ... many priests who see the furtherance and promotion of those ends as paramount in their work. But I don't. I put freedom, justice, human dignity and human development in the broadest possible sense and a host of other things on a plane way above the rest. The Church has survived - even bettered itself - for over a thousand years, and yet all around there are people, God's people, denied not only betterment in their own lives, but also even the basics of human existence. They are being denied life, itself. Now as a priest, I follow Christ. It was his teaching that drew me to the Church, his example I resolved to try to emulate. The Church as an institution was never attractive to me. It has been home, but only a home in the institutional sense. It still remains at least tacitly responsible for some of the forces that oppress the very people it should be seeking to liberate. Christ said human suffering was unjust, and that we should all strive to eliminate it, to further just causes and it has always been this that I have seen as my mission. Now, after ten years of solid work - and I can honestly say I have done my best, John - I cannot cite a single success. I cannot claim that anything I have done has ever turned out to be more than cosmetic. In the meantime injustice has deepened and the poverty of people here has surely increased."

"But Michael, one cannot expect as a mere individual to change the world."

"I don't want to change the world, John. For Christ's sake, I might be unrealistic, but I'm not mad! If I could honestly say, though, that through my actions or my words that someone somewhere might have benefited, then I'd be satisfied. But it seems that whatever I try to accomplish, because I believe it to be right, either backfires on me or just withers away. Sometimes things are undone or nullified by external pressures beyond anyone's control. I can live with that. But in the end, all I can see is failure. My failure." Michael is almost shouting by the end. He stares wide-eyed and agitated at O'Hara, but the Bishop offers no reaction. He continues, "For a start my ideal is to further Christianity and with it the Church through example, through truly Christian work. The starving need food, not prayers. The sick need care, not promises of salvation. How can I teach by example? I must be suffering delusions if I think I can. I have nothing to offer." His arms are outstretched in confession. He is pleading for O'Hara's agreement. "I can dream up health schemes but I'm no doctor, agricultural projects but I'm not a farmer, literacy schemes but I'm not a teacher - what can I do? I can preach, but what good will that do by itself? Nothing, except encourage people falsely to be patient and tolerant of their lot. And what is happening on the other side of the coin in the meantime? People are being dispossessed of their land, their stock, and their entire livelihood. And because they've got to sell to survive, everything becomes devalued because the precious market is swamped. They simply have no choice. So what happens in the good years when the fortunes of the place improve? Who will benefit? The already rich, like Mulonzya, who have the means both to survive and even to profit in these hard times, they find that what they bought for a song during the drought is suddenly worth a fortune. They grow richer, while the poor find they are literally poorer. They have no hope of ever regaining their land, of ever regaining that security. If they sell their land now, they will never get any of it back. If they don't sell, they starve - and still lose everything. Look at my maize growing scheme as an example." John O'Hara nods to indicate that he remembers the case and acknowledges its relevance to Michael's point. "A simple practical idea. Grain is cheaper in Nairobi. I have free access to a lorry. At home there are thousands without enough food. Even allowing for petrol I can provide maize in Migwani cheaper than people can buy it in the market. When people have nothing to begin with, a little more than their expectation can mean an awful lot to them. And what happens? The one man in the town with a licence to deal in wholesale grain bribes his powerful friends to threaten me with prosecution if I continue the scheme. I am told that I am trading without a licence. All right, I say, give me a licence and I'll go into business. But my application is blocked by the same alliance, so our trader continues to profit from people's hardship. He knows that grain is in short supply and he wants to be able to charge his own price for what he decides to offer for sale. And so I try to report him for overpricing. The same rules that grant him the licence in the first place set strict profit margins, and he is clearly exceeding them. I get told to keep out of politics. And anyway I later find that the trader is within the law. His transport charges are so high, he says, that the allowed margin then takes the price of the grain right up. He owns the transport, of course, and is charging himself an inflated figure for that so that he can then inflate the grain price."

"Michael, the Church has too much to lose. We have to be careful. We have to be selective in the battles we choose to fight."

"What have we to lose? We can only gain, unless of course our relationship with the trader is more important than that with the rest of the people. Either we win our case and thereby reduce the burden on people, or we lose and so enable people to see just who benefits from their suffering."

"But the problems were no different in my day." O'Hara's reply is quick and impatient this time.

"Probably not, but less acute."

"You're wrong, Michael. Different, yes, but just as difficult to manage. Now be quiet Michael, it's my turn." O'Hara averts Michael's interruption with a wave of the hand. "You cite the fire in Migwani as an example of your dissatisfaction with the job. To rebuild the mission you had to divert funds and effort from what you considered to be more deserving causes. 'One step forward and two back' is how you described it. What do you think I felt that morning? After all, I built the place. It's about the only tangible result of a near-lifetime's work. What do you think I felt when I saw it virtually destroyed? Do you think that the frustrations which demoralise you don't affect me, don't apply to me? You seem to assume that you are a special case."

***

Permanence had been his mission. When he arrived in Kenya as a young priest, he came to work among a people who had already been converted to Christianity, already been efficiently evangelised, saved from themselves by their paternalistic colonisers. The majority, of course, were Protestants because their Church had been granted a head start by the country's all-powerful but, in this unwanted area, largely unseen rulers. Catholicism arrived much later and at an apparent disadvantage. Missions could be established, said the administrators, but they must not be built within two miles of an existing church. Their motives might have been worthy, but in the end the result was just bigotry. They had wanted as many locations as possible to be developed by the efforts of the missionaries, whom they saw as an essential catalyst in the 'civilisation' of the country. They drafted laws, therefore, designed to avoid what they saw as duplication of effort. Catholics, however, saw it merely as discrimination, and nothing less than true to type, an export of the home country's tradition. Through their shortsightedness, they set a pattern for the future development of the country that would set one town against another.

The Roman Catholic Church in Kenya, as in many other countries, had embarked upon a policy of development from inside, a response to an indigenous movement, not an imposition from outside. The Protestant Churches, on the other hand, encouraged individual allegiance to themselves first, before the community at large. Service to the Church would itself promote material change, but the nature and extent of those changes would be controlled by the Bible's teaching.

Migwani location was a wonderful example of this dichotomy. O'Hara had chosen Migwani market - later to become the administrative centre of the location - as the place to build his church, just over two miles from Kyome rock, beneath whose stark slopes Baptists had long before established themselves. Before Kyome was by-passed by a new road from Kabati to Mwingi, it had been the centre of the location's activity. Higher and more fertile than the rest of the area, it was still the place where the best farming land and hence the largest density of population was to be found. Here the Protestants built their church, a mission house and a school in that order, all funded from overseas money collected in the churches, jumble sales and coffee evenings of Middle America. As the facilities took on an air of permanence, powerful people from Europe and America came to visit the place and were impressed. At home, their reports persuaded others, more powerful and richer than themselves, that they could make a true Christian gesture by donating money to the missions and thereby help the poor and underprivileged in Africa and also promote 'civilisation' of the natives. A better school, a bigger church and a finer mission were what the assistance built, an island of overt relative riches amid an unchanging land.

Students scrambled to get into the fine new school, better than anything the government could then provide in the area. In return for their education they learned to embrace the church with an unquestioning belief, to reject utterly the ways of their parents, to dismiss them as primitive and pagan, to condemn their elders for drinking *mawa* or *uki*, or for smoking *bhang*. Kyome was still a town without a bar, without a whore, where a boy would be expelled from school for being seen out of doors after dark.

But, in a pragmatic mechanistic way, the system worked. It produced results. It provided opportunities that people wanted to take. With the qualifications they gained from school, young men became teachers, administrators and pastors. They travelled to Nairobi to earn salaries. They were sent to study overseas on scholarships provided by the Church. Above all else, they lived this new life successfully and their families, though caused much pain in the process, eventually began to benefit materially. These young men in employment sent a proportion of their money home so that the whole family might benefit from investing in the farm. The money paid school fees for other children, bought fertiliser and good seed, more goats and then more land and so the family would prosper in the market capitalist manner of self-advancement, much to the satisfaction of those missionaries who had set the ideological transformation in motion. No self-doubt allowed here, because religious belief and political philosophy were merely different aspects of the same persona for these people. They truly believed in all they did.

Others, who had spurned the Church and its claims - or who had been spurned by it - were made to see the power of this new religion. Soon criticisms of its rejection of the traditional were silenced by the growing desire to share its adherents' prosperity. All wanted a part of this good fortune, but to attain it they must know the Church and its teaching or remain ignored. In the early days after independence, when even an unqualified secondary school leaver could walk into a white-collar job, the prestige of this church and its workers blossomed. It represented people's aspirations in terms all could understand. Membership was a passport to visit the riches of the Western world and later to share them, those same riches which had built the church and which were embodied in its teaching.

When John O'Hara chose Migwani market as the site for his church, he had no idea that after independence it would become the administrative centre of the location. In those days it was a small group of mud-walled shops on an insignificant track along the top of a ridge.

The main market centre was elsewhere, Migwani being host only to occasional trading in cattle and goats. The main trading centre was a mile or so to the south, where several Arabs and Asians had established shops in a place still known as the Arab *dukas*. These people controlled local commerce and so Migwani proper was not much more than a crossroads and meeting place on the way to watering livestock at the nearby dam.

It served, however, a number of social functions for those who remained non-Christian. O'Hara knew that and had tried to exploit it. Without much external finance, he relied on the efforts of Migwani's own people and he encouraged them to fund their new *kanisa*. It was important, he told them, that they should contribute as much as possible to the building of their church. If they were poor and could not give money, then they could offer their labour to carry stones and sand or make bricks. When the people of Migwani presented him with the results of their collections, he was able to match it with a similar amount from outside, thus making the project a truly cooperative effort.

He negotiated with the Chief and an old man called Nzou, who was willing to sell a part of his land. When complete, the deal was blessed by the Chief, and O'Hara, with his early converts, was able to start building a church. A complication arose when a stranger appeared just a week into the project and claimed that the plot of land in question had never belonged to Nzou, but to himself. Work had to stop for almost a year while the dispute was taken to court in Nairobi.

Since the area never had land titles recorded on paper, the court could not find in favour of any party, however, and left the matter unresolved. It did recommend, though, that the parties should employ an oath taker. The men who laid claim to the land should take the oath of the seven sticks. To lie under this oath meant certain death. With some reluctance - not least on the part of O'Hara, who, though he professed personal respect for traditional beliefs, was not keen to found his church on them - all parties agreed on a place, date and time where the oath would be taken. And then, next day, Nzou disappeared and was never again seen in Migwani.

O'Hara's initial relief that all appeared to be settled was soon forced to admit more disappointment. On a visit to the Chief to begin negotiations with the rightful owner of the land, he found that the price, unfortunately, had more than doubled and O'Hara was forced to start looking elsewhere. His original second choice was plot a hundred metres from the market, at the junction of the track that led from the main road down to Thitani. Though no more than an overgrown cattle track, it would allow sufficient access once it had been cleared.

The owner of this land was willing to sell, or so he said, and so O'Hara finally had his plot. The fact that the man was a crook working in collusion with the Chief became apparent when O'Hara's helpers turned up to begin clearing the land for foundations. "But we cannot build here," they said. "This is a sacred place. It is owned by no one, so no one can sell it and no one can buy it. It cannot be owned."

However, with the help of Catholics from nearby towns, O'Hara began and finished his church. Though made of earth bricks and sisal poles, and therefore appearing like a poor relation of Protestant Kyome, the structure gave great service and his congregation grew. The fact that it had been built on communal land was never forgotten, but it was simply assumed by all that Europeans would ride roughshod over any tradition, so it was hardly out of character.

But the Catholic Church too came to build schools. It encouraged people to improve their lot through their own community efforts and so the process was slow and the results second rate compared to Kyome's market system and foreign money. The real difference, though, was that O'Hara went out of his way to work personally with people. He did not stay at home waiting to receive his rightful respect, quite the opposite, in fact. O'Hara went out of his way to canvass opinion, to find out what people wanted and so people grew to like him. Migwani's mission house was to make the establishment permanent. Again built by the sweat and contributions of only local people, it was the finest house in the town. It boasted concrete walls, a tin roof and iron-framed windows with glass. This surely was what 'development' meant and people were very proud of it. Now Migwani could stand alongside Kyome.

After independence, a local war broke out. The Protestants built a primary school in Migwani, right in the middle of the Catholic patch. The Catholics responded with a new school at Kanyaa. People were happy with the results, however, for while the missionaries effectively competed, every town and village could realistically aspire to found its own local services. Now everyone might share the benefits of development. Schools, both primary and secondary, all with the blessing of the District Education Office grew up almost overnight all over the area. As Kenya seemed to grow richer, more school leavers found employment and there were thus renewed demands for yet more schools, and with them more churches.

And then something changed. The rain stopped. People's crops failed. Migwani families could no longer afford to pay school fees, because what funds families had were needed for food. Interest in schools remained, but no longer was there any local money to fund them. Christianity, in whatever form, had always been associated with increasing prosperity and increasing material wealth. Now times were changing. Life for most people was becoming much more difficult, more of a struggle than anyone in the area could remember. The new youth, educated in post-independence Kenya, having grown up with this association between Christianity and wealth, began to question the Church's role and the motives of the missionaries. They went to Nairobi and saw that there were many rich Europeans who neither attended church nor claimed to be Christian. They became, in effect, the Westernised sceptics, those who eventually came to respect neither the Christian Church nor traditional beliefs. It was a difficult time for everyone, a new age even. Rural society was still split between Church and tradition, and here in Kitui, because of the drought and the poverty it had brought, the traditional was again growing stronger as people sought out any insurance against suffering.

Among the rural educated population, there were some whom the system had rewarded. But by this time there were also many others who had remained unemployed and gained no benefit from their schooling. Some turned to crime and added weight to the arguments of the traditionalists who maintained that education and therefore, by association, Christianity also had harmed their youth.

The towns, on the other hand, were increasingly swelled by those people who had rejected everything traditional in favour of the Western world's cult of the self. They respected neither tradition nor Christianity and for the most part had completely forgotten their rural roots, their families and farms. Many, however, had taken their hardships with them and merely translated these into urban currency.

Privately, O'Hara was afraid that the Church had been superseded by the results of its own work. Could they any longer maintain that personal salvation in the afterlife remained the goal of human existence? The spiritual side of the work had always been his prime concern, but allied with that had been a desire to help people materially, to transform their lives from the old subservience into what he saw as a new kind of freedom. This had proved highly selective, however, and those who had attained it had also forgotten the Church and the faith which had originally granted it, preferring to embrace those things he, himself, most hated about Western society. Privately, he believed that his Church must change its ways. It must no longer strive to build fine houses for its priests and impressive structures to house its congregation. It must no longer be seen to concern itself primarily with the material world, but should seek to redefine the nature of the spiritual kingdom. It must do this, however, as part of the community it was to serve. No longer should the Church deal in currency that fostered false aspirations. But then he became a bishop.

***

"But that doesn't change my views." Michael seems sceptical of John O'Hara's sincerity. Though he has never before heard such a detailed history of the Church's involvement in the town which has been his home, he seems to regard it as unimportant, even irrelevant to his own analysis. O'Hara is immediately irritated. His expression hardens, recreating the attitude of disgust he displayed when he first entered the room to find Michael, apparently oblivious to the results of his own stupidity, dozing over a glass of whiskey. O'Hara, however, as is his habit, tries to hide his anger behind an expression of stolid silent defiance. "Don't you see, John?" When there is no reaction Michael continues. "The fact that you see the establishment of Catholicism in Migwani in terms of the permanence of a mission house and a church... The fact that you see this as one of your greatest achievements whilst by any interpretation of Christian morality the state of most of the people has worsened beyond recall... That is why I say the Church is not serving its people. We expect people to give to us. We demand their attention and their resources and we receive both. But in my opinion we give nothing in return except a pat on the head and a thank you. Our Church, in these times, is as bad as any Mulonzya in the way it treats people. We are merely furthering our own interests."

"Nonsense!" John O'Hara's dismissal is immediately pounced upon by an angered Michael.

"Look at what we've done! Take John Mwangangi as an example." Though John O'Hara maintains his almost defiant expression of disinterest, he is suddenly listening intently behind the mask. He cannot escape the parallel between himself and the young priest. Michael's efforts saved the life of his catechist's child. A year later that life had been taken in tragic circumstances. O'Hara had himself saved the life of the young John Mwangangi and though he had lived to maturity, his life too was cut tragically short in an event which had changed the lives of many who had been close to it.

***

Later, much later, Michael would come to look upon the case of John Mwangangi as one that had proved crucial in forming new attitudes to both his own faith and the way he chose to live it. At the time it was simply a tragedy. He was afraid that August morning, that Janet would never recover from the shock, so deeply had the experience appeared to scar her. Until that morning, Michael had judged that Janet saw life through a filter which categorized all experience into a set of limited types, assumptions which she had been taught by a culture she still thought was both rational and universal. Here was an event that contradicted those values and thus that day her world seemed to shatter. For once, she saw that neither she herself nor anyone else, for that matter, could claim to control what life would deliver. Not only do those who have grown up with the assumptions of Western materialism as the filters through which they sense all experience regard themselves as immortal, they also see themselves as the possessors of the only true reality. By reinforcing this naiveté, their society never allows them to mature. That August day, Janet was certainly confronted with experience that should have ended that false childhood. Later, much later, Michael would still not be sure whether as experience it had registered.

While Michael had been away on leave, she had grown close to John Mwangangi. That morning, so soon after his return to Migwani, he still had not fully understood the sequence of events that had conspired to bring John and Janet together in what was patently committed friendship. All he would remember later, much later, was that John had seen fit to drive the hundred miles of dust-trailing dirt road from Nairobi to attend Janet's leaving party in Migwani's secondary school. Privately, Michael had even been proud of her. Anyone, whoever it was, who received the unequivocal backing of John Mwangangi, as Janet seemed to have secured, was surely by virtue of simple proximity also worthy of respect. Later, much later, Michael would continually remind himself that here he had been using the word 'respect' in a sense that was devoid of fear, quite unlike the Kitui Akamba understanding of its meaning. It was an important distinction, because it was this word 'respect' which also labelled the relationship between a father and son.

He had never known the full story. John O'Hara certainly did, but he had always been reticent about it and had never once, despite Michael's regular prompting, shown the slightest desire to reveal it. Mwangangi always had a problem relating to his family in Kamandiu. On the face of it, he was the epitome of success for the mission school system. A poor boy, from a poor area given a chance in life, meaning of course a chance not to be what his birthright might have presumed, a chance that he had duly taken and used to massive and praiseworthy advantage. After secondary school and university, John had studied in London as one of his country's identified achievers. Exactly what achievements were likely to be his, the country had never specified. In retrospect, what he had received was the ultimate training in individuality, the perfect mechanism to expunge the duties and responsibilities demanded by the collected assumptions of culture, family, nation, or the people, whoever they might be.

When, almost two years after the murder, Michael eventually and surprisingly once persuaded John O'Hara to talk about Mwangangi, the Bishop of Kitui played down the fact that the boy had adopted his own Christian name, but could not expel from his eyes a momentary twinge of sadness, regret, or was it conscience? It was a common enough name, he said, and clearly Michael could only agree. He had denied the fact any significance, because, as Migwani's parish priest at the time, O'Hara had actually been responsible for the boy's prior instruction, and wasn't it very common indeed for those newly admitted to the Church to assume the name of whoever had prepared the path?

But Michael had already established that John O'Hara had been nothing else than Mwangangi's mentor. As parish priest in Migwani throughout the period of the boy's schooling and instruction in the teachings of the Church, he above any other was responsible for the boy's attitudes, the assumptions through which he would continue to interpret life. And John O'Hara had undoubtedly spawned a radical. How radical had the old man himself been at that time? O'Hara was willing to offer not a word of judgment on that.

It was possible that Mwangangi was either in the wrong place or arrived at the wrong time or possibly both. Initially, Michael could not believe his luck, when he had met the newly appointed District Officer over dinner in his Mwingi home. He had arrived expecting a typically perfunctory session with yet another civil servant who would soon move on under the pretext of pursuing that strange latter-day euphemism for life, the career. At least careers merely end. They never die. Or perhaps in some cases they do just that, and not just once. Now that is serious. But Mwangangi was clearly different. Alone amongst all such products of the bureaucracy Michael had met, John had both ideas and a commitment to see them realised, a rare mix in a society which might on occasions choose to see either as subversive.

At that first meeting, John Mwangangi had described visions of exactly the kind of work that Michael for a decade or more had always felt should be the Church's priority. What he was offering Michael was tantamount to a partnership, where he would handle politics, planning and official sanction. He would use his influence and position to help Michael lobby for whatever funds or permissions which might be needed for specific projects, whilst handing over completely to Michael all work related to local organising, day-to-day management and the crucial role of animator, who would canvas opinion and promote action wherever even a seed of interest might be found. But the plan was not merely altruistic. Michael saw that immediately. On the contrary, what Mwangangi described in ten minutes was the most sophisticated plan for political self-advancement he had ever heard, so impressive, in fact, that it might just have worked, had it not been for his own mistakes and his collaborator's background.

The appointment of Boniface Mutisya in Thitani had clearly been a mistake and Michael shouldered all the blame for it. His teaching methods in the literacy classes had definitely gone too far and he should have known better, but in the final analysis it was Michael's fault for not offering the young man adequate advice on how to cope with the instruction technique he was being asked to employ. Overall, his method was perfectly acceptable, but his choice of target was impolitic and it had created entirely the wrong enemy for John too early in the plan he had devised. Michael took complete responsibility for the error, however, because the monitoring of Boniface's work remained his province throughout. He would never be sure how much the eventual battle over Boniface's work contributed to John Mwangangi's move from his civil servant's position in Mwingi to his later highly lucrative position in a Nairobi legal firm, but on balance he would conclude that in the final analysis it had been Mwangangi's self-interest that had prompted the change. He was certainly a man with ideas, Michael had concluded, but without staying power. Perhaps that stated commitment of his had been mere words. Perhaps his initial assessment of the man had been too generous?

Because that was before he knew anything about the man's domestic problems. On that first meeting, which had been quite soon after the Mwangangi's appointment to Mwingi, Michael saw only a happy family life with John more than adequately adopting the role of husband and father. He was husband to Lesley, who generally remained quite silent whenever he spoke, which perhaps had always been an indication of how much John always dominated family life, and a father to Anna, a vivacious young girl whom Michael saw only that once before she went away to boarding school in Nairobi. But what lay beneath this becalmed surface, though, was a web of problems that was soon to bind him to a course of action that could only lead to tragedy.

O'Hara knew why John Mwangangi, right from being a boy, had been virtually at war with his father. By the time he returned to Kenya already a rich man after several successful years in London, he had neither seen nor spoken to his father for at least a decade, whilst some estimated it might have been as long as fifteen or more years. Behind everything John had done, including returning to Kenya to take a job at a fraction of the salary he had commanded in London, seemed to be aimed at reconciliation, between himself and his ideals, himself and his father, perhaps himself and what he saw as his lost identity. His British wife, however, could share none of her husband's ideals and simply did not understand what he was trying to do. What was more, she hated living out of the city. She never coped with the dirt, the bugs, the isolation or, more importantly, the claustrophobia of a small town. John and Lesley had grown apart, but had kept their public face content for the sake of John's career. And was that word here a euphemism for life?

There were some nasty rumours, though, that John had been seen with prostitutes in Kitui town on those evenings when his visits demanded that he stay overnight. Worse than this was the assertion that the girls were under age, merely schoolgirls to whom he would pay enormous sums of money to keep quiet. Not many people, however, believed those rumours, but, guilty or not, they hurt John and damaged him politically. In some places his name had become dirt.

But what really proved to be his undoing was his relationship with his father. The old man was about as traditional as it was possible to be. Perhaps even more so, in fact, because it became increasingly impossible for the son to satisfy the ever more demanding tests of loyalty and commitment which the father set. The final split came when father asked son to see his daughter initiated into womanhood in the traditional manner. Now, not even all the girls in bush places like Migwani undertook that treatment. Not for some considerable number of years had the practice, which always involved the girl's circumcision as well as instruction on a wife's duties, been at all widespread, or at least not many people would openly admit it was widespread.

Of course Lesley Mwangangi would not begin to discuss anything of the kind being done to her daughter. She began to wonder if John had gone quite mad when he revealed that he actually wanted her to undertake the initiation, because that would reconcile himself and his father. It had seemed to her that her husband was fast becoming a stranger again. Lesley suggested that even if they did go through with it the old man would just create some new demand and she was probably right about that. And then she would grow angry because she would then realise she had spoken of the suggestion as if it were possible that she might countenance it. The split effectively left John alone, unable to comply with his father's wishes and alienated from his wife and daughter.

Whether he and his father had been discussing Anna Mwangangi's initiation in that room behind the Safari bar after Janet's leaving party no one would ever know. It was widely assumed, though, that they had and that John had come from Nairobi to tell his father that his marriage and daughter were more important to him than his father's respect. Anna would not become a Kamba girl in the manner the father had demanded. The old man, people believed, had interpreted this as complete rejection by his only son and in a fit of anger had hit him with an axe. Every room had one at that time of year to cut wood for the stove the bar always provided to take the chill off the cool August nights. And so collective conscience put it down to a chance act, a moment of madness, rather than born of alienation, something much harder to explain, which, however, was closer to the truth.

In the morning, to say one final goodbye to her friend, Janet had gone early to the bar to make sure she would not miss him. And so it was she who first saw the corpse, on the floor behind the bed, the side of its head smashed by repeated blows from the father's axe. Not only Janet but also the whole community was in shock. Janet, of course, was to leave that day and leave she did, carrying that devastating experience with her as the final memory of the town. In Nairobi, Michael and Janet had gone to find Lesley, taking it upon themselves to carry the news of her husband's death, but she was strangely passive when they told her, almost disinterested. Janet would never understand that reaction, no matter how many times she tried to replay it in her memory during the long hours of her flight to London, or, indeed, the decades that followed.

Michael, on the other hand, had to return to his mission house in Migwani to share a communal grief that simply would not accept that a father could kill a son. And he too had lost a friend, a partner and a collaborator, one with whom he had shared much of himself. Perhaps most important of all, John Mwangangi had come to personify much of what it was he hoped to achieve through his own mission within the Church in Africa. He was a man whom the Church had moulded, a mind that the Church had nurtured and created in its own image, and ultimately his own family had rejected him as alien, an act that not only destroyed the family but also now had split the community. Where could he start to heal that rift? And what might he say to the next eager parent prepared to suffer years of hardship and sacrifice so that a child might have the opportunity of an education? Yes it would change the child's life. Surely it will affect the whole family, but are you aware of how much it will change you if the child succeeds, and can you cope with having your own values, your life's very assumptions questioned and then remade? Later, much later, it would all be clearer.

***

"So that's what you think." O'Hara does understand Michael's point of view, but he sees it as being at least in part a criticism of his own work and opinions. Michael's implication is that from the very beginning the emphasis of the Church's involvement has been wrong, has done little more than enforce new forms of injustice, the exact opposite of its professed ideal. O'Hara accepts that locally the direction of that work has been set largely by himself. If things have gone wrong, then he is responsible, but he does not yet accept this pessimistic analysis. Nevertheless, he gives it credence by dealing with Michael's opinions seriously and not dismissively. Though it is clear he does not agree with Michael, he is still respectful through his clear impatience. "So, Michael, you want to leave us?" His tone is serious and resigned, as if his mind is already made up. For once he looks directly at Michael as he speaks. He is perhaps asking for Michael to resign here and now, to state his desire to leave, formally and irrevocably.

O'Hara continues to stare throughout the unexpected silence which follows. Michael's eyes are looking blankly into the space before him. He seems reluctant to speak now. It seems, as he sits apparently precariously on the very edge of the settee, that he is unsuccessfully trying to find the right words. He is struggling to find a compromise between yes and no, both of which he wants to use, without either being correct. It is eventually O'Hara, however, who speaks again. He is conscious of Michael's dilemma and tries to offer him a starting point. Throughout he maintains what he believes to be an expression of open reassurance, but the uncharacteristic directness of his gaze lends an air of confrontation to his words, causing Michael to grow nervous and choose to interpret his manner as an expression of criticism. "Now, Michael, we've covered a lot of ground while we've been sitting here. Four or five times you've told me that for one reason or another you have concluded that you have no respect for your own work. You seem to have a very clear idea of what you think you ought to be able to accomplish and you seem to be saying that your objectives are impossible to achieve while you remain part of the Church. Now I don't really care about your reasons. They are your business and yours alone." O'Hara's voice hardens a little, betraying a hint of suppressed anger. "I don't care if it is the lack of what you consider to be worthwhile results in your work or simply your love for Janet which has persuaded you to leave." This last phrase seems to sting Michael with its directness. He has never before heard these words expressed as if they were part of something outside himself and it is a shock. "What I want, what I demand from you and what your faith also demands is commitment to your mission. That, I remind you, is first to the Church and secondly - and I stress secondly - to your work outside it."

Here Michael's impatience shows again. How can O'Hara make such a distinction in an age where the true ministry of his Church lies in the achievement of social justice? O'Hara continues without a pause, however. "Since you seem to have lost that commitment, you force me to consider removing you from your position until you can either commit yourself to it with renewed vigour or embark upon some other course. I cannot ignore what you have said. It is now up to you to state your position once and for all. Is it to be the Church and its work, or another life, either with or without Janet Rowlandson?"

O'Hara is immediately offended by Michael's reaction. He expects the priest to answer solemnly and unambiguously and with the overt seriousness demanded by his precarious position. When Michael falls back onto the settee in a fit of apparently uncontrolled ironic laughter, O'Hara's anger overflows. "For God's sake, Michael! This is not a game. I'm beginning to think I have been wasting my time..."

Michael interrupts. "Oh Jesus!" He shakes his head dismissively. "I'm sorry, John. Don't misunderstand me. I'm laughing at myself - no disrespect, no joke intended. How could I have been so utterly stupid? I've behaved like a child." He sits upright again and his laughter recedes. "Look, let's finish the important stuff first. Let's get back to this morning and finish that once and for all before we change the subject yet again. I've been trying all along to find an excuse for myself, but there isn't one. All I can do now is admit my mistakes and accept responsibility. I've been careless, thoughtless and immature, and it's about time I came clean. Now where did we get to?" He thinks for a moment. His now relaxed air contrasts sharply with O'Hara's continued agitation, which betrays an unspoken but fuming anger. "Right. I was on the way to Kitui to tell you I wanted to leave. Boniface came and asked me to take his wife to hospital. So I went off to Thitani. Obviously there was no point going back to Muthale from there so I decided it would be quicker to stay on the main road and come to Kitui. Selfishness justified again, you see? It was me that wanted to come here. Maybe Muthale might have been quicker, but it was in Kitui mission that Janet's letter was waiting for me."

***

Michael was driving too fast. The car lurched and banged over the eroded ridge that marked the end of the dirt and the beginning of the tarmac road. They had reached Kitui town, much to Boniface's surprise, in one piece. The numerous skids and slides during the trip had frightened him to the bone. Several times he had called out to Michael and gripped the dashboard with both hands, fearing the worst. Michael had simply ignored him, like he had ignored everything else this morning. The priest's head lolled nonchalantly on one side and, as he drove like a man possessed, he sang quietly to himself. Boniface uttered a deep sigh of relief as the noise of the dirt road was apparently switched off. The sight of smooth tarmac disappearing under the car reassured him greatly. For the very first time, he saw fit to turn round to ask his wife in the back seat if everything was still all right. She, however, offered no reaction to his glance. She remained silent with her face set, but without expression. By this time they had climbed the hill and passed by the prison. At last they were getting near the hospital.

"I'm just going to call at the mission on the way," said Michael. These were the first words he had spoken since they had set off.

"But, Father, the child is very serious. There is no time to spare."

"I'll be less than a minute. It won't make the slightest difference."

Michael drove past the road that led to the hospital and on up to the mission. He parked the car in the cathedral forecourt and, without bothering to switch off the engine or close the driver's door behind him, he ran inside.

"*Jambo*," he muttered mechanically to the clerk who sat, as ever, behind the typewriter in the reception.

"*Jambo sana*, Father," replied the young man with some surprise, for even before the short phrase was complete, the whirlwind which was Michael had gone, having first reached over his desk and plucked a letter from one of the pigeon holes on the wall behind him.

Having then slammed the front door shut behind him, Michael sprinted back to the car to take his seat like a scrambling fighter pilot. Boniface was looking round to face his wife in the back and they were talking, almost shouting in their frustration. Michael completely ignored them and immediately drove off down the short steep hill onto the road.

"Father! Stop! Stop!" shouted Boniface and grabbing at Michael's arm, causing the car to veer off course toward the deep roadside gutter.

Michael braked instinctively and immediately the car skidded to a screeching halt in a cloud of dust, half on and half off the tarmac. As Michael turned angrily to see what the problem was, Boniface's wife opened the back door and got out, moving briskly and determinedly.

At first without leaving his own seat, Boniface began to shout at her. His voice conveyed shock, not anger. Then, when she reached back into the car and took the child which still lay on the back seat, still without offering her husband any reply, he too got out of the car to join her. For a moment the two of them anxiously bent over the child as it lay on its mother's breast, but then, as the anxiety melted to resignation, Boniface turned to Michael and said quietly, almost with relief, "Thank you, Father. It is finished." Without another word Boniface watched his wife strap the baby's corpse to her back in her wrapper and then together the two of them set off walking stoically, but with obvious dejection. Neither gave Michael a single backward glance.

Michael beat the steering wheel with his fist in frustration. "Oh shit! Shit!" With his head in his hands, he sat there alone with the car engine ticking over and two doors swinging open for what must have been several minutes before he began to think again of himself and what he might do. He closed the doors and then returned to his driver's seat.

Though it would later seem futile that he should blame himself for the baby's death, his mind began to flood with a catalogue of his own errors. He should never have tried to drive all the way to Kitui. A health centre on the way - at Kabati, say - might have been able to help. He could have stopped there. He should never have made the detour to get Janet's letter when he knew that every minute was precious. Every thought seemed to heap more blame upon his own shoulders and, though he knew it was futile, he could do nothing to avoid this vicious self-recrimination. Even the admission that if the baby were so sick, a minute or even an hour either way would have made no difference in the long run was only partly admitted by his guilt.

Eventually he reached across to check the passenger door was shut and knocked the car into gear. It was then that he changed his mind. There was no point in going to see John O'Hara with half a story so, without switching off the engine, he returned the gear stick to neutral and opened Janet's letter. His intention was to read it quickly. As he tore open the envelope, he suddenly felt his expectations begin to crystallise. During recent weeks when his eagerness to receive this letter had obscured, even devalued everything else in his life, the last thing which had concerned him had been the news he expected it to carry. What he had envisaged all along and what he now explicitly sought in it was something within himself, some reassurance which would provide the final push over the brow of the hill he had been threatening to climb. He had proposed to Janet. She had not believed him, saying that she knew how important his work was to him, that she could never accept the responsibility for parting him from it. Then, in his own letter, he had tried to deny her image of his devotion to duty. He had told her with blunt clarity that he was ready to leave the priesthood. His reasons, he had said, were many, but she, herself, was by far the most important among them. Now in this long-awaited reply, Janet would mend the last flaw in the fabric of his resolve.

He read it many times. It wasn't very long, much shorter than many of her other efforts on his behalf. But under the circumstances it was perhaps understandable. His concentration on it rendered him completely oblivious to all else.

From beside the large new post office building on Michael's right a lank bent figure shuffled unnoticed across the road. When only a few yards from the car he paused to look at Michael, but the priest did not look up from the letter he was reading. Thus, still unnoticed, the old man continued on his way. Some minutes elapsed. A large herd of cows then appeared on the brow of the hill ahead of the car. A troop of boys had the animals well marshalled. They were town boys. They knew that roads were used by vehicles whose drivers became impatient if ever they had to wait, even for only a few seconds. They knew that a blast on a car horn could send some of the animals running and if that happened they might lose control of their herd and have to spend an hour or more collecting their animals together. Thus, the boys worked hard to keep the animals on one side of the road, always allowing enough room for a car to pass on their outside. Their herd was large, however, and the column of bedraggled, almost sleepwalking animals stretched over forty yards from head to tail. Soon they had reached the place where Michael's car stood askew, itself almost blocking one side of the road.

At this point, as the cows loped slowly past Michael's car, a white Mercedes turned into the road and found its way barred by a combination of Michael's car and cows. The driver automatically sounded his horn impatiently, giving three long sustained blasts.

Michael looked up for the first time in some minutes. A glance in his driving mirror revealed the faces of James and Charles Mulonzya, father and son, in the front seats of the family's trademark limousine. Mulonzya senior was gesticulating impatiently at him whilst still sounding his horn. "Get out of the way!" He heard the shouted words clearly through his open window, despite the horn blasts and the rustle of the passing herd at his right shoulder.

Michael's face set hard, infected by the other's impatience. "Oh piss off, you stupid whore," he muttered. His own engine was still running, so in one quick movement he knocked the car into gear and set off, his foot impatiently hard down on the throttle. Immediately he knew something was wrong. A low-pitched thud of impact came from the front of the car and a group of people walking towards him down the hill began to shout and wave him to stop. He slammed hard on the brakes and the engine stalled. What was it? A rock? A goat? The possibilities raced through his mind in a meaningless jumble as he sprang out of the car and stretched to peer over the bonnet. He saw nothing at first, but then as he walked forward, his heart sank and his senses raced in shock. Doubled under the front of the car was a man, an old man, wedged between the road and the underside of the car's bumper.

Before Michael could react, the group of onlookers arrived on the scene. Pushing him aside they hauled the old man free of the car and laid him at the side of the road. He was not yet dead, but obviously close to it. Mulonzya appeared at Michael's shoulder to look on and was immediately engulfed in a fit of rage. He began to shout in Kikamba at the others, too quickly for Michael to follow every word of what he said. The odd word, however, was enough to convey the entire meaning.

As Munyasya gave out long blood-wet groans from deep within his crushed chest, Mulonzya publicly accused Michael of murder. The priest was still too shocked to react, too upset to offer any defence as the other explained to the small crowd that had by now gathered that Michael hated this poor old man. He personally had seen Munyasya spit at Mister Michael and everyone knew that the old man, demented though he might be, had recently set fire to the mission house in Migwani. Even though everyone knew him to be mad, everyone also made allowances for him, would help him to his feet, walk with him to wherever he wanted to go and even let him travel for free on a bus, as he must have done that very morning to reach Kitui town. Everyone knew that the old man often lay down in the road. Surely this priest should know as well?

For some minutes there was complete mayhem on the road before the cathedral. As the pathetic old Munyasya lay in a heap at the roadside dying, but still receiving what all judged to be Michael's hollow concern and futile attentions, James Mulonzya continued to make a politician's speech to the fast-growing crowd. Meanwhile a hundred or more cows blocked the road, or pushed their random way between the blocks of people, one almost treading on Munyasya as Michael placed his rolled-up jacket beneath the old man's head. When two of the now uncontrolled animals, buffeted by others reacting to the noise of a lorry passing by on the main road, walked sideways into the white Mercedes, they rocked it on its suspension, causing Charles Mulonzya, who was still inside, to grow visibly agitated. After opening the window of his car, he shouted at the boys who by then were much more interested in what was being said at the side of the road than in what their cows were doing on it. Though Charles shouted his stern and even angry command to the herdsmen, neither they nor anyone else heard a word of it above all the other commotion, now caused mainly by the continuing speech of Charles's father.

And then suddenly, dangerously, the white Mercedes moved off, at first only to cover a few yards before coming again to a screeching halt as it hit a cow. Then, as the frightened animal panicked, pushing two others and then a group of people off balance, a woman to the left of the car, well away from the main site of commotion also fell to the ground at the side of the road, unnoticed except by just a few of the onlookers, who assumed that she too must have panicked on seeing the frightened animal charge away from the car. And then the white Mercedes screeched into motion again, this time turning to the right and forcing a path through the scrambling herd. And then, in a plume of dust as it left the tarmac on the inside of the corner at the bottom of the hill, it was gone onto the main road and to the left and out of town. Though many may have turned momentarily to look, few noticed it had gone, being still more interested in the fate of old Munyasya and James Mulonzya's merciless interpretation of it.

Mulonzya's speech continued for some time until it was interrupted by the dying man's loud gravelly laugh. This brought a short pause when everyone looked in his direction. Mulonzya then continued, his words tinged with a tragic, almost theatrical bitterness.

"Munyasya, today you have become a martyr. You have shown to these people that what I have been saying is true." There were murmurs of agreement at this. "You will be remembered forever, Munyasya," he said slowly, provoking some to applaud.

"It's true." "We agree." "We can see." The calls began to ring loud in Michael's ears. He was trying to speak, trying frantically but in vain to find words which would explain that he had not seen the old man lie down in front of his car, but how could he not have seen him? When he walked unaided, Munyasya moved so slowly that it would have taken him many minutes to settle down so neatly on the road in front of the car. All eyes turned towards the priest, their gaze unanimously accusing him of the crime Mulonzya had invented.

Michael remained speechless, rooted to the spot and unable to react. Then, just as he began to feel the pressure of the now silent crowd that confronted him, Munyasya laughed. For a while he had been almost ignored. Everyone had turned away, forgotten him for a while. Prostrate on the rutted red earth by the roadside, his limp body moved not an inch, but issued a long, clear bout of liquid laughter. He tried to speak, but his mouth was bloody and the sound became a gargle, spat and unintelligible. The shocked crowd looked on as he was engulfed in a near fit of laughter that was cut short only by the orgasmic spasm of his death.

Michael took his chance. While everyone else turned to look at the dead man, some with pity but most with fear, he got in the car and started the engine. Though several people tried to stop him, he drove clear of the crowd and away up the hill. But there was nowhere for him to go. He had not wanted to try to run, to hide from the responsibility that was obviously his. It was simply that the events of weeks past and especially those of that morning had broken his spirit, had finally doused his desire to try. For the first time in his life he had admitted defeat and turned his back in shame. It was his own conscience he could no longer face.

At the top of the hill, Michael drove straight on over the main road without stopping at the junction, straight into the compound of the

Bishop's house. Inside the house he found John O'Hara reading the Daily Nation before retiring to take his after-lunch siesta.

"Michael, come in." His perfunctory greeting was open and friendly, but automatic. Only when it was finished did he see Michael's tension.

"John, I've done something stupid - they'll be here in a moment. I've just run over someone. I didn't see him - the stupid old whore was lying in the road in front of the car - I had no idea he was there." Michael's voice cracked on the words. He was at a loss as to where to begin his description of what had happened or of how he felt.

O'Hara stood up and slowly crossed the room toward the priest. Laying his hands reassuringly on Michael's shoulders, he spoke quietly, but paternalistically. "Just a minute now, Michael. Let's sit down. You're talking riddles..."

Michael pulled away impatiently, refusing to accept any solace. "John, they'll be here any minute. I've just killed someone!"

O'Hara sighed impatiently and raised his voice. "For God's sake, Michael, that's enough. Pull yourself together."

"What's the point?"

"Michael! Michael!" O'Hara's last words were shouted at Michael's back as the priest turned and made off towards the doorway through which he had appeared only a minute before.

O'Hara hurried after him, making an undignified and unsuccessful grab at his shirt. Michael avoided O'Hara's lunge with a shrug and continued towards the kitchen door and the outside. He had taken no more than two steps beyond that doorway towards his car when he stopped dead in his tracks, distracted by a crescendo of shouting to his right. As he looked around the side of the house towards the noise, he was joined by O'Hara.

A group of ten or twelve people approached. O'Hara stepped forward to greet them, to calm them with welcoming but restraining outstretched arms. But they ignored him, brushed past him and made straight for Michael. As O'Hara looked on stunned, three men began to push Michael, all the time shouting at the top of their voices. The others stood aside and first urged them on, but then they themselves rushed to take hold of the priest. O'Hara acted quickly.

"Stop! Stop! Wait!" He took hold of Michael whilst at the same time shouting at the others. His aging but enormous frame still possessed enough power to brush aside three of Michael's assailants in one movement and, when they spun away to fall to the ground, the others instinctively stood back for a moment. Their indecision gave him the time he needed literally to throw Michael back towards the open door and into the kitchen. Without saying a word to the priest, he slammed the door shut behind him and, placing his bulk before it, turned to face the crowd's anger. When, almost as one, they glanced to the side of the house and made as if to move, O'Hara's hand dipped beneath his white robe and produced a jingling bunch of keys. "It's all locked," he shouted. "You can't get in and he can't get out. Now what's your problem?"

***

With Michael's version of events finished, both he and O'Hara remain silent for some time. They share an impotence. Neither wants to accept what has happened. Privately they each try to see things differently, to search for the kernel of an analysis that will dissolve their shared responsibility, or excuse Michael's mistake. Their silence testifies that none exists. When Michael speaks, he does so merely to relieve the oppression that the silence is feeding. He sounds exhausted, drained of hope. "And that's where we came in." There seems to be nothing more to say and, after this pleasantry, the silence again grows.

When O'Hara finally speaks, he sets Michael's lulled senses racing. It is clear that the Bishop's mind is not yet fully made up. "You've left something out, Michael." He waits for the priest to offer the information he wants, but it is soon obvious that his mind is quite blank. "The letter, Michael. What was in the letter?"

Michael looks at him guardedly. Trust is beginning to evaporate. "I tried to tell you. It doesn't matter. It's got nothing to do with the accident. I..."

"Michael! Stop! You've been consistent all along on several points. One: you were on your way here to tell me you wanted to leave the priesthood. Two: you wanted me to understand the reasons for that decision. Three: your relationship with Miss Rowlandson is the most important factor. Now we've heard about all the frustrations and problems of being a missionary priest. Let's hear from Janet and then together we can decide what we should do."

"We?" The word rings inside Michael's head as he reluctantly takes a single folded sheet of blue airmail paper from his shirt pocket. He exhales a tired sigh as he begins to read. The embarrassment that O'Hara suffers at having to listen to another's personal letter is obvious, though he succeeds in suppressing the emotion for, as he sees it, Michael's benefit.

'My dearest Michael. Just a note to keep you in the picture. Sorry for not writing earlier, but I've had hardly a spare minute for weeks. First my operation. It was horrible! I had a terrible time... It turned out that I was more than four months pregnant. I couldn't believe it. (I still don't!) I was starting to get a little big in the tummy, but not so much that anyone would have noticed, though I did take to wearing smocks for the last couple of weeks, because I was getting so self-conscious. Anyway the 'simple' operation has landed me in hospital for a week. They told me I lost a lot of blood, so they are keeping me in for a few days longer than normal. They started by giving me anaesthetics or tranquilizers - I'd almost lost interest in what was happening to me by that time. Then they wheeled me off into a theatre. I was only there for a few minutes. It hardly seemed worth the trouble. They gave me some injections straight into my tummy. I wanted to cry, because I suppose that was to break the waters and kill the baby, but I was so far gone on the drugs I just let it all happen without any real feeling at all. I felt I should have cried though...

Then I was duly wheeled back to the ward and put back to bed. It wasn't long before the contractions started. My God they were so painful. And they went on and on and on. I was screaming my head off and shouting for them to give me painkillers. After what seemed like a lifetime, a nurse eventually gave me an injection and I felt a little better for a while, but then the pain returned, and if anything it was worse than before. I just couldn't help myself screaming. I felt absolutely awful about it because they had left me in the ward all the time and there were people coming out of the theatre after their operations and they all had to put up with me screaming my head off in the corner. There was one woman who was recovering after a hysterectomy. She had lost a lot of blood and was moaning to herself all the time. It was really awful.

Eventually, when I 'excreted the foetus' as they called it, I was so full of painkillers, tranquilizers and I don't know what that I had hardly any idea what was happening. I was so detached I forgot to push. A great big cow of a nurse started shouting at me to push, but I was miles away. Then she hit me around the face... She described it later as a slap to get me to my senses, but it certainly felt like she meant it. Anyway it did the trick, I screamed my head off and then pushed like hell. My God the pain was absolutely unbearable.

I must have passed out then, because the next thing I remember was coming round a few hours ago and being presented with your letter. Apparently Pete had been to see me earlier, but I was still too drugged to react to him in any way. I'm starting to feel a bit better, but I've got a drip in my arm and I feel as though I've been in a desert for days. My mouth and throat are so dry they feel like sandpaper, and all I've been allowed to have up to now is one small drink.

The nurses have all been terrible to me. They seem to have decided to give me a bad time because I have had an abortion. Well surprise, surprise, who do you think saved the day? Yes, Pete! Honestly, he's been marvellous. We've had a marvellous chat and got quite a lot of things straightened out, at least potentially anyway. I've decided that when I get out of here I'll have a real talk to him with a view to finding a way of making it work between us. He's done absolutely everything for me - really taken me under his wing. He's got things organised for me at home, been to talk to my mother, bless him, because I couldn't bring myself to tell her what was happening. I've been so confused over the last few months.

Sorry this letter is taking so long to finish, Michael. I know you'll be worried and I really should just get myself together and send it. I couldn't write any more in hospital, because as I held the pen I could feel it starting to slip as the sleeping pills started to take effect. I'd already been in for four days at that stage and thought I was getting over everything, but over the next couple of days before I came home I started to feel a lot worse again. I just felt so completely sad and depressed about the whole thing. It would have been so easy to have avoided the whole trauma. And tears still come into my eyes every time I allow myself to think of what I have done.

Pete is still wonderful. I can't get over how much of a help he has been to me. I asked him what had brought about the change in attitude and he said it was possibly because he loved me. I didn't believe him of course, but everything that's happened since then has forced me to change my mind. You know I really believe him! Ever since my operation things have been better between us, better than I could ever have imagined. He even says he wants to marry me now. Funny, isn't it, that something like that has to happen before people know their own minds? Don't worry, by the way, I'm not going to rush into anything - apart from getting myself on the pill, of course. I have decided, though, to move in with him. It seems stupid to keep two flats on the go, after all. It might be that I've been feeling so clingy and insecure since my operation that I've just deferred to him every time when in the past there might have been a disagreement between us. Only time will tell if there has been a real change.

Anyway there's nothing more to tell at the moment. I'll write to you again soon to let you know how things develop.

Love, Janet

P.S. I've just read your letter again before posting this one. I suddenly had the terrible thought that you might have been totally serious... What am I saying? When you say you love me, I know what you mean. I know you well enough to say that I love you in the same way, spiritually, that is. And thank you again for offering to help me out but I could never accept. I would have liked you to be here with me - my goodness it would have made me feel a lot easier to have had you around - but it would have been selfish of me to have had you all to myself. I know how much your offer meant, because I know how much the people of Migwani need you. Anyway now you can rest assured knowing that everything has turned out reasonably well in the end. Write soon.

P.P.S. I feel absolutely awful about this, Michael. The letter's been hanging around for another week and I still haven't got my act together to post it. I am awfully sorry. Pete and I are still on really good terms and I am feeling one hundred per cent better. I almost feel back to my old self. I'm still a bit unsteady on my pins if I have do a lot of standing, but I feel almost back to full strength in every other way. I still haven't booked myself in at the family planning clinic, but I promise you I'll see to that over the next day or two. The stupid thing is that I've been feeling so close to Pete that the very minute I was confident I could do so without fear of problems I wanted him to make love to me. Don't worry, we were only silly twice, Michael, but I am sure that you'll understand now that I really do feel so much closer to him. A lot of that change I put down to the help you've given me, by reminding me that it's what I invest in other people that eventually I'm paid back from them. Let's hope it lasts. Please write again soon. And I really would love to see you again.'

O'Hara silently taps his fingers on the arm of his chair. "So you never told her that you wanted to leave the priesthood to be with her?"

Michael gives an ironic laugh. "Not in so many words."

"And so she thought you weren't serious."

Michael shrugs his shoulders. He is close to tears. It is neither Janet's flippancy nor Munyasya's death that moves him, but merely the apparent helplessness within which he has trapped himself.

O'Hara continues. "Because, it seems to me, that you've been speaking at cross purposes, all this 'communication' between the two of you - yourself and Miss Rowlandson - has been an illusion. You told her what originally was meant for my ears. It was in a code that I could have understood, but not Janet. Once started, the illusion grew, fed off itself. It grew so strong you believed it. As for her, she obviously has no such illusions. What you wrote was completely misinterpreted by her."

Michael interrupts. His voice is breaking with emotion at first but soon grows steadier and flatter, showing that he has already admitted to himself everything which O'Hara has said. "John, I can see all that now. There's no need to state the obvious. I've been stupid, immature. I've behaved like a lovesick child on the one hand, and a spoilt one on the other, trying to be seen to reject what I know I want because I'm denied something else I think I'd rather have. All of this talk of not being able to cope with the work is nonsense. It's just an excuse for my own stupidity."

"The fact remains, Michael, that you said you were ready to give up your work. The illusion is in command."

"No, it's finished." Michael is almost whispering, as if thinking his most private thoughts aloud. "I told you from the beginning that my mind was never made up. I've never been able to write it down. Perhaps I've never believed it. Certainly after talking to you today I've made up my mind once and for all. I do want to stay here - and as a priest." He looks up and stares wide-eyed in innocence directly at O'Hara, who immediately turns away.

For a while O'Hara offers nothing. It is clear that all that remains to be heard is his judgment. Michael realises this and continues to stare anxiously. "What do you think, John?"

O'Hara sighs and turns to look directly at Michael. His blue eyes are open wide beneath their black brows, but they see nothing, for they are focused on an infinity beyond the room. They are searching inwards, but are nevertheless outwardly piercing. The intensity of the stare added to its uncharacteristic directness sets Michael's nerves on edge and he begins to fidget with the bush hat he discarded when he first entered the room.

At last O'Hara speaks. "I'll ring Patrick right away." Before Michael has understood the significance of this, O'Hara has stood and has crossed the room. He pauses by the settee, though, and places his hand reassuringly on Michael's shoulder. "I'll put things to you as I see them. First: I think you need a rest - a long rest. All these things you've created for yourself speak of a mind under stress. You say you're suffering constant frustrations to such an extent that even you, yourself, will admit that they have had a debilitating effect on your work, and they have convinced you that your continued involvement here can bear no useful results. Secondly: there's this morning to think of. When I was outside I heard Mulonzya talk like I've never heard before. He wants rid of you Michael. That at least is clear, and he will use this to get his way. I'll bet he's already at work making a case against you. Even before this morning he was no friend of ours. Now he's most certainly going to be an enemy. With you out of the way for a while, things just might blow over. In a few months we'll look at things afresh and see if it might be possible for you to come back. Mulonzya will remember, though. That is for sure. And as long as he thinks he can use it for his own benefit, I'm sure he'll keep the whole thing alive. He'll never let it drop, Michael. We could be involved with the police, the courts, heaven knows what and that would reflect on all of us, Michael, not just you.

"So I think the best thing we can do at the moment is make a case for you to have a few months leave. We'll say it's on medical grounds. We'll cable to the seminary back home and tell them to expect you. It'll be a marvellous opportunity for you to study for a while, to refresh your ideas and restate your commitment to the Church."

"John, is there any need?" Michael pleads with some impatience. This was not what he wanted to happen. "I've told you I know I was wrong. What more do you want? And I can handle Mulonzya..."

O'Hara rocks slowly from side to side as Michael speaks. He is obviously no longer listening. His mind is made up and he can no longer hide his anger as he says, "Let me put it this way, Michael. If you stay here you are jeopardising not only your own position, but also that of all your colleagues. You will be a liability. Don't you see that? As a Christian..." He lays great stress on the word, "... would you like to see yourself as responsible for the outcome?"

Michael cannot answer. The discussion is over, the judgment cast. O'Hara walks silently out of the room and into the hallway. Michael hears him wind up the telephone and then speak. As the Bishop's echoing voice drifts into the room, Michael takes hold again of the long-ignored bottle of whiskey and fills his glass.

"Long distance please. Nairobi. Person to person. Father Patrick Mahoney. St. Patrick's Mission."

Mulonzya

James Mulonzya was born to privilege, guaranteed at least local honour, relative riches and unquestioning respect. He was thus one of the few Kenyans in a position to assert his advantage when unusual opportunities arose after the hasty departure of the country's colonial masters. He secured more than his fair share of power and wealth, far greater than had even been envisaged by any of his kinsmen. Others like James Mulonzya throughout the newly independent country were able to do just the same. At independence these men sharpened their eyes. Some simply moved in to occupy a niche ready prepared by their privileged predecessors. White farmers, not the settlers of long standing, for they felt they had nowhere else to go, but those who had recently emigrated from Europe to 'pioneer' new land in the promise that it would thenceforth be theirs alone to exploit - many of these people, who had come to grow wealthy and had placed their entire hopes on the success of this new life, left the colony in an angry stampede, pursued by their own fears. Thus vast tracts of prime land, having in the first place been expropriated from the common ownership of everyone and no one, first by settlers and then by the legal system they brought with them, were vacated, left to the mercy of the first person to stake a claim. Although the dreaded word 'compensation' was voiced frequently for some years, it was clear from the beginning that finders would be keepers.

Of course many private deals were done and thus much of the plunder was secured long before it officially became vacant. And there were not only farms to grab. A large slice of the economic life of a nation was to be re-apportioned overnight and like the hopeful dash to stake a claim in a gold rush, the prospective businessmen and farmers grabbed as much and as quickly as they could. What had always been the most lucrative, of course, did not change hands. Much of that which became free was of only marginal importance, but it more than suited the desires of local heroes like the Mulonzya family.

Thus some Kenyans of James Mulonzya's age became rich overnight. Many had originated from the same kind of background as himself. Few, however, had been better placed than he, either financially or in terms of the influence they could muster in the right places. The fact, then, that Mulonzya largely missed his chance and, when life settled down after independence, was found to be 'comfortable' without being wealthy tells much of his personal qualities, or rather his lack of them.

Unlike nearly all his fellows, the date of his birth can be placed exactly. On a registration certificate issued by a Nairobi office, which later Mulonzya had framed for his wall, his first day of life is recorded to have been on the twenty-fifth of September nineteen twenty-three. His father's name, also entered on the certificate - and in the eyes of most people over the subsequent years the detail which endowed the paper with most of its worth - was one Chief Abel Mulonzya Mwendwa of Mwingi location, Administrative District of Kitui. A champion of many causes - and especially his own, Chief Abel Mwendwa rose to a position in life from which he could command the total respect of his contemporaries, who often quoted the local wisecrack, "The father is Abel, the sons not!"

His qualities were many and varied, his achievements beyond number. His greatest talent, however, and the single quality which led to the permanent benefit of his entire family, was his ability to appear to be all things to all men, or, more aptly, anything to any man. He became a champion performer, apparently living one life through the eyes of his own masters whilst furthering quite different interests in the perspective of those he mastered. Forever trusted, for all parties believed him to be on their side, he was able to play an intricate game whereby he pitted one against another, maintaining his own innocence and safety, so that when conflict arose to shatter both opponents and allies alike, he could re-assemble the pieces in his own image, reconstructed according to his needs.

Mulonzya Mwendwa had been converted to Christianity at an early age, long before most Europeans have even considered the prospect. Though he received no formal education in his youth, for his home district was entirely without schools, he was taught to read and write by a Presbyterian minister. A member of the first generation of Akamba born under white rule, Mulonzya Mwendwa - or Abel as he would soon prefer to be called - encountered only one European, his minister-tutor, in his early life.

There were no farmers, no settlers and for the most part no

administrators in his area. The British were not interested in that place for it had nothing material to offer them. There were people there, though, the Akamba of Kitui, who interested the missionaries, whose zealous desire to expand and convert seemed insatiable. They were well received in Mwingi, accepted without necessarily being welcomed. By the time Abel reached maturity, however, much had changed.

The area's people, if not its possible resources, had begun to interest the administration in Nairobi. In order to reap the windfall benefits of the colonies they had found, the rulers needed labour to build railways, roads and the like to serve those areas deemed to be economically exploitable. From the very beginning of the colonial period, the Kamba people had served the Europeans well and, so that this relationship and others like it might continue, it became necessary to establish a chain of government.

Obviously this would cost money and divert precious funds that would be better spent elsewhere and so it was decided that these new administrators in the field should also become tax gatherers. At the very lowest level of each individual, township or location, it was envisaged that a local man, an appointed chief, would execute the dictates of government and, though it was accepted that these officers would have to command great respect from the locals if their position were to remain credible, it was also a necessity that they should be able to communicate with their overseers. In other words they would have to be able to read and write English.

The dearth of people in the bush areas who could fulfil these qualifications led to some younger people having greatness prematurely thrust upon them. By the time Abel was appointed chief, however, the entire process had settled into a semblance of established routine, whilst at the same time retaining its common perception as an essentially external imposition and, as such, resented.

As chief, Abel executed his tasks both efficiently and conscientiously, always striving to achieve the goals that were set by his superiors. Dependability is what he aimed for and without question achieved. He was always a conscientious organiser of tax collection in the area, even when the levy in question was as despised and unworkable as the dreaded hut tax, which forced unwilling peasants into the cash economy, often to the detriment of their essential subsistence.

Even in the north of Mwingi location, where semi-nomadic pastoralists habitually herded their animals, Abel proved to be such a good administrator from the executive's point of view that he, perhaps alone among Kenyan local government officers, managed to enforce the new laws on stock ownership almost without exception. It was widely recognised as an enormous achievement on his part. To have done no more than to introduce such pastoralists to the very idea that they should limit their herds to a level below that which their migration could support, would have been a feat in itself. Abel, however, managed to go much further than this and actually succeeded in reducing these people's herds year after year. The fact that, in order to do this, he had to employ the services of a detachment of the King's African Rifles to direct and carry out the required strong-arm tactics, he saw as mere expediency. By attacking the annual migration of several groups into the north of Mwingi location with salvoes of gunfire, Abel achieved his own and his superiors' end. The *askaris* did all he asked of them, though on occasions they might have been a little over zealous.

Abel's great chance to display his true qualities came later. After central government had deigned that large areas of the country should be set aside as forestry reserves and had designated much of Mwingi location as such, it was necessary to move the people who had settled those areas onto other land which they would then be able to farm. The size of individual holdings, however, would have to be reduced and it became necessary to impose limits on the number of cows and goats a person could keep. Obviously the plan encountered much resistance. Effectively it disenfranchised people. Despite the fact that the majority of land was used by no one in particular, it was seen as the common property of the people of the location, each part to be used until it was exhausted, when again it would be left fallow to replenish itself. Thus the enactment of the plan required not only organisation provided by Abel in his capacity as Chief, but also, because it challenged long-standing tradition and assumption, enforcement by police and later the army. Though the policy was never fully realised, since it depended on the determination of the local chief to achieve its aims, its enactment was continued until the final days of British rule. After independence, people were allowed to re-settle these areas, but in Mwingi they returned to find their former plots not only untilled, but fenced off, Abel Mulonzya having claimed most of them for himself. Since it remained the Chief's duty to arbitrate upon disputes over land, Abel effectively blocked all protest against his actions. Furthermore, the odd complaint against him that was levelled over his head direct to the District Officer was simply bought off with a bribe of money that, of course, ordinary people had never possessed and therefore could not match. Thus, by virtue of position and opportunism, Abel became the largest landowner of northern Kitui. The caveat that history would add to Abel's achievement, however, was that northern Kitui was far from the most advantageous part of the country to own.

There was, however, just one mishap that marred the progress of Abel's brilliantly self-engineered career. Throughout he had maintained the respect of his own people and the colonials by sitting firmly on the fence between them and refusing to climb down. Having successfully maintained this position for some time and convincing everyone that he stood on their side and their side alone, some people began to realise that Abel was working for the benefit of no one except himself. It was too late by then, of course, to make any difference because the chief had already constructed the greater part of his empire, but the mood of the people was such that anyone who had collaborated with the colonialists - and especially someone who had benefited from the arrangement at the expense of the locals, should be seen to suffer for his wrongs.

It was during the Emergency that this mishap occurred. Abel's children had all left home, so he and his wife had the near mansion of the chief's house in Mwingi to themselves. Though as an administrator he was certainly a target for reprisals by the Kenya Land Army, he had never seen the Akamba people of his own district as a possible threat and so the soldiers employed to guard his compound were effectively paid to sleep. Whenever the Chief's eldest son, James, paid them a visit, he would always remark upon the imminence of the possible dangers and urge his father to be more careful, but these warnings fell on consistently deaf ears and were held up to the young man by his father as an example of how little he understood his own people. The aging man's beliefs were sincere, but privately he enjoyed taking this standpoint to remind his eldest son of his inexperience in worldly matters. An education, even an undistinguished one, as his son had received, was a privilege that he, himself, had never been afforded and he rued the fact. It was necessary, therefore, that he should retain at least this claim to his son's respect, no matter how irresponsible the tactic might appear when viewed in cold light of day.

Abel had sacrificed much to provide an education for his sons and, though he desired to see them benefit from the experience in the long run, he was equally determined that the resulting changes in their attitudes would never undermine their respect for either his age or obviously superior wisdom. Thus he actively enjoyed flouting his son James's sincere concern for his safety. As things eventually turned out, the son was proved correct.

With the enforced depopulation of the designated areas of Mwingi well under way, disenchantment with the scheme reached its peak. There were still plenty of people waiting to be moved and thus plenty of people with much to gain and little to lose if they could possibly find a way of thwarting the enactment of the plan by any means, however drastic. Under the cover of darkness, six men visited Abel's house while the family slept and in ten frantic minutes accomplished what was designed to end the career of Chief Abel Mulonzya Mwendwa and also permanently display to others the inevitable consequences of collaboration with the desires of the colonialists. These men, masked and forever silent to deny any recognition, broke down the door of Abel's house and took him and his wife screaming from their beds. While two men first restrained and then gagged the woman, three held the Chief face down and with arms outstretched on the floor.

With Abel's terrified wife forced to watch, her screams muted by a tight gag, the sixth man proceeded to hack through the chief's wrists with an axe until both hands were severed from the arms. There was no ceremony about the act, no attempt by the men to force the Chief to hear their reasons for their act of retribution, everything being accomplished in silence with an air of apparently practised efficiency. Subsequently it would be rumoured that they had been Kikuyus involved in the forefront of the resistance against the British, that they had travelled from Meru to accomplish the specific end of eliminating Abel Mulonzya Mwendwa and him alone as retribution for his long-standing collaboration with the colonisers, but Abel himself would never subscribe to this view, always maintaining that they had been local men motivated by local issues.

Their task accomplished, the attackers unceremoniously disappeared into the night, leaving Abel for dead, with the severed arteries of his arms gushing blood onto the floor of the bedroom. The commotion, however, had been sufficient to arouse the soldiers from sleep in their nearby dormitory and it was through their efforts that he survived. Had they not acted immediately he might have bled to death. But the application of their rudimentary training in first aid was enough to stem the bleeding for long enough for him to be bundled off in a Land Rover down the road to the Mission Hospital for treatment and recovery.

The fact that Abel's performance as the chief of one of the largest locations in Eastern Kenya had won him many friends in higher levels of government was immediately apparent when news of the attack reached the capital via Kitui's District Commissioner. Almost by return of post a detachment, generous in number, of the King's African Rifles travelled to Mwingi and embarked upon a series of reprisals to atone for the crime. Suspects were forcibly moved out of the area and often detained without charge or trial in a small camp for Mau Mau prisoners at nearby Ndolo's Corner. The soldiers worked with such speed and vigour that by the time Abel was fit enough to leave hospital, only a few weeks after the attack, he returned to his desk to find that the process of resettlement was almost complete, having been speeded up by the very act which had been designed to frustrate it. Nothing now stood between Abel and his private plan to claim much of the vacated land for himself.

It was during this period that the chief first made the acquaintance of Major Edward Munyasya. Munyasya's home area was the neighbouring location to the south, Migwani, a smaller and generally poorer administrative area than Mwingi. Munyasya had been a member of the original detail sent to Mwingi after the attack on the chief and, under the strict orders of his superiors, he was requested to stay on to ensure there would be no further acts of terrorism and also that the resettlement programme was effected as speedily as possible. Thus the Major was required to work closely with the chief toward this common end. Gradually their continued professional relationship changed to one of long-standing friendship.

When, in what would prove to be the final days of colonial rule, it was decided to reward those people who had offered friendship and hard work to their foreign masters, Major Munyasya received a promotion and Chief Abel Mulonzya Mwendwa, in recognition of his work and personal sacrifice, received a medal from the Queen of England. Obviously the good lady could not be expected to shake his stump of an arm instead of a hand in congratulation, so, before he was despatched on his trip of a lifetime to London, Abel was equipped with two neat elongated wooden cups to hide his scars. Abel was immediately enthusiastic about his wooden hands and wore them constantly. They became nothing less than his hallmark in his later years and caused his handshake to become regarded almost as a feared weapon. It had always been his habit to greet others by clasping their offered hands firmly between his own. His wooden clubs of forearms meant that the unsuspecting would find greeting him a somewhat painful experience, especially in the later years when, with a new self-confidence inspired by his ever-increasing wealth and power, he would shake hands more vociferously than ever and deliver ever more painful raps to the knuckles with his left club as he instinctively tried to clasp his own hands together.

Abel remained lively and active right up to his death. He bequeathed to his sons immense but not fully developed farms, two bars and two general stores in Mwingi market, the sole rights to buy and sell grain and animal skins in the location, two lorries and the controlling interest in Mwingi's own bus company. Though this was a veritable empire in local terms, nationally it was nothing. Kitui District, itself, held few riches when compared to the vast resources of the highlands and coast and, despite determined efforts on his behalf by his son James in Nairobi to gain a foothold in these areas, he never succeeded to any substantial degree during his father's lifetime.

James, the eldest of Abel's four sons, was destined by virtue of his family's relative wealth to live a very different life from that of his father. In the span of a single generation not only the aspirations but also the expected achievements of the members of the family had been totally transformed. At the time of James's birth, his father would have considered his son lucky if he inherited a small herd of cows and a couple of acres of useful land. By the time the boy had completed his schooling at the age of twenty, his father could guarantee that his son's eventual inheritance would place him among the ten richest men in the entire District. By that time, of course, both son and father had grown impatient with the status of local heroes and aspired to be amongst the richest in the land.

To accomplish this Abel needed access to something, which he knew that he, himself, would never possess. And that was influence outside his home district of Kitui, through someone involved either in central government or law or finance. Now it had been clear to most people for a generation that there were jobs and thence fast promotion to be had in Nairobi for anyone with an education. The catch was that the school places available were both few in number and expensive and therefore effectively open only to the sons of men like Abel. He was determined not to lose his chance and so sent all his sons off to school in Nairobi. Whether through lack of application or talent, none of the boys did very well and only James obtained even the minimum standard required to pass his Cambridge Certificate. While the other sons returned to Mwingi, however, to run the family's farms and businesses, James took a job in the city as a clerk in government service. Unfortunately, the ensuing years did not see him promoted into a position of possible influence as quickly as his father had hoped. In fact James Mwendwa Mulonzya was a careless and somewhat lazy addition to the civil service. Had he applied himself as his father wished and received quick promotion, by the time independence became a certainty James would have been in a perfect position to help his father to invest his money in the right land with the best prospects. As things turned out, the son could not yet help the father.

At this point Abel struck upon a new idea. With independence clearly in the offing and with it elections, he, as the most powerful and widely respected man in the north of the district found himself being urged to stand for Parliament. He would have no serious rivals. There were no nationalists, no former members of the Kenya Land Army in this area to accuse him of collaboration with the colonial masters, no one to brand him a traitor. No one outside Kitui District itself had ever been interested in this semi-arid poor area, and so it had interested neither the rulers nor the leaders of the ruled. There was thus a real prospect of his being elected, and also that his rise to relative power would not be seen as a threat by anyone outside the District.

In fact Abel knew he was too old and slow, too set in his simple rural ways ever to get the better of the highly educated elite which seemed destined to rule the newly independent country. Thus, still believing his son to be more capable than experience had proved, he persuaded the interested parties to back not himself, but James as the candidate for the constituency centred on Mwingi. Once he had accomplished that, the election itself was a mere formality. Being rich, Abel could aid his son's chance of election by giving more gifts and buying more beer than anyone else could afford. In the long term it would be an investment, after all.

The declaration of the result that affirmed his son's success proved to be one of Abel's happiest moments. By then old and already ailing, he believed he had secured the future of his name and line and, when he died, peacefully in his sleep only a few years later, he had already begun to see his idea start to pay off.

Throughout his childhood, James Mulonzya received the benefits that his family's relative wealth could endow. He grew up expecting to receive special treatment and the assumption not only stayed with him, but actually grew stronger into adulthood. His quick temper and the associated ability to invent a suitable tantrum whenever something or somebody stood in his way remained undiminished by age and it was whilst thus afflicted that he at one stage disowned his own father and promised to make his own way in life. The argument revolved around two things. One was his apparent lack of achievement in his chosen career. He had worked for five years since leaving school and still showed no definite signs of being entrusted with the extra responsibility that Abel so desired to be his.

The second bone of contention was James's expressed wish to marry. The woman concerned, in Abel's eyes, was far beneath his son's station. The father commanded the son to wait, for if, in the future, he should become more successful, he might find that so 'bush' a wife might be a handicap. The girl was uneducated and a member of a poor family, but James had known her for many years and, though they had hardly met often, James had made an irrevocable decision to marry her. And so he bluntly disobeyed his father.

He asked for no help when it came to paying the dowry to the girl's father, preferring to save the required sum month by month from his own salary. Once Abel had learned to live with the idea, however, he actually began to admire his son's determination and desire for independence. The aging man thus offered reconciliation, which was immediately and gratefully accepted. In the long run Abel's reservations about the match would be proved justified, but he would be dead before they became public.

The girl, Mbete, was a country girl with a clearly moulded traditional view of a wife's duties. Initially, when all the formalities of her marriage had been completed, she lived with James in the city but found life there dull, even useless. For twenty years she had been brought up to adopt a certain role in life and when she found it denied her, she blamed that which had replaced it.

In their town house, James insisted on employing a 'boy' to do the garden and a 'maid' to do the housework. Chores, he called them. When discussing the business of the household duties with his 'staff', he adopted a confident authority, as if in some other life he had developed an intimate knowledge of the nature of their work. For Mbete - or Rose as he preferred to call her, though she never regarded herself as a Rose - who had grown up yearning to fetch the wood for her own fire, to cook for her own husband, to bear children and tend her own garden, this was simply too much. She thanked God that she had already been pregnant when they married.

Within six months of the ceremony, the child was born and at first reluctantly James granted her wish that she and the baby should return to Mwingi. In her eyes the city was no place to bring up a child. It was far too restricting and far too dangerous. And anyway where in a city like Nairobi could a youngster learn to herd goats? So she moved back to the country into a plot of land with a new concrete house which James had built especially for her and, though he bought a car and promised to visit her and the baby every weekend without fail, they became steadily more estranged from that moment. But since it was considered normal for the woman to tend the farm while the man worked away from home, their growing lack of sympathy for one another remained a private affair, too commonplace to warrant public comment.

Their first child was a boy, much to James's delight. The birth of a man's first son was surely his greatest moment. It demonstrated his potency, assured the future of his family line and kept his name alive. Three more children followed quickly - two more boys and a girl. Though by now certainly not seeing eye-to-eye, Mulonzya and Mbete had clearly managed to agree an agenda through other channels. Children were what Mbete believed life was for and James enjoyed the convenience. For him, however, the birth of each child seemed to mean less and less.

When his wife subsequently had two miscarriages - events which he interpreted as personal threats - he told her he had lost all interest in a larger family and from that day he and Rose were effectively, though never either officially or publicly, divorced. Though Rose had known for some time that James was keeping a concubine - a second wife, in fact - in the city, she offered not a word of complaint. James had given her everything she could want and she was content, after only eight years of 'normal' married life, to live out her days in the enjoyment of those continued benefits. Besides, it was common practice by then among those men who worked away from home in the city - even for professed Christians like James - to keep two wives, always with the 'official' wife at home on the farm to retain ownership of the land and its produce. The second, common law wife in the city could then warm the bed during the week, until such time that she was superseded by new charms in the form of a new and younger body. Rose could therefore be happy that she would always be the 'real' wife, because she had borne the children which would bear her husband's name and would therefore inherit his wealth.

That first child, the boy, ritually and proudly named Mulonzya Mwendwa after his by now illustrious grandfather, was baptised a Christian in the Africa Inland Church whilst an infant. James gave his son the name of Charles in deference to the boy child and future king of that name born to an English princess. She, of course, would later become the queen who would honour his own father, a conjunction that confirmed, in James Mulonzya's self-importance, that his own son would one day be worthy of empire.

As he grew, Charles promised to be everything that James, himself, had not been. After his father had lied about his age so that he could start his schooling a year early, Charles never looked back. He did his work conscientiously, passed all his exams and went on to a degree in Commerce and Business Studies from Makerere University. By the tender age of twenty-one, an age which traditionally would not even have conferred the status of manhood, he had installed himself in an office and taken on the responsibility of running his father's interests, thus allowing James Mulonzya, himself, to concentrate his efforts on the perhaps more important if less taxing pursuit of politics. Charles's business acumen was undeniable, as was the fact that, though he been lucky enough not to have inherited his father's brains, he had certainly inherited his quick temper and idiosyncratic behaviour.

His first major initiative, initially against his father's wishes, was a masterstroke. James Mulonzya's brothers, who had continued to run their own parts of Abel's empire in their own way and according to their limited talents were fast growing disenchanted with their lot. All businesses in Mwingi were performing poorly, since the local economy was in recession at the time, depressed by the effects of the prolonged drought, which had afflicted the area for several growing seasons. Charles saw his chance and bought them all out.

The brothers were all extremely happy with the ready cash which would certainly be sufficient to allow them all to increase the productive capacity of their farms. Charles was satisfied with the deal, not because he wanted two shops and two bars, but because he needed the plots on which they stood.

During his grandfather's day, the majority of the town's shops had been owned by Asians or Arabs. They had initially followed the paid work of building the railway from the coast and then had settled inland wherever the work ran out, intending to exploit the total lack of commerce in the interior at the time. Since they were mainly Muslims, wherever they settled they tended to congregate in a single area, where family, life and business could benefit from mutual support. After independence, when more local people began to set up businesses, the trading centres of these expanding market towns moved away from these small Muslim ghettos a quarter of a mile down the road to what became generally known as the 'African markets'. His uncles' shops, therefore, being quite long established and therefore sited in the older 'Arab town', had rather been left out on a limb and captured only occasional trade.

His father's political contacts told him that a new road was to by-pass the 'African market' town centre and skirt the edge of the old, and it was there that the town's only and ineptly run petrol station stood. Thus, having bought his uncles' shops, Charles immediately demolished them and within a year had replaced them with the town's second garage. Subsequently, just by making sure there was always petrol in stock, which the other station could only rarely guarantee, he cornered a market which was still small, but which was surely bound to grow.

Charles then made his next move. Instead of releasing his uncle's maize marketing licence to one of the other traders in the market place, he not only held on to it, but also bought out one of the traders in the new town. So within two years of having turned over the management of his affairs to his newly qualified son, James Mulonzya found himself the owner of two highly successful and expanding businesses in Mwingi instead of four struggling small shops. Of course the petrol station did very little trade there since the road through Mwingi could hardly be described as busy, but, using it as a base and its cost-price fuel to increase profit margins, Charles was able to expand his father's business into transport, including pick-up-truck taxis to ferry local people to and from market, long distance buses and lorries. It was said at the time that a man could grow rich by operating one taxi for two years. On behalf of his father, Charles operated six and all of them on cut-price fuel.

The young man was certainly ambitious but always chose pragmatic methods to realise his goals. He could, for instance, have bought out his own father at almost any time and rendered himself the undisputed ruler of the empire. Anyone with only limited vision would have seen that as a victory. He was young, dedicated and hard working. The business would surely expand and what is more his father was fast growing tired of the predictability of commerce. Surely he would have leapt at the chance of an early retirement which would have allowed him to spend more of his time on the activity he preferred, being politics, or the Nairobi social scene, however it might be labelled. The son, in fact, would have been glad to be rid of the father in many ways. He knew that the elder man's outmoded, over-simple understanding of business had for years held back the growth of his interests, and felt confident that if he could run his own show, he would counteract the stultifying influence of his father and, furthermore, manipulate his standing to great effect. But the father's contacts and political influence were both invaluable and irreplaceable, so the pragmatic partnership endured.

One typical disagreement between father and son centred upon the son's early decision to split Mulonzya Enterprises into a series of separate, smaller companies under different names. Each part would be registered separately as an autonomous concern. Now James took great pride in seeing his name advertised so diversely in so many places. Mulonzya Enterprises shone resplendently from cars, lorries and buses, over shops, bars and a garage, and, most importantly of all, from a stainless steel plaque outside an undistinguished office on Government Road, Nairobi. His name stood at the foot of a cabinet full of contracts confirming the company as owner or part owner of shops, hotels and bars in Nakuru, Nairobi, Mombasa and Malindi and this knowledge afforded the man great pride, added inches to his stature and oceans to his public credibility. In that sphere, the name was always more important than turnover or profit margin.

It seemed a great shame to James to have to do away with all this, to split up the empire into what appeared to be almost insignificant smallholdings under anonymous names such as Market Trading Company, Overland Transport Services or Sayala Property Company. Try as he might, he could not understand his son's reasons for doing this. To him, it seemed like the dismantling of everything that had taken so long and so much effort to build.

Charles tried to explain numerous times. He offered a myriad of paper calculations to show how it worked. For a period of many months, every time the two men met their conversation would gravitate towards the issue of 'rationalisation of the company' within seconds of exchanging pleasantries. Silence usually followed, as Charles would again offer only few words to illustrate what to him was self-evident in the pages of projected accounts he would show his uncomprehending father.

Take maize, for example. You buy maize in Nairobi, use your own lorry to move it to Mwingi and sell it. People have to buy it, because their own farms are not growing enough in this drought to render them self-sufficient. You make enough profit on the bulk maize to cover your transport costs. Now create a separate organisation, went the argument, to own and manage the lorries and force this transport business to operate at a profit. Legally, your maize marketing licence allows you to pass on your transport costs, so you make no less profit on the eventual retailing of the grain. Don't you see that we've made three profits on the one item, two of which can be passed on into a higher retail price? Meanwhile our transport company and our wholesaling company declare their own separate profits, rather than appear as part of an overall operation of buying and selling grain? But what's the point? It will surely all come to the same figure in the end because the retail price is fixed. A few cents here and there make hardly any difference.

Charles would smile at this point, as if he were condescendingly comforting a naive and innocent child in its ignorance and in passing say just one word to his father. Tax. For James, neither the watertight theory nor the lucrative practice compensated for the fact that his name had disappeared from the landscape, no longer seen painted on signs swinging in shop doorways or in letters a foot high on the side of a dust trailing bus.

One thing James did accomplish which, more than any other single act, proved to be a source of both immediate and immense wealth, was to procure by means part fair and part foul an import-export licence. Charles saw this as a necessity and had pressed his father to act for some time before James finally cooperated. The shops they owned in Mombasa and Malindi had from the start concentrated on attracting tourist money. Stocked with trinkets, game trophies, both imitation and real, ornaments and clothes bought on the open market, the businesses made useful if not excessive profits. With a licence to import and export, Charles could more easily control the cost of that stock and therefore keep his prices down to undercut the many smaller-scale competitors who still had to purchase their goods internally. Soon, of course, Charles's import business had become a wholesale clearing house and these one-time competitors began stocking their own shops from what he could offer. All the special, difficult to obtain or much in demand articles were earmarked, of course, for his own shops and those alone.

The export side of the interest developed slowly but significantly. Charles had developed links with craftsmen living in bush areas so that he could secure a supply of wood carvings, jewellery and other craftwork for his tourist shops, and though the export of such things was never easy, it is through the efforts of men like Charles that a tourist hunting through the souvenir shops of the Bahamas can buy a wood carving for a dollar and find the words 'Made in Kenya' cut into its base.

On paper then, this was a steady if not actually dependable interest. Paper accounts, however, could not be allowed to tell the full story. These same men in the bush who made the trinkets also hunted illegally, poached in the game parks in search of rhino horns, elephant tusks and crocodile skins. With no legal means of disposal available to them inside Kenya, the poachers needed to export their trophies. But they were common folk, usually uneducated and uncomfortable even in Nairobi, let alone Hong Kong or Singapore, where everyone knew the market lay. It is here where men like Charles Mulonzya Mwendwa joined the story, because it was they who possessed the means to accomplish the end. Satisfied with their pay and protection from prosecution, the poachers sold what they had and then, through a system of dealings designed to hinder future investigation, the commodities in question, usually described as 'traditional art objects', were passed from one company to another - hence Charles's real need to split up his father's empire - and finally left Mombasa by ship or Nairobi by air at the bottom of a crate of wood carvings or banana leaf baskets.

Once out of the country the merchandise was safe, being legal trade in the country of destination. Payment of course found its way into a foreign bank account, necessitating frequent overseas trips by Charles. Though illegal, the chance of detection, Charles believed, was minimal and even if they were found out, the profit from one shipment was always more than enough to buy off any small-time official who would be given the job of pursuing the case. It had all grown horribly complicated, much too complicated for James, whose concept of success had never really surpassed that of his own father's generation. He had been and remained a Mwingi man, proud to see his name on a board in his home town. All these dealings in dollars and yen, co-ownerships, part-ventures, shared-liabilities and meaningless impersonal names were quite above him and he soon decided to leave all such things entirely in his son's capable hands.

He would continue to offer support, continue to act as a figurehead, a non-executive chairman, as Charles described the role, as long as his son wished, but would no longer take any active role in the day-to-day running of the business. Charles, of course, had foreseen all of this some years before, when he first took over the management of the family firm. He knew from the beginning that he was very different from his father. Whereas his father had known lowly origins, he had not. The tailored suits, Mercedes-Benz and Parklands house that had been the heights to which his father had aspired, he himself merely took for granted. Charles knew that he aspired to heights that his father could never even comprehend, let alone actively pursue. His ambition would never be limited by unwritten assumptions learned amidst the poverty of Kitui District, a disassociation rendered complete by his decision to use and then formally adopt the name Mulonzya, his father's name, for himself and any future family as if it were a European surname. Wealth and achievement, for him, would always be measured relative to that of the people whom he now regarded as his peers and, amongst that group, allegiance to a home area or that figment of the colonialists' imagination, the tribe, took a poor second place behind that of an international ethic. Neither he nor any other Kenyan could aspire to the concrete and glass heights of the international companies who operated on a level no sane individual could ever hope to reach, but even these giants needed people to occupy the space beneath their umbrellas and the desire to move into that space to share the shade was both the goal and the ethic. Charles knew he was on the ladder and climbing, his eyes permanently focused on what he believed to be the top. (He would not fully realise the limitation of his vision for many years to come.) The fact that he neither noticed nor recognised the existence of a seething mass of millions clutching at his ankles for a pull onto the first rung is not surprising, for having never looked their way, he had never seen them.

***

When James's wife, the near forgotten Mbete, died in November 1974, neither he nor anyone else was either surprised or even saddened. The woman had been ill for some years and, though urged and prompted to do so by her husband during his still-frequent weekend visits, she consistently refused to seek any help from the hospitals and doctors in the city.

She was a Mwingi woman. She was born there. She had lived her life there out of choice and, now that her time had come, she would die there. Though she sought and accepted palliatives from the town's health centre as did most other Mwingi folk, she never once sought a cure, never once paid heed to any offered diagnosis of her illness. She had pains in her stomach and would not eat and that was enough to convince her that whatever a doctor might think, her time was finished, her life was near its end. Though this timid acceptance of fate troubled Mulonzya, personally, as much as on his wife's behalf, he accepted and respected her wishes and over a period of years rather than months watched her body slowly wither to the skin and bone of death. Consequently this final blow was cushioned by a long period of preparation, both material and mental. Before she died, Mbete had already sited her grave and had already fixed the form of her funeral. On the day, again in compliance with her expressed wish, the church ceremony and burial were followed by an immense social gathering in the church grounds with food provided for anyone able to attend. James did not know whether he was correct in believing that this was specifically designed to hurt him and hurt him where it hurt most, in his wallet, but how could he deny his wife her dying wish? It could be that this was simply her way of thanking all her friends for the years of companionship they had given, or perhaps it was merely a final Christian gesture from a devoutly Christian woman. But nevertheless it cost James a great deal of money which in his eyes was offset only by the opportunity to canvas support from within the crowds. Mbete had been a good woman, however, and had lived a good life. Perhaps it was possible to be thankful that she had died relatively young?

With his wife buried, her funeral festivities over and the rest of his family save for Charles back on the road to Nairobi, James Mulonzya and his son again turned to business. Charles had received letters from the recently appointed District Officer in Mwingi whom neither he nor his father had ever met. Mbete's funeral had demanded their visit to Mwingi and both father and son agreed that this presented a good opportunity to meet the man. An introductory letter to him had received an instant reply bearing an invitation to dinner and an offer of accommodation for the night for both James and Charles. They had been pleased to accept and the appointed time had been fixed. Unknown either to father or son, this first meeting would prove to be an important landmark in the furtherance of their mutual cause, both personal and material.

The new man, one James Mwangangi Musyoka who came from Migwani, the location bordering on Mwingi to the south, appeared to possess impeccable qualifications. Like Charles he had been privileged to receive an education and he had used the opportunity to good effect. Unlike Charles, his family had been poor and he had attended mission schools, not, like Charles, prestigious and expensive establishments in the capital. Mwangangi had eventually done well for himself, however, and, although he had taken much longer over the process than Mulonzya's son, he had attained the still rare distinction of a place in an overseas university - London, in fact. This alone isolated Mwangangi in the eyes of both Mulonzya and his son as a man worthy of respect. Following the customary introductions the three men sat down to talk over a beer while Lesley, John Mwangangi's wife went to the kitchen to prepare the meal.

"So, Bwana Mwangangi, you have not yet had time to find yourself a cook?" Mulonzya's words were no more than an introduction, an invitation to his host to introduce himself and offer some reactions to his posting to Mwingi. For people of such social stature, there is no such concept as small talk.

Mwangangi smiled. "We do not intend to have servants," he said.

"Lesley likes to run her own house. Besides," he continued after a mouthful of beer, "I don't think that we could afford to pay a fair salary. I have a daughter, you know, and it seems that young children can be very demanding on one's resources these days!"

The knowing laugh which Mwangangi uttered at the end his statement completely fooled Mulonzya. He had not the slightest suspicion that Mwangangi was sounding him out, laying before him an opportunity to divulge the nature of his political standpoint. Mulonzya took a complete mouthful of the bait. "But surely, Mr Mwangangi..."

"John," interrupted the other.

Mulonzya acknowledged the implied request with the merest nod and then sought confirmation of his newly granted right with a slight pause both before and after exercising it for the first time. "But surely, John, a cook would not cost you much. I might be out of date with the current rates around here, because as you know I spend most of my time in Nairobi now, but I am sure it is not more than three hundred shillings a month for someone to work part time."

"Ah but we don't consider that to be a fair salary, Mr Mulonzya. It might be the official rate, but it's certainly not fair. We are not really interested in what we can get away with paying. What we want to pay is a 'fair' wage and we think we can't afford it on a public servant's pay. Anyway, it is immaterial, since Lesley really doesn't like having strangers about the house all the time."

Mulonzya was slightly taken aback. Not only was it unusual to disagree openly with a person who was clearly your superior so early in an acquaintance, but also he felt there was at least an implied criticism of his own views. His next sortie thus took on the posture of a counter-attack. "Do you not think though that to take such an attitude is to be rather selfish? After all three hundred a month might not be very much to someone such as you... or I, might not even be a fair salary as you put it, but for the family of the man you employ, it could be the difference between life and death, between having something or nothing to eat."

"You misunderstand me, Mr Mulonzya," said John. "In the first place my wife wants to do her own work, so even if I could afford to pay a reasonable salary, I would still not want to employ a servant. The usefulness of three hundred shillings to some poor man and his family is indisputable, but then if one is really interested in welfare, both you and I and all like us could easily afford to give him the money anyway."

Mulonzya gave the slightest of scoffs as he replied without hesitation. "Ah but charity is not good for the soul. It can make people believe that they have a right to expect those things which only hard work should merit. If life is made easier for me today it will be harder for me tomorrow."

John gave a short, superior-sounding laugh that provoked Mulonzya to wonder whether he was being cross-examined by this young man. "I agree entirely, Mr Mulonzya."

"You see, Mr Mwangangi, if we are going to see our country develop, we have to encourage people to work productively by rewarding them..."

"Hence we should make sure that we pay fair salaries, not slave rates," interrupted John.

"Well, yes... I suppose so." Mulonzya was genuinely confused by John's speed of thought. "So if people learn to expect charity then our nation will be poor for ever."

"That is probably all true, Mr Mulonzya..." John spoke as if he was ready to state the essence of his case. "...But please remember that we began by speaking about whether or not I should employ a cook at three hundred shillings a month. Now let us suppose that I do. It is doubtful that the man concerned will come from this town. It is far more likely that he will come from one of the out-lying bush areas, so to hold down a job he will have to rent a room in the town. That for a start will take care of half of his three hundred a month. Then what will he eat? He will be living away from home. He can't expect his wife to come running along the road every mealtime with a plate of beans, so he has to buy food. He would probably eat better food than he would at home, but here in the town it would cost him money whereas at home, if he is at all lucky, it grows in the ground for nothing. After eating, out of his three hundred a month he might have fifty shillings left. An odd beer? Sometimes a visit to one of our town girls? He is living away from home after all... Surely the family would be lucky if it received more than twenty shillings of what I originally paid him. At that rate he would be better employed on his own farm making sure that he had no weevils in his granary." John finished on a serious, but almost cynical note.

Mulonzya, momentarily and uncharacteristically lost for words, could make only a pathetic and rather powerless gesture in reply. Charles, who up to now had remained silent save for a word of greeting, smiled. He still respected his father as a father, but privately enjoyed seeing his own low estimation of the man's intellect confirmed in another's trap. It was John Mwangangi who was first to speak again. "You see, Mr Mulonzya, I have not been here very long, but it has been long enough to realise that everything is very different from what it was when I left."

"How long did you spend out of this country?" asked Mulonzya rather sheepishly, hoping that he could direct the conversation to other matters.

"About ten years. You see I remember this area bearing ample crops, receiving more than enough rain to grow all the grass our animals needed. I must tell you, Mr Mulonzya..."

"James."

Mwangangi nodded. "I must tell you, James, that I hardly recognised this place when I arrived. It was certainly not because it had developed out of all recognition. There are more shops, and there's the new road, of course, but apart from that the entire area, to me at least, seems poorer than I remember it. I have been here long enough now for that initial shock to have worn off, but it is still both obvious to see and saddening to realise that whatever you say about hard work, reward and profit, the possibilities for ordinary people to benefit from such things simply do not exist here. No matter how hard someone in this area tries to work, he can never improve his lot. First, the salaries he can get from what employment there is are just not enough, as I have just shown, to cover the inevitable expenses he must incur. Even if he goes to Kitui to dig trenches or load wood at the ginnery he will be lucky if he gets nine shillings a day. What use is that? Then secondly, if he devotes his time to his farm, terracing, ploughing in fertilizer, harrowing the soil, he finishes with a bowl of dust, two exhausted cows that will probably die from the exertion, and still no profit or even food because there's no rain. What can he do?"

"He can go to the town to find work. There are many who do."

"But the same applies. The earnings are higher, but so are the costs. And what accommodation could he find?"

Mulonzya began to shake his head and smile knowingly. He had obviously concluded that he was dealing with a naive idealist. As he continued the argument, Lesley appeared from the kitchen with a tray laden with food and John gestured an invitation to him and his son to take their seats at the table. "Nevertheless, John, we must be realistic. The employers are paying what they can afford. We are not lucky enough to live in a rich country. Our industries are young, and still struggling to establish themselves. That is why we are encouraged by our leaders to work together in sacrifice to see our country grow and our economy develop."

"Indeed," said John, "but that still does not help fill our friend's empty stomach. As for working together in a spirit of sacrifice, all I can say is that another shock which Kenya had in store for me when I returned - and a shock which I have still not managed to reconcile - was my first impression of Nairobi."

"In what way? Was it that there is so much squalor and so many beggars on the streets? The government is currently very concerned about the impression created by our capital city. Many of us feel it has deteriorated seriously over the past few years. There are more tourists now you see, who bring currency into our country. It is not good that they should be harassed by beggars on the street. It does no good for our nation."

"No, my reaction had nothing to do with any of those things," said John, clearly trying to suppress a resigned laugh. "For ten years I lived in Great Britain. Now most people there own a car. I even owned one myself."

"That's a good thing," said Mulonzya. "I would like to see that here."

"So would I, James, but that's not my point. In Nairobi it seems that every other car is big and expensive - a Mercedes, a BMW, a Jaguar or a Rolls - in short the type of car which only a very few people in rich Europe could ever hope to own after a lifetime of work. It worries me, you see, that the spirit of sacrifice you speak of applies only to the poor and not the rich."

"On the contrary, John, I disagree. All those people have undoubtedly made their sacrifice. They have probably like myself worked hard for a lifetime to achieve their present state. They deserve their reward. Think of all the other people who have benefited from their efforts."

"I would like to believe you, Mr Mulonzya."

Mulonzya was suddenly uncomfortable. He was clearly under attack, perhaps not directly, but still under attack. He turned to his thus far silent son sitting at his side. "You are very quiet, Charles..."

Charles nodded as if in confirmation of the obvious accuracy of his father's statement. He smiled confidently and looked up, his gaze momentarily meeting that of Lesley. He caught her off guard and she quickly looked away, clearly embarrassed. She had been eying him, thinking how he reminded her of her own husband when she first met him. John too had been tall, slim and lithe and had carried himself in the same way as this young man, erect and proud. The difference was that Charles was obviously a highly sophisticated young man whereas in her eyes John had never been able to shrug off the telltale remnants of his poor and humble background. He remained just that little bit 'bush'.

Mulonzya paused over his meal and turned to face his son. "Is there something wrong? I've never heard you so quiet."

The others laughed at the obviously unintentional joke and this diverted their attention sufficiently to allow Charles to ignore the comment.

The conversation subsequently lulled while all four concentrated on their food. Mulonzya ate very loudly compared to the others. It was he, also, who continued to do most of the talking, with John pitching in only an occasional word. Neither Charles nor Lesley offered more than the pleasantries required by table manners, while the others still seemed to be engrossed in what was by now almost their private snippets of conversation. Lesley in fact lacked the confidence to take part. It was not a lack of worthwhile things to say which kept her silent, but a quite inexhaustible capacity for self-deprecation which, in her own estimation, effectively rendered to irrelevance everything she wanted to say. Whenever she did speak in the company of strangers, this lack of confidence and self-respect prevented her from expressing herself effectively and thus the reactions she provoked in others carried a host unexpected and unintended signals. Of course this simply helped to reconfirm her lack of self-belief.

Making things doubly difficult on this occasion was the presence and behaviour of Charles. Though she remained polite and tried not to show her feelings, she felt uncomfortable with him there, almost threatened, in fact. Several times while John and James had been engrossed in their own conversation, she had looked up to find that Charles was staring at her - almost through her - with a vague smile which clearly said something, but exactly what it was she had no idea. It was such strange behaviour that soon she was not even sure whether he was looking at her or simply staring into space while, like a fly on the wall, he listened to every detail of what his father and John were saying. Certainly the young man was more interested in what they were saying than he was prepared to admit, but he also seemed to be expressing an obvious interest in Lesley and was causing her a good deal of discomfort. It is an irony that those people who possess a natural beauty capable of turning most eyes are often least equipped to cope with the spotlight of another's attention.

Quite suddenly, however, Charles's previously bland expression changed a little. His expression hardened. His eyes seemed to give up their analysis of the neckline of Lesley's blouse and darted to focus upon John as he spoke. Mulonzya, himself, had prepared the ground.

"So then, Mr Mwangangi, what are your solutions to the problems of this area? We are agreed that charity is undesirable. There is no rain so there is not enough food and you maintain that taking a job is not a solution."

"No, I didn't say that. I said that with salaries as they are most people are unable to benefit from the employment which is open to them. Obviously people will take jobs if they are there and if they have to survive. Even a few shillings in your pocket are better than nothing."

"So what is to be done?"

"In the future the government must show a greater degree of interest in areas such as this. It is not good enough to expect people here to starve just because there is no immediate and apparent economic benefit to be gained from trying to cope with the underlying issues. We must legislate so that more work - worthwhile work comes into the area so that people do not have to move to the city. If businessmen will not create it then the government must do it. I would suggest, for instance, that farmers could be paid to improve the quality of their land. Give them a real incentive to terrace their land and they will do it. In the long run everyone will benefit. The fields will not erode, what rain there is will not just run away and then another family may have enough food, may even produce a surplus. In the absence of any leadership at a national level, all we can do at present is make sure that what little resources people currently have are used to the maximum effect. That is why I have promised my non-existent cook's three hundred shillings a month to Father Michael's special fund in Migwani."

"Oh? Why? What is he doing?"

"It's a very simple idea he has had and I am sure it can work. Let me try to explain, but I recommend that you get it directly from him if you want all the details." John paused momentarily to find a starting point.

Charles's interest was by now obvious. Lesley was still uneasy. With her plate now empty before her, she was wondering where to place her hands. "At present many people have to buy their food from the traders. They have no choice. It's the only source. Though I respect the trader's right to run their businesses and make their living, they must accept that without the famine in the area they would sell only a fraction of their current trade in maize and beans. What they have come to regard as the normal demand for basic foodstuffs in their shops would in theory dwindle to nothing if people started to produce surpluses from their land as they used to do. Throughout the District people are selling their animals and their land for cash so they can buy food on the open market. If something imaginative is not done, before long people will just not be able to support themselves, even if the rains return. They will just not have the resources. There are many people now who have sold everything and are still starving. Father Michael wants to do something immediate and positive for those people but he has no more relief money to spend. Famine here is now endemic, you see. It would have to hit the headlines for large-scale appeals to be effective, and endemic problems will never be headline news. Also our government would never allow Kenya to be seen internationally as in need of charity."

"So the idea is this," John continued. "The Father has been told he can use the school bus from Mutune once a week for nothing. All he will do is provide the petrol. The nuns have been very generous to us. Without the vehicle we could do nothing. Near Nairobi there is a group of Europeans who are researching into agricultural techniques for some agricultural research agency. Their farm is very productive but is subsidised, so it does not need to make a profit. Michael has persuaded them to sell us their maize and beans at a cheap rate. We will then bring it to Migwani, Mwingi, Mutonguni or wherever in the lorry and then sell off some of it to people who can afford it until we have covered costs and raised enough money for the next trip and then we will distribute the rest free to people who have nothing."

"That is illegal," said Charles curtly. "You need a licence to trade grain."

"Ah, but we are not trading, Charles..."

"You are selling some of it so surely the law would rule that you are trading."

"But that's only to get us started. If we can get enough reasonably well-off people to give a hundred shillings each - and regularly - we will be able to carry on without having to sell any of the food. It could then never be argued that we were affecting the traders' business because we would be supplying only those people who had absolutely no money to buy food for themselves."

"And how would you identify such people? On whose word do you judge whether a particular family can or cannot afford to feed itself?"

"Priests, Chiefs, District Officers, Members of Parliament..."

The argument had suddenly become very serious. "This food... It will only go to Catholics, then?" asked Mulonzya, as usual firmly grasping quite the wrong end of the other's meaning.

"Oh no. To anyone who is in need of it."

Charles spoke again. His voice spoke the words of a mind already made up. "What you propose is illegal. You need a licence to trade grain. Your school bus is licensed to carry children, not merchandise. Mutune is a government-funded school. I am sure that the Ministry of Education would not like to think that their property is being misused in this way. It is definitely illegal."

"You forget that I am trained in law. I would certainly be prepared to test what you say in the courts. Anyway, the whole project would be done in the name of the Church. Would you like to be seen to bring about a case against the Roman Catholic Church?"

"If it is illegal we would oppose it," said Charles. "It would certainly be against our interests. We would have to consult with our legal advisers, of course, but I have no doubt in my mind when I say that, whoever started such a scheme, we would seek to stop it through the courts."

James Mulonzya almost interrupted his son. "Would you, Mr Mwangangi, a magistrate and civil servant openly break the law?" There was some sincere as well as calculated shock in his voice.

"If the law were to stand in the way of a simple, non-profit-making humanitarian scheme such as this, especially in an area racked with famine, then the law must be changed." There was a hint of the beginning of anger in John's voice. "If there must be a test case then so be it. Meanwhile people who would have gone hungry will be fed."

Charles and James Mulonzya began to laugh as he spoke. There was no disrespect, however, only familiarity. Both father and son knew that they had trod this ground far more regularly and successfully than their potential adversary. "Ah John, but now you are talking politics."

When John nodded sagely in agreement, however, Mulonzya's smile faded without trace. "I cannot believe," said John, "that Parliament would want to oppose an emergency measure such as this. I am sure that under the circumstances they would allow such a scheme to take place and succeed. I would also be willing to test that."

Mulonzya began to dither. He had no answer. Charles, however, replied immediately. "Let me put it like this, Mr Mwangangi. As the law stands, your suggestion is blatantly illegal; let us at least agree upon that. Now if you think you can lobby around this issue when it becomes a test case, you are wrong. All the traders will oppose it, and not only traders from this area. They would unite to defeat you."

John nodded in such a way that confirmed he had just heard exactly what he had expected. He himself offered no more and Charles was again silent. Mulonzya was obviously still thinking through the idea. Then after almost two minutes of complete silence he said, "Charles is right."

The rest of the meal was eaten in relative silence beneath a tangible tension. When, over coffee, Charles announced that it was time that he and his father should set off to return to Nairobi, only Mulonzya, who had assumed he was staying the night, looked surprised. Charles offered a clear excuse, saying that he had to attend a meeting in town the following day as John politely showed the two men out to their waiting car. Then after a short and curt goodbye, they left. Back inside the house, Lesley was clearing the table.

"I didn't really understand what it was you were planning," she said, "but did you really expect them to agree?"

"No," replied John with a smile.

"Then why did you bother asking them here?"

"Well I needed to meet him anyway but I wanted above all to check out what I've been hearing about him."

"And?"

"It's all true. He's useless."

"Do you think you could beat him?"

"At the moment, no. But by the time the election comes round, who knows? At least I now know that if I stood against him, the real power I'll be facing is not his, but his son's."

Lesley's body visibly shivered. "You're not kidding. He was really creepy."

"A creep maybe," said John respectfully, "but he certainly knows what he's doing."

Charles drove the car. At his side, his father had begun to nod off to sleep within ten minutes of leaving John's house. Slouched in his seat with his full and ample belly lying on top of him like another body on his lap, James ceased trying to stay awake. There was little sleep for him, however, because there was no comfort with the car constantly jolting on the uneven dirt road. Charles on the other hand was wide-awake and still alert. When he spoke, he shouted above the constant banging of stones in the wheel-arches of the car.

"How long did you say that Mwangangi has been here?"

"A few months - maybe three or four."

Charles bit his lip as he thought. "We shall have to keep our eyes on him. I wonder why he went to the trouble of explaining all the details of the priest's project... He could never have expected us to agree. Neither can he have expected us to take his naiveté at face value. He's not that simple minded."

Mulonzya laughed as he replied quickly. "That priest, Mr Michael, he is the one who is simple minded. It's just the kind of stupid thing he is always talking about." A wave of the hand tried to dismiss the entire subject.

"But, dad, John Mwangangi is a magistrate. He knows the law. He has simply used that story to see how you would react. That is why I took over and answered for you." After a short pause, Charles continued, "Someone like him will not be satisfied with a District Officer's job for long."

"What do you mean, Charles?"

"I'm not absolutely sure, but do you remember when you said that changing the laws was the politicians' job?" He turned momentarily to see his father nod. "It was the way he reacted. His expression seemed to say he knew that all along. I think that before the next election comes round we'll be hearing a lot more about Mr Mwangangi. We had better keep an eye on him."

The car sped on into the night along the orange-coloured dirt road. Eventually Charles spoke again. "What do you know about his wife - Lesley? She's not Kenyan, is she?"

Shaking off his drowsiness, Mulonzya replied. "No, she is from the West Indies or America, I think. They met in London." He paused for a while and spoke once more before slowly drifting into sleep. "I am surprised you can remember so much about them. You were so quiet I thought you were asleep."

Charles smiled ironically and shook his head. "Oh no," he said quietly.

***

James Mulonzya and John Mwangangi did not meet again for some months, until both attended as invited guests a fund-raising *Harambee* day for the secondary school in Migwani. The school's governors, all local men, primary school headmasters, businessmen and councillors plus Father Michael, representing the Roman Catholic Church, which had sought and secured much of the initial funding for the project, had organised the day well. They needed to, for the very survival of their venture was at stake. Their school had been founded some four years previously and had just seen the first of its students, though largely unsuccessfully, sit for the revered East African Certificate of Education. The failure of any of the school's first class to attain even the minimum standard required to obtain the qualification, however, had done nothing to diminish the enthusiasm of the people of Migwani for their school. But, to ensure its future, the project now urgently needed more cash - and a lot of it. A school can exist on charity and collections in its infancy and, for a time, the parents of its students will accept the fees they pay being used to buy cement and sand. If the government could be persuaded to provide trained teachers and pay them according to their own scheme, then the school would be rendered permanent. No qualified teacher, however, would ever entertain a posting to the bush without being provided with a house and building houses costs money. Hence Migwani's *Harambee* day.

Fifty thousand shillings was the target - enough for two houses with a little penny pinching on the finishings. Hundreds of invitations had been sent out, one to every Migwani man known to be earning a regular salary and most of these men had come with their wallets bulging to the degree they thought would be expected of them.

Local people had donated animals, cows or goats, which would be auctioned so that the proceeds could be added to the fund. Migwani's churchmen were there, Father Michael for the Roman Catholics and every single pastor or lay preacher from every outpost of every sect or splinter of Protestantism. Representatives of the traders from the market centres of Migwani, Thitani and Nzeluni were there with at least one shopkeeper from every one of the minor centres throughout the location. Thus on the day five thousand people crammed into the school compound to witness and, where possible, to contribute to the event.

There were many speeches to be made, a few less to be heard, before the day's real business of passing round the collecting tins began. In turn three headmasters spoke voluminously to extol the virtues of education to a crowd that was already convinced. They reassured people of its absolute necessity for the future of both their nation and their children, citing themselves as living examples of education's potential benefits and the starvation of Migwani's people as the fate of those who ignored it. It was an analysis that described all but the select as culpable victims of their own ignorance, and it was meekly, dutifully and guiltily applauded by those whose worth it denied.

Next came the location's Chief. His tack was different. He identified himself as an unabashed moderniser. He saw the expansion of the school and the possibility of its assured permanence as evidence of Migwani's continued development. He praised the farsightedness of everyone who had contributed to the scheme in the past and almost demanded that everyone gathered there should make as large a contribution as possible to the collection. He told the crowd that by doing so they were actively investing in their community, not only in the future of the school, but also in the potential of their own children and through them even their own future. There was great applause for his speech and much nodding of heads in agreement.

Then came John Mwangangi. As Mwingi District Officer he was effectively an overseer for all such projects in the area. As he mounted the low platform to speak, everyone applauded. It was common knowledge that only after his permission had been granted could the collections for the new building programme be made. Perhaps more important than this, however, was the fact that John was himself a Migwani man. Surely his speech, above all others, would address the mood of self-congratulation, which everyone simply exuded and strove to express. His words, though, hushed the crowd into a partly reflective and part angered silence. While recognising the Location's achievement, he tried to temper people's enthusiasm. No matter how much money they would collect that day, everyone would soon have to accept that only a small number of children would receive an education in this school. And only a tiny fraction of those who did would benefit materially from the experience. This, after all, was a *Harambee* school. It catered only for those children who, at the end of their primary education, had effectively failed their certificate examinations. Thus, if you believed that four years later those same children would do well in the far harder secondary level exams, then you would all be deceiving yourselves. Most of the parents who will pay fees for their children will be paying for nothing! Except, of course, to make the traders who supply the school with food and books more wealthy. There were some odd shouts of disapproval at this, though many self-consciously murmured their agreement. Turn back to your land, John said. Don't just sit idly and wait for the rain. Work hard and improve your land. Invest in it before you invest in education. Terrace it. Fight against erosion. Lay earth dams across the gullies on your land to trap rainwater. Then, even if the rains are too little, you can carry water to your fields and maybe, just maybe, it might be enough to prevent your crops from shrivelling. You can do all these things and succeed. You can then be well fed all through the year. And then you can have your *Harambee* days, which would also then be far more likely to realise the level of support everyone desired.

When Mwangangi stepped down from the speaker's rostrum to a merely polite ripple of apparently begrudged applause, James Mulonzya began to make his way forward. During John's speech, no one had noticed a well dressed and extremely fat man called Nzuli nervously passing behind the speaker's platform to seek an audience with James Mulonzya MP. In his hand the fat man carried a thin school exercise book and after a few introductory words had been shared, he presented this to Mulonzya. The MP stared coldly at the book's cover with his face set in an apparently rigid grimace. Though there were no more than a dozen words written on that cover, he read them through, carefully and slowly several times. Having opened the book and begun to read, the expression on his face, if anything, grew steadily harder. From quite some distance it was possible to see the veins in his forehead begin to swell through the skin as rage raised his pulse and made his blood race. It was a clear case of public moral indignation.

After he had read through four or five pages of the book he had seen enough. Leading Nzuli to one side of the group of VIPs who sat behind the speaker, facing the crowd, Mulonzya was seen to question the man. Though no one could hear what was said, the content was obvious, at least to anyone who recognised the source of the small green exercise book.

Several times Mulonzya held it up to Nzuli and pointed to a page whilst mouthing a question. Almost invariably, Nzuli's only reply was a nod of the head in confirmation of something already stated and agreed. After only a few minutes, Mulonzya, obviously convinced of something, thanked the fat man and shook his hand. Grim-faced, he returned to his dignitary's chair, sat down and then for a while simply stared into space, with eyes blank and his face set hard, involuntarily rolling and unrolling the soft-covered book in his hands, Mulonzya awaited the end of Mwangangi's speech. His political mind was almost audibly constructing its tactic.

When a mere ripple of almost polite but definitely not enthusiastic applause greeted John Mwangangi's departure from the rostrum, the school's headmaster stood up and laconically introduced the next speaker and the afternoon's star turn, James Mulonzya. Now every speech Mulonzya made in public was a campaigning speech, designed to show off how his influence in high places had made things possible. From the day he had received the invitation to attend this particular function, he had assumed that Mwangangi would also be present and had prepared accordingly a fighting speech designed to dissuade the new District Officer from furthering his obvious ambitions in politics.

Having now read through the exercise book presented by Nzuli, a long and trusted ally, he decided instantly that many of his intentionally oblique references to Mwangangi should become more explicit. As he strode proudly if clumsily to the rostrum, he was greeted with loud applause and trilling ululations. He raised his hands as far above his head as his over-fleshed shoulders would allow and milked the adulation. Then, as if switched on by an invisible hand, he began to dance. For just a few moments, his hands clapped, his head shook, and his foot stamped out a hollow rhythm on the rostrum boards. His body strained to vibrate the bulk of his hips and exercise the flabby shoulders in this, the traditional imitation of a cock, the ultimate in potency and his own trademark by which the illiterate could recognise his name on a ballot paper. Women's ululations cackled out above the intensifying cheers and applause. This was Mulonzya, his style unmistakable, his power indisputable. When he raised his hands again with open palms forward, it was the well-known sign that his self-introduction was finished and the crowd immediately fell silent. Everyone knew however that the ritual was still far from over and that greetings would follow. This was his style, and his audience was utterly at home with it.

"You are well?" shouted Mulonzya.

"We are well," replied almost everyone in the crowd with calculated restraint.

The figure on the platform then looked aside with a scowl of dissatisfaction. "You are well?" His question is louder.

"We are well." The unison reply is adjudged to be sufficiently loud and enthusiastic this time, it seems, for Mulonzya nods his head and smiles. More spontaneous applause then follows because now the speech is about to begin. Mulonzya's Kikamba is like an old man's language, slow and musical, not like the jagged staccato rattle of the young. Like a grandfather he entertains his audience with stories, but stories pregnant with meaning, simple parables of experience. He clearly anticipates how his words will be received and every time his head thrusts forward as if to propel a final word from his mouth, he knows applause will follow and so he raises his hands whenever he wishes it to be stifled.

"When I was a boy in Mwingi, not Migwani - before you attack me let me say that I have a legal passport in my pocket -." He pauses here for laughter as he pats his bulging jacket pocket. "When I was a boy, there were no schools in Kitui District. There was no education whatsoever except that which our aging grandfathers gave us by the fireside. Now we all remember our grandfathers and their stories. We remember how wise they were. We remember how they could tell us of places and things we had never seen, or of great men from long ago. I would ask everyone to think for a moment of your own childhood. Think of your own grandfather resting by the fire at suppertime. Sometimes, he was funny. How many of you can remember being told 'Don't speak while you are eating millet' and being sprayed with wet flour from his mouth at the same time?" He pauses here to allow a ripple of laughter to cross the crowd. "But did you not also respect your grandparents?" The crowd affirms. "Did you not love them, sometimes more than you loved your own parents? A father must be strict and powerful and a mother should be full of warnings. But grandparents could delegate these chores and tell you what you wanted to hear." Everyone seems to agree. The long flat tone "Ii," "Yes" is almost choral.

"Now everybody - every single person - try to recall your own grandparents. Try to remember them working in the fields before the rains. Try to think of the way you used to help your grandfather break up the clods of soil with sticks and branches." There is a long pause here. Mulonzya, half turned away from his audience, looks sidelong at the bemused and fast saddening faces before him. "Oh, I must explain that I am speaking now only to those people who can remember such things; only those people who are as old as myself or perhaps just a little younger." At this point he looks down at a small boy in front of the rostrum. The child is startled as the practised penetrating gaze settles on his face. Mulonzya tries to look shocked, as if the boy has offended or insulted him. But the act is still deeply friendly and therefore comic. It raises a little titter here and there. He then looks up and, with a flat hand raised to shield his eyes from the sun's fierce glare, he peers over the heads of his audience and then theatrically begins to count all those who might qualify as older than himself.

"One...Two...Three...That's all." This raises a crescendo of laugher and some applause. Among this crowd, age itself is still worthy of respect. Mulonzya raises his arms to request silence and then continues. "Let us be serious, people of Migwani. As I have asked you to do, think back. Think back to your grandfather beating the soil with a stick because he had neither plough nor hoe. And can you remember eating millet?" He seeks and receives another chorale of confirmation. "And did you like it?" Many people burst out into spontaneous laughter. They shake their heads and screw up their faces as memories of millet porridge are raised from the past. "But why did you eat it if it tasted so bad that on some days even dogs would refuse it? You ate it, my friends, because there was nothing else. Now I want the youngsters - and that is nearly all of you - to listen very carefully indeed. There is a lot of talk about famine in the area, but don't you think that it is anything special. There has always been famine here. Not always right across the District, of course, but if you talk to your fathers and your grandfathers, they will tell you just how many times in a year when they went to bed hungry in their youth. They will tell you how many times they took their food to their houses from the family cooking pot and held their noses

133

while they ate it - because it was millet. There was no maize in this area in those days, and very few beans also. All we had was millet porridge, millet stew, millet bread, millet shit and millet everything. We were not fooled, were we?" He pauses here to allow anticipation of what is to follow to grow a little. The expected does not follow.

"We knew why our grandfathers always seemed to be saying 'Don't talk with your mouth full of millet'. We know why. It was because they too had their mouths full of foul millet and when they told us not to speak they could spit it all out because it was so horrible..." He waits for the prolonged laughter to subside. "And what did you do when there was no millet? Did you catch the bus to Nairobi and beg for pennies at the feet of some white men with cameras? You did not. Did you write a letter to your brother who was earning a salary in a government post in Nakuru? Did you say, 'Dear brother, we are suffering so much here in the countryside. Please send us one hundred shillings to help us buy food.' Did you say that? You did not. Did you walk to the Chief's camp with your bowls to be given free maize and beans by the government in the form of famine relief? You most certainly did not do that. The very last thing that concerned our former masters was the fate of a few starving blacks." There are many nods of agreement here.

"So what did you do? Nairobi was too far to go in those days because there was no road. Most people had never been near Mombasa. There were no buses, no taxis or bicycles. And there were certainly no brothers or uncles earning salaries because there had never been any education to allow them to become qualified. So what did you do?" He invites suggestions from the crowd. Several people reply by shouting, "Go to the mountain!"

"Exactly! Boys and girls, do you know what that means? Go to the mountain? Well it means that you walk from here to Meru or sometimes Embu, over there on the slopes of Mount Kenya..." He points vaguely behind his podium to the west, "...where there were some large farms, some great, great estates run by white people where, at harvest time, you could get casual jobs picking coffee or tea, or cutting sugar cane. And you could earn just about enough to stay alive and no more. Of course, by the time you had walked the eighty or so miles all the way home, the rest of your family might all have died - but that was life, and death, in your grandfather's time."

He pauses again here for some moments and looks slowly around, directly into the eyes of selected individuals in the crowd before him. "Yes, I can see in your faces that you are somewhat confused. How could they have walked to Embu? How could they have crossed Tana River? There was certainly no great concrete bridge at Kindaruma in those days. No, they did not swim across. Though people might have been hungrier in those days, so, alas, were the crocodiles."

"Let me tell you youngsters something you might not know. There used to be a ferry across Tana River, a long canoe rowed by Luos. They would carry you across the river at a price and, in times of famine, when many more people arrived on the banks to make the crossing to Kikuyuni, they would charge you twice as much for the service. You would sit in their boat and these Luos would start to row, their bodies grunting and heaving as they paddled into the cascading water." Mulonzya mimics the paddling of a canoe with great swings of his arms and jerks of his torso. "And you would hang on to the side of the boat as it shook and swamped, and would fear that you would surely drown. But was it hard work for them? Do we not know that if Luos are not actually born in the lake, then water runs through their veins? No. It was easy for them but they could charge as much as they liked because they knew that we here had no choice but to go to that mountain for work. Children, those were the facts of life in your grandfather's day.

"But why are things different now? We had to cross the river or starve. Don't try to tell me that you cannot see the reasons! That which you could not do in the past you can do now. Nearly every family in this location has a son, a father or an uncle working in a paid job. Now often many bad things are said of these people - that they go away to the cities and forget about their families at home on the farm. I will accept that this does happen sometimes. But how many of you..." He points defiantly and assertively at various imaginary sections of the crowd, "...would be starving now if it were not for the help of a relative who earns a salary? How many of you would have sold all your land, all your cows and your goats, and thus would have nothing left at all, and still have neither rain nor food? What could you do then, except die or go to Nairobi to stand for a few cents on the tourists' photographs?

"You could, of course, like your grandfathers, pay through your noses to cross the Tana River..." He mimics the paddling of the canoe again and raises a laugh. "...Or maybe you could not." He hushes the crowd. "Those Luos who used to do so well from their ferry have long since

135

gone. They went back to Nyanza and helped to build roads and schools there and now look how prosperous they all are! Especially when compared to people here in this area where there have been neither roads nor schools for so long.

"I ask you again, are your sons and daughters going to be employed in the future if they have no education?" Loud shouts of "No!" answer him. "Will they ever have an education without schools? No! Do you want your children to follow certain advice we have heard to stay at home and have no schooling? No! Of course not! Because then who will move in to harvest the rich crop of jobs and salaries we all know is promised in the future of our country? Correct. Kikuyus and Luos would never be so stupid. You must never be satisfied with only second best for our area. We need more schools and more roads and more hospitals and we need them now. While there is drought we can never hope to grow rich enough to pay for these things if we rely solely on our farms. Why, we cannot even produce enough to feed ourselves, never mind enough to create the surplus we would need to sell if we were to raise enough cash to pay for our development. By the way, I have one piece of news related to this which will interest you."

He pauses to emphasise his seriousness. "I expect in the near future to be able to announce to the people of Kitui District that the main road from Nairobi will be tarred." This raises great cheers from the men and wild ululations from the women. Mulonzya milks the applause, acknowledges people's thanks and then raises his hands to hush the din. When he continues, he speaks very quietly, as if revealing a personal secret to the masses.

"But let me tell you something. There will be some people who would say that tarring a road or building a school is not right. They will say that you should turn your back on such progress and reject it. They will say that you should look back to your land and seek to improve it - a deceptively subtle ploy to take away from you the chance ever to do anything different... Now when they say these things, what are they actually asking you to do? Think back, even in your grandfather's time the rain here was never dependable, never enough to grow a surplus of food - and without a surplus you can sell nothing for the cash you need these days for your own development. And anyway, did we not as a people come this way as the rain-seekers? And are we not still seeking it? Perhaps we have to learn to find our life-giving rain in a different form from that which falls God-given from the sky.

"Now we have a number of people who have never themselves lived off the land telling us to turn our backs on progress, to return to our farms and gamble on their always-fickle fertility. In effect these people are telling you to go back to your homes and to spend your time dancing to make rain." Everyone laughs here as Mulonzya jigs about the platform to ridicule a traditional rainmaker. His deliberately ungainly dance is punctuated by exaggerated glances at the sky and shakes of the head to indicate that despite his efforts there is still no rain.

When he prepares to speak again, however, his expression sets to deadly seriousness and his voice sounds bitter and aggressive. "And when these people who give this advice to you are so obviously not speaking the truth because, when you examine why it is that you respect them and therefore listen to them in the first place, you see that it is because they have education, what do you think then? People who have everything to owe to their education trying to deny you the chance of that same thing... What I would think is maybe that these people have other reasons for saying what they do, that they do not want to see people develop because, in order to further their own political interests, they want to keep people poor. Don't look confused, everyone. Don't ask why these people want this. But you do know, if you take a moment to think. If people are poor, hungry and sick, they will be angry! If they are angry they will seek to make rash changes. In their anger they will change those things which they think are bad, but which in fact are good. The problem then is that in the turmoil many good things are difficult to keep going until the battle is won. Don't let the rumours fool you. Don't let the cheap wisdom trick you into destroying what is obviously good.

"So build up your school and let's all see it succeed." Great applause follows which Mulonzya immediately quells. "And I will begin your fund..." It is here that Mulonzya performs at his best. As the last speaker, it always was going to be his prerogative to start the collection, and it always had been his intention to set both a personal and public tenor with a memorable public statement. The political opportunity that had come his way via the soft-backed exercise book was not much more than a peripheral bonus by now. He dips into his pocket and produces a wad of notes. "...With a donation of ten thousand shillings. Thank you, my friends." As his thanks are lost in the ecstatic and tumultuous adulation of the crowd, Mulonzya steps down from the rostrum and strides up to the headmaster of Migwani Secondary School to present him with a sum of money greater than most people gathered there would hardly aspire to earn in five years. The applause continues as the teacher gratefully shakes the MP's hand for a minute or more.

Mulonzya then returned to his seat to allow the headmaster to take the rostrum again and declare the collection commenced, but the crowd shouted him down, demanding a curtain call from their hero. Not until Mulonzya had stood, bowed and waved his arms in victory did the chanting, clapping and cheering begin to subside. Then, one by one, each of the invited guests was summoned by the headmaster in his newfound role as master of ceremonies. As each donation was made, its value was announced to the crowd before being passed aside to a clerk for counting. Each sight of bank notes or cheque brought forth prolonged bursts of applause and cheering. No one, of course, matched Mulonzya's ten thousand. No one would have dared. As the occasion worked through its pecking order, the amounts announced gradually decreased. Soon the headmaster had discarded hundreds for tens, tens for fives and finally fives for single shillings. The process would take between two and three hours to complete but not one of the assembled thousands would begin to disperse until every last cent had been counted. Then, after the dignitaries had strode in turn up the rostrum to hand over their donations, they would not return to their seats, preferring to mingle with the crowd to seek out their friends and relations.

With his official responsibilities completed, Mulonzya too left his seat and walked through the crowds to the very edge of the school compound where people were more thinly scattered and congregated in small chattering groups. Father Michael and John Mwangangi stood together but apart, so engrossed in their conversation that they did not even see Mulonzya approaching until he was almost upon them. When John saw him out of the corner of his eye, he immediately began to move away, gently but deliberately touching Michael on his arm as a goodbye.

"I'll see you later." John turned and began to walk away.

"A minute, please, Mr District Officer," shouted Mulonzya as he panted his way across the bare earth of the school's playing field. "I would like you to hear something." By now he was close enough and stopped his advance. After waiting for a moment to regain some of his breath, he looked accusingly from John to Michael and back again to indicate that what he had to say concerned them both. He betrayed ignorance, however, of just which one should bear the brunt of the attack. Eventually, he chose the safer option and addressed Michael. "Mister Michael, a friend of mine has brought something to my attention. I understand that it is your doing and I would like to know more about it. I understand that you have a school in Thitani, a school for adult students?"

Michael nodded dispassionately, a gesture that both offered confirmation and yet immediately distanced himself from what might follow.

"You are teaching people to read and write?"

"Indeed we are, Mr Mulonzya," said Michael confidently. "We are trying to provide a little of the education in which you have so much faith."

"But why for adults? Surely education and schools are for children? What can an adult hope to benefit from it? There are no jobs for the old. We have too many young people to cater for as it is."

"This programme is not designed to create employable civil servants with a string of exam passes, Mr Mulonzya." Surely Mulonzya knew what the scheme was designed to do, thought Michael, but nonetheless he began to offer an explanation. "It is an adult literacy scheme. The intention is to teach adults to read and write - especially women - so that they can both write letters to their husbands in the city and also read the ones they receive without having to get one of their children to do it for them. It can be a great strain on a marriage, you know, when personal letters between a woman and her husband have to be read out loud by a child. Sometimes they contain things which a child ought not to hear..."

Mulonzya interrupted with a gesture of the hand. While Michael and John looked on in silence, he dipped his hand into his inside pocket and took out the exercise book that Nzuli had given him earlier. "Then why," he asked, flicking through the book and perfunctorily showing pages to the others, "do you teach this... this cheap politics?" Mulonzya angrily spat the words. "Just listen to this." He turned to a particular page in the exercise book and pointed to a passage in Kikamba neatly written in blue and corrected by a teacher in red. It had obviously been copied from the blackboard since it contained very few mistakes and the writer, who was Mr Nzuli's wife, he knew to be illiterate. As Mulonzya began to read from the book, both John and Michael began to look acutely embarrassed, but more out of impatience than guilt. "When a man has a lot of money he is said to be rich. When a man has little money he is said to be poor. When a man is rich he has plenty to eat. When a man is poor he starves. When a man is rich he has plenty of money. When a man is poor he has nothing. When a man is rich he can help the poor. When he does help the poor he is a good man. When he does not help the poor he is a very bad man. When I see James Mulonzya in his fine car, I know he is a bad man." Mulonzya looks up at Michael and then at John. Slapping the closed book against his leg in anger, he says, "Well? Is that literacy? Or is it something else? What do you think it is?"

"It's just an exercise in the use of the word 'when'," said Michael dismissively.

"Don't play with me, Mister Michael!" shouted Mulonzya, his voice beginning to break with suppressed anger. Presenting the open book to Michael and inviting him to take it, he continued. "Here. Look for yourself. I have not chosen just one isolated case. My name, traders' names - even our President's name - there is something on every page. Look. See for yourself."

Michael thumbed through the exercise book, apparently with little interest, but both he and Mulonzya knew that he did not actually need to look at all, for he already knew what was there. "Hmm," said Michael, "she seems to be making very good progress. See here, she can hardly write her own name on the first page, but later on she's coping even with quite complicated words and phrases." When Mulonzya realised that Michael was reading the woman's name from a page inside the book he snatched the book from the priest's hands. Earlier, he had carefully obliterated the name of the book's owner from the front cover with a ballpoint pen. Michael, however, continued his sentence without hesitation.

Mulonzya again scrutinised the book as he flicked through the pages. He looked as if he might explode with anger when Michael next interjected. "What worries you, Mr Mulonzya, is no more than the method of teaching. Let me explain." Michael began to speak quickly, thus silencing Mulonzya and pre-empting the pending attack. "I have been running these sessions for some years without success. Some people have learned to read and write as a result, of course, but in the past most have dropped out of the classes after only a few sessions. It was obvious that we were using the wrong methods, but no one had any new ideas about new approaches we might try. And then we came across a method which has been used with great success in South America called 'conscientisation'." Michael's voice proudly dwelt upon the word while a hint of a cynical smile played on his lips. He pronounced the word with the emphasis of a teacher who wants his class to repeat it. In the event, he was sure he saw Mulonzya's lips move as suggested. "Myself and several of the other priests in the district, all of whom have similar classes running in their parishes, got together and wrote a course based on this method. You see the idea is to motivate people to come to the classes because they feel that they get something out of them by allowing them to talk about the things that most deeply affect their lives. The classes use people's obvious interest in what matters in their lives to stimulate an interest in expressing what they have learned in writing."

Throughout Michael's short speech, Mulonzya had seemed to be fumbling with the words of intended interruptions. Though ready to burst forth, his impatience was so violent that he could find no suitable expression. "But this is rubbish!" He was by now shaking the exercise book in front of Michael's face. "And what is more, it is libel!" he shouted. "You have no right to teach people lies."

Michael smiled condescendingly. "Lies, Mr Mulonzya? The passage you read, for instance, is nothing more than the teaching of Jesus Christ in plain language."

"Nonsense! The man who brought this book for me to see is himself a man of the Church and he thinks it is every bit as obscene as I do. You have no right to spread such rumours, such obvious lies. If people must be told why they are poor, then tell them. Tell them there is a drought. Tell them about the riches of Europe and America and how white people demand that everyone else lives in slavery. Tell them then what is evil, Mister Michael. Tell them about the colonialists who raped their country and robbed it of its riches."

Michael interrupted here. His patience had obviously begun to run out and consequently his voice had hardened. He spoke slowly, as if consciously spelling out his meaning. Though the other constantly tried to interrupt, the priest subtly diverted every attempt to do so with only the slightest raising of his voice. "Mr Mulonzya, the whole point of teaching in this way is to get people to read and write as quickly and as well as possible. To motivate people to do the necessary work, we have to use the material of their own lives. If they cannot understand the subjects we use, how can they ever read about them or write about them? Now we do discuss the drought, have no fears about that, but how can we talk about Europe? People here don't see rich white people. Neither did they ever see colonialists here. And what's more all of that finished over ten years ago. If we talk about poverty - and believe me, that above all else produces the best discussion, we have to contrast it with what riches people see - and that is clearly rich Kenyans, like yourself, Mr Mulonzya, with your shops and your buses and your Mercedes-Benz. I agree," continued Michael, "that maybe our teacher has gone too far by making his students write these things down as exercises. But don't you see that if we discuss such things we can do nothing to prevent our students regarding you as wealthy? Knowing you like I do, I would have thought you would have been flattered."

"But there is nothing wrong with wealth which has been made for the betterment of the country," said Mulonzya, defiantly shaking his fist. "I have worked for that wealth and through that work, I helped to develop my location. You can see for yourself," he continued, gesturing to the crowd at his back who were still avidly watching the confrontation, "how grateful people are for what I have done for them."

Michael laughed again. He spoke quietly and cynically. "They are grateful for your promises, Mulonzya. How many times in the last ten years is it? How many times have you promised that the road from Nairobi is about to be tarred? And in the meantime we gradually watch it wash away with each new rainy season. And meanwhile the potholes get deeper and the gullies get wider and we don't even get it graded. It's been like this for more than a year now. What are you doing about that?"

At this point Mulonzya turned away. He had had enough. Now facing John Mwangangi, he said, "I shall hold you responsible, Mr District Officer, if this slander is not stopped immediately. This... this priest's school is in your area and so it is your responsibility to supervise what goes on there."

Mwangangi, who until then had maintained a polite silence, now spoke. Straightening his back to stretch himself to his full height and thus accentuating the difference in stature between himself and the rather small and rounded Mulonzya, he spoke quietly but firmly, stating his case so clearly that, for a moment at least, Mulonzya was left speechless, allowing Michael to develop the point. "On the contrary, Mr Mulonzya. My job is to oversee the administration of such establishments, to judge whether or not a project aids the overall development of the District. Father Michael's scheme, like this very school here, is designed to provide education where it is obviously needed. As such I would have expected you to encourage it. Surely if it achieves what it sets out to do and teaches many previously illiterate people how to read and write, then we should not worry too much about how they do it, as long as what they do is within the law, of course. And what is more, I would remind you, Mr Mulonzya, that this scheme is run by the Church and not by government, so even through the education officer, I have no direct power over the teachers or the methods it employs. There are, as far as I know, no rules for such private schemes. If you have criticisms, don't come to me, but go to the next meeting of Father Michael's parish council and take it up directly with them. The fact that I granted permission for the project in the first place does not mean that I am still responsible for it. It was merely recognition on my part that there was no legal barrier in their way. In the same way, though I granted permission for this fund-raising day, I have no control over what is said in the speeches."

"Even if they are clearly political," said Michael, "and directly criticise someone who is obviously doing a good and useful job and who has been denied a public right to reply."

Mulonzya gave out an aggressive laugh before speaking. "If someone tells lies, he deserves all he gets. You know as well as I do that an education in a school like this one is the only way of escaping starvation and poverty."

"And how many families will starve as a result of spending every penny they can get on school fees they cannot afford in the entirely false belief that their children will pass exams and get jobs?" Michael's unanswered comment was effectively allowed to close the matter.

Mulonzya's parting words were then delivered with the vehemence of a curse. "I can see no point in arguing with you. You will both be hearing from me in due course." And with that he turned and stalked off defiantly towards the crowd. He had passed no more than four people when a stranger stopped him, greeted him with a smile and warmly shook his hand. The joy of Mulonzya's broadcast greeting could be heard by hundreds and many turned to watch.

"He just doesn't see, does he?" said John. "Surely he must know that we are not against education? That all we are concerned with is whether or not the money could be better spent at the moment on other things. He seems to think that we want to prevent people from going to school." John was almost pleading with Michael.

The priest, however, was still staring at the now laughing and joking Mulonzya as he began again to play to his audience. "He doesn't think, I am convinced of that. But he has an unerring ability to judge which side his bread is buttered." Then, turning towards John, he continued, "I'd better have a word with Boniface. He might just be taking his instructions a bit too literally."

***

Not satisfied with Nzuli's book full of evidence, Mulonzya changed his plans. He had intended to drive directly back to Nairobi immediately the *Harambee* day was over, but instead drove the twenty miles north to Mwingi to spend the night in his late wife's house just outside the town, which he kept maintained and cleaned daily by a houseboy as a base for his still frequent visits to his home town.

The following morning he rose at dawn and, after a hurried breakfast of maize porridge, which he prepared for himself, drove along the new main road which by-passed Migwani several miles to the west, passing through the now fast growing trading centre of Thitani. Though he arrived there before seven o'clock, the small town was already bustling with activity. A stranger's eyes would hardly have interpreted this occasional and lazy progress of several herds of cows across the main road toward the town's dam as Thitani's equivalent of a morning rush hour, but that indeed is what it was. This heavy traffic certainly frustrated James Mulonzya's progress. Three times within the last mile of his journey he had to stop to allow groups of animals to meander apparently aimlessly across the road. The apparently similar aimlessness of the young boys who herded them prompted Mulonzya to use the car horn repeatedly and angrily.

This, however, had no effect on the third and last of the infant drovers.

The confused boy stood at the roadside not knowing whether to run out in front of the growling car to beat his father's cows with his stick or simply stand aside in fear and hope that they would move of their own accord.

Impatience prompted Mulonzya to get out of the car and threaten the boy with a beating. He began to shout, saying that if the boy could not move the cows immediately he would move them with his car, but the only result was to frighten the child even more and send him scurrying to hide behind one of the nearby shops. The cows, however, eventually did wander off in the right direction as if to prove that they hardly needed tending at all on this daily journey they knew so well.

James Mulonzya was undoubtedly a man in a hurry. He knew he had a deadline to meet and, although he believed he still had an hour to spare, he obviously begrudged every unproductive minute that passed. Having driven straight past the dozen or so concrete boxes that were Thitani town, he turned off the main road and into a euphorbia-hedged compound. With piles of sand, rows of new cement blocks left to dry in the sun and odd lengths of timber strewn haphazardly about, it looked more like a building site than a new primary school, but, having made frequent visits to the project during its short history, Mulonzya knew exactly where to find what he sought.

The only sign of life in the entire compound was a solitary donkey which took time off its grazing to raise its head and watch Mulonzya's white Mercedes grind to a dusty halt beside a house some distance from the classrooms. The headmaster was already up and about and, on seeing the MP leave his car and set off toward his house, he rushed outside to offer a greeting.

Mulonzya apologised profusely for calling so early in the morning, offering the excuse that his time was short, due to the necessity of his presence at a meeting Nairobi at midday. It had been some time since he had inspected the new school's progress so, since he was passing, he thought he ought to call in and look around.

As he expected, the headmaster showed some reluctance to grant his wish, offering the excuse that the school had not yet been swept out that morning since the boarding pupils had all gone home for the weekend. Mulonzya, however, would not be dissuaded and soon the two men had set off for the classroom block. Mulonzya still seemed to be in a hurry whilst the other, nervously jangling his school keys, still seemed reluctant. Mulonzya insisted on inspecting both classrooms before any other part of the school. As the head unlocked and then opened the door to the first, the MP rushed inside and looked about, his eyes darting from wall to wall in search of his prey. Here he found nothing.

Then, as the door of the second room opened, Mulonzya's search was surely ended. Striding slowly but purposefully across the classroom toward a notice board on the far wall, his progress created a slight scraping sound as his soles ground down on the gravelly dust that had accumulated overnight in a film on the floor. There he looked long and hard at a collection of photographs, newspaper cuttings and pieces of students' work, hand-written on lined paper, the whole having been neatly arranged with some care.

Though the display bore no title, the subject was clearly himself. The photographs were all of him. The cuttings from the Daily Nation and Taifa Leo all concerned him, as did every one of the hand-written passages. There was nothing here that could be construed as libellous, nothing that attracted him in the same way as the passage in the exercise book, but he had found what he sought and his suspicions had been confirmed. Clearly the teacher employed by Father Michael for the literacy scheme used this room for his classes in which, during the day, he also taught children. This display was clearly on show permanently. Obviously embarrassed, but doing his best to conceal it, the headmaster showed the now disinterested Mulonzya through the dormitories and kitchen and then finished the tour by pointing to a patch of bare earth and scattered thorn bushes to which he gave the proud title of 'football pitch'. Mulonzya then curtly and laconically thanked the man and left immediately. No longer in a hurry, he drove steadily onto the main road and so on his way.

It was about half an hour later that the headmaster's Saturday morning was again disturbed by the noise of an approaching vehicle. This time, however, it was the growling of a *pikipiki*, a motorbike. Again he went outside to welcome his visitor and was this time greeted by Father Michael and, sitting precariously on the pillion, one of his own staff, Boniface Mutisya.

"Have you had any visitors, Joel?" shouted Michael, without bothering either to dismount or switch off the engine.

The headmaster nodded. "Mulonzya. Earlier this morning," he said.

Michael gave a short frustrated sigh and half-turned to cast a glance toward Boniface. "Okay. Thanks, Joel," and with that he kicked the bike into gear and rode off.

***

Several weeks elapsed before Mulonzya's manoeuvres neared completion. During that period he discovered much about John Mwangangi and this newly acquired knowledge helped a considerable amount in the formulation of his scheme. Though this plan of action was by now almost complete, he still needed the cooperation of one more person, whose link in the chain would be crucial. Without him the plan could still succeed, but with him it was almost bound to.

It was approaching midday when James Mulonzya nosed his car into a space on Kenyatta Avenue. After switching off the engine, he leaned back into the driving seat for a moment and gave out a deep sigh to hide a yawn. Despite being hermetically sealed from the heat and fumes in the comfortable opulence of his car, he was clearly hot and flustered. He was panting quite hard as if he had suffered some exertion. Sweat streamed down the side of his face and stood out like glistening beads of dew caught in his hair. For over half an hour he had crawled along the city streets in his car to seek a parking space and found nothing. Kenyatta Avenue, up Government Road, Kimathi Street, Mama Ngina Avenue, Government Road, Kenyatta Avenue, Muindi Mbingu Street; he had covered every inch of the triangle twice without success. As time passed, he had begun to fear that he would be late for his meeting. He had allowed his frustration to take over and had taken to driving along with his head out of the side window to allow him to shout and gesture at anyone who got in his way. This, of course, completely undid the effect of his car's air conditioning and now he was paying for his actions with sweat.

He had, however, succeeded in finding a space at last and, after handing over a five-shilling note and a stern finger-wagged warning to the parking boys, he walked off quickly towards Government Road. Nairobi was certainly becoming a nightmare. It was overcrowded, noisy and dirty. On every corner there was a group of crawling, limping beggars, accosting every likely passer-by with their jangling tins, sycophantic greetings and offers of bony handshakes. If he, a local man, was embarrassed by their advances, what must the many tourists who walked the city streets be feeling? If he had his way, he would have all the beggars rounded up and sent back to their home areas. After all, why were the families of these people not looking after them as they should do? Undoubtedly they were responsible for the majority of crime, which so deterred honest people from walking the city streets. As a Kenyan, he was angered to know that Europeans commonly referred to his capital city as Nai-robbery.

He felt embarrassed to know that no one could safely park a car without paying for the attentions of the parking boys, the ragged urchins who roamed the streets in packs. If not paid for protecting a vehicle in its owner's absence, they would probably steal it themselves or merely dismantle it on the spot. If James Mulonzya had his way, he would suggest that a special school be built for these boys, way out in the bush so that they might learn how to survive without begging. He would do all these things if only he had the time, but other, more pressing concerns forever seemed to fill his every minute.

On reaching Kimathi Street he turned the corner and looked to his right to survey the crowded terrace of the New Stanley Hotel. Smartly by-passing the lengthening queue of people awaiting a vacant table, he approached a man he knew to be the senior waiter and introduced himself. The waiter shook his head in response to a question from Mulonzya and then obsequiously led him away along a tortuous meandering path across the terrace to the unoccupied table that had remained vacant because it bore a 'reserved' notice. The waiter removed this and left as Mulonzya sat down.

For several minutes Mulonzya remained alone, though obviously expecting company. Craning his neck to peer across to the roadside pavement, he stretched and rocked his whole frame as if trying to break free of the chair's bondage. He sought the face of every likely passer-by and, in a glance, rejected every one and moved his eyes to the next. His worry was that he had been late and might have missed his rendezvous. Despite the widespread belief that in African time, mid-day could mean anything between eleven and four, Mulonzya knew that when George Nzou arranged a meeting at twelve o'clock, he usually meant twelve o'clock on the dot.

He did not have long to wait, however, before a small middle-aged man came into view. As he rounded the corner from Kenyatta Avenue, his eyes had surveyed the hotel terrace, their gaze darting from one table to another, their movement punctuated by occasional concerned glances at his watch. Mulonzya stood bolt upright to face him and raised his arm high. Nzou saw him immediately and offered a wave of acknowledgement. By the time he had threaded his way to the shaded rear of the terrace where Mulonzya sat, a waiter had already been summoned and their coffee ordered.

"Good morning, Mr Nzou," said Mulonzya, standing to greet the other and offering an over-hearty handshake.

The other nodded and replied to the greeting, but in a manner that was more curt and less enthusiastic.

The two men then sat and exchanged pleasantries until their coffee arrived. Nzou had suffered the same parking problems as Mulonzya and apologised profusely but perfunctorily for being so late. Clearly of quite different generations, they spoke only guardedly of themselves, with neither trusting their estimation of the other's views. Their ideas mirrored their different minds. Mulonzya, much older than Nzou, wore a green cotton suit, a 'colonial' type, in which, to the British eye, the jacket is a mere shirt. Designed to keep its wearer cool, the collar was loose and open. The fact that it did not cover the rolls of flabby redundant flesh, which encircled Mulonzya's thick squat neck, was an imperfection which would have troubled George, but which the older and less self-conscious Mulonzya had never even considered.

George, himself, small and in his early thirties, was clearly a city man, closer in ideals to Mulonzya's son Charles, rather than those of his elders. He overtly displayed western standards of dress, a formal business suit, a white shirt and tie, and even, on this hot still day, he would not consider either loosening his collar or removing his jacket. As they sat at the table talking, their manners accentuated the differences between them. George, full of nervous energy, sat on the edge of his chair and leaned forward to rest his forearms neatly on the table, his eyes politely and self-consciously angled down to focus upon the neurotic fiddling of his fingers. Mulonzya, on the other hand, leaned back, almost slouching in his chair, whilst he held his head straight and fixed his gaze on the other.

Within a few minutes, long before other orders taken at the same time would be met, the waiter returned to serve their coffee. While he hovered near the table to off-load the collection of pots from his tray, the two men sat in silence, their eyes independently following every movement of the waiter's arm. His last act, the placing of the bill facedown in front of Mulonzya, prompted both to offer reticent thanks. Then, as Mulonzya milked and sugared his coffee, he leaned forward in his chair and the mood suddenly changed. All subsequent conversation was subdued and quiet, but always utterly to the point, contrasting sharply with the pleasantries which they had shared before, when, leaning back in his chair, Mulonzya had almost shouted his words, apparently so that everyone else on the terrace might hear.

"So, James, what's our business today? Is it another donation you want?"

"No..."

"By the way," interrupted George, "how did your *Harambee* go? Did you raise your target?"

"Well, not quite, but almost." Mulonzya changed the subject quickly. Though he wanted to get down to business anyway, he most certainly did not want to be drawn into a discussion about Migwani School's fundraising. After all he might let slip the fact that he had donated the entirety of the ten thousand shillings in his own name instead of admitting that the sum had been collected from several Nairobi-based people. Thus after pausing to adjust his tack, he began, "George, I have a slight problem to discuss with you. I think you can... I think you will want to help." The other raised his hands a little and shrugged his shoulders. Submissive open palms invited further explanation but offered no promises. "Do you remember that some months ago a Migwani man came back to Kenya after several years in England?"

George's blank expression began to solidify to one of interest. "Yes. That was... John Mwangangi?"

Mulonzya nodded.

"Yes," said George, "I remember him. I ought to. He's in my field, after all."

A hint of a private smile crossed Mulonzya's face.

"He went to Kitui School, didn't he?" asked Nzou, clearly trying hard to remember. "Yes. He took a job in the civil service... But surely you, of all people, should know that. He was posted to your area."

"Oh yes, I know," said Mulonzya. His smile was now openly displayed.

"Well? What has he done?"

Mulonzya paused a little here to collect his thoughts and add emphasis before starting to state his position. With his elbow resting on the table and his head half-hidden behind its supporting hand, he spoke in a near whisper. "I have met Mr Mwangangi several times and have come to know him quite well. The problem is George, he is going to get himself into a lot of trouble if he is not careful."

As Mulonzya paused, George Nzou looked up, his eyes widening a little and silently asking for more.

"You see, George, like you he is still a young man and he is very much an idealist. It seems to me that the most obvious thing for him to have done when he returned from England would have been to establish his own law practice here in Nairobi. It would have been a lucrative business. But he is not a poor man, you see, and he seems to spurn talk of profit and comfort. He practised in England for some years and earned quite a sum for himself.

Nzou seemed a little surprised at this. "You mean that Mwangangi gave up a working practice in England to live in Mwingi?"

"Well it was never just his own practice, so I have been told, but he is obviously a very capable man and it is said he was partner in his company. He has a reputation for working extremely hard and for learning very quickly. He has a doctorate, by the way..."

George raised his eyebrows again, obviously impressed. "Why then did he take a job in the civil service? That will never pay very well."

"As I said, he is something of an idealist. He is determined to work in bush areas and is adamant that he should stay in his home area. His head is full of ideas and schemes that he believes no one else has ever thought of. It seems to me that this job of his is nothing more than a way of earning money whilst he devotes most of his time and energy putting these ideas into practice. What he is really doing, of course, is building up his political alliances."

"What are these ideas and schemes? Give me some examples."

Mulonzya pauses to think for a moment. "There are very many, it seems. Even I only know a fraction of what must be going on. He works very closely with the Roman Catholic Church, though never officially, of course. He offers backing - both through finance and influence - for such things as adult literacy schemes, irrigation projects and so on. In fact, he not only sanctions these schemes officially through his professional work in the District Office, but also offers informal advice and assistance, helps them with planning and makes the required connections to other government departments to ensure they get all the help to which they are entitled."

"In one way this all sounds very good. What Mwangangi is ensuring is that no initiative gets under way in his area without proper support. Where he is wrong, and perhaps this is where you object, Mr Mulonzya, is that he is using official systems to assist private projects. Public servants should not be getting directly involved in such schemes."

"That is the point. This is why he is going to get into trouble. What is more, either he does not understand the political dimension in many of the things he is sponsoring, in which case he is naive and stupid; or he does understand the politics, in which case this must surely be his prime interest."

After a pause, Nzou raised his eyes and looked pensively at Mulonzya. "I don't altogether see what this has to do with me." Then, as Mulonzya described his suggestion, Nzou began to smile and nod. With some resignation, he suppressed the impatience that was his first reaction, and throughout he remained aloof, offering neither agreement nor rejection.

"Ah, George, wait a moment. You have not heard everything. Just listen to what I have to say and then you will understand. It is very clear to me that Mwangangi has ambitions. I am convinced that he regards his present job as a mere stepping stone, a means of establishing himself while he tries out the ground for his schemes. His head, you see, is full of these ideas, all learned from his days in England. But he is not yet fully convinced that they will work. For him this is the testing stage. Within a couple of years, I would guess that he will decide whether or not to continue in this vein. He will make his judgment on the basis of whether he still has popular support. If not, I would expect to see him pack his bags and pursue another career in law here in Nairobi."

"And what if he does have support?"

"Ah, George, may I say that this is my real area of concern. I am convinced he wishes to enter politics."

Nzou smiled. "Ah yes," he said, slowly, "Now I see where your real interests lie. You think he will stand against you in the next election." Mulonzya nodded. "But James, you have been a Member of Parliament for the area for many years. You are a highly respected man and a well-known politician. Surely a young man who has spent most of his life out of the area cannot threaten such a strong position?"

Mulonzya wore a serious expression as he spoke. "George, listen to my argument and my evidence and then make up your own mind. He lives in the area permanently. I have to spend most of my time here, for obvious reasons, but at the moment he is almost a free agent and I cannot even keep track of what he is doing! He is out amongst the people at every opportunity. I have heard it said that he spends barely half of his time in the office. He personally visits *Harambee* committees and local councils to offer advice. Unlike most other District Officers, he not only passes judgment on their requests, he actually puts ideas into their heads, tells them how they should organise themselves and most importantly uses his connections with the Church and the missionaries to get his hands on money, overseas money, to fund their projects."

"Surely that cannot be much..."

Mulonzya interrupted, his voice hardening as he counted out each of the examples on his fingers. "Forty thousand for a water tank in Migwani - from Germany. Twenty thousand for a dam in Mwingi, also from Germany. Thirty thousand for a dam in Kyuso - from America. The list is a long one. There is one priest in Kitui, you see, who knows all these foreign agencies. He can get the money if there are worthwhile schemes to support. What Mwangangi is doing is trying to create the schemes and then, when he is successful, he brings in the priest from Kitui who can then secure the foreign money. At the end of the day, it is Mwangangi who gets all the credit.

"For instance," continued Mulonzya, "take this adult literacy work. There are institutions in Europe that will aid almost any new project. They will pay for fifty per cent of the project for the first three years - but only if it uses a very specific method of teaching. Mwangangi knows this. The priest in Kitui knows this. But in the past there has never been the interest amongst the older people to learn how to read and write. They have always preferred to send the young people to school in the hope that they will be able to get a job and help the family out of poverty. No older people will learn enough to qualify for employment. But since Mwangangi came to the area, he has been promoting the idea of older people going to school. You see, he creates the interest at the local level, puts an idea into people's heads and then presents them with the money to carry it out through his contacts in the Church."

"What about the teachers? How does he get them?"

"This is the neatest thing of all. There are now so many of these schemes in the area that the missionaries have set up a training course for instructors. They do not employ officially qualified teachers at all."

"But what is the problem with all this? What is it that you find so worrying?"

"It's the method he is using, George. I suppose the idea is all right in itself, but the way they put it into practice is not good. The teaching, you see, is nearly all informal. It is designed to motivate people by talking about those things that are important in their own lives. To put it simply, George, they teach politics." Mulonzya paused here to extract the Thitani exercise book from his pocket. "Read this. You will see what I mean."

Nzou read the passage that Mulonzya indicated. When he looked up he laughed at first, but was then immediately more serious than before. "This is nonsense. It is simplistic - like a child would write. You think, then, that this is what they spend their time discussing in these classes?"

"No, George. I am sure of it. And what is more Mwangangi not only knows how the classes are run. He helped to design them."

"What you are saying then, is that Mwangangi is using these classes to put out propaganda against you."

"Exactly. And also against all local people who have done well for themselves, such as you yourself, George. And he is using his official position to create more and more opportunities to carry out this lobbying. In all of this, his ally - and perhaps even sponsor - is the Roman Catholic Church."

"So where do I come in?"

Mulonzya spoke quietly and slowly now. "I am asking a favour of you, George. My problem, you see, is this. Although I am confident that I can easily beat him in a fair fight, he has the big advantage over me in that he is out there in the bush and I am in the city. He is campaigning for himself every day and I have no way of keeping my eyes on what he is doing. If I am seen too much in Kitui, he will just say that I am not doing my representative job in Nairobi properly, so I cannot win. Do you see?" George Nzou nodded. "If the circumstances were more evenly balanced, I am sure I could win. So what I would like you to do is this.

"Now you remember I said I was convinced he would come to Nairobi if his ideas did not seem to be producing the results he wants? Well I would like you to help me to bring him here. I know, you see, that your partner has just left you. You must have much more work than you can possibly do alone. What I want to suggest is that you could write him a letter of introduction saying that you have heard much about him et cetera, and that you might be willing to consider some agreement; perhaps some short-term arrangement whereby he could carry out some specific tasks for you... You need only offer him limited pieces of work relating to, let's say, a particular case, just so that you could lighten the load on yourself. And, of course, initially it need be on no more than a consultancy basis. That will allow you some time to assess whether you might cooperate more, or indeed less, in the future. If things did not work out, there would still be no formal links, so you would simply cease to offer him any more work. If things did work out, of course, you might ask him to take on complete cases to ease your workload. After all you wouldn't want to lose lucrative contracts simply because you could not cope with the workload, would you? In the longer term, if things worked out well, you might be able to come to some more solid agreement with him regarding his status. I know he has some considerable capital to his name, which he retained after selling property in London before moving here. And, after all, George, there is no business under the sun that could not do with an injection of capital, is there? Especially one which has been suffering recent partnership... er ...shall we call them difficulties?"

Nzou looked somewhat confused. "Wait a minute, James. Surely he has not yet finished his work in Kitui. What is going to persuade him to give up so easily?"

Mulonzya smiled knowingly. "Several things, but three in particular. First, I have been doing some investigation of my own. It seems that Mr Mwangangi has a few personal problems to overcome. He and his father have apparently been sworn enemies for some time. They just do not get on together. This friction is having a very great effect on Mr Mwangangi's wife and as a result she has fallen sick two or three times already. Secondly, his wife is not Kenyan. She was brought up in England and hates the bush. I am told she is very lonely and is threatening to leave Mwangangi if things don't change. You see she does not like living apart from their daughter who is at boarding school here in the city. Thirdly, I can tell you for certain that Mr Mwangangi has had his knuckles rapped. The husband of this woman..." Here Mulonzya pointed to the name on the front cover of the offending exercise book "...has written a letter of formal complaint to the Minister. He is one of my strongest allies in Thitani, you see. He has accused Mr Mwangangi of using government property to further his own political ends. I know for a fact that a letter has already gone out to Mr Mwangangi and that he is likely to suffer at least a severe reprimand, and maybe a compulsory redeployment. He will conclude, of course, that he will be unlikely to get much further in the civil service, but there is still just a chance that he might decide to fight it. And then there is the matter of money, of course. He would clearly earn much more money in a Nairobi practice and even the idealists among us are still human, are we not?"

George Nzou took a deep breath and then sighed. He said nothing for a while as he dissected Mulonzya's words. "I can see that you have been very busy, James. I can see the logic behind your scheme. If Mwangangi's personal difficulties are as great as you say, the right incentive might persuade him to come to the city. That is merely what you want, isn't it; to get him out of the way?"

"Yes," said Mulonzya. "As I said before, I don't want to discredit him or take out a legal action against him. All I want to do is make sure that we will campaign on equal terms."

"You would never succeed with a libel action in this case," said George curtly. "Internal discipline within the Ministry on the grounds of professional malpractice, maybe, but not a court action... not, of course, unless there was more incriminating evidence than you have shown me. But suppose I were to help you, James. What is in it for me?"

"George, all I am asking is that you should offer him an invitation to talk to you. You have more work than you can do. I know that. When you talk to him, you can judge for yourself what he is like. He is very highly qualified, would give you more access to high prestige work and, importantly for you, could deal very easily with foreign company representatives and the like. But those decisions would be for you to make later. All I am asking at the moment is that you write to him saying that there is a vacancy and that you are currently seeking a new likeminded partner. One the other hand," he continued, after a short pause, "if there is anything else I can do..."

"Suppose he turns out to be no good? What then...?"

"Then tell him that things would not work out and don't offer him the position."

"But that would not solve your problem. He would still be in Kitui..."

"Ah, but the idea of moving to the town would have been raised to the forefront of his mind and a mechanism to accomplish it would have been identified. With the other things I have arranged, the pressure would begin to tell. If there is anything else I could do, George..."

George Nzou looked down, as if studying his clasped hands. Now nervously, he clicked his fingernails together one after the other while he considered his proposition. "At the moment," he said, "you stand to gain much more from this than me."

Mulonzya interrupted here, speaking louder and quicker. "George, I will gain nothing financially from this and you know it. This is more like an insurance policy than an investment. At the moment, what I am suggesting will be of no cost to yourself. On the contrary, your firm would once again be able to fulfil contracts that it otherwise might lose. All I am suggesting to you is that you should write to Mwangangi to discuss the possibility of a future association. If anyone has anything to gain from this, it is you. I happen to know, you see, that you have already tried once to persuade Mwangangi to join you."

Nzou's reaction was instinctive. "Who told you that?" His voice was tinged with anger.

Mulonzya offered only a gesture in reply. Displaying wide-eyed ignorance, he simply shrugged his shoulders as if to signify that the fact was common knowledge.

"It seems to me, James, that your insurance policy is likely to mature before your investment pays its dividends." He paused here and looked up. Mulonzya, however, offered no reaction. He merely waited. "There is something else, however," continued Nzou, "which might restore the balance a little." Mulonzya still stared back blankly. "I have some item of value which I would like to sell. My problem is that here the market is not too good. There are much better prices overseas."

Mulonzya raised his eyebrows. "Well?" he asked when the other remained silent.

"Oh yes, of course," said Nzou. "They are *mavia*." He used the Kamba word deliberately to avoid running the risk of being overheard by the wrong people. The simple word 'stones' was fast becoming a dangerous one to use too openly.

"You would like me to find a way of exporting your *mavia*?" Nzou nodded. "What are they?"

Nzou leaned across the table before speaking. "There are not many as yet, James. I have bought most of them from people in the bush who

157

have found them on their land. Of course, I can't get rid of them, except to tourists, most of which will not buy because they are afraid to do illegal deals. If I can find a way of exporting them, though, I am sure that my contacts will be able to carry on supplying."

"What sort are they?"

Nzou whispered. "All kinds. Opal, tiger eye, red garnets, green garnets, emeralds, rubies..."

Mulonzya was suddenly interested. He knew that there was no problem whatsoever in either exporting these stones or covering up the deal to avoid it being traced. "Hmm," he mused, "there are many difficulties..."

It was now Nzou's turn to smile. "Come along, James. Don't play with me."

Mulonzya scoffed at this bush talk. "There would be tough penalties for both of us if we were caught, and I would lose my licence."

"I doubt it. There's a lot of money involved." George Nzou smiled and looked Mulonzya straight in the eye. He rubbed his thumb across his fingers to signify that a bribe could be paid.

James Mulonzya bit his lip. He eyed the other pensively for some time before finally saying, "All right. It's agreed then! My company will charge its usual fee, of course." Nzou nodded and smiled as Mulonzya offered his hand across the table to clinch the deal. "Good. I will expect to hear from you within the next month then. I would be grateful if you would let me read your letter to Mwangangi before you send it. I might be able to offer some useful advice."

"Of course, James. I will bring it round to your house personally. I will bring my merchandise as well."

After shaking hands again, the two men rose from their seats. Both reached for their wallets simultaneously, but Mulonzya insisted on exercising his seniority and placed a twenty-shilling note onto the table, carefully ensuring that it was trapped firmly beneath the sugar bowl. Then, after a parting word, they left the terrace of the New Stanley Hotel to make their separate ways through the city, Nzou with his new market secure and a possibly valuable piece of inside information firmly in his mind, and Mulonzya with the increased pressure on his rival now guaranteed, plus commission of twenty per cent gross of any future deal.

Within a few seconds, a party of four European tourists almost dived into the vacant seats. They had been waiting for over half an hour by then. The guidebook, which one of their number so avidly read, invited them to Kenya, where they could leave civilisation behind, find natural beauty and people who still lived the simple life. The waiter, who came to serve them, took the twenty-shilling note with his heart racing. Ten shillings of it were pure tip.

***

Lesley stood and watched the car drive out onto the road. As it turned the corner, she saw the faces of both Janet Rowlandson and Father Michael momentarily turn her way. Their concern for her well-being was clear, though she had tried her utmost to convince them that she would be all right. She wondered whether they had been surprised at how unemotionally she had received the news. It was surely possible, she thought, that she had already got over the worst of the shock because she had already been told by a personal messenger from Migwani, who stood at her side. But perhaps the real shock was still to come. Surely that was it. She would continue to feel nothing until she had become aware of the full reality of the event.

As the car disappeared into the distance, she turned to her right and spoke to the boy who stood beside her. "I am grateful that you came to tell me. Please don't think I am being nasty to you, but I think it would be best if you could stay the night in the hotel down the road. I would rather be alone tonight." Before the boy could say that he had no money, that he had rushed all the way from Migwani at lunchtime with only his bus fare in his pocket, Lesley had spoken again. Laying her hands gently, but without either thanks or affection on his shoulders, she said, "I'll give you a hundred shillings for your room. You don't mind, do you?"

The boy shook his head. The mere thought of a hundred shilling note in his pocket rendered him quite speechless. It took only a minute for Lesley to go inside the house and get the money from her purse. Another minute later and he was gone, already walking down the road. She knew he would find some room behind a shop or bar for twenty shillings or so, and then pocket the rest of the money, but by then she was past caring. She watched him disappear behind the euphorbia hedges of the next house as if to see him off the premises and then turned and left the veranda.

Once inside, her first thought was to pour a glass of whisky, but after taking just a small sip, her face contorted in a grimace and she left the rest untouched on the sideboard. After lighting a cigarette, she sat and lifted her feet onto the low coffee table in a vain attempt to relax. She closed her eyes and took repeated short nervous puffs of her cigarette. Within a minute it had burned down almost to the filter and she again sat upright to lean across the table so she could stub it out. Throughout she wore an expression of self-admonitory disgust. Clearly she felt that she should do something, but what? What could she do? She looked about the room. It still seemed strange. How hard she had tried to feel at home here, and how little she had succeeded. Everything here was John's. It had never been and would never be hers. No matter how hard she had tried, no matter how hard John had tried, ostensibly on her behalf, she had always felt an alien here. She had done her best to understand her husband's point of view, to help him realise his ambitions, to strengthen his sometimes flagging determination with her support, but she had never truly understood why. She had backed him because he was her husband, not because she agreed with his intentions, which she hardly even understood, let alone shared.

It had been so different in London. There he had been the stranger. It had been her responsibility, initially, to make allowances for him, but then he had found it so easy to adjust. After all, it was much easier there, where no one ever made any demands. Kenya, however, had been different from the start. What would never have been an easy adjustment for her to make was rendered nigh impossible by John's uncompromising attitudes, by his determination to fulfil his ambitions, by the ease with which he adopted a lifestyle and its assumptions which she had been led to believe he had never really known. He changed so quickly that his preoccupations had blinded him to her own obvious difficulties. He had expected her to adapt to their new life as quickly as he had done and, because he could not comprehend her fears, he could do nothing to allay them.

And then there were the other demands, those that others placed squarely upon their lives. She had soon realised that her husband's position and past experience would make them both effectively public figures. At first she had rather enjoyed all the attention they received when they moved to Mwingi. Later, though, she had grown to hate the almost constant knocks on the door, regarding visitors and their demands on her husband's time as intrusions on their privacy. Everyone here seemed to live everyone else's life, not just gossip about it.

More directly, and now it seemed with justification, she had feared John's father. John had spoken very little of his own family while they lived in London and, when they arrived in Kenya, the old man seemed to have re-entered John's life like a skeleton from some half-forgotten cupboard, raising old arguments which John had clearly thought he had long buried. Time and again he had tried to force John to submit to his wishes, presumably, she thought, to reassert an authority that had once been flouted, but nothing seemed to satisfy the man. As John became more and more preoccupied with his own thoughts, his ideals, his ambitions, his father, it seemed that he had progressively less and less time for her, simply assuming that in the meantime she would occupy herself with their home and their daughter. All their friends were John's friends. He invited them round to their house. Lesley never had any independent contact with them and anyway did not enjoy their company. All conversations seemed planned. Every one of their acquaintances served a purpose, either for information or for influence, and whenever John spoke, he seemed to be arranging things, planning events or seeking support for his projects or ideas. They had no friends, only contacts.

Lesley, of course, had nothing to say to any of these people. There was no common ground and everything was conducted only on John's terms. She knew there was a widening gulf between them, but could not identify what it was that was forcing them apart. Was it that John was changing and leaving her behind? Or was it that her lack of sympathy for his current priorities was causing her to withdraw from him personally in the same way that she found herself doing socially?

And then one day it all seemed clear. John's father suggested, nay demanded, that their daughter should be initiated into her adult future in the manner which was traditional for his people. It would be a gesture, he said, which would prove his son's commitment to rediscover his true family identity and to heal the personal rift between them which had only widened for over twenty years. Initially Lesley listened to the proposition with a sympathetic ear, since it sounded capable of bringing about at least some degree of reconciliation between John and his father. When the details were explained to her, however, she was immediately horrified and angered that John had even thought it might be possible.

Becoming a woman in the traditional manner sounded a worthwhile thing to do. It was a little bit like confirmation, where you publicly expressed your loyalty to an ideal. But when Lesley was told that the girl would be circumcised in the process, it was not a feeling of disgust that caused her to reject the idea, but simply a profound disbelief. At first, she seriously thought that her husband was joking. And then, quite slowly, it began to dawn on her that he was serious. It became clear that by this act, not only did he want to seek a reconciliation between himself and his father, but also he wanted to place on public record his desire to rekindle memories of those traditional values, which his generation had largely rejected.

Here her private thoughts were interrupted by the sound of another car pulling into her drive. In response, she simply sped to the window to confirm her hope that it was the white Mercedes-Benz she had been expecting. It was. Thank goodness for that. At last she could talk to someone. An hour before she had been horrified when Father Michael and Janet Rowlandson had arrived unexpectedly. She was grateful for their obvious concern for her well-being and was nothing less than deeply touched that they had driven all the way from Migwani to tell her the news, that John had been murdered by his father, beaten about the head with an axe at the back of a bar in Migwani. But it was essential that they should go before this particular invited guest arrived, because they would surely recognise him and, putting two and two together, they would understand what had become of her marriage to John. Lesley had been grateful when they had accepted her only partially expressed wish to be alone and had left, for now she could really be herself.

***

Alone in a crowded room, Lesley stood apart from the rest. Who were these people? Why were they here? Was it because, like herself, they had nothing better to do? Why was it that their mouths seemed to be full of words whereas she felt forever dumb? Why had she spent an hour doing her hair, making up and deciding what to wear to stand like this, detached and unnoticed, outside the party?

The Nairobi social scene was never extensive enough to render her a complete stranger here, of course, despite perceiving herself as one. For the middle classes, Nairobi is a deceptively small city, offering not only just a small number of inhabitable places, but also only a limited number of fellow travellers. So inevitably there were faces here she knew, or rather faces she recalled. She could not even claim recognition of these people, all of whom, if they ever went out of their way to address her, only ever asked about her husband. Never about herself.

If the decision had been left to her, she probably would not have come here this evening. On balance, this 'social' on behalf of some company or other, held in a hotel lounge, was perhaps marginally more interesting than an evening alone with a magazine (except for certain pages, which she always enjoyed!). John, of course and as usual, was away in Kitui, and still trying to do twenty things at once, no doubt. He had been adamant that she should still come along here, not because she herself had said anything about wanting to, but because the company was one that maintained a long-term and lucrative contract with his firm, and it would be politic to be represented.

Cocooned in her unhappiness, Lesley watched the throng as a spectator, but at the same time thought only of herself. Not for a second did she try to admit the possibility that there might be others who, like herself, had come here out of duty. Everyone, except herself, seemed to be talking, laughing or drinking, apparently absorbed in worlds they had created to share. Lesley, on the other hand, was alone, totally alone. She was alone all day, because John was usually at work, and she was alone most evenings because that was the time he used for his other interests and now increasingly at weekends, she was alone because he would use the time to travel out of town to question witnesses on whatever case he was currently preparing. And then there was always Kitui to check out.

Initially she had been overjoyed at the prospect of moving to Nairobi when John changed jobs. Surely there they would have more time together, since they would not be living next door to work. In Mwingi they had lived literally next door to the office. Effectively John had been on call there for twenty-four hours a day. Everyone knew where to find him and thought nothing of bringing their business to the house after office hours. It seemed that her husband's permission and planning were needed before anyone could sneeze in Mwingi. Living in Nairobi was going to change all that. They would live out of town and he would leave his work in the office. Their daughter, Anna, would no longer board at school and Lesley could once more become her mother. It was never meant to be like this, with husband at work all day, sharing his evenings with his 'contacts' and associates and then rushing off to supervise the building of their second home in Kitui at weekends. He had become more of a stranger to her than he had ever been in Mwingi. She was bored. She had no real friends and was a total stranger in the city, a fact that John, it seemed, never understood. And, on top of everything else, John had insisted that Anna should stay in boarding school after all, so that they could be free to travel out of the city at weekends whenever they wished. He had simply refused to listen to any other opinion on the matter.

"Hello, Mrs Mwangangi." James Mulonzya almost sang the greeting. He walked quickly toward her offering his hand. His son followed, taking sips from his brimful glass as he moved. They had obviously just arrived.

With an obvious lack of enthusiasm, she shook his hand and then his son's to return their greeting.

"Is your husband here?" Mulonzya swivelled on the spot like a manic machine to glance around at the other guests.

"No," she said. "He's gone out to Kitui." Had her impatience with the fact shown through? She hoped not.

"Ah yes," said Charles. He sounded suddenly very interested, as if someone had just switched him on. "I hear that you have bought some land. Is that so? I hear that you have several hundred acres and a bore hole?"

Lesley shrugged her shoulders. "I have no idea. John's been handling all the business. I don't even know where it is. I don't think I'll ever make a farmer's wife anyway." She offered a dismissive giggle at this point, but at the same time she could not hide the obvious core of conviction in her words.

James Mulonzya, however, was not listening. "I must ask you to excuse me, Mrs Mwangangi. I have an important matter to discuss with a person I have just seen over there." With that he made off in the direction in which he had been looking. Lesley watched him go and, it seemed, she was immediately returned to her own private, silent and empty world. She had not really wanted to talk to him anyway. Her heart had sunk when he appeared in the first place, but still, as he disappeared to the far side of the room, she almost regretted his departure. He could have protected her from herself, provided a barrier, if only an illusory one, between herself and her loneliness. But then there was still Charles. Perhaps that was the problem.

"So you stayed in Nairobi this weekend?"

Charles's voice, though expected, almost startled her. She was thus dragged, kicking and screaming in silence, back to the present. "Yes," she replied. "I've seen enough of Kitui to last me a long time." Offering a curt smile, she momentarily turned to face him, but the pressure of his penetrating eyes immediately caused her to look away again. Why was it that she never seemed to have the confidence to look people directly in the eye?

Charles laughed. "Same here. As far as I'm concerned, if you've seen one piece of bush, you've seen it all." A sip of his drink marked the full stop.

Again turning towards him and again immediately away, Lesley added her agreement. She was surprised and sounded it. "That's exactly what I think. I can't understand what everyone sees in the place. It's a desert and that's that. The water's dirty. There are too many flies, scorpions, snakes, mosquitoes..." She gave a public shudder here. "Name anything nasty and Kitui's got it like a plague. I'm glad to be out of it."

"I'm surprised you say you hear a lot about it. I can go for weeks without even hearing the place mentioned - and after all, I'm a Mwingi man myself."

"Oh, it's just that John has been very keen to keep up his contacts with his home area. We tend to see a lot of people from Migwani, Kitui and Mwingi - and what's more he goes there quite often to see how his land is coming along."

"I can see that you feel the same way as I do. As you know our family has quite a few business interests in Kitui District, but I only go there when I have to. I'm glad I'm not some teacher or civil servant posted there permanently. I'd be bored out of my mind."

"And you find living in Nairobi different?"

"Well, yes. Of course, don't you?"

Should she continue? She knew she was in danger of delivering a tirade of private disaffection. Should she reveal the depth of her unhappiness to this near stranger? She had met him once before and in this country where, it seemed, that a friend was any person who had shaken your hand at any time in the past, she began to look upon him almost as a confidante. After all, he was one of the few people she had met in Kenya who seemed not to misinterpret her words, who spoke English as well as herself, who would understand her predicament. "To tell you the truth, I've not even seen Nairobi yet. All I seem to have seen is our house and the rest of Lavington. I don't like using the bus because I don't feel safe and John takes the car to work, so I'm stuck there all day. Most evenings we stay in, either because Anna is at home from school or we have some of John's friends for dinner, or perhaps he has to read papers or something for the following day."

"Don't you go to the cinema?"

"I'm not too keen on films. Even in London I hardly ever went to the cinema. And here you have to go all the way into town to go to the cinema. In London there are cinemas in the suburbs as well, but not here. And here, when you get to the city centre, there are all the beggars and gangs. I don't like it. It frightens me."

"Well go out for dinner then. Go out to a restaurant or to a friend's house, rather than having them round at your place every time."

Lesley grimaced. "Remember that all of our friends are Kitui people. They all seem to eat maize and only maize. We did go out once and we couldn't find a restaurant where we could get both bush food and service. We finished up, as ever, eating in a tourist hotel where, at least, you can get a decent plate of oven-ready chips, even if you daren't touch the hamburgers."

Charles laughed. "So you have not developed an African stomach? You cannot eat maize, but neither, it seems, can you eat hotel food."

"No fear," said Lesley, her face contorting in an expression of imagined pain. "Honestly, I could still feel that stuff in my stomach a week later. It's like lead."

Charles continued laughing. "It's all right when there's nothing else."

"But why do people still eat it," continued Lesley at speed, "when they can get anything under the sun here in the city?"

"When people have grown up with a choice between *ugali* or nothing, they learn to like it. Out in the bush - even in Kitui, as you yourself know - it is still a matter of eating *ugali* or nothing."

"I'd take nothing," said Lesley, without much thought.

The two continued to chat, their conversation always residing wholly in the mundane or trivial. Though she remained unwilling to allow this near stranger to draw her into more personal matters, Lesley's single-minded and bleak self-obsession placed herself and her predicament as the subject of all she said. Inevitably, the careless slips of the tongue that punctuated the commonplace began to lodge in Charles's mind. They gradually formed a pastiche of clues, which when rearranged just a little, created the pattern that was the substance of Lesley's inner conflict. As each unconscious slip emerged like a blemish on Lesley's social face, Charles mentally mapped every one and, though individually insignificant, they joined to form a portrait of disillusion and deep unhappiness that lay beneath her elegant and controlled exterior.

Lesley never allowed herself to trust this man. Why should he want to talk to her? She could not accept his confession that he, like her, knew no one else in the room. No, that could never be true. If anything was clear, it was that he was an experienced socialite, quite used to the airs and graces of affluent Nairobi, which she herself was still trying to translate into her own actions. And, if what he said was to be believed, frequent parties, dinner dates at the city's gleaming modern hotels and nights out on the town in the clubs were no more than mundane and expected elements of his everyday life. In her own estimation, she ought not to be capable of maintaining the interest of this man who claimed and appeared to receive the freedom of his world. How could she trust him? Why should he be interested in her? He continued to display the same degree of interest in her whilst at the same time describing his private villa near Diyani Beach, Mombasa, and how he spent most of his week-ends there, and how he flew there every time, and how he would laze in the sun and occasionally swim like a member of the idle rich, with the emphasis on the rich. Why should the man who claimed he could have anything have the slightest interest in her? And why should he still be so interested in her husband? Now that they had moved away from Mwingi, John no longer had any direct contact with the Mulonzya family. Why should he be so concerned at John's plans for his farm in Migwani? Time and time again she asked herself these questions but only ever answered them in the context of her own self-interest. Surely all he wanted was to conquer her and her alone, to add her to what was without doubt the long list of Nairobi socialites he had bedded. She bet he could look around the hotel lobby where they stood and tick off a fair percentage of the women present on that very list, and probably supply chapter and verse of where, when, how and how often in each case. He was that sort of man. Surely he asked after John to test the ground, to seek out her inner thoughts about her husband. Had she told him that

John was away in Kitui? Had she given the impression that she was lonely? Had she led him to think that she was talking to him because she found him attractive?

She was, of course, only partly right in her analysis of his motives. Naively, she did not link her husband's political ambitions in Kitui District with Charles Mulonzya's interest in her. There were two reasons for this. One: John had never really confided in her to the extent of explaining the actual nature of his ambition. He had mentioned his political ambitions, but not clarified the implications of these. Lesley was still largely unaware that standing against Mulonzya would entail their two families virtually declaring war on one another. Secondly: John had never told her or even intimated that the process had already started, and that hostilities had begun. John had not spoken of his ambitions at all over recent months. Ever since they had moved to Nairobi, he had seemed more preoccupied with other things.

"So your husband is going to provide the cash to set up the entire farm and then is going to give it all away?"

"No, not exactly give it away, I think." Lesley tried to explain the planned scheme, though her understanding of it had never been any more than sketchy. "He is going to set it up. That's part of the deal, you see. Apparently no one believes that the land is any good, even with a guaranteed water supply. Anyway, he will raise the first crop to show that it's possible. Then the next stage is to hand over the running of the farm to a management committee. I think I've got this right. They will run it as a cooperative. He then expects other people nearby to join in and pool their land in return for a guaranteed income and other things like access to machinery and so on. When enough people have joined, the idea is then to run the whole thing like a corporation, with a labour pool and large-scale marketing of the produce, but still it will be controlled by a committee elected from its membership." Lesley stared into space as she spoke, counting out each recalled stage on her fingers.

"It's a long story, isn't it?" she said with a smile. "I think that they are going to share out the produce or profit or something according to how much work people put in. John thinks that some people will just sell their share, but he's fairly sure that most people will keep their membership and pass it on like they used to pass on pieces of land. It's all a bit of a trick really, I suppose, because he's going to get them to grow all kinds of things like vegetables and even some cash crops, as well as maize for making that awful *ugali*." Another shudder told of her continued distaste of the idea.

"It sounds like a very innovative scheme," said Charles. His prosaic tone did not divulge how permanently and accurately the words had lodged in his memory. "I don't understand, though, what your husband will get out of it. He must have spent over one hundred thousand shillings already on buying land and drilling the borehole."

"That much?" Lesley silently rebuked herself for showing her surprise. She could see Charles noting every nuance of her reaction. Or was he now touching her with his eyes? "I think he's got it all worked out," she continued, averting her eyes from his direct gaze towards the glass of wine she clutched just beneath her breasts. "Let me see. First of all, he hasn't used our money. I'm sure of that!" She looked up momentarily and with a slight laugh tried to convey a false confidence in herself. When her eyes met those of Charles, however, a tiny shudder passed through her stomach and she immediately looked away. "Well I suppose he has really. He's borrowed most of it from the bank, so until he has raised the first crop, he will have to make repayments on the loan from our money. Before handing over to the cooperative, he will sell enough of the produce to recoup all that money. The committee will then take over the running of everything, including the loan repayments." She was surprising herself with the depth of her understanding of John's scheme. They must have discussed it more than she could consciously recall.

"And what if it fails and they default on the payments?"

Lesley smiled slightly, humoured at her unexpected ability to recall all this detail. "Ah, then ownership reverts to John again - is it called being a trustee or something? - and he decides whether to have a go with another committee, carry on himself for a while, or sell the lot. He's confident, though that it will all work out well. The idea is to show people how they can overcome the drought if they will work together. It's all to do with traditional land use - something like that - where you use communal labour and then share the results."

"But run like a business?"

"That's it. John reckons that he should have most of his money back within two years."

Charles nodded. "He'll make ten to fifteen thousand shillings an acre on tomatoes alone. Just on the first crop, if he were to sell enough of it, he could make a whacking great profit."

"Goodness, I never realised we were talking about sums like that! I thought it would be a few thousand shillings here and there."

"But he's got acre after acre. It's a massive farm, even by Kitui standards, as far as I understand." He paused here to look into Lesley's eyes before continuing. The hint of surprise they conveyed convinced him she had never been to the visit the new farm. "You seem to understand enough about it, considering that you claim to be not the least bit interested in either Kitui District or the project, itself."

Lesley gave a short sardonic laugh before answering. "I've had no choice but to be interested in it. It's all that John has talked about for months. He goes off to Kitui at every opportunity and always comes back saying how well everything is going. And then he describes the progress since his last visit in minute detail, right down to how many courses of brickwork have been added to this building or that, and how many baskets of sand have been moved and exactly where each terrace has been laid down and on and on and on..." Lesley's sigh bore some evidence of her frustration. "I was looking forward to him handing it all over to the committee, but now he is already saying he's going to do it all over again, but next time in Mwingi. I keep telling him that he should get this one properly under way first, but he won't listen."

Charles's expression darkened instantly. For a moment, his thoughts turned to business, but then, with this snippet of information and its associated possibilities duly stored for future reference, he switched back to their conversation. "Your husband is away often then?"

"More often than not these days." Lesley's words were resigned, but still clearly underpinned with cynicism and disaffection. Charles not only took note of this, but also of the apparently greater ease with which she now spoke to him.

It was then that Lesley realised that she had all but admitted publicly for the first time just how estranged she had become from her husband. She had related what she knew of his plans as if he were a complete stranger, and, more importantly, as if they held no place or role for herself. This was no illusion, of course, for she had remained a complete outsider in this aspect of John's life. She was forced by this cross-examination to admit to herself that her difficulty in remembering the details of John's scheme was not because her husband had never explained them, but because she had never listened. She simply did not care. More important and ultimately more difficult to admit, was the fact that she had received more direct attention from Charles over the previous hour or so than she could remember receiving from her husband for many months. He had become obsessed with his ideas and had ignored her to such an extent that she had almost forgotten what it was like to share small talk with him. Everything in their lives now carried an agenda.

Without John, she had only herself to turn to and hence her recent bouts of insomnia and depression. It had taken Charles, a virtual stranger, to make her see all this in its true light. In him she saw much of what John used to be when he was younger, that which she hoped he would rediscover when he returned to Kenya. In the event, it was now becoming clear that Kenya might have changed John and estranged him from her to such an extent that now she felt she hardly knew him.

After a difficult, nervous start, talking to Charles had grown easy, easier, in fact, than talking to her own husband of late. She did not yet apportion blame for their predicament. She was still undecided whether it was John who had changed, or whether, in this environment that she still found oppressively foreign and threatening, it was she herself who had grown selfish and therefore unable to sympathise with his concerns. This place still did not feel in the least like home and it had distorted their relationship, had changed either John or herself, but she had not yet decided which.

She spent the rest of the evening talking to Charles. Neither she herself nor he seemed the slightest bit interested in mixing with others. She began to find his obvious interest in her somewhat comforting, and soon she had quite forgotten that before that evening they had met just once. As the conversation drifted from one aspect of Nairobi life to another, she began to feel quite comfortable in his company. If anything, he was a rather quiet, shy man beneath a very thin veneer of overt sophistication. Yes, he had money. Yes, he flaunted it, but what he seemed to be seeking in life were comforts much more homely than those which were generally on offer in the life he led.

They talked of everything, but discussed nothing. They filled increasingly easy silences with drinks and cigarettes, or merely eavesdropped on the general hubbub to find that everyone else was doing the same as themselves, simply passing the time. Lesley felt increasingly gratified at this. It seemed that at last she had found that reassuring state of hypnosis that is small talk. For once she forgot her cares, she forgot about John's plans and ambitions that had begun to eat at the core of their relationship, and simply enjoyed the ephemeral and indulgent present for what it was.

It was very late indeed when Lesley finally declared it was time she should leave. When Charles offered her a lift, she did not accept immediately. She knew what he wanted. His eyes made everything quite clear. She thus had to make a decision. Twenty yards from where she now stood there was a rank with a plethora of taxis, each of which would be overjoyed by the prospect of a fare to Lavington Green. But here was a challenge, a different kind of challenge from anything else currently in her life. Here was something that promised to be exciting and just a little dangerous, but also completely without commitment. Something to be done for its own sake; not for her husband's sake, and that would make a pleasant change. And then she said yes.

Lesley did not sleep with Charles that night. The idea was certainly at the forefront of her mind, but on the way home in Charles's car she suppressed it, partly out of renewed loyalty to John and partly because conscience reminded her of what a momentous step it would be. And could she trust this man? Of course she could not. But then if they had an affair, would she be looking for trust? In this land, where wives could be bought, why should he be interested in her? He was rich enough to command the most beautiful or the most talented women in the land. What could he want with a married woman in her thirties? When they parted, Charles kissed her politely on the cheek, but placed his hand lightly at the very small of her back, which made her shiver. Instinctively, she drew away and offered a handshake.

Then Lesley was again alone in what was supposed to have been the family home. She was again thrust back on herself, set apart from the humdrum existence she now led. Attacked by conscience, having actually admitted to herself what was bound to happen, she spent a sleepless night drinking coffee, cup after cup, and smoking until, just before dawn, still dressed in her party finery, she fell asleep in a chair out of sheer exhaustion.

The very next weekend, when John again rushed eagerly to Kitui, she went with him. Desperately she tried to penetrate his world. She tried to understand why he worked so hard and so single-mindedly and devoted so much of his time to this cause on behalf of a group of complete strangers. But she returned to Nairobi none the wiser, except that she was now sure that there would never be a niche for her in his work. She also brought back to the city with her a severe stomach upset, caused, she believed, by drinking rainwater out of a tank. Another week later, she stood in the driveway of their home and watched him drive off, bound for a court hearing in Nyanza Province. He would again be away until late the next day. She felt, as always, that he was leaving her behind, driving out of the poverty of their shared life and into the riches and stimulation of his career and politics. He seemed to see her role in his life increasingly as the housewife who tended the home while he won the bread, a duty that was and would always be his by right. What made matters worse was that he had never once asked her what she wanted, not for months and months and months.

Only then did Lesley admit to herself that she really did want to see Charles again, whatever his motives might be. She saw in him a chance to escape from this drab loneliness into another life, the like of which she had once known when she first met John. Strangely, though, as she fumbled with her purse to extract the business card Charles had given her, she felt neither excitement nor guilt at the prospect. This was little more than the satisfaction of a need. John had been gone for barely fifteen minutes when Charles answered the phone to receive an invitation to dinner. Lesley did not tell him that John would not be there, hoping that he would assume he would be one of several guests. She would then be able to judge his reactions later when she told him the two of them were to be alone. As she replaced the receiver, she was fully aware of what she had done. She knew then that Charles would spend that night with her. What she did not know at that stage, of course, was that their affair would blossom, and last.

***

And then, much later, when John died, it was Charles who offered Lesley comfort and sympathy and enabled her to cope with the trauma so well. For a short while he had shared her sadness, but for him the initial shock soon dissolved and self-interest took over. He clearly had known that Lesley and John's relationship had been breaking down. Not only was she having an affair with him, she was confiding in him, telling him every detail of her frustrations with a husband who increasingly took her for granted. Privately, Lesley had spoken of divorce, but both she and Charles knew that if John had discovered his wife's feelings he would have done everything in his power to keep her, if only to spite the Mulonzya family. Though it was clear that all their problems had been caused by John's obsessions with career and politics, had she asked for a divorce, John's priorities would surely have shifted and all Charles would have achieved for himself would have been an act of philanthropy. Obviously he had a vested interest in keeping them together, since that enabled him to continue to see Lesley without any danger of her suggesting he take on some responsibility in her life. It also gave Charles continued access to the inside information on where John Mwangangi was, whom he was seeing and what projects he was hatching.

But then it became clearer every day that things were coming to a head. Reports from Mwingi had told Charles that John's father in Migwani had openly criticised, even disowned his own son. Since the cooperative project relied upon the continued involvement of the much-respected old man, Charles felt quite gratified that the rift between father and son had developed. Within a short time, the rift had grown so deep that John's father was actually making statements demanding that no one continue to cooperate with his own son's schemes. What John was beginning to gain, his father was systematically destroying.

In addition, the more John quarrelled publicly with his father, the less he seemed to think of his wife and thus each new report, every item of gossip was received by Charles with double satisfaction. Without any personal intervention from him, events conspired to further both of his aims, to discredit John Mwangangi in public and to continue to see his wife in private.

Lesley was not sure why she was crying. It seemed the right thing to do, despite the fact that she had privately and angrily wished death on her husband a thousand times in recent months, so distant and unfeeling towards her had he become. In some ways, therefore, her bereavement was hardly a loss. Was it relief that brought the tears, relief that at last everything might be resolved? Was it merely a final thought for the husband she had once known, the ultimate act which would make way in her own mind for Charles to take his place - a parting gesture, a relieved good-bye? Or was it just her body coping with the shock and finding a way to release the tension it brought? Or would she now find that she would miss him? Had she lost him earlier, before they came to Kenya, the sadness would surely have killed her. But now, after the return to his roots had seen him unthinkingly revert to a type which Lesley would never have wanted to have known, she found that her emotions were uncluttered by any love for him. If she cried, she cried because of the trauma of the circumstances, but inwardly she felt as if a stranger had died. She was crying for herself. It was nothing more than self-pity that filled her mind now.

"Lesley," said Charles. His voice was soft and comforting, but also quietly confident and assured. "Take your time. Cry as much as you want. I'll be here all the time. You're crying because you've lost him. But remember, in reality that happened months ago. You've nothing to worry about. You did all you possibly could have done. If communication breaks down between two people, it doesn't mean that both are to blame. You know I want to marry you. And you know I will look after Anna. There is no problem."

Lesley's reaction was violent. Like a cornered dog she struck out. Breaking loose from his light embrace, she stared at him wide-eyed. "You don't need a wife. You need some cross between a mother and a whore. How can you say all that? He's not even in his grave! It's not right, Charles. Look at you. You're enjoying this. All you've wanted right from the start is for John to fail. It couldn't have worked out better for you."

"Or for you. Admit it, Lesley, all you have lost is a headache."

"I loved him!" For some moments she eyed him with a mixture of bitterness and lust. Charles's attitude to her husband was in some ways a public expression of what she felt herself but dare not admit and, like most people, when confronted with an impression of an unacceptable side of themselves, she deeply resented the experience. And the lust was never far from the surface whenever and wherever they met. Their relationship had started with sex and had continued with it, not just ordinary sex, but joyous rich physical love that fulfilled them both almost whenever they wished. But here, she was privately blaming him for the callousness that scarred her feelings. Then, slowly, she admitted to herself that he was right, accepted the fact and buried her face deep in his chest. Her tears were now surely those of relief. There would be problems to be overcome, memories to forget, but she knew that she would have to cope and, without a shadow of doubt, eventually succeed. She was stronger than he. Beneath the elegant and accomplished exterior that greeted the world, Charles was as frightened, unsure and self-critical as herself. If anything, he needed her more than she needed him, for she had learned how to cope with her limitations, whereas he was younger and had not.

But there was one final blow to strike, one last detail which from the beginning had precluded her complete trust in him, and again she struck out. "It won't work, Charles. I don't know... we've been through this a hundred times. Why me? What do you see in me? You can have almost anything in life. Why me? Is it just because I'm married - because I'm an option that's closed to you - that you want me?" The words bit through the tears.

"Now you are being silly. You're not married any more and I'm still here. You know what I feel. I'm not interested in anyone else and never will be."

And then they made love. She cried all the time, and laughed, and kissed, and screamed out her lover's name when she shook with the deepest of pleasure. John, her husband, lay dead in Kitui, murdered in a fit of rage by his own father, but she had never felt more alive than this.

***

"We had better call at the post office first, then," said Charles, almost shouting above the rattle of stones hitting the car's wheel arches.

"You can leave me there if you like. There's no need to wait. I'll walk up to the offices. You can take the car and pick me up when you come back." As he spoke, James Mulonzya kept his eyes fixed on the road ahead. Even after years of practice, he had never quite learned how to drive on a dirt road. A lack of confidence thus always rendered him rather nervous behind the wheel and his posture faithfully reflected his state of mind. Leaning slightly forward and with his short arms stiffened against expected jolts from the uneven road, he held on to the steering wheel with tightly clenched fists, every muscle in his body tense. Just as he began to speak again, they hit a series of corrugations in the road surface. Unlike a practised hand, who would have accelerated to bounce the car across the tops of the furrows, James Mulonzya slowed down, which only made things worse. The consequent shuddering passed through the car and into his body, causing his words to be uttered in a comic, trilling vibrato. "How long will you be?"

"Only an hour or two. I want to pick up the cash books and just see how things are going."

"What do you think we'll make out of this?"

Charles thought for a moment. "About sixty thousand gross, this time. Let's say thirty clear profit."

"And there's still only half of the land planted?"

Charles nodded his reply.

James Mulonzya smiled and shook his head. "That was a really brilliant move you made. If it had been left to me I would have simply sold the lot. I never thought I'd see the day when Kitui land would become such a profitable farm."

"It's not quite profitable yet," said Charles quickly. "We have a lot of capital to recoup first. There's the pump and the piping for a start and we'll need those four or five more water tanks - big ones - before we can plant the whole farm."

"So when do you expect it to be complete?"

Charles shrugged his shoulders. "It depends on how things are progressing. If the contractors get on with the job, we can have the entire acreage under the plough next season. Any delays, of course, will cost us."

"How much is all this costing?"

Charles took a moment to make some rough calculations in his head. "Four tanks, say, and the piping - plus labour - let's say a hundred to a hundred and twenty thousand."

Mulonzya commented with a short, hacking laugh. "My goodness, I'm glad that you're handling all the money matters. I don't think my head is big enough to hold such figures."

Charles looked across at his father, his expression saying, "If only you knew." James Mulonzya saw nothing but the road ahead, however.

"So how long will it take us to get it all back?"

"One season, if we're lucky..."

"What?" Mulonzya laughed and shook his head again out of sheer disbelief.

"Yes, one season, if we're lucky with the weather."

"But you don't need rain. You've got the borehole."

"We still need the sun. And the more rain we get, the less we have to spend on running costs for the pumps and so on."

177

James Mulonzya laughed again. "There's not much trouble with the sun out here."

"Don't forget that we get quite a number of other benefits as well. We have only been running the project for two years so many of the extras are still developing. There are going to be a lot of spin-offs. And then there's always the possibility of starting up similar ventures in other parts of the District. We take very little financial risk because of the way the project is managed and operated, so there is no reason at all why we should not seek to do it again whenever and wherever we want. I must say that I was sceptical at first, but now I have had time to see the thing operate, I am really very impressed with it. Of course, one of the major spin-offs will be political. You are seen to be investing in your home area. You are providing employment and helping development. It will do you the world of good."

"I hope so," said Mulonzya with some concern. Chancing a glance to the side, he saw Charles's eyebrows rise, silently asking for an explanation of his lack of confidence. "How many people will we be employing?"

"About thirty. More, of course, at harvest time, but they will only be casual, paid on a piecework basis. Why? What's the matter?"

"Nothing. It's just that I had an argument with that priest in Migwani. You remember, the one who was running that literacy scheme in Thitani with John Mwangangi. It seems that he knew quite a lot about Mwangangi's plans for the farm and if my guess is right he'll be doing his best to point out to people why our plans are inferior. He has certainly already picked up on the share ownership system which replaced the original cooperative idea."

"Our plans are not inferior," said Charles dismissively. "We're running it as a business. Everything is legal. There will be plenty of benefits for the people in that area."

"It's not that, Charles. Mwangangi was never going to gain anything for himself from this investment. He was going to hand it over to a local committee as soon as he had recouped his capital and I think that fact is widely known."

"But it didn't work. It would never have worked."

"That we will never know. Anyway this Mister Michael will make sure that he finds out exactly how much profit we make and he'll publicise it. If it's too successful, it could actually do me some harm - especially when most of the produce is being sold in Nairobi or Mombasa."

"Nonsense," said Charles with a shake of his head. "It's a business. The better it does, the better for everyone. People will surely see that."

James smiled at this. "Remember, Charles, you handle the money and I do the talking. You know nothing of the bush. You're a city gent. Believe me, if that priest presses me hard, he could do a good deal of damage." Charles clearly remained unconvinced, but his father was adamant. "I think it would be prudent for you to lose the profits of the farm in those small companies you created. I think at last I understand why you insisted that we split up the group." As the car approached the black tarmac of Kitui town, James Mulonzya again turned to the side to glance at his son. This time he was smiling.

Both men sighed with relief as the noise of the dirt beneath the wheels was replaced by the smooth hum of tarmac. Mulonzya relaxed at last and settled his ample frame back in his seat as the car whined up the hill towards the town in the wrong gear.

"Right then. Post office for me," said James Mulonzya. "I'll be in the DC's office when you get back. How long will you be?"

"About two hours. I'll certainly be back before three. I want to get back to Nairobi before dark to give Lesley a rest. Her time is pretty full these days and she's very tired."

"Oh yes," said Mulonzya, reminded of an important, but thus far much neglected duty. "How is little Joseph?"

Charles's face shone with a father's shining pride. "He's wonderful."

"Right then, we're here," said Mulonzya as the car slowed to turn left in front of Kitui's shining new cathedral. As they rounded the apex of the bend, however, they found the road ahead blocked. On their side stood a stationary car and on the other a large herd of cows meandered slowly towards them. Mulonzya braked suddenly and the car skidded to a halt uncomfortably close to the car in front. Without needing to think, Mulonzya reacted immediately in the manner which common practice, both taught and conditioned, would predict and he gave a hard prolonged blast on the horn. In the seconds that followed, both James and Charles spoke, but events progressed too quickly for words to register.

"He's not even seen us. It's that priest."

"There's someone in the road..."

"Hey, *mzungu*, get out of the way!"

"He's going to drive over him..."

And it was done.

"Ah...Ah...Ah..." stuttered Charles. "I could see him. He was just sitting in front of the car. His legs were sticking out at the side. The white man must have known he was there."

James Mulonzya had already got out of the driving seat and set off toward where the injured man lay, beside the priest's car. By the time he had walked the few yards, he was already one of a small crowd and, as minutes passed, other bystanders were drawn to the scene so that by the time the old man finally died on the roadside, some forty people or so had gathered. Mulonzya exercised the prerogative of his seniority and took charge, a manoeuvre that all others allowed, a position that no one present dared to question. While the old man's breath still gurgled in his crushed chest, Mulonzya publicly gave up hope for him and turned his attention to Michael. So that everyone might understand, he used Kikamba to address the priest.

"You are unlucky, it seems, Mister Michael," he said gravely. "You are unlucky that I was here. Had I not been here you might have got away with this." He shook his head and wagged an accusing finger. "We have come to expect 'strange' behaviour from you - drunkenness, lechery, disrespect for our culture and our way of life..." A few shouts of agreement with each point pierced the tense silence that had enveloped the onlookers. "...But who would have believed that a man of God could do this?"

Michael, too stunned and shocked to answer, simply stared at the dying man. "I say it again, Mister Michael, you have been very unlucky. If I had not been here, you might have got away with this."

With a gesture toward the dying man, he half-turned to face the crowd before continuing. He spoke softly, but with an assurance and confidence that convinced all. "I know that man, and I think that also that Mister Michael knows him. He is called Munyasya Nzoka and he is from Migwani town. He has served his country well. For many years he was a distinguished and decorated officer in our army. When my own father was attacked by thieves in the Emergency, it was this man who brought the culprits to justice. Until his illness, until he lost his mind, he worked unselfishly to bring about the betterment and development of his home town. Only I, myself, can testify to the many achievements of this man. But now everyone should listen, because this is very important." He spoke more quietly now, hardly above a whisper, as he looked down at the dying man. Mulonzya's voice, however, was harsh and bitter, its condemnation aimed squarely at Michael.

"For some years, Munyasya Nzoka has been too ill to work. After an accident he lost his mind and entered a second childhood. Now it is common knowledge in Migwani that this man feels he has a vendetta against Mister Michael. I myself saw him - completely without provocation - spit in the priest's face, so much did he hate the man." Even quieter still, barely louder than breath, he continued. "And it is also common knowledge in Migwani that it was this man who set fire to Mister Michael's house some weeks ago." Mulonzya now looked up to face the still bemused and speechless priest, but his words publicly addressed the fast-choking Munyasya. "You saw this man, Mister Michael. You knew he was there in front of your car. Everyone else saw him, including myself, and so must you have done also. I think you did this on purpose, but even if you did not, we will all remember this. Wherever you go, people will remember what you did here today. For many, many years they will remember this old man here..."

Munyasya spluttered loudly and spat blood. Momentarily all eyes were on him, but then returned their gaze to Mulonzya as he continued, "... and when they think of him, they will remember that you killed him, and they will judge your 'Christian' claims accordingly. Here, today, Munyasya Nzoka has helped us to see an important truth. He has helped us to see that our country's future is in its people and its traditions, not in great works such as this." Here, Mulonzya gestured to the giant cathedral behind him. "One life is worth a million churches. We will remember this forever, and here, by the side of this road, so that we never forget our duty to people as we face this great building, I will place here a plaque dedicated to Munyasya Nzoka. All who will enter this great church in the future will then remember this old man, and will remember that simple humanity should always be their first concern."

The old man spluttered again. He coughed up blood again as his body retched its final paroxysm of pain and then, after a final retching fight for breath, he was dead. The onlookers crowded towards him. Some bent down at his side while others at the back craned their necks for a view. Momentarily, everyone had forgotten Michael. The priest, still shocked and unnerved, took no more than a second to get back in his car. Then, having left the engine ticking over, it took no more than another second for him to put it in gear and drive away by pushing a determined way through and past the assembled group of people, some of whom instinctively tried to bar his way by pressing down on the car's bonnet. Only a second or two later, however, with wheels spinning and tyres squealing on the tarmac, the car broke free as Michael's utter panic convinced all that standing in the way of his now admitted guilt might be dangerous. As the car sped away up the road, slowed to cross the junction at the top of the hill and then disappeared through the gateway into the Bishop's compound, no more than two hundred yards in all, everyone watched whilst Mulonzya, thinking quickly, added the commentary. "You see? He has run away. He knows I have spoken the truth."

Then, whilst a small group of people clustered round the dead man, the rest of the crowd with Mulonzya at its head set off in pursuit. For some reason, only an instant later, Mulonzya was suddenly reminded that Charles was there, still sitting in the car. Unexpectedly, he stopped dead in his tracks at the front of his mini-procession and turned round to look towards where he expected to see his own car and son, still parked at the roadside. Those who had followed him were, of course, taken completely by surprise by this unexpected manoeuvre and several people who followed one another too closely stumbled noisily into the person in front, giving the whole group the appearance of a caterpillar coming to rest. James Mulonzya craned his neck to look over the heads of his followers to a spot just beyond the dead man, where he expected to see his own white Mercedes, but he saw nothing. It had gone. Neither he, nor many of the others present at the roadside had noticed a few minutes earlier that the car had sternly pushed its way through the crowd and set off at speed along the main road with Charles at the wheel. Clearly, thought James, it was still business as usual for his son.

Janet

The doorbell sounded its two notes, a C and the A below, with a mild tremolo within the digitally sampled tubular bell sonority, prompting Janet to react immediately. A conditioned response found her untying the vertically striped blue and white butcher's apron that had been protecting her smart casual entertaining clothes, preventing tomato splashes from the pasta sauce she had just invented. Accompanied by the merest of sidelong glances towards Rosita on her left, she said, "That will be them now," and nodded towards the heavy skillet on the gas ring to indicate that its contents would benefit from further reduction and would need some attention. It was a practised perfection.

After over twenty-five years of married life shared with David, she was now physically unable to hear the sound of the doorbell without privately replaying the story he always told to guests about the 'bing-bong' of these notes. Apparently, they are the same tones that are used as a call sign in the cabins of British Airways flights, used to attract the attention of the hordes in economy before in-flight announcements. Once, when he was en route to New York, the system broke down and one of the stewardesses had to be called to the microphone to sing 'bing-bong' every time a meal, a duty-free sale or a progress update was to be announced. His words again ran involuntarily through Janet's mind as she climbed the steep stairs from the basement kitchen, the staccato rasps of her leather-soled boots on the ridged non-slip edging only slowing their brisk rhythm as she reached the top. As was her habit of years, she paused briefly at the mirror near the base of the three carpeted steps, which separated the house's lower rear extension from the ground floor, to check her appearance. She had changed since arriving home from school and so did not see the dark pink and blue floral skirt, slightly flared towards the hem just covering the tops of the black, moderately heeled boots she preferred for her winter walks to the underground. Neither did she see the formal pleated-front white blouse or the complementary floral chiffon at the neck. The work outfit had been replaced, but the enduring memory of her daily check of its correctness in this very place was still there, suffused over the actual picture of the tropically patterned blouse she wore tonight, tucked into her most comfortable pair of denims. The boots are still there, however, poking out beneath the now faded blue, being always more comfortable than anything else she owned. She patted her hair a little at the side. It was greying now, but catching it up in a bun at the back with a giant spring-hinged black grip seemed to minimise the extent of its aging.

She took the three stairs in two steps, a two and then a one with an associated little leap, and then paused. On her left was the open doorway to the dining room. The main part of the house was a single through room of significant proportions running alongside the hall. It had floor-to-ceiling folding doors, originals apparently, which David and she had patiently stripped with Nitromors, blowlamps and scrapers to reveal the greyish knotty pine that the Victorians had probably assumed would always be painted. Looking to her left, she glanced a check that Rosita had set the large round dining table with its high-backed chairs for seven, with an extra place left free for serving dishes and a space for administering to the children, which, as ever, would remain vacant.

Turning back into the hall, the pause having done no more than shortened her next step, she looked down to see the long Kashmiri runner reveal herringboned terracotta tiles at its edges abutting the now stripped skirts and Janet Smythe, née Rowlandson, felt a sudden and unexpected twinge of nerves, a slight tightening of the breath alongside the slightest tingle of the spine, the kind of shiver she thought she used to feel when her first boyfriend arrived at the family home to pick her up. Now more than thirty years beyond such nonsense, the unexpected nervous trill forced a pause, a mere shortening of the rhythm of her step, just as she passed the second door on her left, which looked into the front room, beyond the closed folding doors. There, presenting the back of his large head above the back of a voluminous easy chair that faced into the room, was David, her husband, precisely where she expected to find him, holding the double spread of his broadsheet high up to catch the brighter light of the hallway behind him, absorbed in a minor piece at the foot of page seven, his head gently nodding to the regularity of the Bach fugues that Janet could just hear scratching from within foam pads of his headphones.

"I'll get it," she said ritualistically, as she passed the open door, knowing full well he couldn't hear. Thus she did not even check for a response which even at best would be a minor noise, not quite a grunt and definitely not a word, if, indeed, such a reference to the obvious might merit any recognition.

And so Janet reached the door, a large, wide and heavy hardwood structure, white within and black to the street, hinged on the right, solid panelled in the lower half, but admitting two decorative stained glass panels above, their uneven frosting not allowing any view of those waiting outside, who invariably presented only fuzzed silhouettes against the scattered back-light of the streetlamps. As she turned the latch, Janet's memory momentarily recreated childhood, prompted by the beautiful symmetry of the diffused street lights and thus reminding her of those same shapes her infancy called 'angels' in the frosted glass door of her parents' suburban semi. Swinging the door open, she smiled at the two priests waiting in the cold and dark of a November evening.

***

It had been a difficult day, but no more nor less than most others, each of which generally presented in turn its own unique problems. This day, a Wednesday, had proved no exception and, as ever, her diary would give little clue as to what she actually had done with her time. Its listed appointments for that day caused her to laugh out loud as she automatically reviewed the page before closing the hard-cover A5 academic year planner. It indicated a site meeting at nine, in the real world a discussion of cleaning schedules, malfunctioning light bulbs and the need to re-edge the now sharply eroded path across to the science block. Next on the list, at eleven, there was another seemingly regular commitment, a consultation about school meals with the catering group, but this had been recently rendered more pressing by a requirement from on high to include, identify and monitor consumption of fresh ingredients in her schoolgirls' diet. After lunch, at two, there was an interview panel, nothing major – or so she had thought – just a mandated executive group to rubber-stamp an internal appointment to a B allowance with responsibility for Classics. The fact that Janet's school still taught a Classics curriculum, of course, spoke volumes about the kind of school it was, since most London secondary schools had not offered such options for more than a generation.

But even these seemingly routine encounters had each been complicated by unforeseen agendas. A relief school keeper, still only a stand-in for a trusted and established employee of St Mary's who had suffered a heart attack last term, was currently using consumables at one third of the rate of his now infirm predecessor. One month's freak figures might be explainable, but three months of consistently different consumption rates had to raise fingers of accusation, prompting the joint examination of three years of detailed accounts to clarify the suspicions. And now Janet Smythe, head teacher of St Mary's, was sure that the previous higher rates of consumption represented pilfering for sale. She now felt a certain emptiness of indecision. How would she handle an eventual need to broach the subject with a colleague she had trusted for more than five years?

The school meals debate had dissolved into a time-consuming farce. All present at the meeting had scoffed in turn at their requirement, as a management group, to re-justify what they had effectively accomplished for years. And this was being demanded in response to an ill-informed and opportunistic statement by a politician of national standing that had since cascaded down the usually stagnant pools of administration to present already overworked educators with yet another time-consuming diversion from their desired prime function. "They will have us actually spoon-feeding them before long," Angela Wright, the teacher representative on the committee had exclaimed. After all, St Mary's girls were largely from middle class families – good Catholic families to boot – who could do without patronising advice about their diet from a politician with certainly questionable morals. Perhaps it was all her own fault, Janet thought, in that she had still sometimes did not chair such meetings tightly enough, despite training in how to prompt communal agreement within time limits.

And then there was the 'routine' internal appointment, which ought to have taken an hour at most and had run to more than two. Ellen Price, a loyal servant of St Mary's for over eight years and the effective occupant of the post in question for a year during the absence through illness of the incumbent, ought to have been the automatic appointee. Sue DeVere, the young, attractive and, as yet, hopelessly inexperienced lass whom Janet had persuaded to apply just for the experience of the interview, had performed like a pro, while Ellen, in complete contrast, had been so racked by nerves that she had hardly been able to assemble coherent words in response to the calculatedly gentle questions. Even a reduced governors' selection panel had been difficult to sway. Janet's chair, not the furniture she sat on, but the man, who was not allowed to be called one, was, as ever, dependable and utterly supportive of what he had correctly judged to have been her wishes. But the vice-chair, who took the word 'vice' in her title as a kind of brief, had flicked and re-flicked her pink and purple-tinted locks from her face as she had argued with apparently ever-increasing vehemence that an old subject like Classics needed a younger, fresher approach in compensation and that Ms DeVere, being closer to the age of her students, would provide this. An equally liberated parent governor, meek, mild, middle-class and usually silent, but keen to appear more liberal than her staid upbringing had moulded her, sided with her vice-chair and had rendered the panel impotent at two votes to two, thus leaving Janet to rue the absence of Father O'Kane, uncharacteristically absent as a result of parish duties, but who always voted her way. She had not offered to resign if it went against her – there are limits! – but she had staked her professional judgment and reputation on Ellen Price's fitness for the post and eventually had a unanimous appointment, albeit after the panel had generated heat, argument and voluminous hyperbole. In retrospect Janet would take solace and satisfaction from having observed 'due process'.

But these were only the scheduled tasks, and even these had not gone quite to plan. Absent from the day's recorded running order were the incessant phone calls from parents, administrators, the local press, suppliers and goodness knows who. An hour had been devoted to dealing again with a problem girl from Year Nine who had verbally abused her physical education teacher for the second time in a week. A talented girl she might be, with a flair for mathematics that often left her case-hardened teacher speechless with surprise, and an ability to play jazz piano to professional performer standards that angered the music staff to a person, since it had clearly not been born of their department's conservative curriculum; yes, a talented girl she might be, but her prime disability was a mother who seemed determined to be younger than her daughter. Full of street language, internet nerd speak and pop-star gossip, she would only ever reinforce what her daughter expressed, criticism or correction never being admitted to the heady brew. And when the daughter grew a little quickly, prompting her friends to tease her with references to 'lanky' or 'stringy', she developed a neurosis about exposing her legs and always took the trousers option from the uniform rules. During PE and games, however, her old-style teacher demanded regulation kit for team sports and tracksuit bottoms were not allowed, hence the eruptions.

And then there was a long and difficult heart-to-heart with John Vorster, a forty-ish South African émigré of just a decade or so who was again suffering. He had been a teacher for just two years, after retraining on a government scheme, initially as a linguist, primarily as a German specialist, since, emanating originally from Windhoek, he was effectively tri-lingual in English, Afrikaans and German. But perhaps painfully he soon realised that knowing a language was not the same as teaching it and he had changed his main subject to art as a way of using some of the skills he had gained in a London design studio before, that is, he was made redundant. St Mary's had been his first appointment and he had made a blunder of stupendous proportions early on. A multi-cultural class of students – this is London, for heaven's sake, all classes in all schools are multi-cultural! – had gone uncharacteristically silent when he announced – thinking he was helping his position - that he had grown up alongside 'Africans' and, of course, he said it in that defining and impossible to disguise clipped vowel sonority of South African English. He learned, a few minutes later, just how many of his students understood the word only as an insult, synonymous with 'backward', 'stupid', 'illiterate' and, even worse, 'poor'. Then, after a class wag and search engine nerd had Googled his name to reveal that he was actually a former prime minister of the apartheid state and distributed printed pages from Wikipedia to prove it, things went from bad to worse. Poor John found himself at the bottom of a pit that he had dug, but which had just collapsed into an abyss that would forever imprison him. He had never recovered the ground he had lost with that one misplaced word, but colleagues had been sympathetic and supportive since he couldn't be blamed for using his own name. If anything, however, his position grew steadily worse as weeks became months and months terms. Now, after almost six terms of undiluted professional hell when classes regularly ran riot, individuals confronted him with abuse, pushed and shoved him as he tried to negotiate the corridors and even spat on his back as he passed by, he was reduced to a despairing shell, having lost all self-respect and even energy, save for that he reserved for compensatory verbal aggression towards his students. He clearly was never going to pass his deferred probation and had also taken the last month off on the strength of a single visit to a doctor who had used the term 'nervous breakdown', a word that John had greedily adopted as a label for his condition. Janet had spent more than an hour with him, accompanied by a deputy head, in a potentially frank discussion of his future. Unfortunately, the result had been fraught and inconclusive, since it seemed that John had developed an ambition to prolong his sick leave, whereas Janet and her deputy were encouraging him to apply for posts elsewhere, suggesting their willingness to provide a reasonable reference if he accepted the need to make a fresh start. Long-term illness had to be avoided at all costs, because that would entail filling his effectively vacant post on perhaps a day-to-day basis with whatever supply cover was available. Thus the conflict of interests had endured and the three of them had made no progress towards resolution. This had prompted Janet to allude to a possibility of termination, a development that John initially greeted with silence, but then acted out a feigned surprise, a reaction that suggested he would go to any length to retain the post he clearly no longer wanted. "He'll fight," Janet's deputy had announced after he left the office without saying goodbye.

And so a conspiracy of the scheduled and the unscheduled had made her late for an appointment she always tried to attend. 'Tried' was apposite here, since her presence was neither requested nor expected, but this initiative of her religious education teacher had been such a success that she had made a point of attending the monthly sessions to show support, solidarity, and appreciation, and to endow the event status in the eyes of the pupils. The fact that she also enjoyed them was a real bonus. To address several rather nebulous objectives of the National Curriculum and to enliven a compulsory subject which lacked the kudos of a public examination, the religious education teachers, at the suggestion of Mo Thomas, the head of department, had organised a programme of visits and talks by people who had made contributions of different kinds to society, the arts, science – whatever – through the application of their religious faith, or even their opposition to it. Today's talk was of particular interest to Janet, since she found the subject matter highly unusual. A lifelong and practising Roman Catholic, Janet had never known that there were priests, fully ordained and subject to all the vows, who kept their religious association secret from their acquaintances and from most people they encountered so that they could occupy ordinary jobs, usually low paid and low status, to build solidarity amongst their co-workers. She had assumed, when she first heard the subject of the talk, that there would be a covert evangelical motive somewhere, but the religious education teacher, who knew today's speaker personally, had explained that this was not the case. The priests concerned did it merely to live a life of poverty in an attempt to emulate the reality of Christ's human existence on earth. Whether they privately thought that, by creating the right conditions, they might facilitate a second coming, was a possibility, but, as Mo Thomas observed, when she and Janet had discussed the invitation in principle, her acquaintance had never, in the years she had known him, ever referred to any such ulterior motive. The priest concerned, she had explained, had done exactly what his order required and occupied a low paid job as a council employee for more than twenty years.

But Janet had already missed the first ten minutes of the scheduled session by the time her hand reached for the push-bar handle of the door to the canteen, which, in her school, was always the easiest place to reorganise when seating for a whole year group was needed. As the bar clanked down and the door opened, a hundred and fifty pairs of female eyes glanced her way and then in an instant of recognition pointedly returned to the task of watching the speaker, their speed of action powered by the fear that their headmistress might note their inattention. Janet saw several emery boards, which a moment before had been filing nails near the back of the room, disappear under the cuffs of the school's long-sleeved white blouse uniform, or beneath the sleeve of the tight-knit blue sweater in the case of those girls who still claimed to be cold in the tropical temperatures the school's heating generated. As Janet continued to watch the these attempts to hide miscreance – she was convinced that she saw a pair of white ear-plug headphones being stuffed into a bag - she quietly found a seat near the side at the back, her instinctive choice of a position that would be noted, but would not dominate. Throughout her preparations, during which, as ever, she concentrated on the behaviour and deportment of her students, rather than the subject or object of the occasion, she could hear a girl stumbling through a long and convoluted question to the speaker and, now settled, she transferred her attention from the girls and looked to the front of the room, several seconds after her entrance.

And she almost fainted. And then she stood up, knocking her chair, rattling a clatter through the wooden floor. Again the female eyes all turned her way and the room went quite silent. When Mrs. Smythe called for attention, her school listened, immediately and intently, but she was not prone to interruption, being too polite and considerate, always too measured and in control to cause such a crass intervention, so surely this untimely signal she had just sent meant that there was some very serious message to hear. Surely there was some painful, guilty announcement to be made, which would render the following days more exacting, perhaps more penitential, as a result of some general misdemeanour, the responsibility for which must be communally borne by the whole school.

But her students were confused and then mildly amused by her silence, especially so, since it was accompanied by a clear sag of her lower jaw, a tremble in the cheek and unblinking eyes opened so wide that they might be glaring with anger, if, that is, she were not so obviously in tears. "Michael," she managed to say, haltingly, quietly, creating some seven syllables within the word. Only a few of her students heard the word, those closest to her choice of marginal status in the room, causing and ripple of question and answer whispers to wash back and forth across the group. The gaze of three hundred eyes darted back and forth between Janet Smythe and Father Michael Doherty, as their speaker had been introduced to them. He continued to sit unperturbed before his audience behind the plain dining table that was his proletarian podium. He offered just a gentle wave of acknowledgment and a soft, "Hi," whilst their headmistress continued her impression of a weeping fish, damp-eyed with wordless lips apparently mouthing deafening silence. And then a wave of delighted murmuring washed across the room as the thirteen and fourteen year-olds marvelled at the fact that their headmistress might even be human after all. Friends looked at one another, sharing wide wide-eyed smiles, and then continued their back and forth scan between their calmly seated speaker and their nonplussed headmistress.

It took the organising teacher only seconds to realise that she should intervene. The girl's question had been lost and the event might descend into chaos if she did not act. Standing, she too looked from Michael to Janet and back, asking, "So you two know each other?" Michael nodded. Janet still could not find a single word as she sat down, shaking her head and wiping her eyes at the same time. "Alice," said the teacher above the gently giggling commotion, "you were asking why

Father Doherty decided to give up missionary work in Africa to do an ordinary job here in London..."

As Alice Bains eagerly took up the cue as her right and continued to frame her question, Janet heard every word, but it was as if they were the beads of spilt mercury she could remember from a science lesson during her own teenage years, beads of massive metal which shot intangibly like weightless bubbles across the teacher's desk and then randomly onto the floor as the thermometer broke. She knew the whereabouts of everything, but could pin nothing down. The words washed over her consciousness, registering without fixing. Her heart seemed to have slipped, its heavy thump now surely in her stomach. Some students still turned her way, smiling and nudging their friends.

In an instant she took control, turned on her professional calm, consciously constructed an expression of admonition and glanced it in appropriate directions. As the girls began to settle, she then slightly theatrically transferred her attention to Michael's answer, which was already under way and, obediently, general inattention became attention.

"I lived in Nigeria almost forty years ago," confirmed Michael, "and then I had several years in Kenya. That's where I met Mrs. Smythe..." He glanced at Janet and again three hundred girls' eyes sought her reaction. Every girl in the school knew that their head teacher had been a volunteer in Africa, because one of the school's annual activities had been a charity gala to raise funds for the school where she worked. Pictures of it showing the fruits of their fundraising had their own permanent display space in the library.

"...But it's almost thirty years since I left there. I changed orders, you see, and the one I joined sees its mission as working amongst the poor, wherever they are. And for us it's not enough just to say nice things about poor people. What we have to do is live a life of poverty in the same way that Jesus Christ did. So I became a council employee in the parks department more than twenty-five years ago and that's where I have stayed. I have seen many of you on your way to school. You have seen me, but today is possibly the first time that you have ever thought about what I do as an expression of religious faith and commitment. I am about to retire now, of course, and that's part of the reason why I decided to accept this invitation to speak to you. I noticed, when I came into the room, that some of you recognised me. I could see on your faces something like, 'Why on earth have they got the gardener from across the road to talk to us?' You see, even the people I worked with didn't know I was a priest. They never knew that my faith was anything to do with why I was doing that particular job. And they still don't know, so all of you now have to help me to keep the secret for a few more weeks. To them, I was just another Irish navvy, any old Paddy from the bog country whose rural origins made him feel at home weeding flower beds, pruning roses, cutting grass or picking up dog shit. I bet many of you girls..." Janet twinged a little at this. It was school policy always to refer to students. She was at last starting to feel a little more like herself. "...have walked across that common..." Michael nodded vaguely to his left to indicate the vast plateau of Clapham Common. "...every day on your way to and from school and never given a thought to how it's kept so neat and clean and who did the work. After today, you might think a little differently. I can honestly say," Michael continued, casting a noticeably direct glance towards Janet, "that when I am dressed in my overalls – you know the sort with glow-in-the-dark discotheque decorations – and I am wheeling my bin along the paths, most people I encounter don't even see me. They look away, past me, through me or ignore me. It's as if I don't exist, sometimes. I've even had people right in front of me drop their crap on the ground, had me pause right next to them, sweep it up, bin it, put my shovel and brush back on the trolley and then watch your man drop something else in the same place! And without even any reference to my existence! From today, you girls will realise that all people like me are real. We exist. We are individuals. Just because we are doing menial jobs it doesn't mean that we have no worth."

"But not all the park workers are priests," interrupted Alice, eager to advertise the confidence of her refined elocution and upper middle class barrister family origin.

"That's precisely the point I am making," said Michael. "Neither was I a priest in your eyes until this afternoon, but that should have made me no more or less a human being than I was as a sweeper in the park, no more or less worthy of your respect and consideration. You all know the tea hut behind the bowling green where we brew up. Many of you walk right past it on your way to school. I can even recognise some of your faces," he continued, scanning his audience and momentarily catching Janet's eye. "Well there's a bloke sitting in there right now – one of my

193

mates. He's also ready to retire, just like I am, but he's lucky to have reached that stage. He's Irish like me and been over here for more than forty years. But he's often drunk. He's not very clean... in fact he whiffs a bit on most days..." A giggled shudder rolled through the audience at this, "...and has been in jail a few times for disorderly conduct. The management have tried to sack him several times for drinking on the job, but I have managed to keep his job for him and now he's ready to retire."

"But if he can't do the job..." Alice interjected with confidence.

"Oh, I never said that," replied Michael, cocking his head on one side, offering her overt self-confidence the chance of introspection. "He does his job just like the rest of us. He's not as dependable as most, but then if we sacked all people who were not wholly dependable, how many of us would ever be in work? And think of what he might have done if he had been sacked. Do you think it would have helped him to lose his income, his self respect, his routine, his mates? I am proud I spent time arguing with the bosses to keep his job. I think it was the best way to keep him at least partially in control of his own life. He's a human being like all the rest of us. He's not perfect, but then none of us is perfect. He deserves your respect just as much as I do. I'm a priest. He's not. But we both work for the council, do similar jobs and should have the same rights, the same as anyone else in society, rich or poor, male or female, black or white – even Irish."

"Do remember, Alice," said Mo Thomas, the religious education teacher who had organised the talk, interrupting to fill the miniscule silence that had begun after Michael's last word, "that Father Michael has been doing other work as well. I met him through one of my spare time interests. I have been active for some years with a group campaigning against people trafficking and similar activities. You will remember that we did a session some months ago when a friend of mine talked about a women's support centre."

"You mean the one about the Bulgarian prostitutes," said Janice, a large round-faced girl with a thunderous voice and a penchant for wanting to be the centre of attention. Several smutty sniggers percolated through the group.

"That's it. Well remembered, Janice. You clearly learned a lot that afternoon. Well Father Michael has also done counselling work in his spare time, but aimed at migrant workers, people who might be thousands of miles from home, away from their families, in a foreign country, often doing low paid work, sometimes illegally and often treated very badly."

"But of course I don't do that work around here," said Michael, again scanning his audience. "I do that for an organisation based up in Kilburn twice a week in the evenings. I have often had to write letters on behalf of the people who come in and sometimes – just a few times – I have had to sign them as Father Michael Doherty to get what I wanted on their behalf. I can't do that if people I work with find out that I am a priest. I have to stay plain Michael around here."

"Where are the people from?" asked Janice, forcefully, as if she already knew the answer, which of course, she did not.

"Eastern Europe, Poland, Russia, Africa, Nigeria, Senegal, Somalia, Asia, Indonesia, the Philippines. They're from all over the world. They get themselves into difficulty with their employers, with their landlords – all kinds of things. I got involved with that kind of work through my trade union. I have been a shop steward – a kind of official representative for the people I work with – and the union we join, as public sector workers, has been doing a lot of research on migrant workers, because quite a number of migrants have taken the kind of low paid jobs that councils tend to offer. I got involved many years ago and have even been to visit some of the places where the workers come from. I've visited the Philippines, for instance, to establish partnerships with organisations that campaign for migrant workers' rights."

"Have you had any Bulgarian prostitutes?"

"Janice! Enough!"

"Yes, Janice," interjected Michael. "I've had lots of prostitutes, though not all Bulgarian. But the cases that come to me have more often involved the unwanted attentions of employers. I'm talking about maids or nannies, for instance, who have been indecently assaulted by their employers, or..."

"Let's move on," said Mo Thomas, glancing first at Michael, then her audience and finally towards Janet. "We don't want to get into specific cases." She looked back at Janet momentarily having subliminally registered an intangible strangeness in the reaction she had received. Her interpretation, perhaps correct, was a suggestion that the session was moving in the wrong direction.

"What was Mrs. Smythe like when you knew her in Kenya?" The

question emerged almost anonymously from the middle of the seated students and caused most of the assembly to laugh, just a little, less than everyone wanted. Before the teacher could make the diversionary intervention that was ready to burst forth, Michael answered the question, latching on it with some eagerness.

"Well, she was young, twenty-two when she arrived and twenty-four when she left, I suppose most of you think of a twenty-four year old as nothing less than ancient..." The girls nodded and laughed. "It was only two years, but I would say that she was a lot wiser by the time she left. She worked hard for our school in Migwani. She was very conscientious, very dependable and was very much liked and appreciated by her students. I would guess that nothing much has changed in those areas." Michael smiled an almost proud smile as he scanned the total agreement he sensed. "And... she was every bit as beautiful as she still is today!"

The room erupted in loud laughter, some cheering and not a little applause. The noise began to subside and then reached another crescendo as Janet stood up and, smiling, offered a short bow. "Oh my God," "Wicked," "Raaaas" and an occasional "Cool" could be heard rippling uncontrolled through the group for almost a minute.

Alice Bains then brought the meeting back to order, raising her hand to ask for another question and hardly waiting for the accepting nod of her teacher. "But what really made you want to change? All of us here have seen loads of photos of the place where you used to live because of our charity day and Mrs. Smythe's display in the library. I'm sure I can also remember Mrs. Smythe talking about you when she gave us a class about the school where she worked. What made you want to leave Africa and come to Clapham Common, because it would seem to me that you could have carried on doing really good work there...?"

Michael did not answer immediately. The assembly was perfectly quiet again and clearly interested in his answer. He spent a few moments screwing and unscrewing the end of a pen, which seemed to be stretched between the fingers of both hands. "What's your name, by the way?"

"Alice."

"Well, Alice, that's quite a difficult question for me to answer." He paused again and looked towards Janet. "Sometimes things happen to you in life which are so momentous, so mind-blowing, that you never forget them. You live with them forever, vivid and clear in your mind. It's as if you can relive them moment-by-moment. You are all old enough, I'm sure, to know what I mean. I bet all of you can think of something like that... And I mean something that you find difficult to deal with, not something associated with enjoying yourself. You might have had a death in the family, or an accident... Anything..." A few nods of agreement and a murmur of shared experience filled the short pause. "Sometimes, Alice, people do things they are not proud of. Sometimes, and sometimes even through no fault of their own, people find themselves in a situation where they have to make a decision and they do something they will regret for the rest of their lives." He paused again here and cast a noticeably direct and prolonged glance towards Janet.

And suddenly her heart seemed to drop again. In the five seconds or so that elapsed before Michael spoke again, Janet found herself reliving her abortion, an act for which she had privately but consciously been trying to atone for almost thirty years. She had prayed for forgiveness every day of her life – often more than once – but the guilt still welled inside her, took her breath, flushed her cheeks. And all these years, it had remained a private guilt, never once shared. The governors of the Roman Catholic school of which she was head teacher did not know. Her own parish priest in north London did not know. He not only accepted the leading role she had come to assume in the life of his Christian community, he was appreciative of her efforts, admired her energy and was grateful for her assistance, offered with complete humble sincerity. But he knew nothing of her abortion. Her husband did not know. Neither she nor her mother had ever told him, and her mother had died with the secret. Her two children did not know. But Michael did know because she could remember, even relive, the experience of writing that series of letters that had helped her so much to cope with something that still gave her nightmares. She almost began to speak, but Michael continued.

"There was a death," he said, "and I was responsible." The room was quite silent. "It wasn't my fault, but there again I was responsible. I didn't do it deliberately. At the time, I didn't even know it was happening." Again everyone was listening intently to the silence he allowed. No one noticed that Janet was close to tears. She had grown practised at hiding her feelings. But she remembered his impassioned plea to marry him to save her baby. "In fact, your headmistress, Mrs. Smythe, knows the person who died." A hundred and fifty pairs of eyes turned to her. Could they tell? Could they read her face? Why was Michael doing this to her? A man she has not seen for thirty years suddenly reappears and ...

"His name was Munyasya," continued Michael, the collective gaze returning to his anguished face. "Mrs. Smythe will remember him as a tramp who use to live in Migwani market. He was very old, an alcoholic and a *mwana wa Mungu* – a child of God, a madman – completely off his trolley. He was absolutely bonkers. People were afraid of him, though, because they used to think he could curse them. They thought he could change you into a snake. Mrs. Smythe was cursed by him one day. I bet she can remember it like it was yesterday..."

Again faces turned towards her. The silence Michael again imposed demanded she speak. Her voice was shaking with emotion. This was not the headmistress her students recognised. " I... I... er... I certainly can." She stood, slowly, her tongue noticeably flicking against her cheek, as if it was trying to find words inside her mouth. "I still have bad dreams about him... He was very dirty. And dressed in rags. He used to sleep under the tree in the marketplace. You can still see the same tree in the photos in the library." She was noticeably more at ease and scanned the sea of faces turned towards her to confirm that her students had registered the observation as advice. "He used to shout... and spit... and he hated white people. He once attacked me... in one of the cafés by the side of the market. I was very scared. He also had a thing about buses." She had not been aware of how much of a non sequitur this would sound and was clearly surprised at having to pause to allow the laughter to die. "When they stopped in the town, he used to lie down in front of them, right under the front wheels. It was like street theatre in London, a show that everyone knew about and came to watch. We thought he was trying to stop them from moving."

"That's right," interrupted Michael. A slight rustle accompanied the unison swivel of enthralled heads. "It was some time after Mrs. Smythe left Migwani, where this strange old man lived. But on the day of the accident, I was in town, Kitui, the district centre, thirty miles from Migwani, and somehow, he was there as well. God knows how he got there. I was parked by the side of the road, sitting in the car and reading a letter. In fact - what did I say about being able to remember every detail? – It was a letter from Mrs. Smythe that I was reading..."

"Was it a love letter?"

"Janice, be quiet!" shouted Mo Thomas.

Michael merely continued. "Well he was there. I didn't see him. He must have laid down in front of the car, under the wheels, just like he did with the buses. I couldn't see him. I started the car, set off and ran over him. I killed him. It was an accident." Michael paused here to scan the sea of faces. They all believed him. "There was an inquest. I testified along with all the witnesses and the verdict was accidental death. But I couldn't stay on as a priest in that area with the label of the white man who killed Munyasya… So I took leave of absence for a while to rethink what I really wanted to do and where best I could serve the poor, because that's why I wanted to be a missionary in the first place. I came to London, where I had some friends. It took me a couple of years to refocus my thoughts while I did stand-in parish work, relief work and the like, and eventually I decided to re-commit my life to the achievement of slightly different ends. I have no regrets. And now it's been twenty-five years in the parks department and, because I chose to be a worker-priest, a worker like any other, I have to retire. I can't ask for any special treatment."

There was another short silence. Mo Thomas rose slowly to her feet and faced the assembled girls before she spoke. "It's just about time for the bell. Let's stop there. Thank you, Father Michael Doherty, for sharing your thoughts, your experiences and your faith with us. And thank you, students, for being such an interested and appreciative audience." As she prompted the start of the applause, the school's end of day bell rang, quelling the rising sound so that it took on a rather perfunctory air, but all present knew that the session had gone well. Without waiting to be told, but in an orderly and civilised way, the girls made their way towards the doors, clutching their plastic bags, their heavyweight rucksacks and admixture of hockey sticks, lacrosse racquets and all the other paraphernalia associated with schooling. They were noisy and they pushed and jostled a little, but they also displayed a communal internal discipline and all one hundred and fifty or so had soon filed through the inadequate door with a minimum of fuss.

Michael, Janet and Mo Thomas were left alone in the large echoing room.

"Oh Jaysus, what about all the chairs?" Michael asked.

"The school keepers will stack them," replied Janet. "Well, Mo, that went very well again."

"Thanks, Mrs. Smythe. I'm sorry, but I'll have to dash, so let me just say another thank you, Michael. It was great."

And so together and alone for the first time in thirty years, Janet stood in complete awkward silence for a minute or more. "I've been coming in and out of this school every day since September 1976," she said at last. "And for twenty-five years I have been walking across that common past you without ever realising it..." Michael did not speak. "I can't believe it."

"What did I say about certain people never being noticed, not even seen?" he replied.

"But..."

"I've seen you." A look of aghast surprise hollowed Janet's face. "I've watched you almost every day come out of Clapham South Station in the morning and walk to work... And then back in the evening." Though she said nothing, Michael correctly read the question "Why?" from her visible astonishment. "You knew I was a priest. I couldn't even talk to you. You might have blown my cover," he said, laughing.

"Incredible... I... Oh, my God! Look at the time! Look, Michael, I can't talk now I'm due at a meeting at the town hall in half an hour. What's today... Wednesday... Are you free on Friday evening? Can you come to dinner? Please do." She fumbled in the small bag she habitually carried for a slim black wallet, extracted one of her business cards and pushed it into Michael's hand. "Come at seven. Please come." And with that she turned and almost ran out of the room. She had to make that meeting on time since, unusually, she was asking someone else for something, less than a favour, but much more than routine. Competent head teachers in their mid-fifties were generally no longer even considered for early retirement.

And so Michael was left alone, a visitor, a stranger unguarded and unescorted amidst a thousand teenage girls. He knew the way out, but he also knew that this should not happen. Something special had caused Janet to overlook protocol and forget her duty to see him off the premises. His thoughts drifted to a particular morning a few weeks past. As usual, he had watched Janet emerge from the station but on that morning she had not taken her usual route, itself something of a detour, so that she could walk through a copse of trees on her way to work. But on that morning she had made for the nearest bench, sat down and lit up a cigarette. She had smoked in Kenya, but he had not seen her touch a cigarette for over twenty years, and then suddenly, that day, she did something out of character. He almost decided to approach her that day and surprise her, but he didn't. There was a problem. He looked down at the card and read aloud, "Janet Smythe BA, PGCE, MA: Head teacher, St Mary's Roman Catholic Girls' School." The home address, beneath that of the school, was in Canonbury, London N1.

***

With the noisy and flustered arrival of Janet's daughter, Marie, her husband, Karl, and their two children, Paul, three, and Carla, two, the group was complete. Fathers Michael Doherty and Bernard O'Kane were still chatting, as they had been when Janet opened the door to them twenty minutes earlier. They had met by chance outside, having approached from different directions along Canonbury Grove and arrived at the gate of the Smythe residence at precisely the same time. Bernard had taken the Northern Line via Bank from Clapham South and had walked from Angel, along Upper Street and Essex Road, but privately relishing the experience of the cut through offered by Camden Passage, one of his favourite little bits of London. As he dawdled along, with time in hand, the late rushers from work sped past at a gallop. Michael, on the other hand, had been in the area for more than an hour, having decided, after knocking off from work and having realised exactly where Janet's house was, to treat himself to a pint of Young's in the Marquess. These middle classes would surely ply him with g'n'ts and wine, so it would be good to get a lining in the stomach.

Douglas, Janet's son was chatting with his father, his affected voice always slightly louder than the rest. He was tall, just taller than his father, whose slightly un-made appearance contrasted sharply with Douglas's prim, if over-stated, colourful neatness. Where the father suggested dandruff, an odd spill here and there, down a lightly creased shirtfront across the noticeable but not large belly, alongside a tendency to cough a little to clear his throat after a phrase, Douglas was neat, finely cut, precise and colour coordinated. He looked, if branded by his father seeing him as a stranger, rather 'arty-farty' or 'queenish'. This, in fact, was an exact description of Douglas that, in other circumstances, he often applied to himself. He had declared his homosexuality to his parents while in his first year of his Contemporary Cinema degree and, three years later, the family tended not to make further references to it. Now independent, earning his own keep as a part-time lecturer in the genre of science fiction film while he spent most of his time preparing a PhD in the same area, his parents were merely grateful that he still wanted to keep in touch and that he always turned up for the Friday evening family meal, a family focal point for both David and Janet and an activity that automatically occupied a Friday evening, no matter what else was on offer. Though his father overtly supported his choice of discipline, Douglas was always conscious of the disapproving tone that was never quite absent from David's voice whenever his vocation was raised in conversation. Something more 'down to earth' (no pun intended), something more professional, more respectable and, it had to be said, more likely to earn a packet would have been preferable.

Marie, of course, was the model. Three years older than him, his sister had achieved in the eyes of her father. She had always seemed to take everything so easily, so much in her stride, apparently never doubting that she would get her first in PPE from Oxford. Perhaps she also had always assumed that she would find a husband like Karl, Oxford law graduate, specialising in things corporate, and now about to adopt the status of partner in her father's practice. She, in contrast, degree in hand and qualified to the hilt, embraced marriage straight after college and, after just months of 'setting things straight' in their Islington terrace, decided on pregnancy, achieved it, bore the result and then did the whole thing again. An almost full-time mum, assisted by a live-in nanny on an allowance plus board and lodging, she granted some of her time to the Conservative Party her parents had always supported and, with her background, she had soon become established as a part-time researcher on social policy, specialising in family issues, for which she was now, of course, eminently qualified. Now that was achievement. 'More's the pity that she married such a prat,' Douglas thought. With the world at her feet, or so her parents would lead others to believe, confident, achieving Marie dossed down with a slobbering gut of an upper class twit who even wore those shirts, uniform of his trade, with white collars above dark blue and white vertical stripes, like a butcher playing vicar. But then Douglas would have to keep his thoughts to himself tonight. With two of the priest things in attendance he might even be outnumbered.

"Let me introduce you," said David, gently manoeuvring Douglas towards Michael. "Father Bernard you know, of course, but this, this is Father Michael ..."

"Doherty," confirmed Michael, offering his hand to Douglas.

"Douglas Smythe, Father Michael Doherty," said David redundantly, with unnecessarily huge formality, the full stop at the end becoming a short gruff rolling cough. "He was a friend of your mother's when she lived in Africa."

"I think that might have been before my time," said Douglas quietly, but with an exaggerated trill of the head, which Michael noticed immediately. Douglas was convinced he heard a quiet, knowing "Ah," from the priest. "I have to say that you don't look like a priest. Are you still a priest, or did you decide to join the living after leaving Africa?"

"I was parish priest in Migwani, where your mother worked," replied Michael, noting the prod. "And, yes to both of your questions: I am still a priest and I did something different!"

"So you must have seen quite a lot of Mum?"

"Yes, we became very close friends."

"So where have you been all these years?"

"I've been working for the council parks department. I've spent most of my time looking after Clapham Common, in fact. You know, weeding the flower beds, keeping the paths clear, picking the Coke tins out of the pond, clearing up dog shit."

"But I thought you were still a priest..."

It took only a couple of minutes for Michael to explain his situation, but it was clear throughout that Douglas thought the whole idea was nuts. He picked up on one aspect of Michael's story, however. When Michael mentioned that he had regularly seen Janet on her way to and from school over the years without once making contact with her, Douglas commented with surprised enthusiasm, "That's really cool! Amazing! A Marxist priest disguised as a council worker, who looks like he's weeding the roses, is actually involved in a clandestine, twenty-five year platonic stalk of my mother. As plots go, it sounds like something from a 1960s Italian director, and probably would have finished in a ritualised bloodbath!"

Fathers Doherty and O'Kane laughed. David was horrified, but his words emerged only as inconclusive grunts and were stifled by Janet's comparatively stentorian tone as she entered from the hallway.

"There. That's all finished. We can eat in a few minutes. There's no need to rush, though. You have time to finish your drinks. It can't spoil." Janet immediately gravitated towards Marie and took the two year-old Carla from her arms. "How is my little beauty... mm... mm..." As if on cue, the child burst into tears, its head turning immediately back towards its mother. Marie stood up from the easy chair she had occupied for only a few minutes and took her daughter back. Until then, all the others in the room, all men, had almost carefully ignored the fact that she had spent her whole time organising the children and their associated baggage.

It was Douglas who spoke. "Mum, I hear that you and Father Michael go back a long way."

"Too long, love. It's over thirty years since we met." Her voice gave no clue that they had not been in contact for decades. Janet looked at Michael and realised, in a way that she had not seen two days earlier, just how much he had changed. She remembered him as a plain man, neither tall nor short, not thin, not fat, without any significant feature. He was round faced, rather ruddy in the cheeks, and always wore his black hair short, in no particular style. He had always dressed in jeans and a shirt, always in a neutral shade. He always wore a hat, however. From Kenya she recalled his floppy bush hat, a soft camouflage-patterned, permanent part of his dress. When he took it off indoors she could remember vividly how he would fiddle with it as he spoke, continually rolling and unrolling it, pulling at it, or tugging it into shapes. He had no idea he was doing it. Forty-eight hours before she had registered only recognition, but now it was the differences she saw. The hair was grey, not completely though, and he had a large bald patch, but only evident from the back. His cheeks were still flushed from the cold outside – typically Irish, she could still hear him say – but now his face was heavily lined from his outdoor work and bore light jowls at the side of the mouth. The bush hat was now a baseball cap and it was stuffed in his pocket, not nervously fiddled. He still wore jeans and a shirt (the same ones?) with no sweater underneath the anorak he had removed on arrival. He still looked as fit as he had done thirty years before, with not a hint of extra weight or as yet any slowness admitted to his still mercurial manner. It felt strange, strange, strange to have him here in her own house, like a gateway through which another world admitted itself to her assumed limits. For Janet, memories of Michael Doherty had always been so completely and inextricably linked to her two years in Kenya that now, out of that context, she hardly knew what to say to him. She had not written to him for more than twenty-five years and yet he, it appeared, had constantly been presented with opportunities to greet her, to bridge the years. But because of the needs of his chosen life, he had always kept his anonymous distance.

"So you know all the dirt?" said Douglas, glancing back and forth between Michael and his mother. When Michael did not respond, he repeated the phrase, following on with, "You know about all the boyfriends, the affairs, the wild parties, the sex, drugs and rock n' roll – everything about Mum when she was my age…"

Michael and Janet both smiled. "Douglas, you have such a way with words," she said, quickly taking the three steps she needed to achieve a mother's distance from his face, which she touched and then, moving her hands to smooth back his hair, kissed on the cheek. For a moment and for everyone present he was again the son, the child, the boy, and Janet became mother incarnate.

"Oh yes," confirmed Michael. "I know all there is to know. I know all the stories." It seemed that the attention of the whole group had focused on the way that Janet still smoothed her son's hair.

Douglas had responded to Janet's advance. He had bowed slightly and looked her straight in the eye, her hands still apparently channelling his concentration on her. "So my gorgeous mother had an African boyfriend. Cool."

***

She remembered holding that head, her hands over his ears, her playful attempt to shut the world from his mind, to concentrate his attention on her, only on her. She remembered him laughing as she kissed him, trying to complain that he couldn't hear anything. "Just listen to this," she remembered saying, her lips still touching his, slobbering through the words.

He was older than her, more than ten years older and always reminding her of how different they were. Their affair, he had always said, could be no more than that, so she must not try to make it something bigger, something it could never be. From the start, they had accepted the need for discretion. In Migwani, it seemed common currency to assume that any time a man and a woman found themselves alone yet together then sex would be the automatic consequence, like some form of spontaneous combustion. One penis plus one vagina combined with one opportunity was the perfect and then inevitable mix, the result known, as night followed day. So they could never meet in her house. His place, of course, had been off limits from the start, never possibly private and always likely to admit an unexpected visitor. But then the end of her two years in Migwani began to loom large and she no longer cared what people thought, so their last two meetings had been in her own home, during the day, of course, though she dearly wished he would spend just one night with her. She longed to sleep by his side and wake up next to him so that they could make love again, immediately, without delay, with memories of the last time still fresh in her spine. But he had never relented and she had learned to make the most of the few frantic hours of Saturday afternoons, which were all that the maintenance of what public decorum they still retained, could grant them.

Perhaps she had grown too dependent on Michael. They had hit it off from the very day she arrived in Migwani and had remained on good terms throughout, their friendship, if anything, having strengthened as time passed. So often, and especially amongst the expatriates, it seemed that positive first impressions often faded. Promising friendships did not meld and acquaintances drifted apart. But not with Michael. It was as if, having communicated well from day one, they had since taught one another a whole new language. Of course she had known priests since her childhood, having received a conventional Roman Catholic upbringing from a devout mother, convent school included. But she had never met a priest like Michael. He was a 'free spirit'; he drank, danced and played football for the town team, Migwani Black Stars, the only white man on the field. And he could not only talk, he could listen as well, a skill not commonly associated with men, she thought, and that's why the two of them had spent so much time in one another's company.

She lived alone. She was not comfortable going alone to any of the town's bars after dark, since it was assumed that any woman who did that must be a prostitute and, though most of the regulars knew her and knew that this did not apply to her, it only needed one unfamiliar face to appear and the inevitable glances in her direction would start, making her feel uncomfortable and insecure. So she and Michael had drunk their beers in the mission in Michael's living room, by the glaring light of his hissing pressure lamp, its kerosene signature tainting the air even in daylight.

Often plunged into darkness when a suicidal flying beetle found its way to the lamp's core and self-immolated on the flaming mantle, breaking its brittle silk-ash mesh and thereby killing both itself and the light, the two of them had grown used to sitting in the dark, allowing their eyes to get used only to the starlight which diffused through the mission's glazed metal-framed windows. She found it hard now to remember what they had talked about – the Church, missionary life, education, fellow priests, the Bishop, other volunteers, Africans and Africa, Europe and Europeans, the Irish, the English, men and women. He had taught her some of his Irish songs, often nationalistic and bloodthirsty, some historical, some geographical, all sentimental, and often they would round off an evening together with an *a cappella* medley or, on special occasions, a sing along to Michael's strummed guitar, after, that is, the seemingly regulation half hour he always needed to tune it. She was safe with him. She was safe in the mission because Michael's cook, Mutua, often lived in during the week, walking home to see his family in Thitani only on Saturday morning and usually returning with Michael on the pillion of his *pikipiki* after Sunday mass.

And Janet was usually away at weekends, after dashing the kilometre to town after the school's last class on a Friday afternoon to catch the orange and white Mrembo bus to Kitui or the blue and white Uhuru na Kazi to Nairobi, neither of which could be relied upon to run. As a volunteer, there were always other volunteers to visit, but she would always be home by sunset on Sunday and probably back with Michael in the mission that evening to chat about what she had done.

Time passed, however, and, as her stay in Migwani reached its second year, her ease of familiarity began to widen her circle of friends. She had in no way distanced herself from Michael, nor had they drifted apart. She had just met other people and found it hard to fit in regular social calls on all of them, given that she had no opportunity to travel out of Migwani except at weekends. As her second year in Kenya had progressed, however, she became ever more confident and sometimes even travelled to nearby towns in the evenings, knowing that there was no bus to bring her back. Like a local, she would just wait for the first vehicle, flag it down and, always using Swahili, since she had never even been able to develop an ear for any aspect of Kikamba, except for simple greetings, try to negotiate a lift home. She lived by the main road, with its fifty or so vehicles per day, and also had learned by rote the Kikamba proverb. "A beautiful girl does not pay on the bus," always using it as her opening gambit with any driver who stopped.

It was during her second year that she began to spend more time with John Mwangangi. Paradoxically, when he had lived up the road in Mwingi, when he had been a civil servant at least partially responsible for the efficient management of her school, she had seen almost nothing of him. They had met on just a few occasions, such as the school's *Harambee* day. But then he had seemed distant, so immersed in the responsibilities of his office that he had not had the time or the reasons to mix with the likes of classroom teachers such as Janet.

Now, of course, during the week he was in Nairobi, doing his legal work. But at weekends, he spent increasing amounts of time at his *shamba* within Migwani location, his new farming venture that aimed at creating a new model of development for the whole district. He had bought land adjacent to his family's established smallholding in Kamandiu and had sunk boreholes. He had been lucky and had struck a sweet supply, precious fresh water that he hoped would grow tomatoes, cabbages and other vegetables for the wholesale market. He needed to be there at weekends as often as possible to supervise the pipe laying, the terracing and planting. It had become his pet project and he lavished all the time, energy, money and attention a celebrity's pet might have received. Janet had found the project exciting from the moment she heard about it. Here, at last, was something that looked and felt like real progress and could provide a model for others in the area to emulate. Here, it seemed, was a way out of the poverty, famine and disease that formed such a large slice of life and death in Kitui District. In Janet's eyes, John Mwangangi quickly took on the aura of a visionary, a prophet to foil Michael's sainthood.

And strange though it may seem, she could help him because time he spent with her became an experience that refreshed other aspects of his life, enlivened and energised him. Though he was nothing less than obsessed with his project and completely overworked with his caseload in Nairobi, he needed diversion. Though they had been mere acquaintances for more than a year, now that he was, himself, a visitor to the area, it seemed that Janet suddenly became a friend, someone beyond the machinations of his interests, someone, perhaps, he could trust. He dearly missed London, where he had lived for more than a decade and seemed to gravitate instinctively towards the company of Europeans. Janet never tired of talking with him about her home town, as she put it, despite the fact that her origins were rather more suburban than urban. John had lived throughout in central London, a Southwark resident during his training in Lincoln's Inn. So Janet and he had, in imagined recollection, regularly meandered through the West End together, reminiscing by flickering oil lamp glow about the bright lights, reliving in this desert scrub the rainy nights when headlamps would glare off the road surface of the Strand. He was a sophisticated man, this John Mwangangi, and cultured, sensitive and complex. Just how complex had only become apparent after one Saturday evening in conversation in the back room of Migwani's Safari Bar. Seated at the end of the courtyard, under the stars, with the hotel's scruffy rooms along the sides completely unoccupied and quiet, John had opened up in a way she had never known. This epitome of confidence and achievement suddenly and unexpectedly revealed weakness and doubt. His wife, Lesley, he had told Janet, hated Kenya and dearly wanted to go back to London. Since, after leaving Mwingi, a few months after Janet's arrival in Kenya, she hardly ever visited the rural areas, Janet hardly knew her and had indeed initially assumed that she was, herself, Kenyan and not, as John eagerly told her, a Londoner. Janet had met her only a handful of times and always at large social gatherings, mainly at their house in Nairobi, formal parties where it was possible only to meet and greet. Now compounding this problem were demands that John's father had made in relation to their daughter, Anna. When John first told Janet that the grandfather wanted the girl to undergo initiation via circumcision to demonstrate his own allegiance to tradition, Janet initially laughed out loud, thinking that she had misheard him. When he went on to describe the processes of clitoridectomy and, eventually, prior to marriage, infibulation, she went quite cold, feeling shock of ignorance then cold horror. But how could John even contemplate such things being done to his own daughter? That's what Lesley says, he had told her, thus placing Janet in the same compartment as his wife, a status she found immediately claustrophobic.

She had discussed John Mwangangi's family dilemma with Michael and found herself deeply shocked that he did not also immediately dismiss the daughter's ceremonial circumcision as crazy. Michael had been clear that he did not agree with any form of bodily mutilation, especially of the female genitalia, since his religion had taught him to worship that place, at least in its immaculately unpenetrated manifestation. But it remained a fact that most people did it. An uncircumcised man, he explained, was forever a boy in this culture. When Janet had pressed him about female circumcision, however, he admitted that he knew very little about it, only that it was usually demanded by older women for their daughters. There seemed to be two justifications, the main one being that the young should not get away with not having to go through what the older generation had been required to do, rather like demands for National Service in Britain. The second reason, though rarely admitted, was probably the real reason why it was done. An uncircumcised woman can experience sexual pleasure, like a prostitute, and frozen decency was the more respectable option.

Compounding all of this was the tremendous bond that had developed between John's daughter and her grandfather, Musyoka, during the family's time in Mwingi. In theory, they could not communicate. The old man spoke no English and Lesley Mwangangi had consistently demanded that her daughter should learn no Kikamba. Despite this, grandfather and granddaughter truly enjoyed one another's company. Hand in hand, they had taken walks together, during those months, walks with regular stops so that the old man could demonstrate something via sign language about a particular bush or tree or uncover something repulsively creepy under a stone. But since the family's move to Nairobi neither Lesley nor Anna had been back to visit the grandfather more than a couple of times in almost a year, and it was noticeable that the old man now publicly greeted his son impatiently, even angrily, prompting palpable expressions of surprise, shock and even disgust in those who overheard.

It had been just after Easter, sometime in April, that Janet and Michael had sat up all night discussing John Mwangangi's dilemma. Easter, of course, was one of the priest's busiest times of the year and he had said several masses over the weekend. But now, on the Monday evening, he had done his duty and was determined to have some 'fierce crack' to relieve the fatigue.

Two unrelated events had prompted the opportunity. Janet had uncharacteristically not managed to get away that weekend. Having planned a trip starting on the Thursday evening before Good Friday, she had waited for the bus, but none came. She was to meet friends in Nairobi and then travel together to Kericho, upcountry. Having missed the appointment by twenty-four hours courtesy of the no-show bus, she would have to change her plans to do something alone or stay at home. When, that afternoon, it rained, thus precluding any travel for at least another day, she decided on the latter. So she was at home for the Easter weekend.

The second facilitation of Michael's crack was an unexpected visit from Father Pat from up the road in Mwingi, who was just returning from his three months of biennial leave. He had turned up at the Migwani mission with a litre of duty-free Jameson's, a present for Michael, and the three of them had started on the pale spirit at sundown, chatting about this, that and everything between a few songs. Michael really did have a good voice and Pat was much more than a strummer on the guitar. Pat had set off along the dirt by ten, leaving Michael and Janet to sit and savour the unusual sight of cloud slowly obscuring the brilliant white stripe of the Milky Way across the night sky.

She learned that night that Michael and John Mwangangi had been close ever since his return to Kenya, intent on being an agent for change amongst his own people, and that they had planned and begun a number of joint projects while John had been the District Officer in Mwingi. But that had all gone sour when the local Member of Parliament, James Mulonzya, had made formal complaints about what they were doing. John was adjudged by his superiors of being more political than administrative and, rather than fight his corner against an authority that was unused to question, he had opted to re-join the private sector and pick up his legal career in Nairobi. That, of course, suited his family to perfection since his wife hated Mwingi and longed to live in the city, a place she now hardly ever left. John had privately continued to pursue his own mission to reform his homeland through the establishment of his model farm. But the family's 'retreat' to the city had fundamentally worsened his relationship with his father. The old man, it seemed, could happily accept having no contact with his son and granddaughter if they lived in London, but now they were in the same country, he could see no reason at all why they should not live nearer the ancestral home and have more contact with the extended family.

Michael's analysis of John Mwangangi's dilemma really did enlighten Janet that evening. As the bottle of Jameson's dwindled to half, they said less to one another, preferring to sip their spirit in silence and watch the stunning developing beauty as a gigantic thunder cloud began to mass from the east.

"We might even get some more tonight," said Janet as the cloud, still distant, flashed yellow-white, its internal fluorescence struggling against its starter. In the silence that followed, she mused on the fact that she had not mentioned the word 'rain', but that both of them had understood it as the focus of her statement. And it was such a rare event that, when it did happen, it was to be savoured. She remembered her first storm, in late November after her arrival in the previous August. Her personal rain water tank at home had run out in early September, having not been refilled since the last rains in April and for eight weeks she relied on the forty gallon oil drum by her kitchen door, a rusty, dented but still watertight receptacle that was refilled once a week. She had grown used to the smell of the regular visits from the school's donkey and its full-time handler as the twin five gallon burdens the beast could carry up the steep valley-side from the seepage holes by the cattle dam were emptied into her store. She had grown used to the technique of grinding alum crystals to a powder and adding them to the light mud in the drum. She knew that it was better to wait until the next day, until the dirt had mainly settled to a bottom sludge, a sludge that would not be emptied out until the next rains rendered the drum redundant, before using any of the water. But she also remembered not being able to wait for the next mug of tea and so she also remembered that she must leave the boiled kettle for a minute or so to allow the grit and mud to settle out before dousing her dusty but gorgeous Kenyan tea in her giant blue enamel pot.

From that first storm, her memory could still reconstruct the exact sound of the giant drops beginning their spatter on the tin roof. She was marking Form One essays by the light of her pressure lamp, an appliance she used only when working, since it burnt more kerosene than she could usually afford. But the moment that those drops had registered their significance, she snuffed the lamp's fuel supply and watched, for a moment or two, as its ashy mantle's glow paled to dark. There was nothing romantic in this image. She did it every time, to make sure that the delicate and expensive membrane was still in one piece. By the time she had reached her front door, the noise was growing quickly, no longer that of individual drops. The cloudy night was profoundly lightless, except for the occasional multiple flashes from within the cloud, which lit the streams of water now flowing from the corrugations of her front porch – the only part of the roof not guttered to collect the precious fluid – instantaneously transforming them into icicles, solid and hanging, within her inability to interpret what she saw. Elation took over. She would never remember deciding to strip off and stand in the rain, she just did it. And the shower she took in the line of channels from the porch roof was the most refreshing she had ever known, taking the dust of years, not months, with its flow. A minute later, of course, she was up to her ankles in mud and had to go back inside to wash her feet, but then she returned to the open door swathed in wrappers just to watch and listen to the blackness. She would never forget that first storm, and would be able to relive her feelings whenever there was even the promise of rain, for usually promise was as far as it went, as the cloud she tracked across the night sky continued on its illuminated way to drop its rain sixty or seventy miles to the west on the slopes of the mountain.

An age seemed to pass between Janet's words and Michael's prosaic, but profound response. "Let's hope so. Friday's storm was a real Godsend. Another would be paradise. We might even get a harvest this time…"

Unused to whiskey, she had been careful not to drink too much and had not tried to copy Michael's practice of taking it neat. But the alcohol was doing its trick and she could feel her senses starting to fuzz, so when the unexpected happened, she took time to respond, hesitated, only half-reacted. Somewhere, a long way distant, someone began playing a drum, an African drum, a single note, low and resonant, on a regular slow beat. Michael also took time to respond. "I've never heard anything like that before," she said.

"It's the rain," he said. "Someone is happy tonight. Someone is already sure we are going to get some more." The trickle of recharging whiskey, which followed the clink of glass, seemed almost deafening against the near complete silence, itself regularly punctuated by the dull slow thud of the drum, possibly miles distant. They sipped a little more of their drinks in the ringing silence for several minutes, there still being enough light from the stars to the west of the cloud for them to exchange a knowing glance as the sound of a gentle breeze began to rustle the leaves of the mission's giant mango tree nearby.

"You've been seeing more of Mwangangi over the last few months," said Michael in a tone that suggested mere continuation of a subject.

"We get on well," said Janet. "We have London in common and we both miss it."

"I'm away at the end of the week," he continued, the apparent non sequitur causing no confusion, as the noticeably strengthening breeze touched their faces. The stars directly above were now obscured and fingers of light cloud had spread across the western half of the sky. The night was changing quickly. "I should be back before the end of July."

"I'll be gone in early August," she said, lulled by inaction and thus gulping more whiskey than she had wanted, forcing her to cough and splutter. The paroxysm pushed her forward and she spilled most of her drink. As she coughed, her eyes lifted wide open and her gasping at breath admitted laughter in its rests. That instant, she began to feel suddenly drunk, her head spun and she did not hear Michael's laughter as he patted her on the back during the thirty seconds or so it took the fit to subside.

But by then, his pats of assistance had changed their touch, being now gentler and focussed on the small of her back. A moment later, she was pulled to her feet in his embrace and, as drops of rain began to sound in the dust, he kissed her, clumsily, forcing her lips apart with his tongue, his hand pushing under the waistband of her jeans to find the solace of her behind. Her senses numbed, she did not react immediately, which was her mistake. When she did act, mere seconds late, she over-did her rejection and actually hit him full fist at the side of the head.

"Oh Jaysus!" shouted Michael, reeling away. The thump was not hard, but it was meant. "Oh Jaysus, Janet, I'm sorry. I'm sorry." He paced away across the grassless dust he called a garden but, as the raindrops quickened, he came straight back to face her.

"I'm sorry too," she said and kissed him lightly on the cheek. She wasn't crying, but it was a sad kiss, a valediction. "Michael, we're both pissed. Let's call it a day." And she kissed him again with repeated cool before turning to leave.

She was not quite able to keep to a line, even before the rain really started, after she passed through the gap in the mission's euphorbia grass hedge, well before she reached the main road. A hundred metres further into her short journey, she found herself almost unable to stand, the torrential downpour now all around, with foam-frothing rapids in the deep-cut gully drains at the roadside flashing white in the lightning. Now she was crying, though she was not sure why. Privately she had perhaps always wanted that to happen. He was a truly wonderful man, fun to be with, dedicated, honest, caring and sensitive. But he was not a man, he was a priest, off limits, incorruptible, beyond sex. And now she knew she had taken these assumptions too much for granted, maybe ignoring the need also to attach the term 'human'.

When she reached home, she was in a mess. Drenched to the bone and spattered with mud after a couple of stumbles and slips, she found it difficult even to find the pocket of her water-leaden jeans, let alone extract the key that no doubt was embedded in a mass of soggy paper tissues at the bottom. For an instant, she thought she saw movement behind her. Had he followed her home? Was he there? As she turned, lightning flashed and the roar of rain reached a new crescendo, the storm hammering against the zinc sheets of her home's overhanging roof.

Something moved, but it wasn't him. It was just the donkey that fetched her water from the dam every day. It was tethered just thirty yards away next to the half finished new teacher's house. He looked forlorn and lonely, seemingly up to his knees in mud, displaying his gender. She had noted this some months previously as the animal had passed by, amidst the loud sniggers of her students.

Somehow rationality took over, despite being misplaced. Thinking that she might protect her concrete floors, she decided to undress right there, watched by this apparently intent pack animal in a stroboscope of lightning. She could leave her clothes outside and even try to wash off some of the mud before going inside. But the plan proved a ruse when the newly opened kitchen door revealed that the storm was now so strong that the run off from the school compound had started to drain through her house, attaining its desired down gradient via the gap at the opposite side of the house, under the door at the front. So naked, wet and muddy, she tried her best to dry off with a towel as the pools at her feet grew. She did not even close the kitchen door, because when she pushed, it now scraped on gravel in the mud and scratched to a stiff halt.

What did it matter? He had not followed her. Anyway, here in Migwani, she often left her door open, even when she went away at weekends. It was a safe place.

She woke up with a hangover. The morning was unusually dark under the first wholly overcast sky she had seen for several months. It took two concentrated inspections of her bedside clock to confirm that it really was already after nine. She was usually active by six. When she heard people in the house, memories of her jammed kitchen door leadened her mind. She panicked and, although too afraid to speak, issued a loud involuntary gasp.

"Take your time, young lady." It was Michael's voice. "We're just clearing up a bit."

She got out of bed and quickly assembled a pair of brightly coloured wrappers about her, one at the waist and one about the shoulders before taking the half dozen steps through the dark internal hall to the living room. She found Michael and his cook, Mutua, washing down the floors with vast quantities of clean rainwater.

"At least the rain also filled up your tank," said Michael, looking up from his contorted pose as he used an inappropriately small hand brush to sweep a wave of liquid towards the open front door. "We were OK. The water came down the hill, but the gullies took it all away into the valley. Your problem is that the school compound is actually quite flat and you get a general build up. Mutua, *ingine*," he said to his workmate, nodding at the empty bucket. Without a pause, the wiry old man, his late middle age belying the term 'house boy' still used by some expatriates to label his role, picked up the bucket and set off via the kitchen to the rain water tank at the end of the house. The instant that he disappeared to the left of the doorway, Michael went to her with a light embrace. "I really am sorry," he said. "I want us to be friends."

She kissed him. She shouldn't have, but she did. "It's a deal," she said. They separated and smiled again at one another. "It was all my fault," she said. "I'll never drink whiskey again." And then they stood there in silence, looking their separate ways until a sharp metallic click indicated that Mutua had just replaced the padlock on the tank. The filled bucket arrived a few seconds later, by which time both of them were standing, brushes at the ready, waiting for Mutua to send his tidal wave of muddy water towards them.

It took all morning to clean up after the flood and all afternoon to clear the mud-blocked concrete gutters that ran round the house, unnecessary drainage that proved inadequate the one time it was needed. They had a sandwich and water for lunch and then, late in the afternoon, Michael and Janet shared the meal that Mutua had left in the mission oven, having left them an hour before to prepare it. They chatted, shared a couple of beers and she was back at home, in bed before nine, sleep preparing her for the task of planning her work for the approaching new school term. Michael's repeated words, "I'll be gone by Friday," still resonated in her memory.

And he was. At ten o'clock that morning Janet was in a Form One English class, all sixty-five students – sixty-four boys plus the Chief's daughter – were busily and quietly engaged with an essay, whose just legible title adorned the over-shiny chalk board next to the teacher's desk. The door opened a little and, as always, all eyes focused on the intruder and immediately recognised Michael's ruddy face, topped by his camouflage bush hat. Janet left the still settled students without a word. She said a quick goodbye and then he was gone, the now clanking dark green Toyota Corolla bottoming as it took the ditch by the school entrance too quickly. The cloud of dust it threw hung in the air for a minute after the sound of the car faded behind the hill. And he was gone.

But Janet was not to be alone for long. The Friday evening Uhuru na Kazi took her to Kabati where she waited an hour for the Nairobi-Kitui bus to take her into town. For weeks one of the bars had been advertising a dance featuring the Mwema Brothers playing live, and since the entry of their latest single into the national hit parade, interest in the event had only increased. She met John Mwangangi in the restaurant near the Standard Bank where she usually ate the chicken and rice with soup which was always dependably sustaining and tasty, despite the fact that the chicken always seemed to have needed an extra three hours at simmer. She was actually laughing out loud at it when he appeared at the top of the courtyard steps, the offending chicken thigh held up on her fork for inspection.

"Hi there. Will you eat it or play tennis with it?"

"A tennis ball would be easier to cut," she replied. It was a measure of how often they had met like this that their conversation began without the need to complete their greetings, as if it had simply continued from last time. They did greet, this time, and John ordered food and two cold

Tusker beers. "*Baridi sana*," he reminded the barman, indicating that he did not want bottles taken from the batch he had just seen being newly loaded into the fridge. And so they chatted over their supper. John was earlier than usual. She had expected him to show up at the dance, perhaps around ten, but he had only driven from Thika, where his last appointment of the week had concerned a land dispute between an expanding pineapple farm and a group of local families.

They had never agreed a regular arrangement, however, though they had met on many of the occasions that Janet had travelled into town for the weekend. They had run into one another sometimes as early as Friday evening, such as this occasion, but other weeks it had been as late as Saturday afternoon that he had spotted her emptying the school box at the post office or even Sunday morning by the time she had passed his car parked outside one of the town's shops. In Kitui, where you could walk the entire length of the town's tarmac street in twenty minutes, it would never be long before two acquaintances met.

Janet had planned to stay the night in town, since she knew that the dance would go on until after midnight and did not want to disturb her early-retiring friends at Kitui School. John's food arrived and they chatted for just fifteen minutes or so when, almost in passing, she broke a short silence after finishing one beer and ordering another, to say that she had booked one of the rooms on that very courtyard for the night. She offered mere information, but the statement suddenly became, for both of them, an assumption that they would spend the night together for the first time. They did not even make it to the dance, and were together in the concrete box of a room, with its creaking sieve of a Vono bed and uncovered plastic foam mattress, well before ten. Janet had brought her wrapper cloths, so when four of them were laid down, the bed looked quite pretty. They took their time. There was no frenzy of grabbed moments because they had all night and all the next day as well, if they wanted. In these strange, bare, even hostile surroundings, when the bed bugs entered the equation, they lay naked together, chatting, touching, kissing, behaving like teenagers learning the secrets of the other's body slowly, methodically and by rote. Repetition strengthened their knowledge and somehow the night passed and as dawn greyed the glassless and curtainless window, they realised that they had never put out the light. For Janet, used only to oil lamps and candles, Kitui town's electric light always was a luxury to be savoured, but on this night she had kept it burning to learn more, to feast her eyes on this man she felt she knew like no other. By the time they parted after a breakfast of *mandaazi*, butter, jam and coffee, the wonderful system of a cup of hot water accompanied by a tin of Nescafe powder and a plastic spoon causing both of them to laugh, they had agreed that it would happen again, but never on a Friday. Having neither electricity nor telephone, Janet was not contactable if John was delayed by work on Friday evening. So, to ensure that she never made an unnecessary bus journey into town, they decided that Saturday would be their day and that he would always pick her up from home. By car the detour to Migwani would add on only an extra half hour to the trip from Nairobi whereas the bus often took four times as long. Public decorum could be maintained if Janet was ready to go at any time, so his car would never need to wait in the school compound and thereby attract the recognition of prying eyes from the town. And he would be true to his word. He never stood her up, never missing a visit without telling her the week before that he would not be there.

So April became May became June and July. She had less than four weeks left of her allotted two years doing good works in Africa and she wanted him more than ever. She cared nothing now about what the townspeople thought of her and so John stayed at her house on Saturdays and now Fridays as well. It would be several years later that Janet would re-examine her time with John, after the trauma of their parting faded from empty bereavement to mere sadness at what might have been. She had not seen it at the time, but a cooler analysis placed this relationship with John as something less than an affair. It had become more formal than that. It was years later that the revelation came and she saw their relationship as a 'traditional', but inverted, modern Kenyan arrangement. She was the bush wife, Lesley Mwangangi the city version, one for the weekend, the other Monday to Friday. But whereas the usual arrangement was for the bush wife to be the staid, dutiful preserver of family and property, whilst the town wife provided the sex, with Lesley Mwangangi and Janet Rowlandson, John had reversed the geography, but retained the spirit. Those years later, Janet would feel real anger, not directed against John Mwangangi, whom she had loved, but at herself for being so naïve.

But this latest weekend had been different, breaking a habit just three weeks old. Michael was back from leave. He and Janet had renewed their acquaintance and friendship, but she was ready to go, scheduled to fly just a week after his return. She had changed. And he had changed, apparently re-focussed and re-committed to his work, unwilling to admit any diversion. He had set about his parish work with renewed vigour and enthusiasm. She told him about John Mwangangi and he was visibly shaken, whilst mouthing support for her right to live her own life. There was a barrier now. He couldn't say what he wanted.

At the end of that last week, John came to stay with her on the Friday before the Saturday when Michael was to take her to Nairobi and her flight to London. With obvious duty, they had both attended the essential but over formal gathering to mark Janet's departure, an event that everyone involved labelled 'party' without intending to enter into any kind of spirit. But it happened and Janet was touched by the enthusiastic attendance of over fifty parents and all the students on this Friday afternoon, stolen from the timetable purely to honour her.

And then the guests and students had left, slowly, each wanting to offer their thanks for her time in Migwani, convinced that the local command of English had been eternally improved through her efforts. By five o'clock, the school was largely quiet and by six it was deserted, to remain so until the start of next term.

They had begun their love-making barely minutes after they had entered the relative privacy of Janet's house, the door barely closed behind them, but with all curtains having been carefully been closed by Janet before going to the Form One classroom to attend the party. An hour later, they ate together the meal that Janet's cook had prepared at lunchtime and left on a low oven before walking home for his usual weekend off. At about nine, after another hour together in bed, she had been mortified to hear that John had to leave. "I'll see you in the morning," he had told her. "Your flight is not until nearly midnight so you won't need to leave until late afternoon. We'll have lots of time. Tonight I have to meet my father to talk over a few things. I've taken a room at the Safari Bar and I have to meet him there tonight. Come tomorrow morning at about nine. We'll have the morning to ourselves." And with that he left her, alone on her last night in Migwani, her last night in Kenya, harbouring a growing resolution that one day she could come back and do what she felt was in her power.

At eight the next morning she walked the dusty road into Migwani, a walk that would normally take her just ten minutes. Today she allowed an hour so she could call at every shop (all six) on her way to say her goodbyes to people she now knew by name, by family and by association. She was still early when she arrived at the Safari bar, but had to loiter across the road for a while until old spitting Munyasya lifted himself from his sleep and breakfast on the bar's doorstep and shuffled his way to the shade of his tree where he continued his sleep. After her experience with him in the café, she had learned to give him a wide berth.

She found John's room closed, locked. He had gone out. The barman, however, promised her that no one had yet left from the rooms at the back. The only way out was through the bar where he had slept. He had unlocked the front door at seven and he had been nowhere. He was surprised enough to go and try the door himself. He too found it locked. He went for his key. The correct one located, eventually, from what seemed like a jailer's bunch, he pushed it into the lock. It wouldn't go in. There was a key in the lock inside. The two of them called through the unglazed barred window. There was no reply. There was a cloth hanging over the grid, which they pushed aside to peer into the room, but it was on the shady side of the courtyard. The bed was below the window and it was empty. They could see nothing else in their revealed cone of light. Still no sound came from within. The barman knew his establishment well, however. Standing on a stool from the bar he could reach through the window frame as far as the key. Though unable to turn it, he could rock it out of the lock and soon a reassuring clink of low-grade steel on concrete brought a smile of relief from both of them.

When they opened the door, all they saw at first was Musyoka, John's father, seated on the floor behind the door. He neither moved nor acknowledged their entrance. Turning to her left, she first saw the empty mattress, but then she saw that head, John's head, the head she had held in her hands and kissed, but the mass of protruding bone, white brain matter, bloody flesh and matted hair offered nothing she recognised. The pool of blood had seeped under the bed, almost as far as where Musyoka crouched, still cradling the heavy bush knife he had used to murder his son.

***

Having left the room only a couple of minutes earlier, Janet rejoined her assembled diners with the words, "We can go through now." She waited in the hall as the others filed past, like a dam in a stream, her outstretched arms ensuring the flow went directly where it should. They usually did not open the folding doors between the rooms in winter, since the resulting space was too large to secure from draughts.

It was David Smythe who managed the placement of each person to an allotted setting. He dutifully and officiously directed both son and daughter, despite their obvious familiarity with the setting and their correct assumption that they would be in the same places they occupied every week. These were places that, with only a minor aberration at the time of Douglas's 'coming out', were the ones they had habitually occupied since the first day they were able to sit. Conscious of a stranger in his midst, David needed to show his control, however, and, directed, they paused, their father's duty thus delaying the task. Janet had placed the two priests between herself and her husband at the round table, with Michael next to herself. To Janet's left, and to her daughter's right, she had left a gap for children-servicing but, as had become practice, the children would spend the meal time anywhere in the room except in the space designated for their use. Douglas was next to his father, a proximity that both were clearly used to, but which neither found comfortable. Their antipasto starter was already laid, the gilt-edged white porcelain setting off the rainbow colours of the cold meats, fish, shellfish and salad.

"Jaysus, that looks fierce," said Michael even before he had taken his seat.

Janet burst out laughing and could not stop, prompting her daughter and son to catch the giggles. Father Bernard looked slightly embarrassed, whilst David and his son-in-law eyed one another ruefully, with exaggeratedly long-suffering but gentle sighs communicating 'not again' without words. Without a thought, Michael turned to his left and patted Janet on the back as she coughed a little, and then with fumbling hesitation withdrew the hand, stretching the fingers a little before unconsciously touching his lips.

"Was that in African?" asked Douglas.

"It's as African as Limerick," replied Janet, still recovering and half turning towards Michael. "Just shut up and eat your dinner! Leave the crack till later when your man will play a bit on the old yoke of a guitar," she said to him with a stern elbow nudge into his ampler middle, her attempt at a Limerick accent passable.

"I bet you've got a pasta dish to follow," said Marie, holding out a small piece of Parma ham for the three year-old fingers by her side.

"Yes, darling," said David, mildly annoyed. "You've educated us before about that. Marie is a stickler for correctness," he said to Bernard, "and in her opinion an antipasto should be instead of a pasta dish."

"Then we should call it ante pasta and we can all be happy," said Janet.

"You can tell the ones who did Classics," muttered Marie with a giggle.

"So what about Mum's African boyfriends, Father Michael? Tell us the whole truth and nothing but." Douglas's words prompted a nervous frown and several short coughs from his father, his words never quite getting past the apparent block of his throat.

Marie was not impressed by her brother. "Douglas, really..." she began, but her words were cut short by Janet's question, quick-fired to her right.

"Whatever happened to Lesley Mwangangi?"

Michael remained engrossed in his starter before looking up and instinctively scanning each face in turn. Only he and Janet understood the question, but everyone was keenly interested in his answer. Ever careful in his dealings with people, if not always diplomatic, he knew the topic belonged to himself and Janet alone, but had not considered the ambiguity of the name. "She married again very soon afterwards. She married James Mulonzya's son."

"What?"

The word was said by four people, by Janet because she was shocked by the content and by Marie, Douglas and David because they had all assumed that 'Lesley' had referred to a boyfriend. Douglas was about to say, "Sex change?" but a sidelong admonitory glance from Marie said "Shut up" in silence and he obeyed. The fact that Lesley was a woman sank in.

They were, however, full of surprise and perhaps some momentary insecurity. They had never heard that tone in their mother's invariably measured, planned and controlled voice. As Janet continued, both Marie and Douglas became aware that the person speaking was someone they had never known. This was their mother before she was 'mother'. There was a sense of abandon, youth, risk, even insecurity in her voice. As 'mother', they had never known her admit doubt or hesitation. Their headmistress was always in control, never flustered, ever diplomatic and conciliatory.

"Oh bugger! She married that creep? What was his name.... Charles. I remember. He was the arrogant bimbo who drove the white Mercedes through town and slowed down every time so that people could see him better. What a creep!"

Michael took a mouthful before continuing. "Charles and Lesley had been having an affair for months, you know..." He turned towards Janet. The others waited for her reply, constructing their private, incomplete, imagined scenarios.

"What? You mean they were having an affair before... before... John died." Michael nodded. "So that's why she was so calm and cool that afternoon. I knew there was something strange, but I never thought that... that she had got what she wanted." Janet paused abruptly, her words almost choked back. Father Bernard was the only person who continued merely to eat. "Wait a minute. Presumably John's father went to prison?"

"He was convicted. I went to the trial and read out the statement you made to the police in Migwani. Remember I had to be with you as a witness to what the young fellow wrote down because you were leaving the country that day. Anyway, Musyoka killed himself in jail a few months later. What was left of the family just fell apart. His first wife, John's mother, disappeared soon after John died. No one knew where she went. The second wife was much younger. She re-married very soon afterwards and took her children with her. The first wife's children, of course, left home at the same time that John did. None of them had his education and, I think, none of them were in contact with the parents. Now that was strange, but not unknown. It could be that the mother went to live with one of them. There were rumours that she had gone to Mombasa, but no one knew where she went."

"So who was this John Mwangangi, Mum? How did you know him?"

"Oh, she knew him very well indeed!" said Michael with heavy theatre.

"And since you're a priest, we must assume that the 'knowing' is in the biblical sense," said Douglas, his response immediate.

"Douglas, why do you always..." scoffed Marie. "You're getting prurient in your old age!"

"Oh... oh... oh, prurient, are we?" he said sarcastically. "So my Mum made it with a black man in Africa! And it sounds like he was married as well. Cool! Congrats, Mum. I can't believe it. I just can't imagine you not being my mother. You must have been about the same age as Marie!"

Janet had not been listening to her son. She laid her knife and fork on her plate with a loud porcelain ring and turned to face Michael. "So who got John's land?" Michael leaned forward and bowed his head a little, turning it to face her. Janet answered her own question. "You don't mean... Did Lesley inherit? Yes, she must have done. John would have done everything with proper legal title. So did Charles Mulonzya get it?" Michael nodded slowly. "The bastard!"

Marie exclaimed "Mother!" and David "Steady on!" while Douglas laughed out loud. Bernard had almost finished his plate. Karl, whom everyone tended to ignore, was, as ever, silent.

"So why was this bloke so important?" asked David hesitantly. "Well I suppose he would be important," he continued, "if he really was your boyfriend. And what was he like?"

"He was – or could have been a great man. He had big ideas but enough humility to want to make them work for others' benefit. And what was he like?" she repeated turning away from Michael to look straight across at her husband. "Like you, he was over ten years older than me. Unlike you, he was kind. He was considerate. And fuck me he was good in bed." Karl dropped his knife. Douglas screamed and tumbled backwards off his chair. David's jaw dropped and his arms went limp. Marie offered consolation as the two year-old began to scream a split second after Douglas's developing show was obviously not a threat. Father Bernard readjusted the position of his knife and fork on his empty plate. Janet shed a tear and Michael did not react.

"You never did get over it, did you?" he asked, placing his hand on her forearm. Janet looked towards him, but could not speak. "Douglas, please," said Michael. "John Mwangangi was murdered and your mother discovered the body. It was the day she flew home. It was something that changed her life. I'm sure that your mother's world changed that day and never let her go back to what it had been. It was one of those things that you never forget, something that stays fresh in your mind forever. Some things, you know, are like that. They're so momentous they happen again every day of your life. It's like being haunted. It's all in here, of course," he said, touching his forehead, still addressing Douglas, though it was David who listened intently, "but, for the person with the experience, it's as real as banging your head. It hurts." He turned in the new silence that surrounded them all to look at Janet, offering a long unspoken question with his gently raised eyebrows.

Janet simply stared back. She was not sure which event he was asking about, but she was reasonably sure it did not concern John Mwangangi. She made no attempt to pre-empt the possibility that he might divulge the secret that only he and she knew, because she trusted him. She did not know this Michael, had not seen him for thirty years, but still she trusted him. Almost apologetically she lifted her napkin to her face and dabbed at her eyes.

"That day when you told her that you had found John with his head bashed in, Lesley wasn't planning anything with Charles. They had been having an affair, no doubt seeing one another at the same times that you were with John. But they didn't marry immediately. Lesley's reaction was shock. It does strange things. She was unhappy with life in Kenya, but she wasn't a schemer, or mercenary."

Displaying rapid and accurate insight, Douglas spoke and, in doing so, placed an idea in Janet's mind that she had never once considered, but, once identified, it made perfect, if uncomfortable sense. "So this John was killed by his father?" Michael nodded. "He didn't do it, by any chance, because his son was having it off on the side with a white woman?" Janet was speechless, but not angry. She really had never thought of the possibility that her affair with John might have been the father's motive. When no one answered, Douglas tried to retract. "Sorry, it was just an idea. I was thinking that it would make a superb script."

"We don't know why he did it," said Michael, pre-empting both Marie's and David's intention to scold. "Personally, I'm sure it wasn't anything to do with your mother. When the case was heard in court, it was clear that the rift between John and his father had developed years before, and they were also having a private but bitter feud over the circumcision of John and Lesley's daughter. It was complicated."

"Daughter...?" said Douglas. "I saw a film on the telly about circumcising girls in Africa. I didn't believe a word of it."

"But we were in touch for a couple of years after I left Kenya. Why didn't you tell me all this at the time?" asked Janet, audibly entering a world that only she and Michael could share.

Michael smiled and without looking up from the unrolling of a pastrami slice, the last item on his plate, said, "I thought the emotional space we shared at the time did not have room for more content."

"Is this a bloody crossword or something?" said David forcefully and uncharacteristically without punctuation. "You two are growing more and more cryptic."

And so the subject was dropped. Douglas was firmly seated again and for a moment or two the only sounds were the scratchings of cutlery on porcelain as they all finished their first course.

Father Bernard spoke, an event that surprised them all. It was if he had not even heard what went before. "You told me earlier you were also in Nigeria."

"Yes," replied Michael, glancing for the first time to his right since coming to table. "But that was a fundamentally different experience. It was during the war. I ended up being deported. Like Janet discovering John's body, in Nigeria I had an experience of my own that has stayed with me. I got caught up in the war. I was there, standing in the background while a young fellow too big for his boots shot a bloke through the head. There was a film crew and the whole thing was broadcast on British television. They didn't know what to do with me, so I got deported."

"You know," said David quickly, "I can remember that." Again he was uncharacteristically fluent, suddenly interested, sensing a handle in the conversation that he could grasp on his own terms and exploit to his advantage. "End of the 1960s. This Week... Panorama... World In Action... can't remember which one. But I can remember seeing that on television. Harold Wilson was selling helicopters to the Federal Government... General Gowan, I think, was the name of the Nigerian leader. And what was the Biafran guy called... O ... Ojukwu? It was in the news all the time. But that programme was a bit special. Millions of people saw that poor fellow's brains being blown out. There was a hell of a fuss at the time. And then they court martialled the soldier who did it. I can remember it like it was yesterday. They put him in front of a firing squad." David's memory was perfect, his gaze darting from person to person in his audience as he spoke. "And the television programme...? I can't remember which one carried it. Do you know, one of them had Sibelius as theme music? It was the start of the Karelia Suite. One of the others... Was it Panorama?... Had the opening fanfare of the fourth movement of Rachmaninov's First Symphony as its theme tune. Fancy choosing such an immature work to introduce such weighty content!"

"Well I was the white guy that got shot by the camera, standing in the background, being held up at gunpoint. The bloke being shot with the gun was a man who lived in the village where I was priest. He was travelling with me when we were stopped."

"It's amazing. You were right about some things being momentous enough to live on in the mind. I can remember seeing that on television, but the experience now is still vivid, much more than mere memory. It was the first time I had ever seen anyone actually die," said David. As he spoke, the door to his left began to open.

"Are you ready, ma'am?" said Rosita, carefully manoeuvring the wide pasta bowl laden with farfalle and Janet's new sauce towards the heatproof mats with views of Tuscany that adorned the centre of the table.

Janet was about to say, "Yes, Rosita, that's fine," but she did not even manage a completed syllable. In that instant, Rosita turned momentarily to her left towards Michael, almost dropped the dish and knocked over David's and Bernard's wine glasses as, luckily, the heavy dish, loosened prematurely from her grasp, dropped half onto the intended mats with a loud crash. And then she fled. A moment before, David's face had been adorned with a confident smile which had flashed from one diner to the next to elicit recognition of the accuracy and poignancy of his memory. He had reclaimed what he considered to be his rightful place at the centre of attention and was about to consolidate his hold. But suddenly, there was a look of horror about him, and it was not concern for the spilt wine or rolling glasses that prompted the change.

***

Term ends were always messy, had always been messy and would continue to be messy. Messiest of all was the end of the summer term, year in, year out, a hotchpotch of early closures, class trips, meetings, courses, training days, open days, class parties, home room shifts, refits, valedictory gatherings and conferences. Every year routine was sacrificed. Every time it was different and the three weeks after the exams seemed to drag into an age. And it had been one of these abnormal summer diversions that Janet had just left, a two-day, London-wide gathering of heads aiming to deliver training in the latest nuances of budgetary management. All present had sensed the irony involved in being told in one breath that they were all now in complete control of their school's finances and then in the next that they must follow procedures so rigid that they felt they had no control at all. The head teacher group had begun to ridicule the whole affair by the time it reached its scheduled close of formal business at lunchtime on the second day. There had perhaps been some logic in the early finish, but no one seemed to know what it was. Finishing after lunch at two thirty in the afternoon left no one enough time to go back to work and do something useful at their respective institutions, so they were all presented with that extremely rare commodity, an afternoon off. It did leave time and space, as the schedule had indicated, for the participants to have an hour or two to share experiences, perhaps to bond, to share professional opinion or, in other words, to have a chin wag. Head teachers rarely got the opportunity to speak to others of their kind outside the constraints of an agenda, except at their association's annual conference, but that was always so full of politics and posturing that small talk was rarely small, and words had to be watched as well as spoken.

For many of those attending the conference, the time off was more important than the small talk, allowing them to avoid the evening rush hour for once. For Janet, who was walking distance from home, it was going to be a real Godsend, a precious few hours at home where she could work undisturbed.

So, rather than stay with her peers for the informal after lunch chat, she set off to walk home. The July afternoon was preciously warm and sunny, and it had been purely by luck that this meeting had been scheduled in a large Islington college. The privilege of being able to walk rather than squash into an underground carriage was luxury indeed, despite the traffic noise and fumes of the Holloway Road.

Two days before, having scanned the conference programme in the five minutes a normal school day might allow for such a reflective task, she had decided there and then not to attend that final session. There were too many 'in words', too many buzz words in the rubric. With a rueful smile of experience, she recalled the idiot of a Deputy Head at her school in the mid-1980s. Having been on a management training course and taken to heart the message of the sessions on 'How to motivate your colleagues', he had returned to school with received advice to instigate a buzzword, which the staff would associate with the concept of motivation and teamwork. Teachers were to be encouraged to whisper this word to one another as they passed in the corridor or drank their morning coffee. After concentrated hours of searching for the right word, the inspired Deputy Head came up with what he thought was the perfect candidate, 'buzz'. He didn't last long, thankfully. She got his job on an internal appointment.

So, having decided not to attend that session, two days before she had brought a few files from work and stored them away in the roll-top desk in her study. She would have the luxury of being able to work on them in the peace and quiet of her own home. David had always disapproved of the idea of siting her study next to their master bedroom on the first floor, preferring to maintain a greater distance between himself and his work than was his wife's practice. Janet was quite the opposite in her habits and even did 'bits and pieces' in bed at weekends, so having the study next door was perfect. When at work in there, the cocooning nature of the small room whose window looked along the toast-rack gap between their house and the next towards the back of the terrace opposite helped her to focus, allowed her to concentrate without fear of distraction, something which she found essential if she was to get anything useful done. This, of course, was the principal reason why she often brought work home, since the environment offered by a large secondary school rarely offered periods of undisturbed calm or quiet. Paradoxically, she also liked to keep things compartmentalised and in their place, under control and known, hence the roll-top desk. It was strange how something as mundane as a piece of furniture could physically mimic and thereby facilitate a psychological trait. No matter how hard or long she worked at home, when she decided she had done enough, she was capable of switching off. She never dithered about her work. She concentrated on the task, but when the time was right, she stopped, abruptly, and never fiddled her way back to it. When the slatted arc of the desk cover slid down, thereby hiding the contents of the desk top, it shut them off from her sight and, thus out of sight, they stayed out of mind.

As she passed the queue of bus stops near Holloway Road station, she momentarily considered taking the bus. She turned to face north to check if a red box might be standing at the traffic lights at the Tollington Road junction. It was one of those tranquil moments when the traffic control systems had left the usually bustling road eerily empty, a time when the delivery vans could do their screeching u-turns without pushing their way across angry lanes of drivers. There were buses in sight, but she decided to walk anyway. Her work was not so urgent that an extra half hour would be critical, so she walked on, crossing over the end of Drayton Park to head south, musing on how she didn't do this often enough, despite her habit of always taking a circuitous route across a small enclave of Clapham Common from the station on her way to work.

She was reminded of her three years as a student at King's College on The Strand, a thoroughfare now so supremely inappropriately named it was always worth a visit just to be confronted with the anomaly, a London street called thin but wide, bustling with life, yet famous for a failed cigarette advert she remembered from the early days of commercial television when the product inadvertently associated itself with loneliness. London was a city of allusion, never illusion, which is why she had always loved the place so dearly, and hated to be away from it. Unless, of course, the change was so complete that experience bore nor relation to city life, for what other city on earth could bear comparison to the variety, the sheer complexity of this town? Paris and New York perhaps, but nowhere else. The great Asian cities were larger and, having visited many of them on her regular summer 'jaunts' with the family, she knew they could not compare. She loved this word, David's habitual euphemism for travel, because it seemed to possess an internal requirement to have fun along the way. But none of those cities could claim the variety of London, though most of them had climates that were preferable. From the seething traffic and diesel fumes of Manila, where, over the years, they had visited the family of more than one Filipina maid in their employ, through Hanoi's atmosphere of unburnt two-stroke, via, if that be the right word, the interminable traffic jams of early 1980s Bangkok, to the endlessness of Bombay, corrected now politically to Mumbai, of course, and on to Tokyo, vast and strangely unpredictable in its utterly controlled way, to the order and calm of Singapore, where a fart in the wrong place could be fined on the spot and the humid, cicada deafening sultriness of Beijing in August, where a street vendor offered to cook them 'brief'. David had offered the correction 'beef', but retracted when the portion that appeared was microscopically small. He might appear staid, but her life with him had been anything but. And so to North America, where the cities didn't seem to know quite what they were. "There's no there there," one American friend had said, and the phrase had proved so consistently apt that she retained the temptation to apply it to the whole pair of continents, despite their obvious difference. Nairobi had not really been a city when she lived in Kenya, and she had hardly spent more that a few days in the place. No, it was London that she loved, London that she lived and London where she had always wanted to be, even when she lived in Kenya, the experience of which, however, had always remained vivid, as if lived just the month before.

Though she had been raised in beyond-south London suburbia, where Surrey poked unwilling gloved fingers into the urban environment, the affinity she felt for this city was real. As a student, all she needed to do to get home was cross Waterloo Bridge to the waiting train on the other side, but after college she would often take a diversion and tramp through the West End, noting the details, the minor changes, the continuities that create the fabric of city life. Over the years, she had met many people who had claimed to hate London and only visited out of necessity expressed as duress. But Janet loved the place. She loved its diversity, its ability to surprise and reassure at the same time. It was ever changing, but it was always there. It was always different, but you could rely on its constancy. And for her the city created its image in those who loved it. When she met someone who shared this love, expressed as an affinity with the place, itself, she always felt an immediate ease, a comfort of familiarity, as if you already knew the person at the core, the rest mere details that would find their own places.

Still only half way between Drayton Park and Highbury Corner, her thoughts drifted back again to her student days. She had banked with the NatWest, or possibly, as a student, they had banked with her, eventually to their advantage, via the Long Acre branch. The walk from King's to withdraw the ten pounds that would see her through a week had been a regular joy, even though the drizzle and mist always seemed to come down the minute she set off to walk. She wore a fleece in those days, fashionable at the time in an alternative way, a long sheepskin, white inside with a high collar into which she could nuzzle her face against the rain. It didn't reach the ground and wasn't particularly waterproof, so it got heavier as it dampened, but rain still dripped from the hem. In afternoon lectures it smelled a little on the ever vacant seat beside her in the lecture hall, reminding her of an era when institutions of higher learning were generally and comfortably under-populated. There it would lie until it was time to leave, having done part of the job of keeping her dry, a task completed by her habit of folding her jeans around her slender calves and zipping them inside her trusty and thoroughly waterproof boots.

She remembered Covent Garden as it then was, before the fruit and vegetables migrated to Vauxhall. You could hardly pass along the roads, the lorries delivering their goods already too large to negotiate the tiny streets with their right-angled junctions. The armies of blue-aproned porters with their two-wheeled trolleys would block any remaining space with their queues, waiting for the sacks of onions, potatoes, cabbages, turnips, swedes and greens that would always overload their squeaking, rattling, metal-wheeled carts. She could remember the wooden handles of these vehicles, hardwood handles worn shiny and thin by years of manoeuvring along pavements and in and out of merchants' shops, probably passed down from father to son in the families that kept these desired jobs to themselves. By mid-morning, when she would wander these streets with less purpose than her timetable demanded, most of the work was done, and clutches of porters hung around the sarnie bars, with cups of tea and bacon sandwiches perfuming their cigarette smoke.

Clutches of porters, she thought on this July day, repeating the phrase she had just imagined. How appropriate. As students they had spent too many happy hours in the sandwich bar next to the college sharing the collective nouns they had discovered or invented. It had been a phase, a trivial pastime that had stuck, never to be dislodged from her memory. If governors form a board, witches a coven, monks an abomination, nuns a superfluity, angels a chorus, cardinals a radiance, professors a pomposity and crows a murder, then what might head teachers be? A confusion? A terror? A babble? A babble of heads?

By the time she returned home from her two years in Kenya, Covent Garden was no more the hive of commerce and activity it had been. Almost all of the merchants had moved. There were no more porters and most of the sarnie bars had closed. The bank was still there and she continued to use it throughout the creeping dereliction that infected the area before it mutated into the tourist trap it became.

She was in a world of her own when the noisy traffic of Highbury Corner demanded attention. She always felt that it was miles up the Balls Pond Road to the crossing, so she decided to cross three roads rather than one, availing herself of the pinging green man on Holloway Road, by Highbury and Islington station. After crossing Upper Street, she decided to take the long way round and walk the length of Compton Terrace, rather than going straight onto Canonbury Road. Though she lived nearby, she rarely travelled north from home, even rarer on foot, and could not recollect the last time she passed by the place where she had met the arsehole called Pete, thirty years ago. Whether it was the unusual space created by an afternoon off, the familiar yet rarely visited surroundings, or merely fatigue after a day and half of hot air, she did not know, but, for whatever reason, she found herself in reflective mood, keen to reminisce.

Redolent with the energy and motivation to change the world that only a returned volunteer, a jolly volly, perhaps, could imagine, she had thrown herself at every opportunity she could invent to promote Third World issues, alleviate poverty in Africa, raise money for her old school or educate for development. In this jargon jungle, she had worked with a group based in this very terrace to publicise the need for clean water, a group that employed Pete Collins, himself a returned volunteer, but of the Central American persuasion, a species which proved quite different from the Africa set. She had started in St Mary's school only a month after returning to London and she was still there, now headmistress, some thirty years on.

But in those first few years she devoted all of her free time to her charitable endeavours, constantly updating the clean drinking water exhibition she mounted on self-assembly boards she bought with her own money and driving it from church hall to community centre to teachers' conference to school visit at every opportunity. And it had been Pete's work, the big-talking but penniless programme he managed, which benefited from the funds and awareness she raised.

It took only three months for their shared interest in clean water to extend to sex, an activity she had always been taught to associate with guilt, but which always seemed to envelop her in its own momentum whenever it came near. And so it proved with Pete, as it had done with John before that, and.... But Pete had proved capricious in the extreme. She could never pin him down, never extract that ounce of commitment that might persuade her to trust him. They could do their project work, 'his' project work, her interest, she corrected herself, and they could sleep together, but that seemed to be the extent of their shared experience. Her faith, his atheism; her constancy, his caprice; her responsibility, his recklessness; her guilt, his abandon; all of these traits were in conflict. He was totally with her one moment and then nowhere in sight the next. He surprised her with his affection and then angered her with his absence. But despite her claims of relative responsibility and maturity, she was the one that got pregnant.

She knew what her reasons had been, but they seemed now to be selfish more than honest. In a resurgence of a deeply felt need to conform with the letter of her religion's teaching, perhaps a desire to expunge private guilt with penance, she had shunned all forms of birth control except that advised by the powers that be, but had never since been able to reconcile herself with what hindsight labelled merely crass stupidity. And so into this confusion there grew a foetus, a child born of her need to reinvent the fundamental purity of her faith, a groping for the solace of an honest confession and, in the end, a conception which demanded of her the greatest sin imaginable, a sin for which she knew she could never atone, no matter how devoutly she might devote the rest of her life to serving others.

It was in a small office now to her left where over twenty-eight years ago, a month after she came out of hospital, that Pete announced he was returning to Central America. He didn't invite her either to accompany or to follow, but neither did he demand he would go alone. Like all the so-called decisions he made, it was cast in a vacuum of his own needs, without reference to anything that might have occupied the same space. With her career developing by then, for it had changed from being a mere job, since she had already taken extra responsibility at school, she could not simply up and go. He seemed to say that the choice was hers, but he never used those words, or thought the thought, because it would have admitted her into a universe that was populated only by himself. She let him go and thankfully he disappeared from her life.

She turned left at the lights at the end of the terrace into Canonbury Lane and Square to join the main road, her mind still sifting memories so vivid they might have happened that week. Pete's departure, his rejection, if she were honest, prompted complete immersion in her work. She had been an average teacher for a couple of years, but with new responsibility on her shoulders she strived to become the complete professional. Another promotion came quickly and then a head of department's job became vacant on the retirement of a colleague. Again on an internal appointment, she became a deputy head with the unmourned departure of an ineffectual male. Then, after the school's growing success had made its mark through improved exam results and recognition by inspectors, the headship became vacant, again through retirement, and the post she had been groomed for by the incumbent for some years became hers. And that is where she still was, now almost ten years into her tenure of the post in the only school in which she had ever worked. Her only school, of course, if Migwani was ignored, which it never was, though for her colleagues it did not count.

It was not even a year after Pete left, not even a year after she emerged lighter from hospital, that she met David again. Her mother's health had deteriorated quickly and kind, charitable neighbours regularly called in to check on her. By then, Janet had already bought her first flat on a giant mortgage for the time, with payments she could only just afford, even with an occasional drift into the red some months. It was a lovely place though, and her fondness for those couple of large rooms, one overlooking Nightingale Lane near her school would prove a permanent memory. But it was not an easy journey to see her mother from there. She had chosen the location, after all, with proximity to work as her priority.

The Smythes had always lived near her parents, at least as far as Janet could remember, just a little further into the cul-de-sac and across the road, their inter-war semi a double mirror image of the one she still called home. She had always thought of him as a bit of a goofy, podgy bore. Recollections of her pranks still had a vivid clarity. What on earth must he have thought of her? As a seven year-old she could remember calling him Billy Bunter and running off when he chased her, slowly. At seven she was highly precocious. At seventeen – could she now imagine that? – he was not, and to her he still seemed a young boy, despite his being half way through 'A' levels by then. Perhaps he had never given serious chase. He never came near to catching her and certainly never laid a finger on her. Perhaps he too was playing a game and had merely sauntered towards her determinedly enough to give playful fright. She thought he looked silly in that grey school uniform he wore even at weekends, his v-neck trimmed with yellow and black, prompting her to call him 'bumble'. She would scurry to the safety of front garden to hide behind the privet and stick her tongue out as he crossed the road.

At the end of the 1970s, however, she was so focused on her work, daytime occupation which she now labelled 'career', implying that it should by right be confused with 'life', that she admitted little else into her thoughts. So when her mother was diagnosed with ovarian cancer and needed surgery, Janet hardly reacted, the matter of fact way in which she received the news suggesting to her mother that she had grown callous and uncaring, a state she resolved to rectify. The operation was a success and she recovered, but was weak for some time and then was subject to some months of precautionary outpatient chemotherapy, a programme that took a steady toll, but she did recover. Indeed when she died, having reached her mid-eighties in the nursing home that had been her home for six years, it was not the cancer that claimed her. And a good measure of the success of her treatment was down to David Smythe, who still lived with his parents, across the road. Always having referred to her mother as Mrs. Rowlands, for some reason consistently omitting the final syllable, a habit that continued to this day, David had taken time off work to drive her to her appointments. He had done her shopping, fixed taps and done odd jobs around the house, despite being perhaps the most impractical person that Janet had ever met. Her mother thought the world of him, always had, and saw much more of him then than she had of Janet since she left university and home in the same month.

He was thirty-five by then, already a successful accountant, fully chartered and with his own practice and a solid, satisfied client base. Memories of absence can be stronger than any other, she thought, as she recalled that she had never harboured any kind of feeling for him, never fancied him in any way. He, perhaps, might have been one of the few males for whom she had never even considered the use of words like 'fancy', even in the negative. He was there because he was there and had always been there, like one of the trees in the street, never quite the same on re-acquaintance, but rarely noticed. Her mother's regular and fulsome praise for his contribution to her well being never registered. It was like talking about the weather. You always did it, but never really cared what was said, its only function to fill a potential void of non-communication. Though Janet visited her suburban roots regularly every weekend, usually spending all of Sunday with her mother, starting with mass and then lunch followed by an afternoon in front of the television, and finally tea before catching the train home to south London, she saw little of David, her presence, she assumed, allowing him some space to do what he had foregone during the week. Not only was he still single, Janet could not remember ever having seen him with a girl, except herself, of course, when occasionally he was given the job of chaperoning her to the nearby shops to spend her pocket money.

But on one particular day, one Sunday when her mother was beginning the renewal of her active enjoyment of life as the effect of her treatment waned, she invited the Smythes for lunch, insisting that she and she alone would cook for five. For Mrs. Rowlandson, Janet had been a late and only child. Mrs. Smythe, on the other hand, had borne David at twenty-one, so his parents were actually younger than her mother, despite David's ten years on herself. The Smythes belied the apparent conventionality and predictability of their son and continued to live the comparatively racy life the street had come to identify with them. Perhaps Janet had borne something of a crush for Mr Smythe, a tall, dignified gentleman with a deep voice and reassuring manner, the father, perhaps, that she had lacked from her early teens.

Her mother had cooked a full traditional Sunday lunch with roast beef, Yorkshire pudding, roast potatoes, carrots, apple pie and custard, a combination of tastes Janet had memorised from familiarity, but which had figured progressively less frequently after Daddy died. It was as if, after months of illness, she had consciously decided to reinvent her normal life, to revive it from a distracted drowsiness brought on by her inability to participate. Over lunch she thanked David for his help, clearly demonstrating more than mere gratitude for what he had done. After nobly acknowledging the after-dinner toast, David, who had spilt custard on his college tie and looked the complete idiot in his formal garb, actually wept. Janet remembered him rise from his place at table and offer an embrace to her mother, saying how happy he was that she was back to her old self. Her mother's response was to giggle a little at his attention and attack the custard spot with her napkin as he leaned towards her, an act that released all tension and gave them all a good laugh. It also, for Janet, cast David as the son her mother had always wanted. Her own foetus might have been male.

With parents happily planted in easy chairs with port and brandy, their flushing cheeks apparently the cause of the room's misted windows, Janet had washed up while David dried. They had a common interest in music and, whereas Janet had not been to a concert in years, David told her that he went regularly, at least a couple of times a week and was a subscription holder in some of London's most prestigious venues. By the time Janet had begun to wipe down the cooker, privately marvelling at how neatly and cleanly her mother could operate in the kitchen, he was placing the last of the dishes in the cupboard, into correct places he knew better than she did. As cutlery crashed item by item into the plastic drawer insert, he raised the possibility of their seeing something together in the coming weeks. He refused to give her details, almost insisting that she should come, because he knew she would enjoy it. She agreed for some reason and gave him her phone number. He rang to confirm the next day, just after the six o'clock start of the cheap rate, saying that he had two tickets for the following week. They should meet in the Lamb and Flag, just off Garrick Street near Long Acre at six. She told him with an affectionate laugh, affection for the place and not for him, that she knew it well because it was just around the corner from her bank. His newly confident tone closed the conversation by asking her to dress up a bit, as he put it. When she replaced the receiver, Janet's only thought was a question to herself, asking why she had never bothered to move her account to another branch.

They met and had a pint and a sandwich in the pub over a chat about her mother and her career. She asked nothing of him and he offered it. They found they shared a liking for the uncluttered, uncomplicated and uncommercialised style of the place, and the beer, of course, was always excellent. It was not, as she had expected, to Covent Garden that he took her, but to the other way, to the Coliseum, where English National Opera were to present Janáček's Katya Kabanova. He was a composer she had heard of, but whose music was unknown to her. David, of course, was an aficionado, and explained the plot, with its story of unhappy marriage, guilt at succumbing to an affair and eventual self-destruction, with such sympathy and passion that it was like meeting a new person, someone she had never known. He infected her with his enthusiasm, real excitement at the prospect of seeing this production and drew her into his world so she could share it. After the first act, they went to the bar for the interval scrum. But she refused the offer of a drink with a shake of her head. She said not a single word during the twenty minutes as he sipped his beer with an occasional comment about its poor quality. Janet's mind was full of the stinging pain associated with Pete's rejection of her, reignited by Tichon's selfish treatment of his wife on the stage.

She needed the diversion of work to cope. She also needed a diversion from work, so an interest in something outside actually made her more effective and her regular visits to the opera with David proved the perfect foil to the otherwise all-engrossing career. When he eventually asked her to marry him, they had never shared a bed, made love, or even kissed more intently than friends. Theirs had been a traditional courtship of the kind lived only in the pages of Victorian guides for young people, a kind that had probably never been lived even by the intended readership. And neither of them regarded themselves as particularly young any more.

She surprised herself by accepting without hesitation, as if the response had been pre-programmed in her subconscious, an immediate reaction to a stimulus, like scratching an itch. He said, "Will you marry me," and she said, "Yes" and that was that. She felt as if she had switched off a gushing flow within her that was always meant to be stifled, a fountain of youth that had to be drained with the purpose of achieving the conventional respectability for which she always assumed she was destined. And now that appeared in the ample shape of David Smythe. They had a simple ceremony in the parish church they had both attended as children, but in different decades, and honeymooned in the Seychelles at a time when it cost an arm, a leg and considerable other limbs to visit that place. He had suggested the Kenyan coast at first, but had rejected it when he immediately and correctly surmised that she wanted to refuse but could not express her reason. She sold her flat, whilst he liquidated some of his investment property. They pooled the considerable sums and added another huge mortgage, this time based on two substantial incomes, and bought, at the start of the 1980s, the elegant, tall mid-terrace in Canonbury they still owned, and where they raised their two children, the first of which was probably already on its way by the time they were married. Once released from the cage in which David had caringly confined it, his passion proved almost insatiable. Though a Roman Catholic like her, he was also a pragmatist and he insisted they use birth control like everyone else to ensure they created only what they planned. Even in love, he remained the accountant. That is how he lived his successful life, calm, measured, controlled, except, of course, when within embracing range of his wife, a region in which he displayed an abandon of gluttony she became ever happier to feed.

And they had over twenty wonderful years of marriage, raising two children, Marie, obliquely named after Janet's school and Douglas after David's father, thereby perpetuating a tradition of the initials DS in the male line. They lived in a wonderful house, had the privilege of accomplished and respected careers plus a considerable income which allowed them to amass very early a large retirement cushion. If that were not enough, the continued success and achievement of both of their children, as far as Janet described it, and certainly of one of them from David's perspective, was a constant and ever gratifying joy. Janet simply could not see that a career in the media, with its unknowns, its risks, its potential for unpredictability, was anything to be ashamed of. These, of course, were the very characteristics that completely undermined it in David's accountant's eyes. The waning of Janet and David's shared star had begun before Douglas came out with his confession, but its cooling had certainly accelerated when Janet offered support while David's instinct was to reject. It had taken four years for the process to register a truly tangible chill, during which time the demands of Janet's headship only grew, while David's involvement with the practice gently waned according to his own plan. He was, after all, sixty years old by then and ready to start running down the flag, as he put it, despite the fact that, as Janet reflected, he left the pole pretty much erect. Her menopause had begun in her late forties and she had to fight herself to remain calm and level headed at times, an encounter she always won within the school compound but sometimes lost by the time she got home. She sought and received surgery, just minor pickings, as it turned out, and it had been delivered easily and quickly, needing only a couple of days off work

But then she lost interest in sex. And, though David by then seemed to be accelerating towards the slippers and fireside of his retirement, no longer putting in any of the extra hours he used to give to ensure he delivered ahead of schedule, as he had done throughout his working life, he still displayed a thoroughly active interest in her, an interest that could not cope with what was interpreted as rejection. Douglas was at college, doing what his father labelled a 'fake' degree, a comment that provoked anger and tears in a nineteen year-old who was still accurately labelled a 'boy' by his parents, because Janet wanted to hold onto that status while David, perhaps, without admitting it, recognised an aspect of himself. A few weeks later, as if to counter his father's perceived ridicule with a blow he knew would hit its target, Douglas announced to the assembled family that he was gay, and adopted every mannerism, accessory and trait, always thankfully understated, that might advertise the fact. David was furious and didn't speak to him for a whole term, threatening to cut off the allowance that sustained his attendance at college. Janet had managed to persuade David to relent, but not without feeling that David blamed her for Douglas's 'condition', accusing her of having been over-fussy and encouraging the effeminate side of her son's character. For her, work again became the solace, devoting as much of her time to it as she could, while David pursued his own interests, his music above all, more often than not now enjoyed from radio or compact discs from his expensive hi-fi via headphones. These usually went on straight after dinner. They still loved one another, but the complications and pressures of their lives, professions and perceived aging in competition, left no space for expression.

She was still walking briskly, having turned right into Canonbury Road and picked up more pace on the downhill. She meandered to the other side of the usually busy road during another period of traffic light sequencing tranquillity and, fifty metres before she reached her own street, the bus that she might have preferred, one which went all the way, sped past to stop at the place where she would have alighted. She was glad that she had walked, the mental space the exertion created having prompted refreshing introspection, an activity for which she rarely found time any more. The journey had taken just over half an hour, but she had relived most of her life above these countable steps.

But as she strolled more slowly and apparently without purpose down the street towards her house, she realised that she had found no space to reoccupy those two Kenyan years. They were years where the exigencies, no water, no rain, no electricity, no telephones, a shortage of real friends nearby except Father Michael, a gas powered fridge that was hotter inside than out, all of these were easy to communicate and consistently elicited suitable admiration from people who could not conceive of life without their dishwasher. But the true magic of the experience defied description. In those two years she had felt closer to life and certainly closer to death than before or since. It was life intensified, concentrated, magnified, even more so in its elusive memory. The tragedy of her last few months, culminating in her discovery of John Mwangangi's smashed head on the day she left was still a chasm in her conscience, a sore that would not heal, a hole that would not fill that she had learned to walk around. She could avoid falling into its still devastating sadness, but it would be with her forever, like that child she had killed.

But she had such a wonderful life, with two marvellous children, now both, thankfully, at ease with their parents, two gorgeous grandchildren at an age when she could also enjoy their infancy, a wholly comfortable life in a picture-book house with a husband she still loved and they were at least, unlike the parents of most of her pupils, still together. But at the end of this summer term, the end of another school year, there was a dawning realisation that she needed some new challenge, some new motivation to reclaim her life from the encroaching humdrum of merely doing it all again next time round.

It was only just three o'clock when she turned the latch and opened the wide panelled black door of the Smythe family home, a door which she carefully and silently shut behind her, even rotating the latch so that it made no sound whatsoever. Used, as a teacher, to the noise of slamming doors for several hours a day, she took every opportunity to demonstrate, even to herself, that it was possible to close a door quietly and gently, a practice that became a habit long ago and a habit she never broke. She walked along the hall as far as the top of the stairs that led down to the basement kitchen and, without descending, paused to listen for evidence of Rosita at work down there. But everything was silent. To be sure, she leaned into the stairwell, just where the triangular top steps did their ninety-degree turn, and said her name, softly. There was no response. She must be upstairs. And so she made her way back along the hall and turned right to take the stairs up to her study. They had renovated the old house with such a sense of quality that the stairs did not even creak beneath the handmade carpets she still preferred to the modern echo of polished wood floors. By the time she was half way up, some eight counted steps, she knew what to expect. She had suspected as much for some time, so it was no shock, as it had not been even the first time. The shock was to arrive later, like the day she found John Mwangangi, nothing at the time and then the dawning of life changing memory weeks, even months later. When she reached the top, turning back towards the front of the house near the three steps of the half landing, she stopped, not turning left to the study as she had planned but staring straight ahead where the bedroom door stood ajar leaving a six inch gap through which she could see her husband's ample and rippling buttocks ramming back and forth into Rosita's behind. She was standing, supporting herself with both hands on the waist-high horizontal bar across the base of the bedstead. She was naked, her small breasts being tugged by David's podgy hands as he worked her from the back. He's up her fucking arse, she thought, as she turned, still unnoticed, to retrace her path back to the street, closing the latch silently from the outside with her key.

She turned right and walked briskly, as if with purpose, to the end of the road and there, as if abruptly beached by the wave that had driven her, she stopped dead. It wasn't in her to cry, though she wanted to. She couldn't be angry, though she should have been. She wasn't even surprised. Why should she be? It had happened before. But in this place where she had lived for a quarter of a century, she felt newly estranged and alienated. She fumbled in her bag for her mobile. She would ring him to say that the course had finished early and she was on her way home. She dialled the number, but paused on the last digit and then cancelled the call. She set off back towards the house, though this time she would slam the door and see what happened, but she stopped after a few hurried paces, unsure of what she might do next, whatever reaction she might provoke. So she turned again and walked slowly to the end of the road where the open door of the Marquess seemed to invite her inside. She rarely went there, limiting her visits to an occasional Sunday lunchtime in summer when she and David could sit outside and watch their small world go by in this giant city. But the bar-staff knew her at least by sight and greeted her as if she were a regular. She ordered a gin and tonic and sat down, only to spring back to her feet immediately to buy a pack of cigarettes from the vending machine. She checked with the staff that it was still acceptable to smoke and then realised she had no lighter, so another visit to the bar was needed, each petty interruption to her dismay pushing thoughts of the here and now to the fore. She had not smoked since she had left Kenya, thirty years less one month before. But this afternoon she smoked three, one after the other in a chain and finished a gin and tonic alongside each one. Her mind felt strangely empty, as if her experience had been anaesthetised. Her head was beginning to swim as the narcotic mixture made its mark and for some reason best known to someone who was not Janet Smythe, née Rowlandson, she started to laugh a gentle sustained laugh. There was no hint of a tear, not a trace of sadness. Irony, yes, that quality writers should not try to write because readers always miss it, as she had taught her English Literature A level students throughout the years when she was a 'mere' classroom teacher, a term she had disastrously used to her staff soon after taking over the headship, an error that had taken a year to undo.

She hardly noticed him sit down. So inwardly focused had she become that he presented only vague shape, a darkening in the unseen field of vision, which offered a polite gesturing question about the chair opposite. She had even completed her confirmation that it was vacant before she recognised him.

"Gerry! Well I never. How are...?" Presented with the bent double stoop of a man she only just recognised, she clipped the question short, in case its intended platitude was interpreted as a genuine request.

"It's good to see you again, Mrs. Smythe," he said, offering his right hand with exaggerated clearance above the level of his pint and her tall glass. His hand and arm shook gently, steadying only as she grasped to shake and began again on her release. "It's my local. I knew you lived down the road, but I've never seen you in here before."

She knew his exact age. He was thirty-nine and looked seventy. About seven years ago, soon after her 'mere' teacher gaff had faded into memory, one of the toughest decisions she had ever made as a head related to Gerald Knight's career. She had pursued early retirement on health grounds on his behalf, having to stick her neck out some distance to secure a deal for him at the time. Newly diagnosed with a debilitating and ultimately fatal disease of the spine, he had been a small man, but very solid, a well-built rugby halfback, as he always used to describe himself. A real ale type, bearded, always conventionally dressed in non-matching jacket and trousers, never jeans, he had given St. Mary's ten years of service, having joined the school as a probationer, straight from college. She had been sad to see him go, not sad on his behalf because of his illness, but perhaps sad for herself and her school, because he was a good teacher whom she knew would be hard to replace.

"Would you like another?" she asked, nodding at his near empty glass.

"I'd love one. Ordinary, please."

Back in her seat, their drinks refilled, she took a moment of silence to compare the then and now. He had lost weight, disastrously. His spine was a complete curve and he had developed a pronounced hump a third of the way down from the neck, which he held almost horizontal. It needed only a glance at the shape to know that it was not a result of stooping, or of occupation. The full beard she recalled was now wispy, long at the sides but almost bald on the point of the chin. His jacket and trousers were as she remembered, perhaps even the same ones, but now they were sizes too large and hung in surprising folds and gathers.

"I should have bought that for you," he said. "I've never said thank you for what you did."

"At the time you thought I was pushing you out."

"I know. Judgment was never my strong point. Had I not at least taken leave of absence for treatment, I would have been dead within a year."

"So what's the prognosis now?" They were already speaking as head teacher and staff member, colleague for want of a better word, if it were not too pejorative a term, as if seven years of non-relationship had never existed.

"I've not got long left. I wake each morning and thank God for just one more day. I have a routine where I try to move all the bits, a checklist of exercises and, touch wood, everything is still there, but not very comfortable. I'm not in pain. Whether it's the drugs I take or the nature of the condition, I don't know. Sometimes I just can't do something, like lift my arm or grasp, but up to now, it has always come back. I am very lucky. I don't function too well overall, but I can keep going. I'm clumsy and I can't walk very far, but at least I can make it here and have a few pints of nectar."

And it was then that image of Munyasya hit her, a decrepit old man with a beard confronting her in a public place. A nightmare she had never fully relived gripped her gut. She turned white and lost her breath and, momentarily, felt herself faint.

He stood, in pain. "Mrs. Smythe... are you all right?"

And the moment passed, leaving its taint as a ponderous hesitancy in her speech, as if the memory of that cursing old man had its finger in her mouth, tugging. As he sat again, she stroked her hair and sighed a little.

"Goodness, I don't know what came over me. I'm sorry. I felt a little unwell for a moment."

"That is your fourth gin and tonic and I have never seen you smoke." His eyes were the same. Piercing green with brown flecks at the rim. She remembered them penetrating her honesty on the day she told him she was seeking severance on his behalf. He hadn't completely trusted her then, and the eyes had cut through the message. Today their penetration was different. He was on her side, and, though their concern questioned her integrity again, this time it was on her behalf, not his. "You acted on principle on my behalf, made a decision I was not capable of and, as a result, have probably given me years of life I had no right to expect. I wanted to carry on as if nothing had changed and I was wrong. Whatever is troubling you now, Mrs. Smythe, think it through and, like you did for me, make your judgment. You will be right."

She left the fourth drink untouched, but took the cigarettes after bidding Gerry Knight a fond farewell and, against all odds, wishing him the best of luck. But she did not go home. She walked for an hour around the quiet triangle of streets between New North Road, City Road and Essex Road, the simple repetition of low London-brick terraces not intruding into her thoughts. She smoked a few more cigarettes and paused occasionally on benches installed by the council in places no one else would ever think of using and then she went home, close to the time she would normally arrive from south London. Rosita had cooked the meal and had left a note on the kitchen pin-board. It said that she had left food in the oven, that she had gone to visit friends and would be back by ten. David arrived home from the office just before seven, after which they spent a normal evening.

She left early for work the next morning and took extra time to stroll a little further across Clapham Common on her roundabout way to school. Usually, this was her way of finalising any outstanding decision to be made that day, a few minutes of undisturbed contemplation of the issues, the strategy, the final decision and the possible consequences. She hardly ever changed anything, but sometimes in that open humming quiet a nuance had emerged which later transformed her intended action into complete, rather than partial, success. But on this morning she stopped to sit on a bench near the bowling green and smoked the last of her cigarettes as, for once, she contemplated her private dilemmas, not someone else's demand. Seeing Gerry had put things into a different, larger context. She had so much to be thankful for and so much to lose with a rash decision. His thanks for what she had done had been profoundly moving, despite her recollection of only being half confident that it was the right course. The summer term, and with it another school year, was nearly over. There would be a summer break, that frantic time of planning, recruitment, initiatives and exam results, passing and failing, smiles and tears, a space to think things over. It was time to move, time to reclaim that chair behind that desk, time to attend to those things that others presented. She had finished the last cigarette a few minutes earlier and, like the previous two, had stubbed it out inside the packet she had prematurely emptied for that purpose, just like she used to do when you could still smoke on the upstairs of a bus, when there was that one car on each underground train where the atmosphere was pea soup. But as she stood, she forgot about the packet, which lay now closed on her thigh, charged with its smoker's trash. She had remained seated on that bench for several minutes after the last stub and now, with horror, she realised she might be in danger of being late. A glance at her watch confirmed the possibility and prompted her to rise and walk in a single hurried movement. She had already taken several steps, her mind on the new tasks ahead, before the hollow clatter of the flip top box on the macadam path registered and caused her to look back. As if by divine intervention, a maintenance worker with fluorescent green strip across his jacket and trousers was already preparing to sweep it into his pan with a long-handled brush. She watched him empty the pan into his dustbin on wheels, balance his tools across the contraption and then move on, pulling his cap further down at the front as he stooped to inspect the ground for more of his prey. It was his job.

***

Having scanned the table and declared nothing broken, Janet glanced towards Marie and indicated with the slightest nod that she should clear up. Then she left the room, turning right to follow Rosita back to the basement, her boots giving clatter on the uncarpeted stairs. Marie stood immediately and walked around the table, her utterly awake two year-old's eyes following her hawk like, the mind clearly deciding if this might be a moment to cry. She stayed quiet, deferring the intervention to a time of greater potential profit. As Marie righted the glasses and mopped the spilt wine with her mother's discarded napkin, David fussily positioned the pasta bowl exactly in its appointed space and announced he would serve, inviting the guests to pass their plates. Distracted, the guests complied, but slowly, as if reluctantly. When Marie announced that she would take the merely damp napkins downstairs, Karl sensed his opportunity and took it. Silent until then, he began to speak as soon as his wife was out of sight.

"Just a thought, David. Must catch up with you sometime this evening for a word. Slight problem to clear up before Monday and tonight's as good as any ..."

David placed a liberal helping of farfalle with their indeterminate clinging red coat on Father Bernard's plate and set it down to his left. He accepted Michael's plate and began filling it. As he replied to Karl, various forms of "Oh Jaysus that's enough" issued from his left. "Problem, Karl? Did something crop up after I left? Can't it wait?"

"It's a little sensitive," said Karl, the speed of delivery and false stress suggesting rehearsal. "Let's chat after dinner."

"Now is fine by me," said David confidently and insistently, "if our guests would excuse the imposition of our talking shop at table." David pivoted and turned stiffly to pose an expression of silent question to Bernard and Michael, to whom he also handed a plate of pasta. As the guests grumbled personal varieties of assent without actually saying anything, David reached over the table to take Karl's plate and, with raised eyebrows and the slightest angle of the head, commanded him to speak.

Outmanoeuvred, Karl had to respond or perhaps let the matter drop, possibly to fester again as it had done for months. His voice communicated both acknowledgement and acceptance of challenge. "I spoke with Sanjit Singh of LCN this afternoon. He told me they were getting pretty miffed with our failure to deliver. We promised..."

"Karl, with all due respect," interrupted David, his voice now displaying none of the hesitancy it always bore when dealing with merely personal issues, "I have been dealing with LCN for years. I've known Sanjit's father ever since he established the company. I've seen it grow from a sweatshop with two sewing machines to a multi-million pound business. Believe me, there is no problem with our relations with LCN."

"On the contrary, David. Sanjit is as good as saying that our contract won't be renewed. The father does very little these days. He's hardly involved. Sanjit runs the place now and he's a stickler for the letter of the law. If we say we'll deliver by such and such a day, then that is precisely what he wants us to do, no more, no less. He's not interested in *why* we are a week or two late, especially when members of our practice cancel meetings at the last minute…"

"Karl," said David, his dismissive tone exaggerated for the name, "it's not a problem. I have missed a couple of consultations but the work is done. I'll ring the old man on Monday…"

"David," said Karl, duelling names, "it's Sanjit who runs the business now. He's the MD. He's not like his father. He's got an MBA and wants things done according to an agreed plan. But that's not the only problem. There have been other times when people have wanted to contact you while you were out of the office, especially in the afternoons, and when we've tried to contact you, your mobile has been off and you have not been at the appointment in your diary. People are losing confidence…"

Marie and Janet arrived together, Marie carrying the salad bowl that Rosita should have delivered after the pasta. Before either had begun to take their place at table, David spoke, addressing his words directly to the two women, his head turning from one to the other as they moved along adjacent sides of the room. "My son-in-law is putting the boot in again. Anyone would think he is trying to kick me out."

Marie smiled ruefully, since for her this was not news. Janet merely ignored her husband and spoke to Michael as she sat down, unfolding a clean, but non-matching napkin onto her lap. "How long have you known Rosita?"

"Quite a while," replied Michael after a short pause, during which he gave a long and direct stare towards David, noting his feigned disinterest. "She's been coming to me for several months, close on a year in fact."

"Bloody hell!" said Douglas, as if newly interested. In fact he had noted with care, and perhaps stored, every word that had been spoken. "Marxist worker priest stalks headmistress mother of two for twenty-five years before illicit liaison with family's Filipina maid!"

"Shut up, you arsehole!" It was suddenly quiet. It was Karl speaking out of turn, his voice laden with frustration. Uncharacteristically, an omission noted immediately and simultaneously by both David and

Janet, Marie did not scoff, did not admonish. She overtly ignored his comment and ate some pasta.

"Takes one to know one, darling," replied Douglas, with heavy camp.

"Oh, the joys of family life," said David, as he completed his allotted task of service with the loading of his own plate, which he set down with a light but noticeable and intentional bang on a picture of the Campo of Siena that adorned his placemat. It was Janet who spoke next. Ignoring the contests at table it was again to Michael she turned.

"So tell me about Rosita's money problems."

"The money?" He seemed genuinely surprised, so much so that with a subsequent little jerk of the head, wide-eyed, he repeated the question. When Janet did not respond, he continued. "OK." Michael's tone indicated the start of a story and prompted a temporary truce amongst the factions. "The money's a problem. She's a Filipina. Money is always a problem in the Philippines. There's not much of it about. She's a single mother with two kids. The husband worked in construction and died when a hoist full of concrete lintels got a bit too close, caught him on the arm and knocked him off the eighteenth floor of an apartment block in Dubai. The company paid no compensation, claiming that he had broken site rules by not wearing his hard hat. They gave Rosita a pay-off to keep her quiet, about five hundred US, I think. But she had two kids in school, one about eight and the other five, just ready to start in primary. She struggled on for a year doing any casual work she could get, but the Filipino middle classes generally don't pay their domestics enough to cover school fees, so she used what was left of her five hundred to pay an agent who promised her domestic work overseas."

"That would be Pacific People," David interjected. Michael nodded confirmation. "I remember dealing with them. Have they been a problem?"

"No," said Michael. "Strangely enough, since the agents are often the devils in these stories, this particular one seems to have been well paid, but also delivered exactly what she wanted, which was a secure domestic job overseas. She had wanted to go to the US, of course. All Filipinos do. But the UK was a fine second best and being based in London was a bonus."

"And so she came to chez Smythe," said Douglas, "and, don't tell me, we aren't paying her! We are unscrupulous capitalist bastards exploiting a poor and vulnerable Third World woman, thrashing the victim daily, raping her, selling her on the street, feeding her salt, and forcing her to sit in comfy chairs."

"That's some list," said Michael, as the others, in their variety of ways, told the young man to keep his mouth shut. "And it's partially correct…"

"Don't you think we should talk about this later? It is, after all, a family matter." David inserted an impatience to quicken his words, the phrase thereby revealing his intent to place a full stop to end the discussion. Michael ignored the prompt and addressed the son.

"You're partially right, Douglas," he repeated, the young man now displaying considerable embarrassment that his intended flippant joke had struck a nerve, somewhere.

"How long have you been seeing Rosita?" asked Janet, unsure that she had registered his original answer correctly.

"For about a year. She comes regularly…"

David's grunts and fidgets prompted Janet to interrupt, turning to her right, whilst placing both hands on Michael's arm with noticeable tenderness, her action utterly controlling her environment in that it placed Michael on pause, froze Douglas and demanded the attention of the rest. "Michael is involved with an organisation that campaigns for the rights of migrant workers. He does counselling sessions for them in the evenings. Mo Thomas – my head of RE – also does some work for the same group." A dismissive expression saying, 'Bloody do-gooders!' in silence fixed in David's face. "It was Michael's contact with Mo that led to his invitation to speak to year nine last Wednesday, otherwise I would probably have never met up with him. It's all very fortuitous. And if I hadn't invited him tonight, we probably wouldn't have known anything about Rosita's problems, which we should know about."

"You've spoken with Mo, then, since Wednesday?" Michael asked. Janet nodded, turning to face him again and letting go of his arm. "Well Rosita first came to see me about a year ago and she's been back about once a month ever since. She has two children, currently living with her husband's parents. As you know, the older one is secondary school age now and in the Philippines everyone wants the best education they can not quite afford. When you know that paying just a bit extra will get your kids into a better school which, in itself, will have a major impact on their eventual chances of getting work, you do everything you can to make it happen. So she's enrolled the boy in a Catholic school in Quezon City…

You've visited the Philippines, I think? Rosita told me that you and David went with her when she made her last visit in August last year, so you know the place where she lives."

Both David and Janet confirmed, but David continued, interrupting. "Look. We pay her the rate for the job and always have done. In fact, we have always paid her extra. We've never once missed a payday and always accommodated any special requests. And if you saw the place that she calls home, made of tin sheets and hardboard in the middle of what looks like a rubbish dump, I reckon she has nothing to complain about."

"She has never complained about her terms of employment," said Michael. "And she is certainly not complaining about the pay. We have hundreds of Filipina domestics visiting our resource centre in Kilburn and when Filipinas get together, they talk. Believe me, they talk," he repeated with emphasis, noting the calm that David maintained. When would he go for it? "And Rosita, financially, has one of the best deals in town. And unlike many of the others, she feels quite secure. You have been excellent employers and she would not dream of leaving. She would never want to give up conditions like these. But she is short of money because secondary schools in the Philippines can be fiercely expensive. There are the extra school fees, of course, but there's also money for travelling, uniforms, books and everything else you need to go to school. She's not doing anything extravagant. She just wants something better for her kids. So she has been trying to earn a bit extra on the side..."

"We'll give her a rise," said David. So out of character was this apparently spontaneous and bounteous gesture that Douglas, Marie and Karl all stopped chewing at the same time, froze and then eyed one another with blank-faced surprise.

"The last time you gave anything a rise was in 1963, when you tried to bake bread," muttered Karl, prompting Douglas to choke on a farfalle.

As his face turned red above the napkin he held to his mouth to hide the doughy laugh, Marie said with her own playful giggle, "Pasta is supposed to choke priests, Douglas, not you."

"Darling, there are farfalle, butterflies. Priest chokers are strozzapreti and they tend to be short and fat," corrected Karl.

"As are some priests," said Michael. Janet's silent prompt registered a moment later. Throughout the banter, she had continued to face him,

253

eager to air the rest of the story. "Where was I? Yes. She's been trying to earn a bit extra money on the side by doing a few things in her spare time, but the…"

"Such as?" asked David, a new brusqueness, a directness crystallizing in his manner.

"Favours mainly. Favours for people," replied Michael without hesitation. "Just favours. But some of the favours proved to be a bit bigger than expected."

Janet fell into a fit of laughter. Father Bernard, who had quietly picked away at his meal since receiving his loaded plate suddenly put down his fork with a clatter and stared at her. He had known this wonderful, this amazing, this dedicated, this committed, this competent, this professional woman for years, during the entirety of his decade of involvement with St Mary's governing body. He had helped her through troubled times. He had marvelled at her achievements. But in all that time, she had never been just a woman. And now, as she laughed with abandon, he saw for the first time her stunning beauty, her overt and inviting eroticism, her capacity for ecstasy.

One by one, everyone at table caught the same bug. Janet could not stop laughing. She went on and on. Even David, who suspected he might know the joke, joined in, just a little. It took minutes for order to descend by degree and, still not quite able to speak, Janet tried to say, "And from personal experience I can confirm that it is a big one," but her words were indistinct, clouded by new belly laughs. Douglas and Marie jerked to face one another, silently asking if the other had caught what their mother had said, but shrugs and shakes confirmed confusion.

Shock can play its tricks. When confronted by the abyss, people cannot predict how they will react. The day Janet feasted her eyes on John Mwangangi's smashed head, her first act had been to laugh. She had never known why, but she could always remember that laugh, relive its involuntary command of her body. And it was not just an instinctive intake or expulsion of breath. It had been a real laugh, a sustained reaction lasting several seconds. In the movies, of course, it hams its way into tears, but her reality of laughter on that day subsided to a blank silence, a dark unfeeling, perhaps anaesthetised pit in the memory destined for eternal emptiness.

But at table, it was not Janet on whom shock played its trick. The game was up. David's face changed, as if in slow motion, from displaying its share of the communal hilarity, through a dawning confusion that publicly confessed self-doubt and finally setting in a blank tensionless glare that contrasted with the hyper-activity of his neck, as it turned jerkily to share the expression with Michael, Karl, Marie, Janet, Douglas, Janet again. He knew his wife never laughed like that unless sex was near, usually accompanied by copious use of the word 'fuck'. This stranger, this left-wing religious paddy, bog country, bleeding Marxist, Irish bastard, shit face of a priest who had invaded his home was a confidante of Rosita, the maid he had screwed whenever the opportunity arose, and his opportunity, despite his advancing years, seemed to be rising all the time. And Janet knew, because he, that red-faced bog country Catholic hypocrite, he knew. And Karl knew. Time out of the office, indeed. Mobile switched off. Not working to his diary. He knew. And no doubt the soft fart of a school governor on his left knew, because his faithful pious wife had probably confessed to him, in the interests of the school, of course. And Marie knew, because Karl had obviously told her. And she had tried to hide the fact. That's why Karl had only broached the subject after she left the room. It had been a way of keeping her nose out of it. The scheming little bitch! And now she would want her pound of flesh, no doubt cut from his most sensitive spot, his bleeding wallet. And who the fuck cared if his pervert of a son knew? Who the fuck cared? And I don't care either.

But whatever reason plodded through David Smythe's privacy, his body did what shocked reaction demanded. He stood up, slowly, as if preparing to deliver a speech. And then he stood there looking lost and confused, his head still turning to interrogate reaction. The laughter, save for a stifled gag, stopped. For a minute or so, they grew steadily silent as the sensation subsided. And then they were silent. David's mouth opened a few times, and then closed, determinedly. But he stayed on his feet. And they all started laughing again, this time at him.

"Dad, if it's Grace you want to say, I'd ask one of those two over there. They are more qualified," said Douglas, again hardly able to stay on his chair. And then David Smythe spoke. Turning to Janet and reaching across the two, seated priests, he tried to touch her. "I'm sorry," he said. "I'm sorry, darling."

Janet's reaction surprised everyone, but not herself. She continued to laugh but, holding David's hand so that his arm had to pass over the heads of Fathers Michael and Bernard, his down-facing palm apparently blessing their holiness, she stood and passed behind her guests, who had to duck a little to keep out of the way. She needed three steps to approach him, taken like a medieval courtesan pacing the angular formality of a distorted dance. And she hugged him and he kissed the top of her head as she buried her face in his chest. He had turned bright pink and looked as if he could be employed as space heating. Janet too was flushed and bright eyed from her bout of laughter. There was not a hint of emotion when she spoke. "C'est plus la même chose. At least you were paying someone's school fees. It's not the first time that international aid has screwed the recipient, but usually the aid comes first."

Realising now the seriousness of the occasion, Douglas and Marie were silent, watching their parents, privately knowing what was never expressed between them. Michael took the opportunity to have a final mouthful of pasta and crushed the new silence with the clatter of fork on pot. Bernard, who had already finished his meal, readjusted his neatly placed cutlery, adding chorus to Michael's lead. And then, with what seemed strangely like determination, Janet disengaged, returned to her place, sat down and replaced the napkin on her lap. She had already taken two fresh mouthfuls of pasta by the time David had returned, slowly, to his seat.

"Well how's that for a bunch of donkeys?" said Douglas.

"You can have a herd of donkeys, a drove of donkeys or a pace of donkeys, darling, but not a bunch," corrected Janet. "Bunch of keys, flowers et cetera, yes. But not donkeys."

Marie looked across at her mother and smiled. She loved her mother. She loved her so much she had no words to express it. And then, for her, reality again prodded. With a sudden start, she looked up to locate the children she had momentarily forgotten. And by God they were both asleep. Carla in her pushchair, where she had spent the entire evening and Paul sprawled across the floor cushions in the corner, cushions that Janet always left there so her grandson could play during the family meal.

"All right. Plates please," said Janet, inviting the guests to pass over their plates, which she took, carefully scraping any leftovers, of which there were few, into the empty serving dish, before stacking them neatly. Though they had not called her, Rosita reappeared in the doorway, as if by divination, with a tray on which she had arranged seven large wine goblets in a circle, each with foaming yellow zabaglione. Duly served with sweet, the guests leaned slightly and politely back in their chairs while the last remnants of the main course were piled officiously and with exaggerated care onto Rosita's tray. It was as if she, not the tray or the crockery, was being protected from damage. Throughout, David said nothing, but he did look at her and give a discreet smile.

And then they ate again, the first spoonfuls for both Marie and Douglas prompting prolonged "Mmmms" of satisfaction, joy that communicated more than taste. "Mum, it's the same every time. You are absolutely wonderful," said Douglas before starting to lap his next spoonful like a dog in an attempt to make the sensation last longer. The new course seemed to restart the evening, as if the new taste drew a curtain that started a new act, the previous one complete if unresolved, its drama yet to be fully explained and its consequences still unknown.

"So what's next?" asked Marie, her manner newly relaxed by the children's slumbers. The unexpected directness of her intervention required repetition to make it clear. "Mum told me that you are ready to retire, Father Michael. What are you going to do next?"

"Now there's a question," he said, smacks of his lips testifying to his own satisfaction with the sweet. "A complete change. I can't continue with what I was doing as a worker-priest. It's a rule for us that we have to work like anyone else and be subject to the same conditions. I can't be a special case, so I have to retire. I've got several other interests, such as…" He looked up to see if the conversation might force its way back to his dealings with Rosita, but the business was clearly to remain unfinished, compartmentalised perhaps for later examination in private. They had moved on. "…Well several things, but none of them is enough for me. I need a new challenge, so I'm off back to Africa." He sat up a little and beamed a proud smile that elicited no active acknowledgement, except, he unexpectedly and slowly came to realise, from his right, where Father Bernard stiffened to sit right back in his chair, turning his way, as if to get a better view of his fellow guest against the strain of his long sightedness, "I left unfinished business in Kenya and I'm going back."

It was Janet, of course, who ought to have reacted, but she remained stolidly unmoved, calculatedly and carefully re-instating her headmistress persona, her feelings well covered by a public presence of calm and control.

"I had to leave Kenya after my road accident, at least for a while, and then my priorities changed. My faith changed as well, and I never went back. But things are different now. I won't be doing any missionary work. The priests in Kitui are all Kenyans now. When I was there we only had two Kenyan priests in the whole diocese, one of whom is still there. It surprises me that he's even still alive, given the speed at which he used to ride his motor bike on those whores of roads."

"Father Peter," interrupted Janet, her tension palpably released, no longer being able to control the swelling frustration to speak, just to say something so that when the real words came she would retain control.

"Wow, you have some memory," he said, turning to face her and inserting his last and only flat-filled spoon of zabaglione into his mouth.

"He was fierce crack altogether," she told him with a smile which he returned, amplified.

"So there's no need for missionary work like I used to do at the parish level any more. But there are other things that need to be done. The world has changed in the last thirty years. Things have moved on and, if anything, they are a bit sadder. When I worked in Africa, we were enthusiastic. We talked of 'development'," he said, indicating the quotes with two fingers of each hand, "and we talked of 'progress' and ending poverty. In Africa today, the issue we now have to cope with is AIDS. So I am going to work full time in a hospice in Nairobi where they care for terminally ill AIDS patients."

When Janet pushed her chair back and bent forward to thrust her face into her hands, they all thought she was ill. Or perhaps it was the delayed shock of David's revelation that he had been unfaithful to her again. Slowly she sat upright, breathed very long and deep several times, flexing every muscle in her face as if they needed exercise. From where she had pushed her chair, she could look across Michael's back, half turned towards her, to Father Bernard who, concerned, had turned in his chair to face her. He was still sitting bolt upright, his chair pulled back from the table.

"How did it go on Wednesday?" He had said so little during the meal and its prelude in the lounge that the others found themselves momentarily stunned as they were reminded of the power of his voice. That evening, Bernard's previous contributions had all been polite mutterings, soft punctuation of other's conversation. Now speaking for himself, his voice was full, sonorous and highly musical, capable of delivering a sermon to a large congregation without a microphone. "I couldn't get into school to see you either yesterday or today. I had assumed that your invitation tonight was to clarify things. You don't need me to tell you how important this is for the school."

"They agreed," she said flatly, if somewhat cryptically, stretching the two words into a string to bind her.

"So when is it to happen?"

"We start the process immediately with a view to appointing by Easter."

"And you are still convinced that we can appoint internally if there are no reasonable external candidates?"

"She can do the job. Whether she should do it is up to her. It must be her decision. But I'm confident that she will apply. Whoever else applies, she will be short-listed and then it's up to the appointment panel. If she decides she wants it she will interview well and she'll get it. Only a superb external candidate could possibly be better suited to the job and in either case the school wins."

"Let's hope so."

"What on earth is going on?" asked David, each apparently private interchange between Bernard and his wife ratcheting up his nervously wheezing frustration.

Janet pulled her chair forward, back to its place at table, and answered, her voice so completely matter of fact, she might have been addressing a staff meeting to convey the most mundane of routine arrangements. "I've been granted a sabbatical. I applied at the start of term, I've done thirty years of service. I've been head for a decade and it's time the school had some new blood to keep it fresh. I've not gone stale, but I want to make sure that I don't. I can't have early retirement, because they don't give that away too easily nowadays. I'm still too young."

"You're fifty-four, not sixty-bloody-four," shouted David, a plea implied somewhere within.

"I'll be fifty-five before the end of the second term. I've been granted a two-year sabbatical. That will make me fifty-seven when it's over. They may ask me to do a year or so as an adviser, or I could go freelance and do some inspection work. But I think the most likely outcome will be that after the sabbatical they will grant me early retirement."

Janet and David had both noticed how little reaction there had been from Michael. He had listened intently, absent-mindedly tracing the edges of his place mat. Realising that both of them were now staring at him, he looked from one to the other, shrugged his shoulders and returned to his self-appointed endeavour to fray the mat's edge with his finger. There was a long pause.

"It's a terrific opportunity, but..." Bernard's words were cut short by Michael.

"Kairos." It stopped the show. "Kairos," he repeated. "Not a revelation, like St Paul suffered on the road to Damascus. There's nothing dramatic or particularly sudden about kairos. It's a lovely word, a theological term meaning a moment of opportunity, a chance to be grasped as it passes, for pass it will if not taken. I once heard a talk by a genius of a man – also a priest – who had been a political prisoner for years. When he was eventually released, he gave a lecture tour. He told a simple story, a parable, about some people who rented a bus to go to market, but it broke down on the way. They waited for help, hoping that another vehicle would pass by but, like when we were in Kenya..." he nodded toward Janet without looking at her, "...there was very little traffic on that road and nothing came along for hours. They waited in the sun getting more and more depressed when a bloke on a motorbike came along and told them that the market was finished and that no one would pass that way until the next day. So the people from the bus got together, talked through what the problem might be, pooled their skills and fixed the bus. They had missed the market, but at least they got home and they had solved their own problems. They had learned to work together to achieve things that otherwise they would have deferred to others and so they had become empowered. And the moral of the tale? The guy on the bike was the Messiah. They heard his words and acted on them. They took the opportunity that presented itself and changed their own condition. That's kairos, the moment of opportunity. It sounds like Janet has one of her own."

"But..." David managed no more.

"That just about sums it up," said Janet, checking that her words had registered with each of the others before turning to face Michael. "I saw an advert in the Times Ed at the end of last term. It was for a new campaign by the people who originally sponsored my time in Kenya. It said they were now looking for experienced people to do quite specific professional jobs. And there it was in black and white, a full page spread. As I read through it, I saw myself written into the text, my name already attached to one of the jobs they had on offer. It was giving me the chance to do something I have dreamed about for years. So I applied."

"Bugger me," muttered David. "When was that?"

"I had the interview in August and they offered me the job there and then, on the spot. It's taken me three months or so to work out the exact conditions with the authority. I obviously didn't want to prejudice my pension and I didn't want to let anyone down. But, like Michael says, now is the right time for me to act. Everything is possible. All the pieces are in place. I have the experience to contribute. Thirty years of service easily qualifies me for a sabbatical, though, I must say, two years is a very generous offer. I have a talented, loyal, ambitious, young and capable deputy, so whoever applies for my job from outside the school, we will have a serious candidate from inside. They need someone to play a role that fits my skills and experience perfectly. I am solvent and have precisely no financial worries. My children are both well established and independent. And," she said, turning full face towards David, "I have a kind, caring, considerate husband who loves me enough to want what I want, to grant me my wishes, to support me and to continue buggering the maid in my absence."

He knew it was coming. At some point she would strike and now it was done. So it was with new composure that David posed the question he had to ask and, as he spoke, his eyes glared a question at Michael, whose head remained bowed, offering no contact or clue. "So pray, dear wife, our very own headmistress, pray tell us what you are to do."

Janet giggled again. Was it shock at the revelation, or the joy of victory? "Well, dearest David, for two years I am to fulfil the role and function of an advisory teacher, to implement a programme of secondary school management reform in Africa, based in the Ministry of Education, Nairobi, Kenya."

Bernard straightened further in his chair and shook his head. But he also smiled, because he knew that this is what Janet wanted. He wanted what she wanted. David was flabbergasted. He could not have spoken even if he had tried. Marie, Karl and especially Douglas almost applauded her, but they did not, accepting the gravity of her words with personal sadness mixed with joy close to elation. Their father, after all, was clearly excluded from the celebration. Michael simply did not move.

"Coffee, ma'am?" were the words that preceded the re-opening of the dining room door and the emergence of Rosita bearing another tray with all the accoutrements needed to serve the after dinner beverage.

As Rosita set down the tray on the table and began to collect the zabaglione glasses, a strange normality reasserted itself. David rose, mumbling something about brandy. Douglas and Marie whispered to one another. Bernard shook his head, though not in reply to David's implied offer of a drink.

Janet turned to Michael, who had still not raised his head, as if concentrating on the detail of San Gimignano towers pictured on his place mat. "Did you know? You work with Mo Thomas, don't you? Had I let something slip to her? Did you know?"

He did not answer, but he would, later.

Boniface

Boniface ought to have been a priest. As a schoolboy in Mwingi Junior Seminary, his heart had indeed been set on this one ambition, but despite the fact that he himself and several of his classmates openly expressed their desire to join Holy Orders, neither he nor any of his peers saw the idea through. Many in the school, of course, had espoused the idea as a concubine, adopted it for a while out of mere pragmatic convenience to secure their privileged place in Father Patrick's secondary school. Others, with similar end result, had professed the ambition of joining the priesthood with neither the maturity to comprehend the difficulty of the task nor the mettle to see it through. In their eyes it was merely a job and a job worth doing, demanding and receiving almost unqualified respect from others. In this poor area where, through the example of its fine schools and towering new concrete cathedral, the Church was effectively the vanguard of modern life, where the priesthood was a job fit even for a European, where every priest had a car, a motorcycle and at least one radio, in this place boys wanted to be priests like those elsewhere want to be pilots, astronauts, film stars or sometimes even dustbin men.

For Boniface, though, the priesthood was neither pipe dream nor ruse. With all his heart and mind he strove towards his ambition, guided by Father Patrick's considered advice. Having administered the school for twenty years since its foundation, the priest had seen many students come and go, but in all that time only a handful had made the transition from junior to senior seminary. Only two of those had as yet been ordained as priests and he prided himself that even in their earliest months in his school, he had earmarked both of them as probable candidates. Such cases were rare, and Father Patrick was rarely wrong. Though he was responsible for the running and development of the school and also for parish work besides, it had always been his practice to provide extra tuition and counselling for those boys who, in his opinion, promised the most. From the very first day that he entered Mwingi Junior Seminary, Boniface Mutisya had been identified for this privileged treatment. He had given the boy four years' special catechetical and theological instruction at the rate of one hour per day during term time. Boniface, though never a bright child, had been pleased to be so treated and had stuck to his appointed task diligently and enthusiastically without a single word of complaint.

In return for the boy's extra studies of the Bible and catechism, Father Patrick had given up much of his own free time to ensure that the boy would surmount the formidable but necessary academic hurdles. When, at the end of four years of arduous and self-disciplined study the boy seemed destined to obtain the leaving certificate passes he needed to progress to the senior seminary in Nairobi, his path in life had seemed ready-prepared. All Boniface had to do was keep standing. The momentum of his ambition would surely see him through.

From the beginning his credentials had been perfect. His father, a trader in Thitani market, was not only a devout Roman Catholic, but also, at least in the public eye, possessed a near guaranteed cash income from which he could provide school fees. As a patron of the Church he had constant dealings with first Father John O'Hara during his many years of service in Migwani and then later with his successor, Father Michael Doherty. His infant son thus received his early teaching from a future bishop. The child had sung in John O'Hara's choir, had learned to don a fine white surplice to help at services and later, when he began his schooling in one of Migwani's primary schools, had lived in the mission house itself for some months until a boarding place within the school's compound became vacant.

John O'Hara had thus become in part a father to the boy and, when news arrived that the long-standing parish priest was to become Bishop, it seemed only natural that Boniface Mutisya, suitably groomed and surpliced, would share the platform at the investiture. As he stood aside, proudly holding the heavy gilt cross high as if it were feather-light, and saw a grave-faced O'Hara bedecked with the resplendent robes of his office, the boy wept out of wonder. He was a still slightly built seventeen by then, though in the eyes of his mentor, still very much a primary school child. Within a year, however, he had made the desired transition and had embarked upon his four years of study and instruction in the Mwingi Junior Seminary. The new dignity with which the now enrobed O'Hara had greeted the boy that day, however, lived on in glowing memory and, if anything, grew both brighter and stronger with the passing of time, until he himself began to see it as nothing less than a blinding revelation. Exam passes, and, on Father Patrick's recommendation, a guaranteed place in the Nairobi Senior Seminary reinforced the vision. So by the time Boniface Mutisya, now twenty-one, made his way home from Mwingi at the end of his final term, both his heart and mind were set, firmly cemented on his one and burning ambition. Over the following years, he would begin to see that moment of homecoming as the high point of his life, a watershed from which he had subsequently drained to be captured in the insignificance of the general flow. Indeed he would look back and conclude that he had been denied the one extra step, which would have permanently raised him to a higher plane, a plateau sanctuary that, once achieved, would have sustained itself.

***

Boniface Mutisya sat proudly upright in the front passenger seat of Father Michael's rattling Toyota. Not once did he turn to check the comfort of Josephine, his wife, as she struggled to hold their sick child steady against the constant lurching of the car. This apparent lack of concern was no mere sham. Today Father Michael, a reckless driver at the best of times, was truly excelling himself, propelling the car sideways as much as forward along the pot-holed dirt road at over sixty miles an hour. Boniface was simply terrified, so terrified for his own safety that any consideration of his ailing child could take only second place behind an undiluted and all-consuming self-interest. And, so strong was his need to maintain masculine dignity before his wife that he dare not turn to face her lest she should see the helplessness of his fear. Thus, with consciously imposed control, he faced only forward with head held high and hands clasped on his lap, successfully suppressing each frequent and fearful compulsion to close his eyes and grab something solid.

There were times, surely, when Father Michael had fallen asleep at the wheel, when the car momentarily lurched sideways or sped defiantly towards a seemingly bottomless pothole in the heavily pitted road. Then, desperately trying to swallow his apparently rising gut, though offering no external clue to his inner plight, Boniface would steal an occasional sideways glance out of the very corner of his eye, if only to reassure himself that Father Michael was still there. On each nerve-racked occasion the picture was the same. With his head lolling on one side and camouflage hat pulled low over his eyes, Michael leaned towards the open side window, where his forearm rested. With silent nonchalance, he mouthed an Irish nationalist song through lips still pursed by the same impatience with which he had greeted Boniface's urgent plea earlier that morning. The violent, radiant red of the priest's sunburnt face heightened, Boniface believed, by anger, which he himself had caused, seemed to demand silence, or more accurately, amid the bangs and crashes of this now loose car on the quite awful road, seemed to demand that no one should speak, even in the odd moments when the young man's fear subsided and allowed him to find the necessary words.

***

Knowing that he was about to receive the praise and adulation of his entire family, Boniface stood and watched, as the bus from which he had just alighted set off on the long road to the south with its gears clanking and its exhaust spouting irregular clouds of rolling black smoke. And still the owners of this heap of cream and orange rusty scrap had the cheek to name it Mrembo, a handsome young man.

Every day this bus ran from Mwingi to Mombasa, or from Mombasa to Mwingi, one of a pair of almost identical buses that operated the service. The three hundred miles took over thirteen hours, mainly because the first hundred and fifty were on dirt roads, where the buses could do no more than sixty miles per hour between pick-ups - and this often sideways! Most passengers, however, used the service only for local journeys, which was better for both the owners and the operators of the Mrembo buses. To travel all the way to Mombasa, Boniface would have needed only twenty-five shillings, whereas the ten or so miles from Mwingi to Thitani cost him almost five. It might have been relatively cheaper per mile to travel all the way to the end of the route - Boniface knew this because his mathematics teacher in the Junior Seminary had used the Mrembo bus journey to Mombasa as a means of teaching averages - but he was glad he was getting off in Thitani. Not only was this home, but he was still in one piece, which he might not have been had he taken Mrembo all the way to Mombasa, as demonstrated by a secondary school mathematics class on probability. This company had a reputation for employing very poor people as drivers and there were always many stories of the buses running out of fuel or crashing.

With his mind aglow with the joy of achievement, but also tempered by a sadness born of a nagging fear for his future, he waved goodbye to the school friends with whom he had shared his last end of term journey from Mwingi. They all knew that the day was a landmark. From here their lives would separate, quite possibly never to cross again. For four years they had travelled to and from school together, had shared the same Sungura dormitory during term time and had attended the same classes to achieve their very different ends. Now, with the departure of this particular bus of the Mrembo company, a division of Mulonzya Enterprises of Mwingi, into a growing cloud of dust of its own making, the pattern was set for change. As Boniface watched it disappear into the near distance, and with it also the happy if somewhat obscene gestures of his friends through the back window, he knew he was waving goodbye to an era, finally dismissing his youth.

Still casting frequent glances toward the fast fading growl of the Diesel engine, as the bus laboured to the top of a shallow hill to the west of the town, Boniface ambled across the hard-baked bare red earth of the market place. He walked as quickly as he could, but was constantly hindered by the swinging of the large wooden box he carried. Such boxes, strong, dovetail-jointed structures, finely made by local carpenters, were one of the constants of school life. Every student had one, invariably padlocked through a steel hasp on the front and kept tucked away beneath the bunks in the dormitory. In it were stored a student's worldly possessions, which always made the ritual termly trip to and from home in their entirety. Thus, inside this strongbox which now Boniface struggled to carry, there were two complete school uniforms, that is two pale blue shirts and two pairs of grey shorts, four books which Father Patrick had given him during his time in the seminary, exercise books full of copied text book notes for each of the subjects he had studied, and a few toiletries, a toothbrush and a half-used cake of soap. It was the paper of the exercise books that made it heavy. He had made a lot of notes, especially during the evening prep sessions in the library, when he had almost succeeded in copying out in his meticulous if rather fussy hand a complete geography textbook. The information was useful for the exam. Boniface now knew everything there was to be known about the Saint Lawrence Seaway, its construction, method of operation, cost, uses, advantages, disadvantages, maintenance and its possible future development. He had developed an intimate understanding of the Great Lakes of North America, the economy of the towns on their shores and of their vast hinterlands in both Canada and the United States of America. Boniface had understood all this, despite himself never having seen a stretch of water wider than the cattle dam in Migwani and never having visited a town larger than Mwingi, whose four hundred or so inhabitants had never regarded themselves as urbanised.

But after four years of travelling back and forth on occasional weekends as well as ends of term, the box that he struggled to lift was now much the worse for wear. It now looked nothing less than battered, with evidence of recent repair. Its swinging dead weight seemed to stretch the young man's thin arm and impart a limp to his walk as its bulk impeded his step. By the time he reached the shade of the neat concrete cube which was his father's shop, his beautifully smooth skin was dripping with sweat and shone black in the fierce light of the afternoon sun. Then, having reached the building and sighed with relief as he stepped inside, he could only watch helplessly as the box flew open. The padlock itself had held, but the strain on the lid had broken the hasp, ripping the securing nails from the wood and splitting the frame. The resulting crash shattered the silence inside the empty shop and brought both his mother and father rushing in to investigate from the rear of the building. Almost together, but from different sides, their faces appeared in the open doorway behind the shop's counter to peer through the relative darkness of the interior.

Their initial concern immediately turned to smiling joy and both came forward to greet their son. They shook his hand, embraced him and offered hearty if premature congratulations for doing well in his examinations. Though the boy was careful to remind them that no one would know the results for some months, the obvious solidity of his confidence made his warnings sound more like acceptance of their praise. Soon his mother had returned to the rear of the shop to brew a pot of tea and the boy set about the task of repacking his scattered belongings back into the broken box.

"When will you get your results, my son?" asked the boy's father. It was clear that he had only just registered what Boniface had said some moments before about the inevitable delay.

"In about two or three months," answered Boniface, kneeling whilst he carefully folded a clean and pressed pair of shorts.

"And what are your plans until then?" The father felt the strangeness of this question deeply within a psyche that denied that such a position was possible. Until that moment, he had always looked upon Boniface as a child. He had never before sought an open opinion from him, having always merely imposed his own.

"There are many things I could do, but there are two in particular. I could certainly help here in the shop..." The boy's voice tailed off into silence, thus transforming the statement into a question.

The other shook his head gravely. "You can see for yourself what business is like. No one in this place has any money these days. What little people have buys them food, maize and beans, not these things." With an almost cynically dismissive gesture, the man waved an arm in the vague direction of his shop's sparsely filled shelves.

Boniface complied with the unintended direction and looked about the room. The four walls of the box were all shelved now. The town's carpenter had done a wonderful job. They were fine deep shelves, made from new wood, unpainted. True, the hardboard did bow a little here and there under the weight of the goods displayed on top, but that could always be repaired. And there were now goods on display on all the shelves. Not one of the shelves could actually be described as 'stocked', but they were not empty. There was at least something on every surface. A small pile of tinned fish here. A pyramid of match boxes there. A fine display of eight tins of Kimbo cooking fat at the back. Bags of sugar and wheat flour. Everything, however, was coated in a fine layer of red dust, thrown up from the road outside by the six buses that passed through Thitani each day, a dust borne on the incessant wind to every corner of the town. Only the open packet of Sportsman on the shelf behind the single glass display cabinet looked as if it had been touched recently. People would always want to buy a cigarette or two.

"We haven't needed to re-stock the shelves for ages. And we're not even taking enough money to cover our costs at the moment. I want to sell some new lines, but we've no capital."

There was a pause here. Both Boniface and his father wanted to speak, but it seemed that both knew that whatever they said would be misinterpreted by the other. For Boniface there were only possibilities, whereas his father could see only difficulties.

"Could you get a job as an untrained teacher for a while? Then you would be earning a salary..."

Boniface again set about the repacking of his box as he began his reply. "That was my second option." An expression of profound relief spread across his father's face as he realised that there might after all be some agreement, some release from a predicament which threatened to be insoluble. "Father Michael came to see me in Mwingi last Sunday. He said that the new primary school is finished and will open next term. He asked me if I would like to teach there until my results come through."

"Boniface, that is wonderful news." Julius Mutisya, the boy's youthful-looking father, was clearly overjoyed. Privately he had hoped and prayed that things would turn out like this. But there was still that little area of nagging doubt. He thought for a moment before saying more. "So it is to be for just two months until your results are published? Why can't it be for longer?"

Boniface looked up and smiled. Only his deep respect for his father stopped him from breaking into laughter. "Because he is sure that I will pass all my exams. Of course if I don't then I'll have to think again, but both Father Michael and Father Patrick are convinced that I will have no trouble in getting the grades I need to enter the seminary."

"You are still sure that you want to be a priest, Boniface? You don't think that it would be better if you trained as a teacher and went on to earn a good salary?"

Boniface made no attempt to answer this. Never before had his father so directly questioned his oft-stated ambition and the boy simply did not know how to react. Initially his father, a man of the Church all his life and a devout Roman Catholic, had praised his son's professed intentions, but had also always responded with a slight smile and that gentle, if metaphorical, pat on the head with which a parent publicly excuses a child's naiveté. Having been convinced that his son would somehow grow out of his ambition to join holy orders, as time passed he had been forced to give the often expressed proposition more serious consideration. Father Michael had even begun to take him aside after Sunday mass to discuss the boy's future. But even when Boniface took up his place in Mwingi's junior seminary, any thought that he might actually still want to become a priest four years later was inevitably dismissed as utterly implausible. After all, most boys at the seminary regarded it merely as another secondary school, and a very good one at that, in an area where there were too few such institutions to satisfy demand for academic education. There was always great competition for places in Saint Patrick's Junior Seminary and whatever his son's eventual ambition might be, he had surely been right to grasp the opportunity which presented itself when he was offered the chance to study there.

The fees had been no problem then. Business, whilst never particularly good, had been adequate, and had provided enough of a return to satisfy all the family's modest needs as well as a small surplus to invest in more stock. Before long, however, the dry spell which had affected the whole area for some time was renamed a drought and showed no signs of relenting. Life grew tougher for everyone. People needed food rather than new cooking pots or clothes and Mutisya's small but once dependable trade deserted him. He had no licence to trade grain, none to market animal skins or meat. He could not even deal in the sisal fibre that all his customers were trying to sell to raise those few shillings needed to supplement a poor harvest. Those commodities were not the province of the small shopkeepers. Instead they were traded exclusively by the managed shops, which were part of larger businesses whose interests stretched across the length and breadth of the District. Only these larger concerns had sufficient capital to effect the bulk buying as well as selling of staple produce, which made dealing in such commodities worthwhile. Mutisya's shop could no longer offer what people wanted. After all, he could never have been described as a trader. Julius Mutisya was merely a shopkeeper and, under these new conditions, he could keep his business alive, but its revenues could no longer sustain his family, for he was effectively excluded from the major economic life of the area.

The foodstuffs he could sell, the pre-packed or tinned products of the food industry, were all too expensive even to be considered by his clientele and, because he was forced to rely on other people's transport for his deliveries, he could no longer compete with the larger shops in Thitani market. Their proprietors also owned the lorries and the profit they made from running his orders paid for their own transport. Effectively he paid their costs and this inflated his own prices relative to theirs. The fact that Julius also had a young family to support compounded the problem and gradually over the last two years he had been forced to sell off much of his existing stock at a loss in order to raise cash to pay school fees. Father Michael had helped by putting two hundred shillings of his own money towards each year's seminary fees for Boniface, but the bulk of the burden remained on Julius's shoulders. If anything, this burden had increased, as local conditions had further worsened.

For some time Julius had looked forward to the day when Boniface would complete his schooling, for only then, when this greatest of his financial burdens was lightened, could another of his fast-maturing children have his chance of an education. Even then, the spectre of hunger would never be far away. Things would always be difficult, at least until the area began to prosper again, even in some small way, but so deep was his conviction that a worthwhile future for his children would be secured only through their education, that he remained willing to make almost any sacrifice short of death to accomplish this end. And thus the day had arrived when the first stage was complete. In his eyes, Boniface, his first-born son, had been granted his rightful turn and the privilege would now pass on to another. But, and here was the worry, from what Father Michael had told him over the previous weeks, he had begun to see that things were destined not to be quite that simple.

His son was determined to enter the priesthood. There could no longer be any doubt about that. Boniface was now mature enough to know his own mind, a fact that Father Michael had been keen to point out repeatedly, and at length, perhaps after every Sunday mass Julius had attended for a year and a half or more. Julius, though equally keen to praise his son's motives and proud to think that one day he could be a minister of the Church, had been forced to divulge to the priest the financial difficulties he faced. If Boniface were to embark upon what could be several years of extra study, his younger brothers would suffer permanently. The fees for the senior seminary were high and would not be paid entirely by the Church until Boniface had completed two years there. Michael, of course, tried to dispel the father's fears, saying that, in his son's case, the Diocese would be able to provide a special grant to cover all expenses. He could make no firm promise at that point, though, for the eventual decision was not his to make. The priest, however, was about as sure as he could be that he could secure such a grant for Boniface.

For Julius Mutisya, however, that was never going to be good enough for it solved only part of the problem. In his opinion, it was Boniface's unquestionable duty to share responsibility for the family's welfare. Julius had looked forward to the time when Boniface would earn a school leaver's salary, help to pay school fees for one of the other children and even invest in the family business, possibly by becoming a partner alongside himself and thus help it prosper again. And that was not all. Boniface was his first-born son. When he married, his own first-born son would take his grandfather's name and thereby give that name new life. That grandfather would be Julius Mutisya Maluki, himself, and the continuation of his name and through it a family line could only be guaranteed by him.

Again and again Father Michael had tried to dispel the fears. He pointed out that Boniface knew all of his father's concerns and was determined to treat them with the respect they undoubtedly deserved. He tried in vain to reassure the father that the boy had not taken the decision to enter the priesthood lightly, that all possible consequences had been explained to him, that all possible pitfalls had been clearly described. But deeper down within himself the priest knew he was but skirting the major issue, that he was never confronting Mutisya's real fears directly, for the man would not admit them even to himself and thus, never openly expressed, they lay beneath a sheen of public identity which itself would not admit to the existence of deeper fears.

The boy's duty to the rest of the family was only part of the story. What really lay behind Mutisya's reluctance was a fear for the boy himself. Without marriage and therefore without a legitimate child who would bear his name, he would himself always remain a mere boy according to the rules of a culture which had been absorbed rather than suppressed by a veneer of Christianity, whatever that might itself be. As a devout Christian, Mutisya could never openly admit this point - even to himself - but yet it underpinned his deepest fears for his son. Perhaps it was also responsible for a number of his own fears, but he was never going to admit to any of those fears while he could continue to project all of his own unwanted emotions onto those of his son.

What Boniface proposed would result in a form of eternal damnation. Like a Christian child who died without a name, his own son was destined for a kind of non-existence. And in true Christian spirit he saw this cruel limbo as the worst possible state, worst of all when the non-soul in question apparently tolerated the process. Better damned than ignored.

Julius could not see why his son refused to train as a teacher. It was a profession that carried great respect in the community, as well as a regular income. Someone as academically accomplished and now highly qualified as his son could surely expect to become a headmaster within five years of joining the profession, and that would lead not only to greater earnings but also even greater respect from the community. And, as the son often admitted to his father, the teacher is a great moral leader, occupying a position of potentially unrivalled importance in the personal development of his pupils. In many ways, it was a role not far removed from that of a priest. Indeed in some schools, the teacher was a preacher, whether or not he had been officially trained as a priest, so central to the life of those schools was the study of religion. Boniface had resolved to enter the priesthood, but why could he not find a similar fulfilment in a teaching vocation?

And this is where Julius always became utterly confused. He had tried on many occasions to discuss this with his son, never directly linking it to his own son's vocation, of course, but at least attempting to address the intellectual dilemma it presented. Julius had been a Church member for long enough himself to have understood that today's priests, such as Father Michael, were now more interested in their work directly with people, in schools, in health centres and agriculture than they were in the more usual duties of a cleric. He knew that if his son entered the priesthood, he would be trained in this mould, not in the older style of Father O'Hara, who had preceded Michael as parish priest in Migwani. Now Father Michael was always expressing his preference for pastoral work, and said that he saw that as his prime mission. Church work, he had once heard Father Michael say, bored him. He only did it because he had to.

Then why, Julius would ask Boniface, is it not possible for the same pastoral vocation to be pursued with equal effect outside the Church? Why go inside something, just to project yourself out of it all the time? Why become a priest so that you can do God's work through teaching when you can teach anyway and therefore be doing God's work? Now if it was the case that his son saw the Church, itself, as the central pillar of his desire to become a priest, he could accept it - accept it, that is, in theory rather than practice. But in his son's own words, this was not the case.

And then, of course, there was the crucial point of a person's Christian duty to the family. Training as a teacher outside the priesthood would enable Boniface to earn a salary of his own. He would not only be doing God's work for his pupils, he would be able to help the other members of his family to have a chance to develop themselves as he had done, and surely this was also God's work.

At first Boniface could not take his father's dilemma seriously. Perhaps in the past his father had simply not understood what he had so frequently tried to explain, that he could receive any training he needed for a future profession during the years in the seminary and he always intended to be a teaching priest. But also he thought he had successfully explained to his father many times that above all else he wanted to teach the word of God through the Gospels, as he himself had been taught by Father O'Hara and the priests in Mwingi. Surely his father had registered the fact that his salary would always be paid to the Church? And therefore that the Church, itself, was central to everything he wanted to achieve? The more people worked within its structure, the more work it could do and the wider its teaching would spread.

So it was that, during the short pause, which father and son shared, both recalled and re-examined the issue of Boniface's future. Both of them believed they knew every detail of the other's position. Somehow it seemed futile to go through it all again, and yet both father and son knew that here and now they would have to revisit the argument, if only to restate their entrenched positions. Eventually Boniface dared to speak through the growing tension of the silence. "But Father, I can train as a teacher at the seminary. I've told you that before."

Mutisya knew the time had come. Raising his voice to shout, he rapped his hand on the shop's counter to emphasise his conviction. Once broached, his views, which he himself still considered vague, seemed to state, even over-state themselves. "Boniface, you cannot go to the seminary. It is simply out of the question. Why is it that you never listen to what I say? I can't pay the fees."

"Then Father Patrick can get the fees. He has always said that he would help us to pay them if we found it difficult to raise the money. He has said on many occasions that the Church needs people like me and so the Church might even look upon my training as an investment for the future rather than a cost for today. I am sure there will be no problem." Boniface still spoke with great calm. The apparently practical solution he offered, however, did not even begin to address the deeper contradictions that provoked the anger in his father's outburst.

"Why is it that you always think only of yourself, Boniface? Why do you never think of your brothers and sisters? Or your mother? Or even me? You are still young and yet you have had seven years at primary school in Migwani and four years in Mwingi. During all that time you have been a boarding student. You have always eaten well, when here at home your mother and your sisters have often gone hungry. And why? So that we could save the money to pay for your school fees. Now I am not saying that you can never go to the seminary in Nairobi, just that you should be more grateful for all the help you have had and that you should make some attempt, for a while at least, to make some sacrifices of your own. If you go to the seminary, you will effectively deny your brothers and sisters any access to the privilege of education you now seem to take for granted."

"But they could still go to school..." The interjection raised the pitch of Boniface's thin voice. "If the Church will pay my fees then what you would have given to me can go to them."

Julius Mutisya hammered the counter with his fist. The resulting crash was so loud, and his father's words so fierce, that Boniface jumped with fright. "But who will feed you? And who will clothe you? Who will pay for your bus fares and lodgings? Your Church might pay for the tuition, but who will pay for the rest?" A wave of his arm vaguely towards the shop's almost bare shelves ordered Boniface to take notice. "Look at all the stock I've had to sell off at a loss just to bring you this far! I can hardly sell anything over the counter these days except for an odd cigarette and a box of matches, but keeping things on the shelves would be better than losing money on them. The way things are going I will soon be paying people to take it away! No one wants to buy these things. No one here has any money." As he spoke, he took a tin from a shelf behind him and derisively held it up for Boniface to inspect. "Look at this. Tinned mackerel... It's very good food. Very good food indeed. Selling this ought to be very good business here and there's a good profit to be made on it. But I can't sell it. It costs fifteen shillings a tin. Now who is going to pay that much for some strange type of food they have never eaten before just because some government poster they cannot even read tells them it is good for them? In Kitui town I could sell this. There are some Europeans there, and lots of Luos in the District Offices They eat fish all the time. But here, who wants it? No one."

"Then why do you stock it?" There was a hint of impatience in the son's voice, just a suggestion of the dismissive arrogance that sometimes grows hand in hand with the perception, however false, of intellectual superiority.

"Why do I buy it?" Julius Mutisya now almost roared with anger, thus meeting his son's challenge head on. "Look! Look around you!" Again he gestures vaguely at the near empty shelves. "Is any of this going to sell here in Thitani when everyone in this place is now so poor? Never? What on earth do you expect me to stock? Now if I could sell maize, beans, cow peas, and what's more, if I could transport all my stock here myself instead of having to pay someone else to do it, then our troubles would be over. But I can't sell those things. I've no licence. So all I can offer is whatever I can get my hands on at a reasonable price at the wholesaler in Kitui. And just at the moment it happens to be tinned mackerel... that no one wants to buy. But remember, Boniface, that the very people who supply me are also themselves retailers. I can't match their prices, so they get whatever trade there is."

"Then sell the shop."

Julius laughed. "And who would want to buy it? Who would pay good money for a failure in times like these? Physically you might be an adult now, Boniface, but you are still a child in here," he said, condescendingly tapping his finger on his forehead. "I would have to give this shop away under the present circumstances... and then what would I do? Would I simply turn and wave goodbye to all the money and work I've put into it over the years?" He shook his head in answer to his rhetorical question, but in so doing also communicated some of his growing disdain for what he considered to be his son's single-minded selfishness.

When Boniface remained totally silent for some time, Julius continued in a low quiet tone, which quivered with suppressed emotion. "You have had your turn, Boniface. If you really have grown up, if you really are a man now, you would see everything that I have said is true and you would want to begin to stand up for yourself. You would be eager to take on a man's responsibilities and to fulfil your duties to your family. The fact that you seem to be intent on starting... what would it be? ...another seven years of schooling suggests to me that while outwardly you may appear to be a man, in your mind you are still a child, living in a world which is only your own."

Boniface countered quickly, his stuttered words pointing an accusatory finger at the other. "But Father, if you are the Christian man you claim to be, you know that serving God is more important than anything else in life. It is not something that anyone can do. The chance to serve God is a greater privilege than any other a man can receive. I have that privilege. I have been summoned by God to do his work. If I ignore His call then I will have rejected Him, and that is something no man should ever do." He shook his head and finished on a grave accusatory note.

What Boniface was trying to do was bring to the surface the deep sense of guilt that underpinned his father's Christian faith. He hoped that latent responsibilities and duties to the Church would surface and, amplified by the awakened guilt, would convince his father of the imperative nature of his own calling. The strategy was not only convenient, but possessed an internal truth that was also implicitly believed by Boniface. Unfortunately, it failed.

"I am not saying that you can never be a priest. What you decide to do with your life is your own business, and I accept that it would be a tragedy if you were to waste what is surely a very special opportunity. Make no mistake, Boniface, I am indeed very proud that you have been offered the chance of attending senior seminary. But at the same time what I can say is this. All of us here have made great sacrifices to make this possible for you. Now if all you can do is say 'thank you very much, but I need to go on for another seven years', then I will have to say 'no'. We will make no more sacrifices for you unless at least for a time you are willing to do the same for your brothers and sisters. Then, when we have helped them as we have helped you, when maybe things here will be a little better, then you can do with your life what it is your own wish to do. Then you can give your life to God, but first, please Boniface, first give some of it to your family."

Julius Mutisya was right. Boniface could see that clearly, but only in the shallows of reason. In the stranger depths where stronger feelings lie, his conviction remained. If anything, his father's attack strengthened his own resolve to see his ambition through to its conclusion. Surely this was the devil speaking through his own father's mind in order to pose the first of the pitfalls that Father Patrick had described and had warned him to avoid. Christ, himself, had suffered temptation so that he could prove his worthiness to proceed along the path of his life's work and thereby to strengthen his mind in readiness for the even greater tasks ahead. Like Christ himself, he would not be moved; he would not succumb to these crude temptations. For ordinary men, his father's words would be true, but for Boniface, whose calling raised him above ordinary matters onto some higher plane, the words were surely no more than a temptation to test his worthiness to assume his rightful place. No matter what his father demanded of him, whatever his worldly duties to his family might be, he would never ignore his calling. Now he was answerable to God and to Him alone, and so the kernel of conviction could never be cracked.

Boniface offered his father no reply. Having re-packed all the spillage from his box that had lain on the floor between them throughout their confrontation, he slapped the lid shut. Then, with a silent, slightly superior air, he walked out of the shop, and away across the market place, keeping his eyes fixed firmly forward, perhaps focused on his imagined future. Though Julius rushed out onto the veranda to call after him, the son offered nothing to his father, neither a word nor even a single backward glance.

The Mutisya homestead, a cluster of circular earth-brick huts surrounding a tin-roofed concrete house, stood quite near to the main Mwingi road, a mere hundred yards from the shop, though already quite apart from the town. Boniface went straight to his own house, one of the smaller huts on the edge of the group, brushed past the hanging sackcloth which was its door and, after carefully setting down his box on the floor, took up his copy of *Waklisto Wao* and began to study. Before long he had become completely engrossed in his task and lost to time. Whilst reading the Kikamba catechism, he sought the advice he needed and found God's clear command alive in his memory. The message it conveyed was the same as before and demanded continued resolution to see his mission through.

Darkness fell with the passing of unnoticed hours, but Boniface worked on by the flickering light of his oil lamp. Then he remembered the letter, addressed to his father, Julius Mutisya, which Father Patrick had asked him to deliver. In an act of self-satisfying defiance he retrieved it from the disarray of his box, broke the seal and read it.

As expected it contained much praise of himself, high praise indeed, not only of the standard of his academic achievements, but also of his commitment to the Church and his chosen vocation. But also there were words of thanks for his father's cooperation over the years and recognition of the fact that his school fees had always been paid in full and on time. Then there was a section that detailed all the tasks that he should set himself and complete before the exam results were published. He was still reading the letter with great concentration when his father entered unannounced. As he held aside the sackcloth door, the man began to speak, but his words were drowned by the vehemence of his son's reaction.

Boniface sprang to his feet and shouted. "You should not come in here unannounced like that! This is my house! Get out!" He lunged forward to push his father outside, his actions justified by his right to defend the sanctity and security of his own personal space, but the confidence with which his action had begun soon dissolved to fear. For the first time in many years, Julius took hold of his son. Calmly, he grasped his son's wrists, drew them together and gripped them firmly in his left hand's manacle grip. With the slightest of twists that had caused the boy's slight frame to tilt in sympathy, he coerced Boniface into a child's submission until the tantrum passed.

"So you still understand family responsibilities enough to know that I should not come in here without asking. It's strange, Boniface, how you manage to remember all the things which benefit yourself." Julius almost ignored the letter whose pages lay strewn over the dirt dappled foam mattress on his son's bed. He cast a glance toward them and then turned away, ready to continue, but his words were stifled. He looked again at the typed sheets and, after a short silent pause, bent to the side to pick them up with his free hand. There followed a lengthy hush while the barely literate Julius struggled to read the text of the letter. Boniface made no attempt to move. Though angered at being treated like a wayward child, he now neither complained nor struggled against his father's continued grip. He knew that in the letter he had a powerful ally his father simply could not ignore.

"Why did you not give this to me?" By now Julius had read as much as he needed to understand that the letter should have been delivered directly to him and to him alone.

"I was going to give it to you..."

"Thank you. That would have been very kind of you," said Julius, cynically. "The letter is addressed to me, not to you. Why did you open it? Were you afraid that it might contain something inconvenient for yourself?"

Boniface was now a child again, helpless and speechless in guilt. He said nothing as the weight of culpability bowed his head. His defiance soon began to return, however, when he felt his father's grip on his hands loosen. Julius began to crumple the thin sheets of airmail paper in his free hand. Then he let go of his son's wrist completely, so that he could free his other hand and then tear the sheets. The violent anger, which his long-running frustration had produced, now began to show as his breathing quickened and grew louder. His eyes, which, after scanning the letter had fixed firmly on his son, again glanced back at the blue sheets in his hand. Boniface tried to act. Under no circumstances could he allow his father to destroy that letter which might serve as a reference when he applied for temporary jobs.

He lunged forward and tried to grab the letter, pushing his father in the process, but he managed to achieve nothing, for Julius was so much bigger and stronger than he. A mere wave of the man's arm sent Boniface staggering across the tiny room and into the earth-brick wall beyond the bed.

Having cast the torn letter onto the bare earth floor, Julius raised his arm to point an accusing finger at his son. "You have sinned, my boy. You had no right to read my letter. No man would ever do such a thing. It is a child's prank. Father Patrick is a good man. This letter speaks very highly of you. What he has written here is high praise indeed, for Father Patrick is a man of God. But it is now clear that he has been deceived by you. What you have done proves that you are not worthy of his praise and so to protect him from your lies, I have destroyed his letter to make sure that you cannot misuse it." Julius's gesture invited Boniface to look at the torn and crumpled pieces of the letter on the floor.

Boniface reacted with great speed, and his instinct led him to commit a callous act, to deliver a biting insult much favoured by educated youth. With overt pride designed to belittle his father, he began to speak in English, using only words that an educated man would understand. "I suppose I should have expected you to react like this. It is my opinion that your beliefs are too backward to comprehend my intentions."

Though Julius could not understand the words themselves, he was in no doubt as to the meaning their manner of delivery was intended to convey and, now too saddened by feelings of rejection to be angry, he eyed his unrepentant son in silence to offer him ample time for an apology. When none came, he revealed his final weapon. He had hoped that it would not come to this. He had hoped that Boniface would see reason before he needed to broach the threat, but clearly he had overestimated his son's maturity. He spoke in the slow musical Kikamba of an old man, lengthening vowels almost into sighs which were intended to reflect age and experience, neither of which he had as yet fully attained. First he prepared the ground, still hoping albeit in vain that Boniface would see fit to apologise.

"I had hoped, Boniface, that I would not need to threaten you. But now there is nothing else I can do. For years I have provided for your every need without a word of complaint. Now I have made a simple request. I am asking you to do no more than your duty to your family and I am receiving only insults from you." He paused here, but still Boniface was determined to offer nothing. He stared into space, but with eyes firmly and consciously fixed on something only he could see. Julius then quickly stepped forward toward the boy's desk and took hold of the smoking kerosene lamp, which needed to burn even in daylight within this windowless hut. Movement caused the low flame to flicker and its yellow light to fade momentarily. "This is your last chance, my boy. Swear on your name that you will promise to fulfil your duties to your family. If you refuse, then you are no longer a son of mine and I will put this flame to the thatch. I will burn down this house of yours because it will no longer be needed." A quiet and disappointed self-pity had replaced the violence of anger in his voice.

Boniface said nothing. Whilst he remained rooted to the spot, his still defiant gaze fixed firmly on the lamp and then rose to meet his father's eyes. Beneath the boy's calculated attempt to project a sense of strength, there reigned a fearful terror whose only but still clear outward sign was the quivering of a muscle in his cheek. After a prolonged silence, Julius Mutisya shook his head and began to raise the lamp's unguarded flame toward the tinder dry thatch above his head.

Boniface lunged forward and grabbed his father's arm, knocking the lamp onto the floor. On impact, the frail tin can that formed its body, split open, splashing its contents onto the bare earth floor and plunging the interior into near-total darkness. In a split second that seemed like an age, the lightless wick flickered blue. Then, quite suddenly, the argument dissolved, rendered insignificant by the urgency of the present. As Julius began to move, the spilt kerosene lit, sprouting geysers of flame through a dull thud of sound. Boniface screamed and fell, but Julius, better positioned to act than his son, dragged a blanket from the bed and in the same movement cast it over the flames, onto the floor where the lamp had fallen. In an instant they were doused.

When shock waned and control of his senses returned, he was confronted only by impenetrable blackness, behind which a memory of the kerosene flame occasionally flashed. Through this wall before his eyes drifted the muffled murmuring of his son's voice. This darkness was an oppression. Where was Boniface? Standing in front of him? Lying on the floor? Was he hurt? Light! He must have light! Darkness is evil; he must have light! "Rose, bring light," Julius screamed as he found his way out of the house and ran across the starlit compound towards his own house. After mere seconds he had already returned to his son's hut carrying his wife's storm lamp. Rose Mutisya followed closely behind and arrived in her son's house to find Boniface whimpering on the floor and her husband bending low over him. The boy appeared to be unharmed, but the more comfort his parents offered, the more he screamed. "I am blind! I am blind! I am blind!"

When belief rules the mind there are no questions, only answers. Only reason allows the impotence of not knowing. Belief explains all, provides a cause for every event, whereas reason, through its reliance on collective experience of limited minds must sometimes admit failure. This was to be an occasion where belief would triumph.

Prompted by fear, the explanation seemed obvious and soon had occurred to all three. Boniface, Julius and Rose thus began to think the same things, but for different reasons. For Julius and Rose it was a sign sent by powers greater than themselves to protest at a father's unthinkable threat to disown a son. For Rose in particular, it was an ancestor's warning against conflict, to remind them that their prime duty was to preserve the family line and continue the name, a role the prime responsibility for which fell to the first born son.

For Boniface it was nothing less than a revelation. The Lord had spoken directly to him, had accused him of disloyalty and questioned his worthiness to become His servant, since for just one moment, the boy had wavered and had almost succumbed to the pressure of his father's argument. In retrospect, he saw the week of illness and fever that followed the incident as his own body's fight to expel the evil, which its momentary weakness had admitted. The fact that he soon recovered both his health and his sight further convinced him that he had won the battle and had thus defeated this first attempt by a powerful devil to bar his way. And he had prevailed, just as Jesus Christ himself had done when he was first tempted. Self-fulfilled, he thus became even more convinced of his resolve to fulfil all of his ambitions.

Reason demanded that Julius should not believe that his son had ever lost his sight. After all he himself had been as close to the flash of flame as Boniface and he had suffered no ill effects whatsoever. Indeed so great had been his concern for his son that he had not even noticed the persistent flashing white patch in his own vision that lasted for over an hour after the event. It took a few days, but eventually it went of its own accord, apparently without any long-lasting effects. Fear gradually gained the upper hand, however, and began to control his thoughts. When, after two days, his son still offered neither recognition nor reaction, he began to believe what he saw, though subsequently he was never openly to confess it. Thus, it was in this manner that all discussion of his son's future was rendered taboo. Julius Mutisya decided that it was best to leave the matter alone for a while, at least until the boy's examination results were known. After all, it just might be that he would not have the grades he needed, and in that case the problem might just solve itself.

In the event, the future would allow them all to see that Boniface's ambition had in fact died that day, apparently never to be raised again. It did live on, though, in the minds of both father and son like a half-remembered skeleton in an unmentionable cupboard, a potential threat to both of their lives to be avoided at all costs.

***

A violent crash shook Boniface out of his dream. He had seen it coming for almost a minute, but had not prepared himself for the shock. The car had laboured to the summit of a shallow rise to reveal a view of the road ahead. In a broad curve it swept across a wide valley, at the bottom of which a grey and narrow concrete bridge contrasted with the brown unedged earth of the rest of their route. On the down slope, Michael pressed his foot to the floor and the car quickly picked up speed. Boniface knew that at the bottom of the valley, where the road crossed a riverbed, the junction between the murram of the road and the concrete of the bridge had worn badly, leaving a vertical step between the two surfaces, several inches high in parts. Everyone who travelled the main road knew the spot. Even the more irresponsible bus drivers would slow to a crawl here to negotiate the bump, but could still not prevent the flow of abuse from the rear seats when their vehicles lurched as they crossed onto the bridge and threw the most vulnerable passengers momentarily into the air. There was simply no way of avoiding it.

By the time Michael's car hit the ramp, it was doing fifty miles per hour, but of those inside the car only Josephine, Boniface's wife, seemed concerned by the looming danger. Not until the wheels hit the step and lifted the entire car into the air did either of the men in front of her show any reaction. A split second before impact, she tried to utter a warning shout, but it was already too late. The car hit the ridge, flew into the air and came down with what seemed like a gigantic crash, flinging her from her seat and transforming her intended shout into a long high-pitched scream.

Boniface simply held on. Michael's previously vacant expression disappeared, transformed by the widening of his eyes to one of undiluted shock and surprise. After only a short skid, which the priest quickly and easily controlled, the car sped on without either a word or glance shared. Some moments later, Boniface did turn to face his wife who was bent low over the child in her lap and holding the top of her head which had bumped hard against the roof. He offered a short comforting smile to ease her discomfort and said, "Don't worry, Josephine. Father always drives like this." His words did nothing to ease her pain or her nerves and, almost ignoring him, she continued to rub her head and grit her teeth. Though Boniface continued to stare at her for some time, their eyes did not meet and she offered him nothing.

After only another half a mile, the monotonous banging of the car over the rutted road regained its regular predictability. Still, however, it apparently demanded the total concentration of Boniface, as he sat bolt upright and newly afraid in the front seat. Soon, his mind again began to wander.

***

The three months between Boniface's homecoming and the publication of his exam results passed quickly, all too quickly for his father. As expected he joined the staff of Thitani's new primary school as an untrained teacher on the joint recommendations of Father Michael and Father Patrick. There never had been any doubt about his getting the job, since the Roman Catholic Church was officially sponsoring the new school and both of the priests had long before identified him as a potential employee to the school's hand-picked governors, but this had done nothing to reduce the pride with which Boniface adopted his new status. For the first time in his life he had money in his pocket, money that he could rightfully call his own. He did not keep the full salary for the job, of course, since he had publicly and conscientiously undertaken to pass on half of his earnings each month directly to his father for his own food and also for school fees for his brothers and sisters.

It was thus with some trepidation that Julius Mutisya again awaited the arrival of his son from Mwingi. During those months, he had grown used to the relative comfort that his son's regular income had made possible and privately he found it difficult to admit that it might not continue. There was still time, of course, for Boniface to change his mind, since the seminary years began in September and not in January, as did the schools. So whatever happened, he could look forward to at least another six months of his son's help and thus there was ample time to seek to change his heart. In the event there was no need to pressurise his son into waiting.

When Boniface returned home on the afternoon bus, he went to his own house and stayed there until nightfall. Julius interpreted this at first as his son's final rejection of his family duties and, determined to see the matter closed one way or the other, he again violated his son's privacy and entered his house. This time, however, Boniface reacted differently. Whereas before he had vehemently challenged his father's intrusion, this time he hardly seemed to notice. Bending low over the scattered papers that covered his small table, he was so engrossed in study that his father had to speak before Boniface would even acknowledge his presence.

"Are you studying for the seminary already?"

"Yes." The reply was clipped short by embarrassment.

For several uncomfortable quiet moments, Julius toyed with the prospect of another confrontation. Eventually, however, he judged the particular moment to be inauspicious and opted for safety. "When will you start?"

Boniface offered no reply as the apprehension on his father's face grew. Matters had certainly reached a head, that at least was clear and Julius felt a new determination to assert his authority begin to grow inside him. He was about to speak as firmly as he dare on this foreign territory when Boniface turned to face him and answered the question.

"I failed in mathematics." The statement was utterly flat and overtly accurate, as if offering indisputable but, from Boniface's point of view, inconsequential fact.

It took a few minutes for Julius to interpret both the meaning and the consequence of his son's words, but once their full implication had been realised, he was unable to hide the almost joyous relief he felt. With a broad smile spreading across his face, he sought confirmation of the obvious. "And without mathematics you cannot go to the seminary?"

Boniface shook his head and eyed his father with growing cynicism. Within a couple of minutes the two had been joined by Rose Mutisya, called by her husband to share in his increasingly private celebrations. Boniface, however, begrudged him his joy, which clearly was a celebration of his own failure. "Father Patrick has told me that he will enter me for the exam again this year. And as you can see I have already started studying." His final gesture, as before, was specifically designed to insult, but this time his father ignored it, for now he had surely won the fight. Turning away from his parents to face his work again, Boniface said in English, "Please leave me alone. You are wasting my time."

With a slightly derisive but definitely satisfied laugh, Julius held aside the hanging sackcloth that covered the doorway to his son's house and invited his wife to pass. Thus they left Boniface in peace to chase what they both now saw as his impossible dream. Already disappointed, Boniface found that he was deeply hurt by his father's obvious delight at what he felt was his own misfortune. Even then he knew that this memory would live for the rest of his life. He had truly hated no one in life until then.

Until November of that year, Boniface lived according to the strict confines of a self-imposed timetable. His teaching, of course, occupied all of his working week. Also two evenings a week were set aside for work with the adult literacy scheme which Father Michael had been keen to set up for so long. Only the lack of a suitable and dependable teacher whom he could trust had thwarted the priest's plan thus far and, with Boniface now available for at least a year, Michael decided that the time was right to make a start. Boniface had at first been undecided, regarding the two weeks compulsory training during the Easter holidays merely as wasted time, but soon the extra cash in payment for his work began to find its way into his pocket, and all seemed more worthwhile.

Sundays remained sacrosanct. They were set aside for the Church, as was half of every Saturday, when voluntarily he took on the training of the choir and, afterwards, met with Father Michael to receive instruction in the catechism, or more frequently to discuss ideas and theology informally. Just occasionally, such discussions might even touch upon visions of his own future. All other time, save that set aside for taking sleep and food, he devoted to study, and study he did, like he had never done before. His only diversion from this rigid routine was provided by occasional trips to Kitui town or even more occasionally to Nairobi to buy books.

He developed quite a reputation among the other schoolteachers in the area. Since most primary school teachers were untrained, Boniface's studying was certainly nothing out of the ordinary, for without the necessary academic qualifications, none of them could apply for the in-service training which could raise both their status and their salary. What was different about Boniface was the fact that he studied seriously rather than simply talked about it over yet another beer in the town's bar. In the first few weeks he was cajoled by his colleagues to join them for a drink but, though tempted, he never once accepted. He thus became branded as selfish, since his refusal was interpreted as an unwillingness to share his pay packet. This in fact was an accurate assessment.

Nothing could ever persuade him that he had studied enough. Even when he had repeatedly completed without a single mistake the revision papers which Father Michael both set and marked, he would not allow any slackening of the pace, since his life's one failure had so severely shaken his confidence.

The months passed with apparently exceptional speed. It seemed that he had no sooner started studying than it was time to take the exam. On completing the paper, every reasoned self-analysis told him that he had passed, but no reassurance was great enough to outweigh the millstone of doubt that he permanently carried. Memories of the intensity of his vision, its force and its malevolent anger lived on and so above all he feared a repetition of failure, for then he would surely be subject to another attack. He would have again failed God, and His wrath was great.

With his exam behind him and therefore the need for study removed, he found he had time on his hands. His routine had been broken and he was left with no interest to absorb the resulting free time. After only a handful of evenings, he ceased trying to convince himself that he ought to stay at home with his parents. With the possibility that he might leave for the seminary again raising its head, his relationship with his father, having been kept by default rather than through agreement on an even keel for some months, suddenly deteriorated, rekindling the tension with which neither of them could adequately cope. The only other thing to do, of course, was to go to the bar with his friends and colleagues. This he did, and soon, where before he had studied, he drank, except, of course, for the two evenings each week which he continued to devote to Father Michael's adult literacy classes.

The priest had been well pleased by his prodigy's performance in delivering the intended content and the preferred style of his classes exactly as the philosophy of the project had demanded. Slowly, small step by small step, Boniface had thus been entrusted with more and more responsibility. Recognising that, with no studying to do and much free time to fill, Boniface might just start to drift and lose his enthusiasm for his vocation, Michael decided to hand over to him the management of virtually the entire project. As ever, Michael seemed to be trying to do too many things at once and he had begun to begrudge time spent ensuring that the classes progressed properly. Handing the responsibilities over to Boniface and adopting a merely occasional supervisory role enabled him to divert his attentions to reproducing the apparent success elsewhere with the help of the Northern District Officer, John Mwangangi.

For Boniface, however, time now began to crawl. The months between the exam and the publication of the result passed so slowly that they seemed more like a year. He was bored, uncomfortable and filled with doubt, not only as a result of his father's behaviour but also by his own reactions to the often pointed comments of his fellow teachers. These friends, whom he had adopted in the first place only in preference to solitude, gradually became more important to him as communication with his father withered to merely an occasional glance. At least they were of his own generation and had shared experiences thus far in their lives similar to his own. But there all similarity ended. Their ends in life were clear, but not, like his own, guided by any ideal other than self-interest. To a man they all professed Christian faith and attended their respective churches regularly. Some of the Protestants even conducted or inflicted Bible readings on a captive and largely deferential audience from an upturned box on market day. Their interpretation judged the Thitani custom of market on a Sunday as fundamentally in error, incurring nothing less than damnation on anyone who took part. Since this classification included everyone in the town and its environs, there was certainly adequate scope for further evangelisation.

The aim, then, was to save the souls of those who mistakenly traded on the Sabbath and therefore violated God's written laws. The fact that none of these same people lived the rest of their week according to God's law devalued, in Boniface's estimation, every belief they professed. Inevitably, then, conversations they shared often revolved around the differences between the two interpretations of Christianity, that of the Africa Inland Church on the one hand and that of the Roman Catholic Church on the other. Boniface, though the only confirmed Catholic in the group, was usually more than a match for the combined efforts of his opponents.

It was during one such argument that engrossed them one sweating February evening when, after the searing heat of a rare windless day, they slaked their thirsts together in one of the town's three bars.

"But why do you want to become a priest? Why not just be a lay preacher like me? After all you would still be serving God." Samuel was the only one of the group apart from Boniface who took his convictions seriously. And he never drank beer, only lemonade.

"I have told you before...", said Boniface with obvious conviction. Out of the whole group, only the two of them appeared to have the slightest interest in the conversation. "...that to serve God in my Church, I must devote my whole life to Him. What is more, I have had a vision. The only time I can remember trying to reject the idea, I was thrown to the ground by a blinding flash. I was very ill and only when I strengthened my determination to become a priest did I get better."

Samuel shrugged his shoulders in disinterest as if to say, "So what? So you have had a vision... so have many other people, but it does not make them want to become priests." For a moment he was distracted. He looked across the bar to what had attracted the attention of the other two men and then, preferring to ignore the diversion, he continued, "But if you become a priest, you can never marry. You can never have a son..."

"Of course," replied Boniface quickly. "How could I devote my life to God if I also had all the responsibilities of a wife and family? This, Samuel, is one of the most basic ideas of our Church. A priest's duty is to God. His attentions must not be divided."

"Mister Michael's words?"

"*Father* Michael's!"

"But taking a wife and having a son is also important," said Samuel, still somewhat distracted. "It is not our culture to reject the importance of this duty."

"It is also against our culture for a man to limit himself to just one wife, but your own Church condemns polygamy." The final word, spoken by Boniface in English, pricked Samuel like a thorn.

"But you can't call such evil things a 'culture'. Taking more than one wife is simply pagan. And it is not condemned by our Church, but by the Bible. That is the law."

Boniface laughed. He pitied Samuel, believing that he was incapable of seeing through what for him was obvious trickery.

"Listen, Boniface. I can show you how unnatural, how wrong your belief is. If I was to call over one of those girls..." He pointed across to the far side of the bar where a trio of nervous and apparently self-conscious girls sat around a table littered with Coca Cola bottles. "...and arrange for her to become your girlfriend, you would have to refuse. Do you call that a natural reaction for a healthy young man?"

Boniface inspected the prospect before replying and thus he joined the other members of his group who had been eying the girls for some time. "No," he replied. "I would not have to refuse. I am not a priest yet.

291

I have taken no vows. I don't even know if I will ever have the chance of entering the seminary. That is for God to decide. At this moment I am as free as anyone to have a girlfriend if I so wished, but if I still wanted to be a priest, then I would have to confess all my sins before I took my vows, and then I would have to be prepared to live out those vows for the rest of my natural life."

Almost before he had finished, Samuel had risen from his chair and crossed the room. That was obviously what the girls had been expecting, because almost as one their eyes lit up with mischievous but accommodating smiles. During the previous hour they had received numerous attentions from interested admirers, but they had consistently met invitations with a good humoured but cutting and dismissive defiance. After all, they were educated girls. They were worthy of more than the attentions of mere common men. Thus, when Samuel introduced himself as a teacher and invited them to join himself and his friends in a drink, they seized the opportunity with obvious eagerness, whilst at the same time displaying a disinterest that suggested that this was no more than their right.

Clearly Samuel was intent on proving his point and Boniface immediately felt his heart sink. Surely he was going to be put on the spot and whatever happened he would have to make sure that he did not lose face in front of the others. It was obvious that Samuel knew at least one of the three girls and he made it clear from the moment he introduced her to his friends that she had once been his girlfriend. Whatever happened, Samuel was surely going to provide Boniface with the opportunity of practising what he was destined to preach. If he refused he would suffer not only the sarcasm and ridicule of his friends, but also intellectual and personal defeat. His actions would have proved Samuel right, for what could be more unnatural than a fit and able young man refusing the obvious invitations of a young and willing girl? On the other hand, if he were to accept the expected challenge, he would be acting contrary to his own deep convictions and thereby committing a dreadful sin, something which he would surely pay for dearly in the future. As the evening progressed, however, his reluctance to participate in what had developed into a wager was gradually eroded by the inviting, beautiful smile of Josephine Ngao.

She was eighteen years old but looked younger. Even in comparison with the thin short frame of Boniface, she was small and slight. When, after only one more drink, the groups began to intermingle so that each man sat next to a girl, she set the young man's heart and expectations racing when she showed a positive eagerness to be at his side. He bought her another drink, beer this time, and proudly stretched his back straight to emphasise his relatively dominant stature. They talked playfully, at first only as members of a group, but later to one another, without the unwanted intrusion of having to maintain a social identity. Boniface was pleased when she told him that she was a Form Four student at Mutune School.

"Ah, so you are a Catholic?"

She nodded.

Though undeniably attracted to her, Boniface was almost visibly relieved at this revelation. It was his answer to the riddle, his face-saving way out of the predicament. This girl who was surely warned by the nuns in Mutune every day about the dangers of sin would surely never be willing to sleep with him anyway, and so he had surely foiled Samuel's plan. He was sure that Samuel did not know that she was a convent girl and so he made not the slightest attempt to enlighten him. He would save that joy until later. Whatever happened from now on, he must surely stick to her. In this particular predicament, she was surely his potential salvation!

"So you will take your EACE this year?"

"Yes."

"Do you think you will pass?"

"If God is willing. Did you pass your certificate?"

"I failed in mathematics, but I have just taken it again. I spent a full year just studying that one subject so I am sure I will get it this time."

"And what will you do then?"

"I hope to go to Nairobi to study in the seminary."

The girl's eyes lit up with both surprise and admiration. "You want to be a priest?"

Boniface nodded, smiling with pride. Josephine eyed him with wonder, as if inspecting some precious but absurd rarity. She spoke again. "When I leave school I would like to go to Nairobi more than anything else."

Josephine Ngao willingly answered all of the young man's questions. She was the daughter of a sub-chief, an old man whom Boniface had met several times, since he had been asked by Father Michael to sit on his school's board of governors. The old man was nothing less than a local celebrity. A professed Roman Catholic, he somehow managed to maintain six wives and fourteen children from his meagre public servant's salary and yet the family never went hungry, despite the fact that he was also paying school fees for some eight of his offspring. Josephine, however, still habitually described her father as very 'bush'. Occasionally she had even gone as far as to use the term 'primitive'. She hated going home because he was always too strict and insisted on treating her like a child, which she felt she most certainly was not. And so, on this night as always when she was at home from school, she was staying with her friend Regina, and indeed hoped to stay there throughout her half term holiday. Regina's father was dead and her mother was already growing old. She needed more looking after than Regina, herself, could provide, so Josephine often volunteered her help. For his part, Josephine's father was actually proud of his daughter's good work and raised no objection to her spending much of her holidays away from home, provided, that is, she always kept in touch and made frequent visits to her brothers and sisters. The best thing about staying with Regina, though, was that her mother's home was quite near to the town, not miles out into the bush like that of her own family.

"I like school very much, but the sisters are very strict with us girls."

"But surely they have to be. It is a poor school where the teachers are not very strict."

Josephine agreed but qualified her opinion. "I understand that, but the sisters don't seem to realise that Form Four girls like ourselves are different from primary school children. We are almost adults, but they still treat us like babies. For the last year, for example, no one has even been allowed to go into Kitui town, not even on Saturdays. And for those of us who have the bus fare, the town is no more than a few minutes ride from the school. We can be there and back before the sisters have even missed us."

"They must have a reason for doing that. Some of the girls must have misbehaved. After all, being allowed outside the school compound is a privilege, not a right."

"But I think that in Mwingi, Father Patrick did not force the boys to stay in the school compound all the time."

"That is true... but then it is different with boys."

"Why? Why should boys be treated differently? If you are in Form Four in Mwingi and I am in Form Four in Mutune, why should I not have exactly the same privileges?"

Boniface answered quickly. He had obviously thought about this point at length. "For two reasons. First, girls need more protection than boys and second, because Mutune is so near to Kitui town, you need even more protection to make sure that bad men from the town do not cause you problems."

Their conversation had drifted word by word away from the Kikamba in which it had begun, so that by now they were both speaking almost entirely in English. Boniface was impressed by Josephine's command of the language, but immediately took offence at the independent way she reacted to what he said.

"That is complete nonsense! We are old enough to look after ourselves. How do they expect us to learn to live our lives properly as adults when they keep us locked up like babies?"

He countered in similar serious fashion. "I have heard some very bad stories from Father Michael about Mutune School. He told me that the sisters have been forced to make a special arrangement with the police so that they will patrol the road from Kitui to Mutune in Land Rovers every night. He said that there are many men with cars in the town that drive out to the school to meet with girls there. They go off and play sex and then the men pay hundreds of shillings to these girls. It is very bad, Josephine. That is why the nuns are very strict."

Again she dismissed his words. "But that proves what I have said. Even now, the nuns are very strict, but the bad girls you speak about - and I shall not play with words, I shall call them prostitutes - these prostitutes still manage to behave badly and do their business. They know how to pick the locks on the dormitory doors and bribe the prefects to mark them present at lights out, even when they have been gone for hours. They stay away all night and then, very early in the morning - at dawn or even earlier - when we all get up to go to the dam to collect water for washing, they come out from their hiding places and join in. Then, of course, all the girls walk back to school together and the nuns are none the wiser about who was in school and who was out of school the previous evening. All the girls know who they are. They have no secrets." She paused here for a moment while Boniface, grave faced, continued to shake his head in an expression of sincere disgust. "But what I am saying is that even though the sisters are very strict, they still cannot control these prostitutes, so then the rest of the girls, the good ones, are really the only ones who are being punished."

"Then you should tell the headmistress their names."

Slightly embarrassed, Josephine fell completely silent for a moment. "We cannot do that," she said nervously. "These girls are very skilful. Most of them are friendly with the boys from the bar in the town. If you say that you are going to tell Sister, they just threaten you, saying that if you do anything, then they will tell these boys from the town to find you. And if they do find you, it is very bad."

"But you would be safe. You are in school all day, and then in the dormitories all night."

"And what about when we go to church? Or when we go home for weekends or holidays? Where do we go to be safe then?"

If not yet enough to convince him, this was enough to surprise him and consider things differently. He had never thought it might be possible that these girls from the stories could seriously threaten the others to keep them quiet. It surely was the kind of act that no woman would be capable of carrying out. His silence brought the matter to a close.

For a few minutes both Josephine and Boniface paid more attention to the others around the table than to one another. Alexander, as usual already too drunk to care, had been counted out. Slumped forward in his chair, he dozed, quite oblivious to his surroundings. Samuel and his charge were clearly ready to leave. Staring almost with concentration at their empty, froth crusted glasses, the couple exchanged neither a word nor a glance, either with each other or anyone else around the table, while his hand haltingly found its place of rest on her thigh. Justus and Mary, however, had not yet passed stage one of the almost ritual progression. His small rather rotund body comically leaned across the corner of the table toward her immense frame at exactly the same angle as she leaned away. Thus, in their parallel but unsympathetic inclination they were still playing out only the preliminaries of a possible encounter. He stared at her whilst she looked absolutely anywhere except at him. He spoke to her whilst at all times she tried her utmost to join any other conversation on offer. He was still interested in her, but she tried her best to give her attention to anyone but him. As time had passed, of course, things had grown ever more difficult, since the number of words shared had sharply decreased as either incapacity or other interests had taken over. And so, with Samuel and Regina otherwise engaged in their concentrated and palpitating silence, and Boniface and Josephine becalmed in wordless doldrums, something simply had to give. With an exaggeratedly bored, but genuinely relieved sigh, Mary stood up and announced that she was ready to leave. When Justus also stood, her face dropped. Looking at the others and, finding them still otherwise engaged, she looked ready to make a dash for the door, but decorum and good sense persuaded her to wait for her friends. There might still be safety in numbers, but it was a deflated young woman who slowly sat down again without a word. Justus followed, offering an ignored question.

Alexander snored a little. Then without a word, Regina stood and grasped Samuel's hand to lift him to his feet. Josephine now stood up quickly and, taking Regina by the arm, led her aside, a pace or two apart from the rest. They proceeded to exchange a few words in a whisper accompanied by frequent nodding, as if what was said could have been as effectively communicated in code, as part of an assumed prior agreement; and then they rejoined the group. By then Mary had already made her move and, with Justus mirroring her gait in pursuit, she waddled hastily towards the door. Alexander was by now asleep and took no further part in the proceedings. When at a suitably respectable distance, Samuel and Regina began to make for the door, Josephine and Boniface found themselves momentarily alone in the corner of the bar, which only a few moments before the whole group had occupied. She spoke just above a whisper.

"Regina will go to her house... and we will go to yours. Come on."

With that she set off, turning her back on Boniface who, for a few seconds, was simply too stunned to follow. Surely he had misunderstood. He followed.

Outside he was surprised to find himself alone. Looking around, he saw nothing. There was no moon and the shaft of soon fading light that filtered through the bar's open doorway rendered all darkness darker and his eyes useless.

"Boniface! Here!"

The voice from the shadows startled him. Peering into the night, he was able to make out the dim outline of Josephine set against the paling grey of a wall. He went over to join her intent on asking her to repeat what she had just said to him inside the bar, but time was obviously short and, before he had time even to open his mouth, she had embraced him and pressed the whole length of her small but solid and lusciously smooth body against his. Whatever words he had intended to speak stuck deep inside him as a sensation he had never before known filled his body and coursed like a drug through his veins. She kissed him and rubbed his limp hand hard against her breasts. He felt himself swim in their softness and suddenly his mind cleared of all other thoughts except desire for her and growing pride in himself.

Then, as abruptly as she had given herself to him, she pulled away. "We can go to your house."

Again the words took some time to register. He had kissed her again and pulled her hips hard against his own before he dared admit that it would be impossible. "No, we can't do that... my mother and father... they are still there."

"But you are a teacher. Surely you don't still live at home with your parents?"

"Of course I do. What is the point in paying for a room in the town when my parents are so nearby?" The words flowed quickly. Without any conscious decision they had begun to speak to one another in Kikamba again.

"Come on. Follow me."

Before Boniface could speak again, Josephine had set off and was pulling him along behind by the hand. They walked, almost ran a hundred yards before she stopped on a patch of open ground some distance from both the bar and the road. They immediately kissed again, but again Josephine quickly broke free of his ever more passionate embrace. Before Boniface could phrase the words that ached to be spoken, she had grasped his hand and thrust it firmly between her thighs. With surprising violence and a single mindedness that shocked the words from his mind, she held his wrist hard and pushed his hand against her. Somehow she placed his fingers into a seam of wetness so divine that for a moment he was sure he could feel God in his bones. Her face was pressed hard against his and she began to moan a little. Boniface tried to say, "No! No! This cannot be..." but she touched him and he dissolved in senseless ecstasy. When he eventually spoke, the words were subtly transformed by a new expectancy. "No, not here," he said. "I know where we can go. There is a good place. Follow me."

Then, as she smoothly disengaged herself from him, he led her off into the darkness, back towards the town. Josephine made a few impatient remarks, questions that he now neither heeded nor heard. He felt for a small bunch of keys he knew to be in his pocket and found them. He smiled a proud smile and ignored what sounded like growing protests from behind. "Here," he said, unlocking the back door of his father's shop. "We cannot be disturbed here - and there is a mattress which my father uses for his siesta."

Primarily it was fear of discovery that kept Boniface awake for the rest of the night. He was up and about long before dawn and, having lit and kindled his mother's charcoal stove in the kitchen, he was able to rouse Josephine at first light with a welcome cup of sweet tea. After one sip she seemed ready to continue where they had left off just a couple of hours before, but Boniface was obviously too nervous to respond.

"I shall come again in two weeks," she said in English. She meant to Thitani.

Boniface smiled and nodded, having not misunderstood. He was deeply and quietly happy.

She eyed him curiously for a moment and then said, "Will you buy me some tea? And my bus fare back to Kitui town?"

After at first being slightly taken aback by the request, Boniface reacted quickly, clearly thinking that it was the least he could do after such a momentously wonderful night. He then took a twenty-shilling note from his pocket and handed it to her. She smiled and, after taking it with thanks, dressed and placed it securely in the left cup of her bra.

She will have to iron that note back into shape by the time she gets back to Kitui, thought Boniface.

"Until two weeks then?" she asked as he showed her out of the shop's back door.

He nodded. How would he manage to wait that long? Then, with a strange formality, they shook hands and she was gone in an instant. Now safe as well as proud, he went back inside and surprised himself by immediately suffering fears that she might never return. He had hoped to go to Migwani for mass that morning and so, after grooming his hair with a plastic comb taken from an open cardboard box on a near bare shelf, he locked the shop behind him and set off on his walk. His head was high; his stride long, confident and contented.

When Boniface's pass in mathematics was confirmed by the expectant congratulations of Father Patrick's personal visit to the Mutisya household, a number of old and partially suppressed conflicts began to reappear. Communication between father and son immediately diminished to the level of mere greeting and stayed there. Boniface, of course, began to make preparations for the new term at the seminary that was due to begin in September. He formally submitted his notice of resignation to the headmaster of Thitani Primary School and thus set the entire town into a gentle but noticeable turmoil, since everyone knew that as a result their children would probably have no teacher until after Christmas, when the next batch of school leavers and therefore potential untrained teachers would be released by the examination system.

After all, why should Boniface, who had received a good salary from the school for more than a year simply be able to leave without finding a replacement for himself? - and in the middle of a school year as well, with CPE, Certificate of Primary Education exams only a month away...

Boniface, however, took no notice of the gossip that filled the town. Neither his heart nor his mind had any time to digress from what was still the sole aim of his life. It was now July, and only a month from his departure for the seminary in Nairobi. And then the bubble finally burst.

Thitani Primary School, like all other schools in the District, had just begun its holidays, and so Boniface was again regularly helping his father in the shop. That day, however, was a Sunday, and therefore a market day in the town. As a consequence, and unlike other days of the week, a large number of people wandered the hundred-yard length of the town's main and only street, intent on at least visiting every shop to view its wares. Thus, with morning service over, Boniface bid Father Michael goodbye and, after collecting all his choirboys' robes together and stowing them away in his classroom cupboard, he made his way toward the market place to fulfil his obligation to his father.

There was quite a crowd in the Mutisya shop, though clearly from the blank depressed expression on his father's face, no one was buying anything. It was at that moment that the chirping tones of Sub-Chief Kimanzi Ngao silenced all the chatter and set Boniface at the centre of all attention.

"Bwana Mutisya!" he shouted. His subsequent pause created both the silence and the drama he needed. "Your son has raped my daughter." The silence was heavier and more threatening now.

After casting a condemnatory but frightened glance toward his son, Julius Mutisya, still remarkably placid, eyed Ngao with suspicion. "You say he has raped your daughter?" he said calmly. "When did this happen?"

"When?" screamed the old man. Several people jumped with fright at the vehemence with which the word was spoken. Sub-Chief Ngao's face was almost glowing with anger. "When?" he repeated even louder. "He has been raping her every two weeks for the last six months! And he has been doing it right here on the floor of your shop!" Here he pointed defiantly to the spot where he himself stood. A babble of disgusted murmuring rose from the assembled witnesses, who almost in unison stepped aside to examine the nondescript patch of offending concrete indicated by the insistent thin-air prodding of the old man's cane.

"Sub-Chief Ngao," said Julius Mutisya, trying his best to retain all manifestations of overt respect for the other's position, "please bring your daughter to my house tonight. We will discuss the matter."

Then, after offering his thanks, the wiry old man bowed and stalked out of the shop, punctuating his still sturdy stride with neat clicks of his rough walking stick on the bare concrete floor. He was satisfied that the public claim he had made had been dutifully and publicly acknowledged by Julius Mutisya. As for the son, that was neither his concern nor his responsibility now.

Boniface fixed his gaze on his father, but the other simply went about his business, apparently neither surprised nor ruffled by the incident. It was understandable. A man of dignity like his father ought to react that way. Even if there were recriminations to be made now that their secret was made public, they would surely be done in private in front of the girl's father and not here, in full public view. So stunned was Boniface initially by the dreamlike events that he did not even notice the smiles and nudges of a couple of his peers on their way out of the shop, as they followed in Sub-Chief Ngao's wake. Clearly they looked upon Boniface's position with some envy, since, like all the young men in the town, they regarded the prospect of marrying Josephine Ngao as something very desirable indeed.

A few minutes later, however, he was behind the counter, doing the job he always did as if nothing had happened. His father would surely sort out the confusion with Sub-Chief Ngao. The girl was no more than a common prostitute and her father ought to know that.

Within three months of that day, Boniface and Josephine were married. That evening meeting which Boniface had imagined would settle the matter once and for all in the event did no more than agree a bride price of fifteen thousand shillings; itself a compromise fee which, in Ngao's eyes reflected both his daughter's immediate and potential worth and which, in Mutisya's eyes, would not prove to be too great a burden on his son's finances and would therefore enable him to contribute also, out of his teacher's salary, to the school fees for his younger brother. Instalments were worked out there and then and, on payment of the first one, the wedding day was fixed. Though the idea of running away to Nairobi did cross Boniface's mind, he was eventually far too sensible a young man to give the option much credence. How could he take the vows of a priest seriously with this behind him? This matter would surely have to be settled first, but, contrary to his expectations, the passing of time merely complicated the matter and instead of reaching an agreement with Ngao to pay damages and forget the matter, Boniface found that his father merely accepted the other's words and played whatever game he demanded.

"Damages would be the same as the bride price. Who would want a bride such as my daughter now that she is no longer a virgin?"

"She wasn't ever a virgin... not even on our first time."

"She was certainly no virgin after you had raped her."

"I didn't rape her. If anything she raped me."

"Aiee!!"

"And she asked for money the next morning."

"You must have offered it first. We are poor people and it is easy for a salary earner like yourself to buy just what you want. When a person can buy things, he thinks he can buy anything."

And so the wrangles continued until, by the time the appointed day arrived, a thousand shillings had changed hands and, whether spurred by sheer resignation, social pressure, default or still latent desire, Boniface and Josephine stood side by side facing the makeshift altar which Father Michael had erected as usual in the schoolroom which served as Thitani's parish church. And so they were married, for better or worse.

Of course, Julius had previously spoken with his son's headmaster to obtain a reassurance that his job as an untrained teacher was still there for the taking. Obviously there was still no one else in this small place who could possibly do the job, so there was no problem to be envisaged there. In desperation, during the intervening period, Boniface had visited

Father Michael and implored him to come to Thitani to speak to both his own and the girl's father, but the priest had refused, saying that he, Boniface, should settle what he had brought upon himself. There was no help to be found. He was quite alone, and therefore well beaten.

At the end of the wedding ceremony, Father Michael's congratulations sounded more like condolences aimed purely at Boniface, almost publicly regretting the demise of what might have been and yet, at the same time, expediently praising the young man's good fortune to be marrying such a beautiful bride. From within the solitude of his own thoughts, Boniface found that he could only laugh in reply to the priest's words, since the unreality of the whole affair still prevented his full appreciation of the permanence of the change. This episode of marriage, in his eyes, was still merely another complication and, just as his initial failure in mathematics had delayed his plans by a year, then also this problem would turn out in the long run to be no more than a temporary hitch. In the event, however, his wedding was to turn out to be only the start of his problems.

***

In her final year at secondary school, Josephine Ngao found herself a member of a small group of pupils in whom the nuns invested their complete trust, respect and even, to a small extent, power. It was a position of privilege she would never again in her life enjoy, though at the time she believed this experience was to be but the beginning in miniature of what she might come to expect as she grew older. By virtue of her continuing education, it was surely almost inevitable that one day she would be invested with ever more responsibility and therefore ever increasing personal stature and worth. This particular year was to be the culmination of eleven others of determined effort, not only on her part but also on that of her whole family, who had supported her throughout her time in school. This, then, was to be the final hurdle beyond which the way would be clear for as far as the eye could see.

"It's five minutes to nine."

Josephine Ngao looked up from her studies of the Saint Lawrence Seaway to see Maria, her friend and fellow prefect, propping open the classroom door. "I'm coming."

"What are you studying tonight?" asked Maria as she crossed

the room to her friend's desk.

"Geography. Have you used this book yourself? It is very difficult to understand." Josephine closed her textbook to display the cover to Maria.

She shook her head and smiled. "I have not even started my geography yet. Sister has been giving me extra mathematics all term. It seems to take up all my prep time every night. I have to do it because Sister takes my book every morning after assembly to check it."

As Maria spoke, Josephine placed her books carefully inside her desk and then secured the lid with a padlock through its wire hasp. "Right. I'm ready. You go off and do Saint Peter and I'll do Saint Paul. Did you ask Sister?"

"Yes. She says it will be all right."

"Good. I'll see you by the main gate in five minutes."

Once outside the two girls set off across the school compound in different directions. Knowing that she was already late for her duty, Josephine ran to the open doorway of St. Paul's dormitory.

"Lights out in two minutes!" Framed in the doorway, standing completely alone and apart from the rest, she possessed a quite different presence from anyone else there. Not only did she silently seem to demand attention, she also received it and, thus, her words had an immediate effect. Where a moment before there had been complete chaos, there was suddenly a hushed and perfect order. All talking and laughing ceased and the resulting silence which replaced it was punctuated only by the comic slaps of plastic sandals on the concrete floor as each of the thirty girls took up her individually appointed position at the foot of her bed, facing into the room. By the time Josephine had sought and found a green-backed exercise book in the small wooden cabinet by the door, all was quiet.

Satisfied that she was ready to begin, Josephine took hold of the pen which swung from a string knotted through a hole near the spine of the book and turned to face the forest of two-deck iron bunks which filled St. Paul's dormitory. Then, walking slowly down the length of the room as she spoke, she called each girl's name in turn and entered a tick in the book only when the summoned replied.

With the last name duly called and acknowledged, Josephine retraced her steps and replaced the book in the cabinet, before again turning to face her assembly. "All right. You can go to your beds now." The words were almost sung, with a change of key towards the end.

The relative silence was suddenly shattered by the creaking of springs and the scratching of loose bolts in metal frames as members of St. Paul's took eagerly to their beds for the night. Josephine waited patiently for the commotion to subside, and only when she had re-established total silence did she try to continue. "Now I want you all to listen very carefully. I have an announcement to make and there is not much time. First, I have to visit Mr. O'Brien for extra tuition in geography this evening..." A few half suppressed sniggers greeted the remark, prompting Josephine to peer accusingly down the row of beds in a vain attempt to identify the culprits. She knew who they were, but elected to say nothing when the minor disturbance quickly waned.

"Secondly," said Josephine with calculated vigour, "I shall leave you, Regina, in charge of the dormitory until I get back. I ask everyone to remember that if you make a noise, we will all spend tomorrow on manual. Sister has said that there is a lot of grass to cut in the compound after the rain and she is looking for volunteers. If you make noise in the dormitory, you will be those volunteers and I will have to miss all my lessons to see that you do the work properly. If that happened, I would not be pleased and I would therefore make sure that everyone worked her hardest."

Valiantly, Josephine tried to harden the edge of her soft, slow voice with the sternness her authority should warrant, but she knew that if the girls were to follow her advice, they would do so out of their fear of Sister Augustus, not out of any respect for her, their prefect.

Before delivering what were clearly to be her parting words, she took several steps down the central aisle between the bunks and turned to face one particular girl. "Remember, Regina," she said, pointing quite rudely at the girl, "that you are in charge tonight." It was a serious, but also slightly theatrical gesture, carrying undertones of meaning, which clearly many of the other girls were able to interpret.

And with that curt reminder her job was complete. After bidding everyone goodnight, she closed the door of Saint Paul's behind her and strode off across the school compound beneath the shining silver of a resplendent full moon. Within a minute the laboured clatter of a single cylinder Diesel engine behind the science laboratory was stilled by an anonymous hand and the sprawling buildings of Mutune Girls' (note the position of the apostrophe, girls) Secondary School were plunged into immediate and complete darkness.

Lying in her lower bunk, Regina waited for a respectable time before making her own move. It was about five minutes in all, long enough for most of the simply frivolous after dark comments to have subsided, before she enacted the next part of the deception which by then had become no more than mundane for the residents of St. Paul's. The various rattles and creaks which accompanied even the most careful of her calculated movements raised half-muted giggles from those amongst the girls who knew all too well what was happening and wide-eyed interest from those who merely thought they did.

It was with nothing less than practised efficiency that Regina first vacated her bed and then placed her rolled up dressing gown and clothes and then finally her pillow beneath the single sheet which covered her foam mattress. Then, without either a response to the stirring about her or even a moment's hesitation, she made her way unerringly in the dark to the head of the dormitory and climbed into the lower bunk on the immediate left of the doorway.

Regina, like all the other girls, would be sound asleep by the time Sister Augustus came to check that Josephine's prefect's privileges had not been misused. Permission to visit Mr. O'Brien was only ever granted on the understanding that the girls in question would be in bed by ten o'clock at the latest. If the agreement were broken by any of the parties, by Mr. O'Brien or any of his permitted visitors, Sister Augustus would see to it that the privilege was withdrawn and would certainly punish all concerned, even Mr. O'Brien, who would probably look upon such a proposition with more trepidation than any of Mutune School's girls.

Sister was undoubtedly very strict indeed and furthermore was renowned for her ferocity. But imagination had never been one of her virtues. Thus Regina could sleep soundly knowing that when the door of St. Paul's inched open at ten to allow the most discreet and least disturbing view of the interior, her body, anonymous in the darkness, would become that of Josephine Ngao in Sister's eyes. Augustus was certainly as fierce as a lion, but, like that very beast itself, she was always easily fooled.

By the gap in the clipped euphorbia hedge, where two white gateposts marked the main entrance to the school compound, there stood a group of chattering girls. Though anonymous in the night to anyone beyond a few strides distant, an in-built fear of recognition still muted their voices to a whisper. The fact that they all had permission to visit Mr. O'Brien after lights out did little to suppress the guilt which their current position invoked.

Had the patrolling Sister Augustus appeared by the main gate at that moment to search out and identify those who apparently loitered there with the penetrating glare of her torch, each and every one of the girls would probably have rushed off back to their beds at speed and without a word of complaint, for their right to be here in this place depended upon the presence of one who had not yet arrived. Without Josephine, the prefect invested with both the trust and the authority of the Sisters, themselves, they could do nothing at all. In their defence, they could not even safely cite the permission they had already been granted, for without the presence of Josephine, even that was annulled.

Thus, when the sound of footsteps on the gravel path reached their ears, their previously excited but still muted chattering momentarily hushed to an immediate and complete silence. Their eyes pierced the dark for clues as to the identity of the moonlit figure that approached, their hopes willing that person to be Josephine Ngao and their fears dreading the sight of Sister Augustus.

"I am coming," called Josephine softly. Her words drew an audible sigh of relief from the group and restrained cheers from one or two of the individuals. Within a few seconds, she was among them and, as if by instinct, they gathered round her to await the leadership they all knew she would adopt. Before directing them all out of the compound, however, Josephine had something to say. "Girls, please listen carefully. Sister has given us permission until ten. She will come to the dormitories to check that we are all back by then. If you do not obey her, we will all be on manual tomorrow." She paused here to look at all about her, as if she was checking on how intently they had listened. Only when she was sure that they had all understood did she continue.

"Now listen very carefully indeed."

Her voice was now little more than a whisper and her entourage huddled closer as if to form a barrier, which might exclude all but themselves from the secrets within. "I myself must leave Mr. O'Brien's house early because I have to be up very early tomorrow. We do not have long - only half an hour or so - so I will leave at about half past. I am telling you now for two reasons. One so that you will be sure if you will be asked tomorrow and two, so that you will all make sure to leave

Mr. O'Brien's house on time because I will not be there to remind you."

With every detail of Josephine's words duly noted, they set off through the gap in the hedge. Keeping close together they passed between the gateposts, which, during term time, were a symbol of the great divide between school and life outside, a worldly manifestation, therefore, of good and evil. (Might that have read goods and evil?) Out here they were free but alone. In school their lives were restricted. Their movements, the clothes they could or could not wear, their entire lives, in fact, were dictatorially governed by the strictures the nuns imposed. Their judgment was fixed and left nothing to doubt. The sisters' wrath was fierce, their instructions always obeyed without question, their authority unquestioningly acknowledged, and their sincerity never seriously questioned. In school they were absolute masters, the often-resented wardens and yet the much loved protectors of the chosen girls.

Once outside, however, once through that gap in the hedge, the girls stepped out from beneath the umbrella of both the authority and its protection, but not for a moment did they forget the demands it made on them.

By the time they mounted the steps onto the open veranda of Mr. O'Brien's house, the expectation of promised entertainment lit the face of every one of the girls with a happy smile. The voice which greeted them with such demonstrative pleasure caused several partially audible giggles. "Ah... good evening, ladies. Make yourselves at home. Good evening Josephine. And how is our prefect?"

"I am fine," she said.

"Would you ladies like a drink? You can take your choice, we have Fanta, *chai* or Tree Top."

Every one of the six girls opted for a bottle of Fanta and, while, with an air of relaxed familiarity, they settled themselves onto their seats, Martin O'Brien went off into the kitchen to fetch the drinks.

"Is Mrs. O'Brien here?"

"No, she is visiting Father." Punctuated by the sharp clicks of a bottle opener and the hiss of fizzing lemonade, O'Brien's resonant voice echoed along the hallway from the kitchen. The near singing tone of voice which he automatically and unconsciously adopted whenever he addressed a prettier than average sub-set of his pupils, rendered everything he said almost comical and always guaranteed great entertainment for those privileged to share his late-night tutorials.

On the surface, Martin O'Brien was a free-living type who, by his midthirties had worked as a teacher in three countries and had travelled to twenty more. On the face of things, always bright of manner and never less than enthusiastic for whatever he did, underneath he was regularly afflicted by an almost complete inertia capable of generating a self-doubt that could render even thought a burden. His remedy had become to seek constant company so that he might never find himself alone to brood.

He had married young. He and his bride had been school friends and had 'courted', because in their home town in Ireland that was what one did. Eventually they married for similar sorts of reasons and suddenly realised that until then they had hardly known one another. So, after nine years of childless marriage, they were still very much a couple, but at the same time still the same strangers they had been on the day they first met. Above all, Martin O'Brien wanted to be liked.

After finishing the last of her lemonade, Josephine rose from her chair and announced, to Martin O'Brien's surprise and disappointment, that she was very tired and ought to go to bed. Had she not learned earlier that Mrs. O'Brien was, herself, visiting the mission, she would instead have announced that she wanted to visit Father before going back to school and would indeed have looked in there for a few minutes, a time span which, if need be, could be stretched on report both at its beginning and its end. That avenue, however, was now closed, since Mrs O'Brien, though a rather small rotund and apparently insignificant woman, was known for her ability to note and recall every detail of her own actions. She, unfortunately for Josephine, would be able to vouch for any time of arrival or departure she, herself, might later claim.

"It's unlike you to be tired, Josephine..." said O'Brien.

The girl shrugged her shoulders and replied, "I have been doing too much work this week. Even today, Mr. O'Brien, you have given us too much homework. I was still trying to finish it at five minutes to nine..."

"Ah now... Don't you try to blame me." He was smiling as he spoke, but it was clear that he had taken the comment to heart. He dearly wanted to be liked.

"It's true!" said Josephine in an animated voice through an innocent, playful smile. "But I still have to go now. Thank you for the lemonade and good night, Mr. O'Brien," she said politely, as she rose to her feet. Turning to the others she continued, "Don't stay later than we are allowed, girls. Remember that Sister will be checking the dormitories by ten o'clock."

She departed with a wave, knowing that all the girls still seated in Martin O'Brien's sitting room would do as requested and return to their beds within the half hour they had been granted for their visit. But how much did they know about her? Did they know what she was about to do? She was sure they did not, so carefully had she bought the loyalty of just two trusted and eternally silent accomplices.

After descending the veranda steps, she set off as if apparently to retrace her path back to the school compound across the road. Always carefully calculating exactly how far the shaft of electric light from the O'Brien house illuminated the road, she walked twenty yards or so as a perfunctory gesture. This took her almost as far as the two white gateposts of the school compound, itself, and thus almost rendered her visible in the bright cone of light from the night watchman's hissing pressure lamp, which spread white through the gap in the hedge between the gateposts. But those few yards made all the difference.

On the other side of the road there was a gap in the hedge and a path that led away from the school and also away from the O'Brien house. It dipped steeply at first down a rain-cut gully that threatened to undermine the road itself after one or two more seasons. Having travelled that way many times, she had grown to know it well and, after a few brisk and confident strides along the steep, narrow and stone-strewn path, she knew she was safe and slowed to the confident stroll which was her preferred way of carrying herself. This habitually slower speed generally allowed her to assess the reactions of those around her to the overt and magnetic sensuality of her body. It had been even before the onset of puberty that she had noticed how men's eyes followed the movement of her hips, and now only a few years later she was no longer conscious of there being anything special about herself, but unconsciously she had learned to expect and therefore receive attention.

In the past many girls had been unlucky with their dash through the hedge and had been seen, but it had yet to happen to her. Possibly those others had suffered from nerves at the critical moment and had broken into a run. In this breathlessly quiet place at the head of a valley running north from the edge of Kitui town, there was surely no surer way of attracting attention than making a noise. The incessant wind that blew in noisy gusts across the higher lands to the north did not even rustle leaves here. There was nothing more likely to attract the attention of Sister Augustus, therefore, than an unexpected or unexplained noise. After years of patrolling the school compound after dark, she knew every sound which penetrated the night, knew the sing of every breeze through the eucalyptus trees and the habits of every red-eyed animal which might cross the beam of her torch before retreating to the cover of darkness.

People made very different kinds of sound, however. Human sounds were always heavier and more complicated than the others. Anything suspicious was therefore noticed by Sister immediately. In an instant she would focus the ranging beam of her torch on the source of any disturbance. More often than not, of course, even her extensive experience had been deceived by this place that she had inhabited but never fully known, but just occasionally her fears were confirmed by the recognition of a glanced body fleeing into the dark. This she found gratifying, especially on the following morning when she could confirm that she had tracked down some heinous misdemeanour, rendered infinitely more serious by her internalised fears of its imagined motives.

Josephine would never make such a mistake now. In the past she might have panicked, indeed she had panicked on many occasions and had come close to being detected by the bright shaft that tried to search her out. She had, however, always been lucky, and now she was more than that. She had grown experienced and practised in her art. She knew exactly what she could accomplish and precisely how she could do it. And even if she were to be unlucky enough one day to be caught in Sister's beam, she would surely still be safe. She had never had to try it out, and perhaps could only ever do it once, but she could always say, "Sister, I was with Mr O'Brien and I saw one tall girl coming this way. I felt I had to follow."

She would surely be criticized for not reporting the matter before acting, but the potential truth of her statement would not be questioned, for Josephine knew of the sisters' mistrust of one particular girl and of their desire to find any excuse to be rid of her. The ploy, however, had yet to be tried and, as she picked her way purposefully between the thorn bushes that lined the sides of the deepening gully, she hoped that the need to use it would never arise.

After a short difficult stretch near the road, the rough and narrow path slipped quickly into the deepest part of the gully. The trick, which she had learned only after several attempts at the route had provided her with some nasty scratches on her shins which had to be hidden from the sisters with knee socks for a week or more each time, was to walk along the sandy bottom of the gully, actually away from the small group of shops which was to be her eventual destination, until its sides began to grow shallow. There, close to a large rock that protruded from the loose dust, a cattle track crossed the riverbed on its way from the main road to the smallest of Mutune's dams. From there, the walk to the shops was longer and all the way uphill, but the path was well worn and easy to walk at night, with neither potholes nor loose stones to cause problems.

It took her about ten minutes to make her way up the side of the narrow valley to the half dozen or so shops which comprised Mutune market. Here they were not real shops, but merely staging posts that sold nothing but soft drinks. One of the shops, however, was a bar and sold only beer. It therefore always had its regular clientele. In this almost private cluster of buildings, the many people who lived nearby and who relied upon the sale of their produce in nearby Kitui town market, would assemble during the day to await one of the many pick-up truck taxis which ran a shuttle service into the town. At night, when there were no waiting travellers, there were no soft drinks to sell and thus all the shops, except the bar, closed at sunset.

Josephine's path described a neat circle in order to avoid the voices that filled the cone of light spreading into the road from the open doorway of the bar. Walking behind the row of closed concrete box shops, she avoided the piles of sand and cement, the partly dug foundations and the Diesel-engined mixer which encroached onto the track and made for the junction of the main road to the town and the side road which led down to the school, the very road her dart through the hedge had left behind. It was there that she saw, as expected, a large white car parked by the roadside.

After quickly glancing about her to confirm the privacy of the place, Josephine crossed the road to the car and, after a light tap on a side window had attracted the attention of its occupant, she opened the passenger door and got in. Without any discernible hesitation - but then there was no one watching who might discern such a thing - she closed the door quietly behind her and then slid down in the seat until she could rest her head against the door's padded inside panel, beneath the level of the window.

"And how are you?" asked the man at her side.

"I am fine," said Josephine, as expected.

After a growl from the engine, the car's headlights lit and, within seconds, it had turned round and sped along the road past the dark silhouettes of the sleeping shops toward Kitui town. She did not try to sit up, even when, a few minutes later, the interior of the car was periodically flooded with the relative glare of Kitui town's sparse street lighting.

"Where are we going tonight?"

"The same place as last time."

"Where are we now?"

"Don't get up!" He spoke to her harshly, but the words were aimed at his own fears. "I have just turned the corner at the cathedral."

"It is quicker to turn by the prison."

He did not reply immediately. "We have to go past the police station if we go that way."

"But no one can see me if I crouch down here. Anyway, we are doing nothing wrong. All we are doing is riding in your car."

"It is better to be discreet, even when you have nothing to hide. Besides that, I am well known here. If I go past the offices and the police station, someone may recognise the car. Someone may try to stop us so that he can greet me. It would be very suspicious if I were simply to drive on."

His explanation did not satisfy Josephine for a moment, but she decided not to pursue the argument further. She knew from the beginning that she would always be a liability to John and that the only way she could be sure of prolonging their arrangement, which was proving to be so important to her, was to accept everything he said, and to do everything he asked without question.

After slowing down to turn left at the brow of the hill, the car took an immediate right turn and then stopped. They were there. Leaving the engine running, John got out of the driver's seat and walked into the broad beam of the headlights. Here Josephine risked a glance above the high dashboard immediately in front of her and she saw him remove a padlock and chain from a pair of iron gates. Then, after driving into the enclosed compound that Josephine had come to know so well, he drove the car under an open shelter where the air was thick with the smell of Diesel oil. She did not try to move until John gave the word, but she did not have to look to know what he was doing in the meantime. After switching off the car's lights and engine, he left his seat without even a glance in her direction. She heard the gates close and the rattle of the chain as he replaced it. Then, after a few seconds of silence, another key turned and a door opened. She heard John call a name several times but, thankfully, there was no reply.

"It's all right, you can come now."

Without waiting for her, he set off to retrace his steps across the unlit compound. At last Josephine sat up in her seat and watched as he picked his way carefully across the open ground. Like a cat, his eyes tested every footfall for safety, examined every inch of ground for sources of grime. Solid objects such as the old cans and odd pieces of metal which littered the place were easily seen and avoided, of course, but one could not be too careful, for the mechanics who worked here during the day drained the oil sumps of trucks wherever the driver happened to park his vehicle. If John were to tread on a patch of such ground, it might not only delay his departure in the morning - how could he possibly leave with dirty shoes? - but also might even ruin his clothing. She followed him, step for step.

They reached the doorway together. Josephine let him go in first as she always did. "Remember that you should not switch on the lights," he said softly.

She already knew what she should and should not do here. What she would do was, of course, presumed. It angered her that he insisted on treating her like a child, that even now, after so long, he appeared not to trust her to remember the conditions under which their arrangement could continue. If ever he brought it to an end she would tell him in no uncertain terms exactly what she thought of his condescension.

It was obviously an office. Each time she went there, in those fleeting seconds it took to feel her way to the door in the opposite corner, she tried to imagine herself at work behind the desk. Without those dreams, she would surely have turned back before this point on every occasion. It was behind such a desk that she could easily picture herself sitting in the not too distant future. In just a few more years, after finishing school and progressing through college, she aspired to be nothing less than a full-time assistant to a manager of an office like this. She would be polite and efficient and those whom she dealt with would respect her not only for her undeniable beauty, but also for her status and achievements.

Merely imagining the pride that this would bring made her feel inwardly warm and satisfied.

John opened the door and peered into the silent and total darkness it revealed. A cursory glance set his always troubled mind more at rest and audibly he began to breathe more slowly as he felt for the oil lamp he knew had been left for him on a small table by the door. A metallic crack echoed from the bare concrete walls as his fingers made contact with the handle.

"I have no matches," he whispered to Josephine.

It took her only a moment to retrieve her own box of Kuni *kibiriti*, full of long thin red-tipped sticks, of which about one in three was capable of lighting when struck against the side of the box from an attack distance of about two feet. She always carried a box of matches inside her bra and occasionally its cornered cuboid would press against her blouse, but here this was to be expected and would go unnoticed. As she handed them over to John, she felt a lingering touch of his hand on hers and she instinctively resented it.

The lamp was soon burning steadily. Its low yellow flame cast a dim flickering light and deep dark shadows about the room. The wire surround of a small electric fan on the desk near the lamp projected onto the bare concrete of the walls, making them irregularly patterned with criss-cross lines.

In an instant, as John ushered her aside so he could close the door behind them, she looked about and pitied herself. Like a closed corridor that led nowhere, the narrow stock room was cluttered and oppressive. The blank pitted concrete of the long wall opposite the door seemed to mirror her own lack of inner feeling. The first few times had been exciting. She felt that at last she had penetrated the other world and in John had gained a passport, which would guarantee her future admission to its ways in her own right, but time and experience had taught her that he was ashamed of her. He wrote the terms. She must accept them all or be rejected. Her acceptance of the role he offered had long since rendered their meetings as humdrum as their surroundings. Like the filing cabinets and cupboards that crowded this stock room, the things they acted out together were merely the trappings and details of a business transaction. They gave nothing to one another, but took whatever they could. Everything, though, happened within defined limits which both of them understood, he because he had laid them down and she because she had never been offered a choice. What she received, she needed and it benefited her; she had long since ceased to speculate about what he wanted. He still came to her, and that was all that mattered.

With the door now safely and securely locked behind him, he breathed a long and almost tired sigh. Now when he turned to face her, he smiled. He seemed suddenly relaxed, as if relieved of a long and tortuous tension. At last in this new guaranteed privacy he could begin to enjoy those comforts for which he had striven so hard and risked so much. Thus, by the time he came forward to embrace her, he seemed like a man who felt he was safe, at least for a while.

As ever, she responded immediately. No matter what disinterest she might have felt before this moment, once his body touched hers she was ready to play the game on his terms. Whatever she did, she knew that he would enjoy her and so she would enjoy him also, or at least try to. Before she met Boniface, it had been easy to trick herself into thinking that John saw her because she meant something special to him. It had been easier then to convince herself that she really did enjoy what he did to her, but now it was different. Everything had changed. Now she needed to work hard with John. She needed to act out a role to satisfy his demands for she knew that he listened to her intently and registered every movement of her body in search of what he might interpret as a compliment to himself.

Soon her blouse was undone and her bra hanging loose beneath it. Having been explored by his hands, her breasts were immediately neglected and thus the ritual progressed as his hands moved to press her bare thighs ever more roughly. This, the first encounter in what was becoming an ever greater battle with herself, had thus been won and, still according to the ritual, she broke free from his embrace. John needed no prompting. A broad smile spread across his face as he started to undress. His eyes, however, still followed every minute detail of Josephine's movement as she lay, now naked, on the low camp bed by the wall.

It was as usual some hours later when John left her. There were no smiles now. Josephine lay back and watched him dress in the now almost intense light from the oil lamp's flame. Why was he always in such a hurry? It made no difference to her. She lay back and watched him button his shirt. As ever, he seemed to resent her watching him. It troubled him, made him feel uneasy. It was as if this was not part of their unwritten agreement on what should be given and what could be taken and thus it threatened to jeopardise the future of the contract.

"Come on now. It's time to go," he said curtly.

She did not even try to mention that she was tired, that she had studied right up to nine o'clock that evening after starting classes at eight in the morning. That would have gone far beyond what both of them perceived as her rights. She simply did as he said and dressed.

They were soon ready to retrace their careful steps to the garaged car. John lifted the glass surround and blew out the oil lamp, plunging them both into a familiar but still claustrophobic darkness. From that moment, it seemed that the ritual ran in reverse until, some fifteen minutes later, it entered its habitual last phase as the white car crept to a halt near the shops at Mutune, almost the very spot where earlier Josephine had made her rendezvous.

John turned to face her. As he spoke in a whisper, he felt in the inside pocket of his jacket and took out a long leather wallet. "I will be coming to Kitui again in two weeks. I'll see you here at the usual time." With that he pushed a hundred shilling note into her hand. She did not bother even to look at it, but immediately pushed it inside her blouse and into the elastic safety of her bra.

"I will need to go home to Thitani for one week-end..." she said. It was delivered as an announcement, but like everything she said to him, contained at least an element of pleading.

"Then go next week-end. Then I can see you as usual in two weeks time. Here is an extra ten shillings for your bus fare... But remember Josephine..."

Though she heard these words that had been spoken so often in the past, she did not listen to them.

"Our arrangement can only continue if you are faithful to me. If you see any other man, no matter who it is, then I am finished with you. Do you understand?" He was not even looking at her as he spoke these last words, his attention having already moved on to the next part of their ritual encounter. "Right. Wait here a moment."

Without giving her even a second to react to his words, he got out of the car and closed the door behind him. She looked across at his broad back in the moonlight as the sound of his urine hitting the ground began.

"All clear," he said a few moments later.

She reacted like clockwork. As he again reclaimed his seat in the driver's side, she opened the passenger door and smartly got out of the car. Closing it firmly but quietly behind her, she walked ten brisk paces across the road and into the black moon-shadow of a large mango tree. She did not even look back. It had always been one of the unwritten rules that they should neither communicate nor even acknowledge one another's existence in any situation where others might see, and that inevitably included an open road outside Mutune market at two o'clock in the morning.

Not until she had reached the safety and anonymity of the shadows did Josephine turn to look back. For some reason she suddenly remembered standing there on the first few times she watched his car, KPY, she called it, after its registration mark, as it scythed its way through the night, casting a billowing mass of dust into the air which obscured the stars. She remembered how special she felt then, how much older and prouder she became as a result of thinking that now she knew all that was to be known and that no longer could her elders claim she was a mere child. Above all, however, she had seen then a vision of some new, almost tangible power. John had become hers. She possessed him. It was he who travelled to see her. It was he who lay after his invariably hurried and snatched ejaculation into her, as if he could no longer control even his own breathing. For some minutes, every time they had intercourse, it seemed she totally controlled him, ruled not only his passions but also, for this short time, his past, his future, his marriage and every inch of his flesh. She remembered still with deep satisfaction her discovery that during the lost dazed minutes that always followed his withdrawal from her that, with just the slightest touch of her finger, she could induce near convulsions in his body. Since then, the revelation had become a commonplace. Now she just wanted him to wake up and talk to her, which still he never did.

In those early days, she had also wondered if John thought of her in the way that she thought of him when they were apart. At one stage she began to wonder how she might exist for the two weeks until he came to her again, but now she suffered no such illness. These days the only real thrill he ever gave her was the rubbing of his crisp folded bank notes against her breast and the only satisfaction she gained was the knowledge that a little more of her future had been bought. Was this what as a child she had heard adults refer to as 'maturity'?

***

By the time her dream dissolved in a crash, as the car hit the step up onto Kitui town's tarmac, the baby was already dead. Perhaps it had been dead ever since they left Thitani over a half an hour ago. The strange thing was that she could not even remember having checked whether it was still breathing. She could remember, early that morning still calling her child "my little boy, Muthuu," but at some point, a point which she could no longer fix either in time or experience, she had started to think of her child as 'it', a mere object. Surely she had known for some time that it lay dead in her arms, but at the same time, could she still not hear the cries of her little Muthuu, if she so wished? So completely had her dreams removed her from the hectic reality around her that it seemed she had completely shut the immediate present out of her mind. Perhaps, for the last half an hour or so this had been her own sub-conscious way of protecting herself from a reality she could not face. And this reality was the pathetically small bundle, enclosed in a bright blue and white floral wrapper, which lay lifeless against her.

The bounce and slide of Michael's car over the rough dirt road had become almost hypnotic. At first she had tried to resist the pitches and sways which the car's over-tired suspension transmitted to its occupants, but soon she had simply given up, had relaxed and allowed herself to be thrown from side to side like so much luggage, surrounded by a cocoon of noise which drowned everything outside of herself. Not being able to see forward past the high headrests of the front seats from the slouched and burdened position she was forced to adopt in the back, she had looked to the side, where speed had blurred her eyes. She could have moved to a position of greater comfort, but that would have taken a conscious effort, and would have demanded that she instinctively uncover Muthuu to check on his own comfort during the process. This she simply was unwilling to do. Better that she should leave him - or it? - alone.

There had been nothing to do but dream, to allow herself to drift in the ever-present past of memory. It was not the first time she had relived her experiences with John Mwangangi, nor the first time she had tried to imagine how things might have been. She had no illusions about him that was for sure; at least none since those first few encounters when either he had tricked her or she had tricked herself into believing that he wanted her because she herself was special, or that he had found something special within her. It had not been long before she had learned to laugh at such delusions, before she had learned to laugh at herself for even thinking them, but now she was far beyond laughter. Perhaps that is what people meant by 'growing up'?

"Shit!" Michael's exclamation was delivered almost under his breath as the car hit a pothole in the road. From the newfound smoothness of the tarmac, Josephine was suddenly and violently jolted back in her seat and momentarily she let go of little Muthuu in his blue flowered bundle. The wrapper loosened, exposing a clearly lifeless face, now so small and screwed into a tiny and ugly knot by the pain of dying. It was dead.

In shock, she immediately felt strangely liberated, almost beyond her own life, as if her continued existence could serve no further purpose while this curse of death lived on inside her. And then her thoughts were suddenly sour. She had done nothing to deserve such a fate, of that she was sure. Why then should she be punished like this? It seemed that her life had never offered her a choice. Throughout she had merely followed orders yelled at her by necessity. She had been born into a large family. It had always been a supportive family, that was true, but was it her father's fault that he therefore never had enough money for her school fees? Was it her fault that the nuns would not allow any of the girls to work at weekends to earn their keep? Was it her fault that there were hundreds of school students like herself looking for work in the holidays and was it her fault that as a consequence all she could get was five shillings a day? Even if she had been able to find a job every day of the school holidays, she would never have been able to earn enough to pay all the fees she owed.

Was it her fault then that she had decided to sell the one thing she had for which people were willing to pay? In a country where enterprise in the market was encouraged as a means of achieving wealth, not only for individuals, but the nation as a whole, what could possibly be wrong with a woman selling a service to customers willing to pay? Why should anyone mind whether that service is delivered by hand, mouth, brain or vagina? Are bankers condemned by the Church as usurers? But which women are not seen as potential whores? For Josephine, selling her services to John Mwangangi - and, indeed, some other men like him whose need for gratification was channelled through their wallets - provided her with the only means at her disposal to become independent of the needs and desires of men. It was a means to pay her own way to a personal independence promised by the passport of education. And now it angered her to think that the only thing that allowed her to stay at school eventually banished her from it. After nearly eleven years of primary and secondary schooling, at a point when her goal was all but within her grasp, a man-child began its life within her.

***

A minute after the bell sounded the start of break, Josephine Ngao joined the straggling queue of sad-faced girls that had already formed outside the school office. None of them particularly wanted to stand there by the open door, but everyone wanted to be first when the cry of "Next" echoed forth from within. When Josephine appeared, however, all the girls immediately stood back to allow her pride of place. It was not fear of her that caused them all to withdraw from the doorway, but the simple knowledge that their prefect shared the sisters' power. The next turn would therefore be hers by right. It was not an egalitarian faith that these nuns taught, but a linear hierarchy at the head of which sat a God, male but de-sexed, sometimes in the form a Christ, who had defiled himself by becoming a man.

It was a small Form One girl who emerged from the head's office. Her face wore a blank expression of disappointment. Clearly Sister had refused her leave to defer payment of her school fees until the end of the month when her relatives' salaries would be paid. The story was common to all but a privileged few of the girls in this place. The knowing glance that she dared to cast towards Josephine said no more than, "Don't expect anything from her today..."

"Next!"

Josephine entered the office, taking care to close the door behind her. It scraped noisily on the concrete, having expanded after the recent rain. The sound caused an involuntary shudder in her spine and a weakness at the knee, like an orgasm without pleasure.

"Leave the door open, will you? It will stick and we won't be able to get out. I must get a man in to do something about it." Sister Augustus did not even appear to look up from the letter she was writing as she spoke.

Josephine hesitated at first. Looking at the concentric arcs of smudged brown earth the door had left on the floor, she feared that she might already have jammed it. She gave it a little pull back toward herself, but it did not move. Were these nerves? The instruction from Augustus, however, took hold of her actions, prompting her to leave the door and begin to speak. Still Sister had not looked her way.

"Sister Augustus, I wish to speak..."

"Oh, it's you Josephine." Augustus now not only looked up from her desk, but also immediately replaced the top on her fountain pen and set it aside carefully into a small storage rack on a shelf to her right. "It's all right. Leave the door. You can close it if you need to." It was suddenly a different person who spoke. Though Sister Augustus only rarely raised her voice and never lost her temper, her usual voice embodied a severity of tone that could arouse guilt in the innocent. When she spoke to Josephine, however, the hard edges softened, as if she were acknowledging that one day this girl might be her equal.

"Sister," she began, "I have come to see you because I am feeling very sick. I think I have malaria."

Sister Augustus eyed her carefully, but still without the suspicion which any other girl would have provoked. "And so you want to go to the health centre?"

Josephine paused almost imperceptibly here. Augustus noted that, but as yet did not interpret it. "No, Sister. I want to go to the hospital in Kitui town. I have been treated there before and I am known by the doctor. Anyway, the health centre has no pills these days. It is closed down until more supplies come in."

Augustus was silent for a while. Her inquisitive eyes held Josephine's unwavering gaze. Though it was obviously more convenient for girls from the school to be treated in Mutune's own health centre, she acknowledged that the place had descended to a pitiful state under a nurse who spent most of his time drinking with the primary school teachers in the local bar. As a result, it was always short of basic supplies and was therefore making her own job that much more difficult. If a girl were really ill, she would now have to go into the town to the hospital, because treatment was simply no longer available locally. Knowing this, however, all the girls seemed to want to be treated for something and most of the requests, as far as Sister Augustus was concerned, were mere excuses for a day out in town.

In this case, however, she knew that Josephine had always worked as hard as any girl in the school, and that of all her pupils, Josephine was one of the most highly motivated and trustworthy. It was to create a role model for others in both of these areas that she and the other nuns had made Josephine a prefect. Thus, after this short concentrated pause for thought and then judgment, Augustus turned to the side and retrieved her fountain pen from its stand. "I will write a note for you, but remember that the longer you stay away, the more work you are missing." Sister's slight frame bent forward over the desk as she took a sheet of headed notepaper from a tray on her left and began to write. She was more shortsighted than her thin-framed glasses could correct and so habitually had to bend her head right over to bring her eyes closer to the paper. From where she sat, Josephine would have been able to have a full view of the bald patch she knew to be there, on the very top of Sister's head. As it was, of course, Augustus was wearing her veil and, like all the other girls Josephine was left to merely imagine whether all white women lost their hair as they grew older.

"I will do extra prep next week to make up for it, Sister," said Josephine, acknowledging the obvious. It was with great difficulty that she suppressed the expression of the deep relief she felt.

She was lucky. When she arrived at the nearby shops, there was a pick-up truck already laden with people ready to set off for the town. The one shilling coin she gave the driver was apparently enough to persuade him that the trip as a whole would be profitable and so the truck set off immediately.

Some three hours elapsed before Josephine walked away from the hospital with her bottle of pills. After the sweaty stuffiness of the crammed waiting rooms and corridors inside, the cool breeze that whistled through the tall trees by the entrance to the compound came as a welcome relief. It had been a very long wait, certainly longer than she had anticipated, but she had no choice but to stay. Sister Augustus would undoubtedly want to see some proof that she had been to the hospital and that her mission had been accomplished successfully.

The walk back to Kalundu market, where the pick-up taxis awaited their business, took her from one end of this District Centre town to the other. She paused only once in the mile or so she had to walk, only yards from the hospital gate to cast a short emotionless glance at a wire-fenced compound where a group of workmen were servicing a lorry. Just behind the lorry, and obscured by it, was the low building where the bus company's office was housed, and beyond that was the stock room with its mattress where she had so often offered herself as a vessel for John Mwangangi's sperm.

Within ten minutes she had reached the open market place, walked straight across it, ignoring both the pick-ups and the buses, and set off alone and on foot along the road to Mutune.

Nestling behind Kalundu market's shops and tea rooms, up and over the low hill with is cluster of ragged banana plants, and only just visible through a gap in the high euphorbia hedges which edged both sides of the road, was a small neatly kept group of small hutch-like houses which had become one of Kitui's most notable sites. Surprising herself, Josephine felt no guilt whatsoever as she walked down the almost manicured, white stone-edged path which led to the place which had all along been her journey's prime destination. She knew she had been utterly stupid to have put off the decision for so long, and began to curse herself for having been so afraid of lying to Sister Augustus. In the event, it had all been very easy. So it was now the light-headedness of sheer relief that caused a broad smile to grow as she rapped on the door of the first of the small, strange houses.

There was no answer. "*Hodi*!" she shouted again and again, but to no avail. It seemed there was no one here to rouse. Standing back to survey the scene, her smile broadened further as her eyes scanned the wonderful paintings that covered the wall before her. Here, a laughing woman receives the attention of a highly aroused and quite enormous man. In her hand she clasps a small medicine bottle. There, two men shake hands across the table strewn with beer bottles. Beneath the table one stabs the other in the groin with a spear.

"Your business, young lady?"

The sharp words made her jump. She looked back at the door where she had knocked. It was still shut. There must be another door or a window on the other side, she thought, and set off to walk round the house. She had taken only a step, however, before she was stopped in her tracks by more words from this disembodied voice, this time angrier and louder than before.

"State your business, young lady."

With at first wide-eyed disbelief and then almost uncontrolled amusement, she stared at the painted skeleton by the side of the door which, apparently, had uttered the words. She had not noticed before that its eyes and mouth were holes in the wall.

"I have come for some *dawa*," she said. She felt strange, almost as if she wanted to laugh at the comical image she faced. But equally, it could have been her nervousness which caused this unexpected and for her almost unnatural behaviour. When she was really afraid, she often gave the impression she was laughing. It was certainly not this silly cartoon that caused fear to start to well inside her; rather it was the sudden realisation of what it was she was about to request that darkened her world like a cloud.

"You can buy aspirin from the shop over there in the market," said the skeleton, impatiently. "I am busy. Don't waste my time. It could be an expensive mistake for you to make."

"I have been told that only you can give me the medicine I need."

"Then state your business," said the skeleton. "Is it a lover you want to woo? That's my speciality."

Josephine smiled again at the irony. "I have already wooed my lover, but too often, I am afraid. I have a child." And the smile faded again.

"But that is good news, young lady. Your lover is now your husband." A skeleton's eyes flashed a glance at her for an extended moment and then withdrew.

"I cannot be married yet. I am a student. I have to finish my education before I can even begin to think about such things."

There was a short pause before the skeleton spoke again. "It seems to me that you have at least thought about such things already."

Josephine did not respond, unable to decide whether what was said was meant as a joke of some kind.

"The *dawa* costs fifty shillings." The skeleton's eyes flashed again. She could not even tell if the voice was that of a woman or a man.

"I have it here," she said in reply, quickly, thrusting her hand inside her blouse to extract the crumpled and sweaty bank notes from her bra.

"Ah, my fool!" The skeleton almost sang its words. "I am hungry. Feed me!"

Josephine strode toward the wall and pushed her money through the skeleton's gaping mouth. She felt a hand grasp the money and pull it from her fingers.

"Your bottles?"

Josephine looked confused. The skeleton's eyes flashed inquisitively at her again. "Bottles?" she said, nervously imitating the strange disconnected way in which the word had been said to her.

"Young lady, what you are asking for is powerful *dawa*. You must carry it home before you take it. I need two bottles. Do you have them?"

She did not answer.

"If you have no bottles, I will provide them, but you will have to pay a five shilling deposit."

"I have only two shillings."

"Not enough."

"Can you wait a few minutes?"

Josephine turned away before the answer came. It took her only a minute to run back to Kalundu market and into the teashop. Here one shilling and fifty cents was enough to buy the smallest bottle of lemonade the shop had to offer. Her bus fare was gone as a result, but after all this it was better than going home empty handed. By the time she returned to the skeleton's house, she had not merely drunk the lemonade, but also emptied out onto the road all the anti-malaria pills from the small bottle she had been given by the hospital doctor.

"I have the bottles," she said, expecting an immediate reply, as if she had never left the place.

It took a minute or more, plus several ever more impatient repetitions of Josephine's claim before there was any response. The skeleton's eyes reappeared and looked at her long and hard. "I can eat bottles as well."

It took her a few seconds to interpret the words, but then all became clear. Nothing more came from the skeleton before she had fed both bottles through the mouth-hole cut in the wall of the house. Then, after she had stepped back to await the results of feeding time, several minutes elapsed. By that time she had grown quite worried. On several occasions, she was convinced that there had been stirring inside, but throughout she had been too frightened to approach any closer than to within ten yards of the house.

Momentarily, she was tempted to peep inside through the skeleton's now vacant eyeholes. Hesitantly, she edged forward, but she had moved no more than a full pace when she was overcome by a fear of the unknown and retreated. She was in no position to take such risks. Without the medicine only this person could provide, she would certainly lose everything she had, so she remained at a safe distance. Almost twenty silent minutes passed before she was again summoned by the rattle of glass in the skeleton's mouth, but during that time, none of the nervous expectancy left her.

"Now you should listen to me very carefully indeed," said the skeleton, as the bottles spewed from its mouth. "First of all remember that this is very powerful *dawa*. It can do the job you wish, but you must follow my instructions to the letter. Do you understand?"

"I will do as you say."

"Good. Now there are two bottles. In the small one there is a powder and in the large one there is a liquid. You are to go straight home from here without pausing on the way and it is important that you should run all the way. Be sure that when you reach your destination that you have run all the way and as fast as you can. You should be completely exhausted when you arrive. You will be very thirsty and will have sweated very much. But you must neither drink water nor wash your body. Then wait until sunset and go immediately to your bed. Lie down there without removing your clothes and concentrate very hard on the thing you are about to do. When you feel you are ready, take a glass and mix the powder with the liquid. You must first place the powder in the glass and then add the liquid a little at a time, always making sure that you stir them so that they mix properly. When you have added all the liquid, put away the bottles in a place where they will not be found by any stranger. Then you should begin. Using your left hand only, you should rub small amounts of the liquid onto your vagina, making sure that it mixes well with your body's own juices when they start to flow. Soon you will start to feel the same pleasure that he gave you when he planted his seed inside you. You will feel it start to grow, but as you use more of the *dawa*, you will also feel yourself going more numb between your legs. It will take some time for the waves of joy to come, but when they do, even as you gasp for your breath, you must immediately drink all that is left in the glass. Is that clear?"

Josephine eyed the bottles with some confusion. She had not expected to feel so afraid of this man's power. "But how much will I need? And how much of it should I drink, and how much should I use down there?" The sound was pathetic and confused.

The skeleton laughed long and hard. "Ah, my pretty young woman, that is for you to decide. It depends on the size of the man you slept with. If he was tall and strong, with a penis that filled and stretched you, then use it all. If he was a weakling with a matchstick tool you could hardly see, let alone feel inside you, then a mere sip would do. The child of a strong and powerful warrior could withstand all of my medicine, but you yourself might not. The child of an impotent boy on the other hand would run away at the first sniff of the stuff. It is you who knows the man, not I. And remember also, that the more you run and tire yourself, the better and quicker my medicine will act on you."

When Josephine finally looked up, the eyes had gone from their sockets. She called again to the painting on the wall, but the skeleton would not be cajoled back to life. It was much more complicated than she had been led to expect. Regina, in whom she had confided, had described the treatment like something which you took for malaria, but then she had admitted that she had never seen any of the medicine herself and was only going on what she knew from talking to the bar girls in Kitui town, who out of necessity had to do this kind of thing all the time. So, as she walked slowly away from the house, still examining the contents of her bottles, she began to doubt the wisdom of her decision.

"Remember to run... to run... to run!" came a voice from behind her, making her jump with fright. She turned round but saw no one. Even the skeleton's eyes were still empty. As much out of fright as compliance, she broke into a run and, turning right out of the compound onto the road, she set off for school.

It was not easy to run along this road. It was quite narrow, and there were quite frequent pick-up truck taxis which ran along there linking Kitui town and Mutune market. As each one approached, Josephine had to slow down and get right off the road to the side to allow it to pass. Most of them, of course, also stopped right next to her, thinking that she would want to board for a ride back to school and every time she had to explain at length that she did not want to ride home. The ones that did not stop, on the other hand, showered her with a cloud of dust that the vehicles threw up as they progressed along the dirt road.

Now in the event, whether it was doubt, growing fright, a new feeling of guilt, or merely a fear of discovery, she would never remember. Perhaps it was her inability to decide which man it was she was trying to overcome. Throughout her headlong dusty dash back to school in the fierce heat of the late afternoon, she tried in vain to reconstruct the already dimly remembered events of the previous weeks. She knew she had seen Boniface three times recently, but could not decide if John had visited her once or twice since her last period. For some months past, time spent with him had been so featureless, so completely matter of fact and predictable that she found it difficult to remember anything but the last occasion.

She knew, however, that it was important that she should remember, because the two men were so completely different. If it had been Boniface who planted the child in her, she thought she might need only half of the medicine to uproot it. He was a nice man and she liked him. He was always warm, kind and respectful to her, but she knew that without her help he would never have found his way around her body. John, however, was different. He was a hard, unfeeling man, tall, strong and extremely virile. Memories of how he would almost order her to respond to him sent a shiver down her spine. And she could remember the wonder she felt the first time she took his great thing in her hands and found that it filled them both and still stuck out at the top. Boniface was a nice man, but he was not a big man in that way. And might it make a difference if she had taken the man in her mouth as she had with John so often? How would that affect the amount she should drink? Why had she not asked all these questions when the skeleton had asked? The mere thought of having to take all of the doctor's medicine to loosen John's child make her feel horribly sick. The mere smell of that oily liquid was enough to turn her stomach.

Whoever she chose to treat, she knew, however, that she simply could not risk taking the medicine at school. She had nowhere private here to do it and, even if she were to find some out of the way corner, she would never be able to concentrate on what she had to do. Surely she would be constantly afraid of being discovered. It would have to wait until she went home to Thitani at the weekend. She would still make sure that she followed every instruction she had been given, so what possible difference could it make? There was the complication of finding somewhere to hide her bottles and their smell until then. And the lemonade bottle with the powder did not even have a stopper. Where could she possibly keep that safe? There was only one answer.

When she neared the school, her pace slowed to a walk, so that she might enter with the decorum demanded of her position. But when she reached the gap in the hedge that many of the younger girls used to sneak out of the school compound, she was still panting, partly out of nerves and fear of failure, as well as a result of her exertions. The school was empty. She knew it would be. They were all at prayers, the Roman Catholic minority in the Church by the mission house, the Protestants in the school hall at the other end of the compound.

Josephine covered the twenty yards of open ground between the hedge and the main school block at speed. No one saw her. Within seconds she was sitting at her desk in the Form Four classroom, casting a studious but nervous eye over a mathematics text. She had already acted quickly and precisely. Everything had gone according to the plan that she had so carefully thought out and now there was just one more hurdle to be overcome.

The door opened with a sharp click. Josephine looked up quickly from her book with a calculated expression of guilt on her face.

Sister Augustus looked quizzically into the room at her. Having been distracted from her labours over the school's cashbook by Josephine's rather noisy return, she had left her office to investigate. "Josephine, why aren't you at church?"

"Sister, I have just come back from the hospital in Kitui. It was very full and I had to wait a very long time indeed before I was seen by the doctor." Sister Augustus raised her eyebrows. Josephine knew she would expect more than this. "I tried to get here as fast as I could, but the taxis were all very full and anyway I had to use all of my money to buy the extra medicine the doctor said my malaria would need. So I had no bus fare. I ran all the way, but I was still too late to go to church. The service had already started. So I thought that because I had missed my classes, I should come in here and try to catch up with the work."

"Did the doctor give you pills for the malaria?"

"No, Sister, he gave me an injection instead. It was very expensive. He said that I should wait for three days and then if I am no better I should go back for more treatment and perhaps pills as well."

Sister Augustus nodded sagely. Since she never seemed more than half convinced even by the truth, the mere second-long glance she cast toward Josephine as she closed the classroom door was interpreted by the girl as confirmation of victory. When the door opened again, however, her heart momentarily raced with fear. Had there been some tiny error in what she had said? Had Sister found some crack of inconsistency through which she might prise her way into the chasm that was the vast world of Josephine Ngao's lies? But indeed she was safe. "Look, Josephine, don't bother with that now. You're hot and tired and just look at the dust from the road all over you. Go over to the washrooms and get yourself cleaned up."

"Yes, Sister." Not until the nun's light, quick footsteps had faded into silence did Josephine risk a self-satisfied glance inside her desk. There, propped upright for safety between the side panel and piled copies of 'The Moon and Sixpence', Wilson's 'Simplified Swahili' and The Bible, nestled the two bottles that would save her life. As she closed the desk lid and replaced the securing padlock with meticulous care, she finally allowed herself an at least partially relieved victory smile.

By the end of the week she had lost everything, except, that is, for the baby and Boniface, who was thus in the process transformed from a boyfriend into a husband to be. The weekend had arrived and, as planned, she had travelled home to Thitani with her medicine bottles safely corked and stowed securely inside her padlocked school box. As usual she had arranged to stay at her friend's house close to Thitani market and, since it had been too late to take her medicine that night, she had gone to the bar to see Boniface and, almost inevitably, she had spent the night with him on the floor of his father's shop. After all what was already done could not be made worse now. The experience, though contracted willingly and enjoyed, convinced her that the child inside her must be John's. Boniface, unlike her mature lover of some time past, filled the grasp of only one of her hands, with about an inch protruding from the end. John was at least three inches longer, she thought. Boniface imagined that the shudder which ran through her body as she pumped what little remained of the foreskin of his penis with her hand might even be a sympathetic twinge of feeling caused by the excitement of touching him, but thankfully he remained blissfully ignorant of the real reason which, of course, was that Josephine had felt suddenly afraid of the size of the dose she must now take.

Thus, on the Saturday, as she began the preparations for her treatment by convincing her friend that she felt too sick to go to the bar that evening, she had grown resigned to the fact that half measures would have no effect and should not therefore be risked. Once alone, she set about her task with unshakable confidence and without a single second thought, but still harbouring a multitude of ill-defined fears. What if this medicine did not work? What would she do then? What would happen if she were disturbed and thus forced to swallow the mixture before the crucial moment and therefore before the job was complete? Whatever her fears, there was surely no going back now.

She followed the instructions to the letter and, to be safe, used all the medicine she had been given. But she did forget one thing, and only realised this much later. What she did not do was completely exhaust herself by running and sweating. Perhaps this might have prevented the treatment from entering her blood quickly enough? She would never know.

In her friend's plastic cup she carefully mixed the powder and the liquid and washed out both bottles with water to make sure that every last drop and grain had been extracted. Was this another mistake? Might the water have diluted the important ingredient, whatever it might have been? She waited until darkness fell before she lay down on her friend's bed. By then the interior of the low mud-walled house was completely black. She dare not light a lamp in case someone else in the compound noticed it and came in to investigate. Neither dare she pull back the sackcloth that covered the doorway to let in the moonlight. At all costs, she must preserve her privacy. But really none of this mattered, because she had already made up her mind to drink everything that was left in the cup when the moment came.

She began by dipping her fingers of her left hand into the liquid. It felt strangely cold when it met the air, and her fingers began to feel numb even as she moved her hand the short distance from the cup onto her thigh. Then, using the three middle fingers levelled together as had become her preferred habit, she began to rub the outer lips of her vagina. Another dip in the cup and a more determined push parted the lips and let her fingers find the inner flesh that grew to the touch. She felt strangely cold again, as if her damp flesh were being drained of life's heat, but soon, as her own fluids began to flow, the sensation eased.

And then the pressure of her touch found the centre of her sensation. She closed her eyes and settled down in the bed a little. Dearly she wanted to press her breasts with her other hand, but she dare not let go of the cup she held so firm in her right hand. Another dip with her fingers and more gentle pulses through the wetness. A little harder here, softer there, a finger inside, around, flat, pointed, soft and hard.

Soon she felt herself open. Her legs started to stiffen and stretch in the way that they always did when the muscles in her buttocks began to squeeze their involuntary rhythm. It was almost time. Another dip into the wet and more coldness, and another pause to regain her readiness. And then she felt she was there. She raised the cup to her lips and drank in gulps as her hand worked itself flat against her swollen clitoris. The taste was vile, like earth mixed with water; but so cold on her lips and in her throat. Why so cold? Pieces of grit seemed to stick in her mouth, under her tongue and between her teeth. Her body tried to cough but she suppressed it.

Suddenly her head began to spin in a way she had never felt before. Though now retching and coughing, she fought against the complaints of her own body to complete the task. Still there was more to drink as her hand worked hard against her body. She was there and cried out as one giant convulsion and then another and then a smaller one and another and another and another and another filled her stomach and spine. A gasp sent some of the liquid up her throat and into her nose. It stung, and in less than an instant ecstasy crossed that narrowest of thresholds into pain. She couldn't breathe and, while inside her nerves rejoiced at the relief the orgasm had granted, an uncontrollable reaction simultaneously emptied her stomach and throat. She even tried to seal her lips, but consciousness no longer had any power over her body, and she was just able to turn to the side before the foul smelling liquid flowed from her mouth as if propelled by the death-like gasp that came with it. In one great stream everything she had just drunk spilled out of her and, just seconds later, through a muted scream, she fell back onto the bed, exhausted, her left hand still cupping the comfort of her pubic hair. The smell of her own vomit continued to make her retch for some time, but there was nothing left inside her to expel. Where the vile medicine had touched her between her legs, she now felt nothing at all through the numbness that had grown there. Suddenly she was thirsty and she tried to stand, but when she did the house moved around her, spinning at first and then turning upside down before blackness came...

It was some twelve hours later when her friend's mother found her on the floor, lying in her own vomit. Even then, she took some time to come round and was still not fully aware of what was happening to her even when she was being lifted back onto the bed. She was conscious only for a short time and then slept again. By the end of that day, a Sunday of all days, her father had been told of her secret. Her friend Regina had grown so afraid that Josephine might die that she had thought it best to tell all so that whatever might be done to help could at least be attempted.

In his inimitable way, Josephine's father acted immediately and, even before she was well enough to be told what he had decided, he had written to Mutune Girls' School, informing Sister Augustus what his daughter had done. In addition, that very afternoon, the old man went to Thitani market to confront Julius Mutisya with at least the gist of what his son had accomplished inside his daughter. He knew this was the right way to conduct himself in the circumstances. He should address the father of the son, one of equal status to himself, rather than approach the son directly. This surely was the right thing to do. Both Julius Mutisya, himself, and his entire family were respectable people. They surely would respond to fair treatment and accept what was now a collective family debt in relation to his daughter. In the event, Sub-Chief Ngao's analysis proved to be utterly correct in every detail.

An expulsion letter arrived from Mutune by return of post and so Josephine never again even visited the place. Augustus had the girl's remaining possessions heaped into a cardboard box and sent on to her via one of the priests from Mwingi, who happened to be passing through on his way home. Though the nuns would live to regard the loss of Josephine as a great shame for all concerned, they believed as one that she had only herself to blame.

It was to be sooner than either Josephine or Boniface could have thought possible that they were declared man and wife. Now, protests about intended careers or a calling to the priesthood were not only scoffed at, they were positively derided, to the extent that neither bride nor groom felt able to raise the slightest objection to what was now inevitable. And so they were married, at a simple ceremony, itself hurried, in Thitani's converted classroom. Father Michael, who conducted the proceedings, was as embarrassed as everyone else who attended and simply wanted to get the thing over with as quickly as possible. Less than four months later, when the child aborted itself after Josephine had walked home the six miles from Migwani market on a hot and dry Friday afternoon, Boniface cried with a mixture of disappointment, pique and shame. Josephine, however, though outwardly as grieved as her husband, inwardly gave thanks to God for answering her prayers.

***

With this, the death of her second child, however, it seemed that all the guilt which her life as a prostitute ought to have provoked, but never did, was suddenly given form within her. It was as if she now knew that she and she alone had been the cause of the misfortune that had beset their marriage. In the past she had been too willing to blame Boniface for spending too much time at school or in the bar. Now she knew that the fault was within her. Inside her, there was a poison, a spell that had infected her womb and all that grew there. She could never be a true wife to Boniface, or to any other man for that matter, because now she was capable of giving birth only to sterility and death. The confusion that she still felt unable to express thus transformed into anger.

"Let me out!"

Boniface turned to look at her quizzically. "But we are not yet at the hospital, Josephine. Father will come back in a minute. I am sure he has only gone inside the mission house to do some very quick job..."

"Boniface, you don't understand. Let me out. How do I open this door?"

"Josephine, it will take you too long to walk around to the hospital from here. Look! See, what did I tell you? Here comes Father Michael now. I told you he would only be a few moments."

"Boniface, I want to get out of the car," she repeated defiantly as she reached around the side of the still vacant driver's seat to search for the lever which would release its fixing catch. Boniface, however, was much more interested in how quickly Michael would get them under way again and he completely ignored what Josephine said and did.

For his part, so oblivious had Michael become to everything outside his own inner thoughts that he did not even realise that he very nearly trapped Josephine's hand in the door as he slammed it behind him. She, of course, reacted instantaneously and withdrew it with an angry cry. Neither of the two men in the front seats paid the slightest attention to her. "Why is this man always in such a hurry?" she screamed to her husband in Kikamba, as the car lurched from reverse into a headlong screech down to the road. Michael could only understand a word or two of what she said.

"Stop! Stop! Stop! Please stop the car and let me out!" she screamed as the car reached the tarmac.

This time the outburst prompted Michael to slam hard on the brakes, causing the car to skid across the sharp lock he had steered to turn left onto the road. By the time they had ground to a halt, it had slid down off the tar and onto the rutted earth next to the roadside gutter, casting a swirling plume of dust skyward.

Almost together, Boniface and Michael turned round to confront Josephine with their combined inquisitive and impatient stare. Boniface, the one that was her husband, she thought, looked both naive and immature. He had still not grasped the truth that ought by now to have been obvious. His expression quizzed her, as if inquiring after the comfort of the car's back seat. Michael's face, however, was bright red. His eyes were angry and impatient, as if challenging her very right to speak. He made her feel like a child who had trespassed on a neighbour's field and who was about to be accused of stealing maize.

"It's dead. Finished. Why go on?"

Her husband showed not a sign of either shock or grief. His blank eyes simply carried on gazing at her. Michael's expression, however, suddenly changed. No longer did his manner seek to challenge her. His assertiveness seemed to dissolve and like a chameleon, he changed colour, turning completely white, as if he had suddenly seen some great fear. He cast a quick sideways glance at Boniface, and then looked down at the still-wrapped baby and then back to Boniface. There were no clues to be found, it seemed.

"I want to get out," she said firmly. Her hand began to tug and pull at anything that looked even vaguely like a handle at her side. There was a click.

"The stupid fool," she thought. Why had her idiot of a husband made her crawl into the car through the front door when there were special ones for the back seat?

In a moment she was out of the car and, without a single backward glance, already on her way. Her child felt far heavier in death than ever it had done in its short life. Perhaps it was more of a burden now. For some reason, she set off at a high pace, but within a few strides it quickly slowed and her step shortened. She began to feel just a little faint.

"Josephine! Wait!" shouted Boniface.

She stopped, but did not turn round.

"Josephine, wait! Don't be angry," said Boniface, as he caught up with her. He had left the passenger door of the car swinging open. Michael still sat motionless in the driver's seat as if already haunted by what had just happened. "Don't be angry, Josephine," said Boniface as he moved to stand directly in front of her. It was as if he was trying to bar her way. "Perhaps it was never meant to live?"

An aching guilt suddenly flooded her eyes with tears. Boniface was right. She was surely to blame. She had infected his child with the poison she had planted within herself and which surely flourished in the pathetic deceit which had been her life.

"Please sit down, Josephine. I think you are not well." Boniface helped his wife to a place where there were stones and bricks strewn in a pile by the side of the road. Here, almost in the shadow of the cathedral, on any normal day, people would assemble to wait for the southbound buses to Mombasa and Mutito and would pass the time of day sitting on these stones to chat whilst they surveyed every vehicle as it passed smoothly over Kitui town's hissing tarmac.

Josephine sat and buried her face in her hands. She cried out in anger, not grief, at the sight of the inanimate bundle of cloth at her feet. She was angry with herself, with Michael, with Boniface, but above all she was angry with the spirit that had infected her womanhood and taken it away to use for itself. She prayed that a knife should appear in her hands so that there and then she could cut out the death that surely lived inside her. If there had been such a knife in her hand, surely she would have taken her life and thus would duly have returned it to its rightful owner like a mother who had preserved a father's sperm until it could breathe for itself.

A vehicle passed by and stopped. She did not look up at first. A horn sounded angrily. She heard the growl of a revving engine and screech of brakes as a single sound. It made her look up. There were several shouts and people were running down the road towards Father Michael's still stationary car. Having had her head buried in her hands, she had not seen it momentarily set off and then immediately stop again. There was suddenly a lot of noise, a lot of shouting.

And then she saw KPY. The white Mercedes stood close behind Father Michael's car and was now blocked in by a herd of cows wandering down the road. It was KPY. It took some minutes before the confusion born of shock and grief began to dissolve and thus allow her to apportion blame. Surely this was God's work. Surely only He could have presented her with such an opportunity.

In a shocked instant, all her grief dissolved. Her tears dried and all the hate and anger, which her self-pity had enclosed for over two years, begged for release. It seemed like instinct itself, which brought her to her feet and demanded she walk briskly but with dignity intact toward the car she knew so well. Boniface was so surprised by the speed of her movement that he did not even have time to call her name as she left him. He began to follow, but her shouted words stopped him dead in his tracks.

"Take it! Take it!" she screamed at the man inside the car. The window of the passenger door was still closed, but from his agitation, it was clear that he could hear what she said.

Charles Mulonzya wound down the window and reached out towards her. With a defiant shove, he tried to push her away from the car, but, belying her small and fragile frame, she was now surprisingly strong. His hands slipped awkwardly as she sidestepped his lunge toward her.

With lightning speed and single-minded accuracy, she shoved her baby's corpse into the car through the open window. "This is what you planted inside me, John! Take it! Take it! It can replace the one which really was yours and which you never wanted to know!"

Charles Mulonzya squirmed sideways across the front of the car and bundled himself into the driver's seat. He shouted something out of the window that only those people on that side of the car heard above the rest of the commotion. "There seems to be some mistake. This woman thinks I am someone else..." And then the Mercedes' engine started. The windows began to rise by themselves as if by magic, and threatened to trap Josephine's arms as they reached across to try to catch hold of the jacket of the man she knew as John. And then KPY lurched forward, knocking over three of the assembled onlookers. They were not hurt and immediately got up and ran aside, out of the car's way. The others also got the message and rushed as if with one mind out of the obvious path of the car. With Josephine momentarily disengaged, her continued attempts to grab something which the side of the car might present were rendered futile by its immense power, Charles took his chance. Reaching across to the passenger seat, he took hold of the bundle that had fallen onto the floor. Reluctantly, as if handling something that was fundamentally and inherently dirty, he picked it up. With a simple manoeuvre which never actually exposed any part of the wrapper's contents, he opened the driver's door and dropped the whole thing onto the road, an act which very few - but at least some - of the onlookers registered. With a dull, almost silent thud, the dead child fell into the road and the white car sped off with a screech from its tyres, forcing its way through the milling people and cows which now filled the road. While Boniface continued to watch and listen to the now constant repetitions of his wife's words, he became oblivious to the nearby plight of Father Michael, to everything in fact, save his own latent desires.

Munyasya

Munyasya troubled people little. The less he interfered in their day the better it was for everyone. Nevertheless, he was never ignored. He had become a part of the town, an apparently permanent feature of its life. Wherever he went, all attention was automatically his. His every wish or whim was answered, though usually he demanded nothing, and his every incomprehensible word was heeded and interpreted by anyone who might hear. He was capable of talking continually to himself in a gravelly speech, which, for the most part, was no more than a breathless whisper, a mumble whining from the chest. Hidden beneath the lank strands of saliva-matted hair which formed his full, but straggling moustache and beard, his lips could often hardly be seen to move as he spoke, so his voice seemed more of his body than his mouth. His chest, naked and hairless, possessed the concavity of decrepit old age, his entire body appearing bottom-heavy as if the organs it once held and supported had slipped to the depths of his distended belly, the breath fuelling his words coming more from the gut than the lungs. If he spoke louder, his stomach would heave, swell and contract like a wrinkled balloon, mimicking the rise and fall of his voice.

This was Munyasya, old, weary and weak, his blank, dark eyes clouded red with drink, dressed only in torn shorts and the brown remains of a raincoat; but always all this was proudly topped by an army officer's hat, with a resplendent shiny black peak. The regular polishing of this, with spit and a vigorous rub with a torn flap of his coat, was his only, but dutifully, if sometimes inaccurately, performed daily chore. As a result, though the peak still shone, the rest of the hat was blotched with stains where wayward gobs had been rubbed into the felt. Thus he sits each day beneath the shade of the broad acacia in the market place, his spidery legs spread like broken twigs from a felled bush that was never quite a tree, until the bottle that he never releases is again empty.

Then he rises to his feet and, with the slow laboured deliberation of the destitute, he begins to hobble, to shuffle short step by short step, his movement so heavy that the dust beneath his feet might be mire. Without his stick he could surely never walk. It seems to take the entire weight of his double-bent body, so that his legs might be released from their burden to edge forward, hindered only by their own weakness. Slowly, deliberately, his bent form crosses the shadeless open ground of the market-place until he reaches the bar, his goal, towards which surely only instinct guides him now, since there can be little sight left in his eyes.

This bar, whose crude, rusty tin roof cracks and creaks in the ever present Migwani wind, whose mud walls melt with each storm; this is Munyasya's goal. He is known here. This small rectangular hut, windowless yet draughty and cool is his only true home now, the only sanctuary that he himself knows. Inside it is surprisingly light. Walls, which appear from the outside to be featureless and dark, are transformed on entering. In fact they are painted white, though a white which in places has faded badly. Near the earth floor, the walls display brown rivulet stains where liquids of various types have spilled or splashed. Higher up, a grand repeated image contrasts with the stronger, less discoloured white. A gaping wide-eyed hunter is wrestling with a snake that is coiling both its body and its absurdly long tongue about his limbs. Waving above and below this painting is a motto in Kikamba that roughly translated could mean 'One finger alone cannot kill fleas'.

On entering, he says nothing, yet, as always, he appears to speak constantly, thus demanding the attention of all assembled there, but never quite divulging the only part-heard secrets in his voice. Having crossed the room in his methodical, machine-like but stalling step, he habitually slams down his empty bottle onto the plastic-topped counter, always neatly avoiding the wide metal grille which stretches from bar to roof (there is no ceiling) to protect the till from those who, in the past, have been tempted to grab what they can and run (but never very far).

Maluki, the barman, and the latest in a long line of renowned brewers of *uki*, a home-brew of sugar and water, then fills the bottle from his apparently bottomless jug and places it on the counter. Not a word is said. Sometimes, there is not even a glance of either greeting or acknowledgement for Munyasya. The sooner the job is done, the sooner the old man will go and leave the customers in peace and untroubled.

Two heavy raps of the bottle on the counter is the sign that it is full and then, somehow, the old man's hands grope and feel their way until they find their prize. And they grasp it. Then, like clockwork, he raises the bottle to his lips (to check that it has been filled to the top?) and with a new smile lighting his entire face finally turns to begin his shuffling hobble back to the tree, his shade, his rest.

There he dozes away the long hours of daylight, occasionally drinking his beer, taking no more than a sip each time, until the shivering cold of darkness forces him to cross the square back to the bar once again. There, after another refill of the bottle, he sits in a corner on the bare earth floor and sleeps, untroubled and ignored, still grasping his beer bottle as if he dare not let it go.

When morning comes, he awakens at sunrise when the first warming rays from the east filter through the bar's holed and unhinged door. He gently pats the rough ground at his side with the palms of his hands until he finds the food which Maluki always provides, unasked. Always ignoring the spoon, which nevertheless the barman never forgets to supply, he eats his daily ration of boiled goat's liver and bread with his fingers. It is his only meal of the day, indeed of any day, and it is consumed, without enjoyment, but with gratitude and vigour. He knows that this food is expensive and in limited supply, much sought after by all those who over the years have lost their teeth and cannot chew tough meat or grains and pulses. But this gratitude never overflows into expressions of thanks to Maluki. After all, as an old man, destitute perhaps, is it not his right that the young should tend to his needs?

At last, amid grunts of morning stiffness, he empties from his bottle of beer any dregs remaining from the previous night before presenting it again at the bar for another charge. Now ready to begin his day, he again stumbles across the market square to the shade of the acacia, now known by everyone as 'Munyasya's tree', to mumble, drink and doze his way through the hours of daylight, always unhindered and untroubled by those going about their business around him. There he remains, apparently ignored, but yet inevitably the focus of many minds that privately fear him, or, more accurately, what they believe lives within him.

It was not Munyasya the decrepit old man whom people feared. Munyasya, the old, weak and destitute alcoholic, was no more than part of the landscape here. For all people cared about this bone-bag, he could have been just another of the acacia's spindling roots, as he sat beneath his tree through the heat of the day. Neither was it Munyasya's seniority in the community that called for respect. He was old, perhaps the oldest man in the town, who could know? But though age alone is worthy of some respect, it is the wisdom which accompanies it which provokes the greater part of people's fear of the old and, in this state, no one could claim wisdom on his behalf. It was another Munyasya, unknown perhaps even to himself, that people feared. He was not seen often, this other Munyasya, but whenever he showed his voice, people would listen, and invariably scoff at what they heard, but they would keep their distance, never contradicting, never intervening.

Once a renowned officer in the King's African Rifles, he had fallen victim to a purge after his country's independence from colonial rule. Somewhere within complicated layers of internecine conflict, a number of important strands combined to result in Munyasya and many other senior figures like him being swiftly replaced. It may have been that the dominant Kikuyu power block within the new government saw the mainly Akamba and Luo officer class in the army as a potential threat. It may have been that Munyasya, and others like him, were seen as too imbued with the very essence of British militarism and all that went with it, such as assumptions about class, fitness to rule, worthiness to act. Surely here was a group that would act collectively, itself, in the future, if the nation did not appear to be upholding those values that they themselves held in unquestioning esteem. Or perhaps it was merely that a new nation needed a new beginning in all manifestations of its identity. A new nation cannot be built on old ways of thinking.

Whatever their motive, the new rulers, with a swiftness of action which in later years they would sadly lose, pensioned off many existing army officers and commissioned those of similar minds to their own from the ranks to replace them. Brigadier Munyasya (when he, himself, told the story) or Major Munyasya (when others repeated it, later) was one of those removed after a long and distinguished, if somewhat servile career. He was already long past retirement age, of course, but then no one, not even the man, himself, knew exactly how old he was. He had certainly served at least forty years and probably fifty, because his name - or at least variants of it - could be traced through various identities right back to the East Africa Campaign during World War One, when, as a boy, he had been drafted as a porter to trek after an army which searched valiantly, but found there was no war to fight. He survived the cholera, dysentery, influenza and malaria that killed so many of his fellows and saw the campaign through to its conclusion. Unlike the vast majority of his fellows, however, he was filled with awe and ambition by the experience so, when the Carrier Corps was disbanded and, almost to a man settled new land near Nairobi, thereafter known as Kariokor, Munyasya joined the army proper as a private. His progress at first was slow. He never had an education, could neither read nor write his name, could not even remember, after spending three formative years of his youth trekking the plains of German East Africa, how to plough, tend animals or weed a field of millet. But after the arrival from England of one Major Thomas Cunningham, Munyasya's combined life and career took an important turn.

Munyasya Maluki became the young officer's personal valet, a post to which he was admirably suited in the opinion of his Commanding Officer. "Munyasya is a true Mukamba," the CO told Major Cunningham. "He is happy, polite, well-disciplined and docile. He will serve you loyally and well, but never once let him forget his subordinate status. Treat him as you would treat a child, because too much freedom is not good for these people. They have not yet learned how to handle it or use it." Major Cunningham never forgot this advice and, over the years, followed it to the letter and hardly a day went by when he was dissatisfied with his servant.

Munyasya was both privately and publicly proud of his position and saw it unquestionably as a privileged promotion. Not only did it release him from much of the inane drudgery of day-to-day army life, but also, in time, afforded him numerous material and preferential privileges which came as reward for his continued, dedicated and faithful service. He gradually began to look upon Cunningham as a kind of substitute father, a replacement for the now shadowy stranger of a stepfather he had left behind in the bush those years ago when he had first enlisted. Major Cunningham was rock-solid in his belief in the universality of Anglican high-church morality. Its culture had moulded his entire life and beliefs, with the persona he presented to the world nothing but its manifestation in miniature. He thus felt privileged to adopt this role of joint commander and guardian of his own Munyasya. After all had he not already had the experience of bringing up his own children to appreciate what was right and wrong? Thus convinced of the absolute truth of his own convictions, Cunningham became a stern but concerned teacher, a rigid but caring father, a demanding but understanding superior. In Munyasya he found a pupil eager to learn, a ward eager to imitate, a subordinate eager to share the rewards of coordinated effort. In some not too distant future, the young man saw what he believed were the inevitable rewards of self-advancement which would flow from his opportunity. After all, it had worked for his master, and it would work for him.

Soon, on the advice of his master, Munyasya was baptized a Christian, taking the name Edward as his reward, naming himself after the English King, whose so memorable photograph had hung on the wall of the District Commissioner's office he had once visited as a child. He had accompanied his stepfather, who was trying to lodge a claim to a piece of land the family thought they already owned. The boy's jaw had sagged at the sight of that giant face framed in black on the wall, a face he saw as upside down, with all the hair at the bottom. The stepfather, amused at his son's immediate fright, had bent over to bring his own face to the boy's level and pointed, encouraging him to say the words, "King Edward." From that day until his enforced retirement many years later, he himself insisted that he should be called Edward and only Edward. He had also later tried, for decades, to emulate that beard, a style named *king'ethwa*, King Edward, in his own language of Kikamba, but had managed only a straggly, and now matted and dirty fuzz.

He even insisted on having Maluki, the name he had been told his own father had borne, erased from his papers, replacing it with Nzoka, his proud step-father's name. Soon, however, an idea came like a revelation, a vision revealed through his contact with his European masters. After all, he had never known his father, or hardly even his stepfather, for that matter, and could see no reason to retain an identity that he had long since left behind. So Private Edward Munyasya, he became, dropping any reference to father or stepfather, thus turning his back on any identity other than his own. And so he stayed, until many years later. Those who ignored his wish, and continued to link him by name to a paternal identity he now wished to deny, he would learn to shun, as unworthy of his friendship. Of course, it was the Europeans in his life who more readily used his Christian name, whereas his fellow Akamba would invariably use the name that more easily rested on their ear. And so Munyasya shunned his original identity and became Private Edward in another world. As years passed, and as those who had known him dispersed or died, new generations knew him only as Edward, but by then his rank had changed and so, therefore, had his name. All those years later, as an old alcoholic, arguably insane and mouthing again the name of a father, he would be heard to deny that any Christian baptism had ever taken place.

Under Major Cunningham's tuition, Private Edward learned quickly, religiously upheld all the virtues he was taught and, in time, gained not only the confidence but also the friendship of his master. For some years he followed Cunningham from one posting to another throughout East Africa, but never, it must be said, home to England during the periods of leave. It was during these months that Private Edward first mischievously and then at others' behest, played at being his superior, taking on the airs and graces and even some of the functions of his master, in order to keep the office running. It was during these periods that the now literate Private Edward identified himself for the promotions that soon followed.

Then, suddenly, Private Edward's life was changed. Harry Thuku's words aroused a nation and transformed discontent into revolt. Major Cunningham entered active service, commanding a force that was now solely concerned with security, not defence. At his request, Private Edward became his personal assistant, entrusted with an ever-increasing amount of Cunningham's command, thus releasing his superior to address greater, more pressing deeds. When the immediate problem was solved and disturbances died down, the real troubles began. A nation's conscience had been aroused, its pride fired, and for the colonial masters, control was the only possible solution, the only way of avoiding continued embarrassment. Thus the future role for Cunningham, Edward and their army was defined, as was the need for more recruits to carry it out.

Impressed by his protégé's work, Cunningham recommended Edward for training as an officer, which he duly received. It was perhaps not the formal structured training that the graduate of an English university might have received, but it satisfied local requirements, which demanded the promotion of 'natives' as both a practical and political necessity. Thus the beliefs that Cunningham had imparted over the years came into their own as Edward strove to become, in his own career, the very image of his master. Edward Munyasya had followed the example faithfully and had thus now received what he judged to be no more than his just rewards.

It was the Second World War that irretrievably transformed Edward

Munyasya's career and his life with it, though perhaps long before career and life had intertwined to the extent that they were no longer discernible as separate entities. He began in the Sudan, on the southern front of the North African Campaign and continued into Abyssinia. Later, he saw service right across North Africa to the Middle East, but not then as a member of the King's African Rifles, a secondment enabling him to continue his support of Major Cunningham in his campaigns, an arrangement that could not survive his master's crossing of the Mediterranean to Europe. His efficiency and effectiveness as a soldier were recognised and noted by his superiors, wherever he served. This, added to his proficiency with the English language, which, after Major Cunningham had sown the seed, he made it almost his life's work to achieve, attracted responsibility. His accent was an image of Cunningham's, Guildford crossed with Oxford, nasal vowels mixed with a pretension that endowed class, thus marking him as one worthy of command. And so he was promoted again, and repeatedly.

By the time he returned to Kenya, battle-hardened and further estranged from his roots at the end of the war, he was Major Edward Munyasya, Major Edward, as he was invariably known in formal circles. He returned to his homeland ready to assume the proud public role to which he had been assigned. In fact he was eager, if not impatient, to seek out and renew his acquaintance with Major Cunningham, but it was not to be. The man was dead, killed in action in Italy. Perhaps for the first time in his life, Munyasya felt himself alone.

Within a year Major Edward was abroad again, this time in India, again seconded from his own regiment, but this time on his own behalf, in recognition of the fact that he had become an efficient, effective, professional soldier. It was not war which required his services, but civil unrest and for two years he delivered training to local recruits, with those he commanded convinced by accent and action that this man had been trained at Sandhurst. With his job completed, he returned to Kenya, only to be posted again, after a few uneventful years, to Malaya, to a modern conflict that taught him new skills. In the mid-1950s he returned to Kenya again, this time never to leave, not yet quite a stranger to his homeland, to find that the things he had learned could be employed at home and, during the years that preceded independence, the Kikuyu and, on occasions, his own people, became his enemy.

The foe was to be contained, not killed and it was in part Edward

Munyasya's command which effected the policy of resettling whole communities of the Kikuyu people, to scatter them across the still artificial but now institutionalised country. When it became clear that the policy would not have its desired effect, the measures became harsher and their enactment tougher. Kikuyu men folk were to be moved from their home areas and held in camps where they could be 'protected' from the potential horrors of the Land Army. Major Edward, after first leading a transport section, was eventually transferred to become the commander of one such internment camp, incurring not only the undiluted wrath of its inmates, but also the unquestioning trust of his Commanding Officer and through him the respect of the administrators who directed him.

And then, as they had left India, the British left Kenya. Though on the surface there was more decorum surrounding the hand-over of power than in India's chaos, behind the scenes there was nothing less than panic. Major Edward, at the behest of the departing power, was granted the rank of Brigadier. It was little more than a parting gesture, a way of both rewarding friends and also a last ditch effort to demonstrate to an increasingly hostile populace that the changes they demanded, notably independence, Africanisation and equal rights with the settlers, would have been granted in any case, in time. But it was this qualification that was the real bone of contention and the politicians knew it. Expediency ruled the day and the colony became an independent state. The British establishment, after accepting as a condition of American victory in the Second World War that their Empire would have to be dismantled, had convinced itself that it could hold on to at least some large tracts of territory, which as yet made insignificant contributions to the world economy. The status of the Indian sub-continent had to change immediately, but there was just a chance that quite large areas of Africa might be retained. They were wrong.

In the whirlwind of activity which followed KANU's victory in elections, men like the now Brigadier Edward, those who, in government service, had collaborated with the British and enacted their policies, were ousted quickly and in most cases painlessly by prior agreement with the departing colonial power.

So, having had greatness thrust upon him by one hand, Munyasya was immediately stripped of the same by another. And so it was that the career army officer reluctantly retired to his homeland, which by and large he had never known, accompanied by his relative wealth and the security of his guaranteed lifetime pension to dull the sting of rejection. Amongst his own people, whom he had effectively left decades before, though he had never deserted nor even shunned them during his long years of absence, he immediately but reluctantly adopted a position of great social standing. With almost radiant pride, he continued to wear the uniform of his rank and thus both demanded and received a degree of respect within the community at least commensurate with that afforded to the country's new administrators.

For some time he remained a public figure, but after unsuccessfully seeking appointment as a chief, he resigned himself to his old age and began to devote himself to farming the large tract of land he had bought and cleared. It became a full-time job. Being now too old himself for physical work and having no family to do it for him, he employed labourers to carry out his plans. He thus assumed the role of a manager, indeed a more fitting position for one of his standing in the community. The farm, however, soon began to run itself. As a farmer he was no more than an ignorant novice, whereas those whom he employed had many years of experience. So, gradually, Edward Munyasya's role diminished, even became redundant. For the first time in his life, his days were empty. He had time to tell the tales of his life, of other lands and of the ways of the British, which he had come to know so well. But stories must have an audience, and Munyasya had none. Tales of the old are for the ears of the young, but Munyasya had no family. The only place which could offer him a regular and dependable audience in this, his home town, was the bar, so Munyasya, whilst his labourers worked unsupervised, began to spend his days drinking in the half-dozen bars which encircled Migwani market.

There he renewed relationships with old friends whom he had previously seen only during his brief periods of leave. Unlike him they had no great stories to tell, having spent the entirety of their lives in their home areas. But, as time went by, their words began to affect him more deeply, to captivate his imagination far more than his fast-fading tales had ever affected them. Over the many years during which Munyasya's life had been totally governed by the pressures of the present, he had ignored and thus almost forgotten the truths that he had been taught as a child, the same truths that still not only affected but governed the lives of his people. It was as if the unacknowledged and ignored fears of his own childhood had been raised from some neglected backwater of his mind. Common knowledge that he had ignored for decades came flooding back to him and privately he began to find it an increasingly painful process.

He had never married. Who would care for him when he fell ill in his old age? Who would mourn his death and, more importantly, who would continue his father's name and line in his own memory? These were questions he had not considered for decades and, when his friends in the bar continued to press him for answers, eager to know how he could come to terms with his unenviable position, he began to see perhaps the first time just how important these considerations had been before he left home to join the Carrier Corps.

Of course, he answered these questions by re-affirming his Christian faith. Publicly it offered a solution to every problem he might be called to face. It rationalised death, gave meaning to life as a progression to something greater, justified all he personally had done in life and, most importantly, excused his failures. But his adopted beliefs had never before been seriously challenged from outside in this way and the self-justification he offered his peers began to ring increasingly hollow in his ears.

He had in fact planned to marry before he left home to join the war effort. Virtually everything had been agreed, but at the time the adolescent Munyasya could not afford to pay the required dowry. He had persuaded his future father-in-law to be patient for a few months to allow himself time to earn the money needed to buy the cows which were being demanded for his future wife's hand. Munyasya thus left for the war planning to save his earnings during the months he would be away. He would then fulfil his promise and have his wife. It would have been better that way, rather than to marry immediately and spend several years paying off the dowry piecemeal whenever surplus production on his stepfather's farm allowed. This way would also allow him to pay everything at once, but neither he nor any of the others who had enlisted in the Carrier Corps knew in advance that their work would take them away from home for years rather than months of trekking through German colonial territory.

By the time he returned, his fiancée had married another and borne him a child. It was no consolation to learn that it had been the girl's father who had insisted on the union, fearing that, as the months passed into years without sign of Munyasya's return, he might be left with a completely unmarriageable daughter unless he acted quickly. The fact that he had already received several payments towards the dowry, which after all had been his only true desire, had made no difference. Saddened, Munyasya had returned to Nairobi after that short period of leave and enlisted in the army proper, determined to make it his career. As the years passed, even though he unquestionably put the disappointment behind him, it seemed that the opportunity to marry never again presented itself. Thus an old man, who possessed many grandfather's tales to tell, had no grandchildren to listen.

As his dependence upon the company in the bar and with it his dependence on the beer he drank there both increased, continued reflection and thought prompted by his friends made him feel ever more cheated by his own life. The obvious differences between himself and those around him gave rise to deep private feelings of loneliness and isolation that, unrelieved, bred cynicism. Having had no family of his own and, over the years since independence, having either lost contact with or suffered estrangement from all his surviving relatives - none of whom had been close for over forty years anyway - he was left quite alone in what remained of his life. He began to shun contact with others, to avoid their increasingly painful questions and, for a short while, even toyed with the idea of leaving his farm to live in the city. But he had no friends at all there and he could not bring himself to desert the community, which for some years, had sought his advice, respected his wisdom and gratefully accepted his participation on councils and committees. People here seemed to need him and constantly encouraged him to stay. Loyalty, a quality he had always possessed in good measure, still governed all he did.

Until his accident, he had appeared to be in fine health. When he did not recover, it was assumed that his injuries had been very serious, but most people who knew him at all well saw that the deterioration in his health was inevitable and directly attributable to his alcoholism. What was surprising, however, was how quickly the changes happened. In the space of a few days he was transformed from an old but still overtly strong man to a broken and weary destitute. He stopped eating completely for some months, preferring to live on beer and, when he no longer had the strength to walk to town to buy it, he took to sleeping under the tree in the market place so that he would never be too far away from the bar. Surely this complete and unexpected transformation could not have come about as a result of mere illness. When the old man lived on in this state for year after year, however, it became obvious that there were other forces than simple sickness or old age at play.

His constant murmuring surely held the key to what had afflicted him, but then no one could ever quite discern what he was saying. Neither was it either desirable or possible for anyone to sit and talk with him now, nor to try to offer help for his condition. He seemed lost to the world. He could not be helped because the old man had grown so cynical that he flatly refused to enter into any communication with others and, more importantly, it was not possible to offer any assistance because the Munyasya that he had become was now sometimes a man to be feared. Most people, therefore, kept their distance.

The accident had changed his mind. He had always been a mild-mannered, even-tempered man, but now he was irascible and unpredictable, to say the least. By some strange feat, this bedraggled bundle of bones, which he had become, could transform itself into something fired with tremendous energy and terrific rage. His limbs would grow stiff and strong and his body would grow stunned and straight. With his back erect, his entire frame could seem almost restored to youth, boasting the power of a man in his prime. His voice, no longer an indiscernible murmur, would bellow out at great volume, speaking clearly of things from the depths of some unknown past, far beyond the scope of his own memory. He would speak of his family and his children, of which, of course, there had been none. He would sometimes challenge passers by at random. On those occasions he would square up to his target, stretching his body to its full height and speak in a declamatory way very close to the other's face, so close that his fetid breath would bring an immediate grimace from the other. He had even once or twice physically attacked people, something that the ever mild-mannered Munyasya would never have done, at least outside active service.

And his eyes that normally were surely sightless would pick up smallest details of behaviour, even the slightest changes of expression in the faces of those he confronted. It was this man whom people feared so much. Opinion around the town was that he had been infected by some spirit and later, when he began to proclaim curses upon those he confronted, this was surely confirmed.

He became obsessed with the paintings of snakes on the wall of his favourite bar. The word *nzoka*, 'snake', seemed to be constantly on his lips and often emerged from within the otherwise toneless and indiscernible murmur he constantly mouthed. But then it was his stepfather's name, which he himself had once opted to bear. To name a child after an animal, contrary to the tradition of using those of close relatives in a fixed and known pecking order of familial proximity to the newborn child identified a family that had suffered infant deaths. The spirits clearly knew the family names and could call their victim with friendly persuasion, so they must be tricked with something they would not recognise. And so it was that many people in a community which accepted child mortality almost as the norm that there were many people named after animals - snake, hyena, lion, cheetah, elephant and rhino, places, mountains, trees or even the weather. So when Munyasya Nzoka spoke of snakes, he could just be talking about himself. But soon he had taken to tying a length of string to his thumb of his left hand. A foot or so long and usually left to dangle limp in the air, it was generally not noticed, even by those whom he confronted. But this was his own snake, the pet with which he would constantly play whenever the work '*nzoka*' lay on his lips.

After the women who sat all day in the market place with their piles of tomatoes and onions had packed away their wares and gone home, Munyasya would scour the earth for new pieces of string, discarded from sacks and bundles which had been considerably larger when they had arrived in the market than they were in the evening after a day of trade. If small, he would tie them to the end of what was already hanging from his thumb, an operation that might demand an hour or more of concentrated application. If, on the other hand what he found was long and still in good condition, he would reject the old concatenated knotty twine and replace all of it with this newfound treasure. On most occasions, however, he found it quite impossible to untie the existing knot. It was a fool trying to untie another fool's knot. So for a while old and new co-existed side by side in an uneasy and unequal partnership until one or the other simply frayed and wore off his thumb.

It was on the occasions when this string became nothing less than the object of his obsession that Munyasya was feared. With his right hand he would stretch it out to its full length between finger and thumb and then flick it loose to loop its way through gravity. This was Munyasya's own snake, with whose power he could curse others. The word '*nzoka*' was always clear and indeed emphasised during such episodes, and thus people who witnessed them generally interpreted this behaviour as an invocation that those whom he assailed should themselves be turned into snakes. It was in such circumstances that his body would reverberate and indeed physically vibrate with the awesome power of a voice that surely was not his.

These aberrations, however, were relatively infrequent. His usual self was this broken, mumbling old man who troubled no one and, even when he did revert to his other, threatening self, he was rarely interested in anyone other than strangers in the town, so most people allowed him to live his simple life unhindered and even untroubled. As an assumed child of God, however, his assumed desires were always respected.

***

Munyasya had decided to go home, where he would be alone. The company there would be better, he thought. It was not far, just across the market, along the road past the mission house and then just two cigarettes' walk, twenty minutes for someone like him, who had a watch. But as he stood to steady his swirling head before setting off, even the first step seemed impossible. The path was straight, but the way tortuous. Too much beer and too little food caused his head to swim. The starlit town seemed to shimmer before him. Buildings seemed to move, transforming the gentle, cold and corrugated moonlit glow of their *mabati* roofs into a flashing glare that hurt his eyes. But he was still walking, slowly but surely, and in the right direction. His mind, though, was straying from its purpose. Drunkenness usually flaunts itself by demanding total concentration on the trivial. What would normally be controlled merely by instinct becomes a conscious act, requiring thought, precision and, unfortunately for the drunk, awareness.

The act of walking, the simple process of standing upright and placing first one leg and then the other thus becomes an operation that demands forethought and planning. In a well-lit room, the drunk considers his path, mapping out both his route and even the very placement of his feet, before he even rises from his chair. The fact that the body will surely enact what the mind has planned is no more than is to be expected. In the drunk's case, however, the body will invariably fail to respond, but the drunken mind still plans its course with apparently unwavering devotion. It was this single-mindedness, this need to concentrate on the job closest to hand that Munyasya sadly lacked. His thoughts were focused only on what had been said in the bar.

Until that night, Munyasya had not known why Mbuvu was such a well-respected man in the community. As their long argument in the bar had developed, the old man began to realise that the townspeople's respect for the man was borne of nothing but fear, fear of his vicious tongue. There was nothing in the town that did not receive Mbuvu's attention, nothing about which he did not have an opinion, and those opinions, when publicly voiced, were not noted for the gentility of their expression.

Munyasya had taken the full force of his attack that night, and the words they exchanged rang through his head even now. And then, whilst he tried to answer a conscience that demanded to be noticed, the inevitable happened. He tripped over an exposed tree root and fell, crashing to the ground by the base of the great acacia in the corner of the market place. There he lay, not fifty yards from the bar, dazed by beer and stunned by shock, half awake, half asleep, only partially conscious. It might have been possible for daylight to re-form everything he could only partially see into shapes he could again understand, but he would never be allowed to judge that for himself. This was to be as far as the old life of Munyasya would go.

The argument with Mbuvu, however, continued to ring through his head. He felt as if during the night he had been plucked from his body, as if in his dreamlike agility, it had sprung away from the useless limbs that constrained it. Thus the meeting had been strange, but no less real for that. When the figure appeared out of the night, Munyasya stood to greet him, but the greeting handshake was withdrawn, when shock saw it being offered over his own still prostrate body.

It will be better when my eyes are accustomed to the dark. There are stars tonight. They will help me to see my way. Not that I need to see where I am going. I could get home from here with my eyes closed. I often do. If I stayed here I could have another beer. There's more beer at home... Ah, that man! It's all his fault. If he weren't so stupid I would stay in the town, as I have stayed here so many times before. It's easier than trying to walk all the way home. Easier to go home in the morning... But I will not be under the same roof as that imbecile! Who does he think he is? He has no education, no wealth, and yet he speaks as if the world is his, as if all men are his cattle.

Good evening, my friend. How are you?

Me? I am fine. A little tired and perhaps a little weary of the world. What brings you here at this late hour? Or perhaps I should say so early in the morning!

You, Munyasya. Just you.

The man was much younger than Munyasya, barely sixty, he thought.

You are troubled by something, my child?

The man's smile was broad and his face was lit with a knowledge he was sure Munyasya desired.

Ah, you are playing with me. And who might you be to call me 'child'? If I am troubled, be sure that my worries are only those of an old man and are caused by the sins of the young, such as you. You should beware of talking down to your elders, young man!

The other simply laughed, ever harder, slapping his bare legs with his hands. Munyasya felt himself stiffen with rage. His eyes were surely now glaring at the other. How dare this stranger insult an officer of the King's African Rifles?

Munyasya, let us not fool ourselves. If you think for a moment; that is, if you can rid yourself of the effects of my family's beer just for a moment, you will see who I am and you will see that you have known me for many years. Let me come closer.

The man began to move towards Munyasya, but simultaneously and involuntarily, Munyasya felt himself move as well, to maintain the distance between them. It was as if the two of them were stalking each other around an imaginary circle, like two frightened goats about to lock horns. Munyasya looked hard at the other seeking the promised recognition, but he found nothing to spur his memory. The face did seem familiar, and yet it was unknown to him. And why was the man's dress so strange? Not for many years had he seen someone dressed in unfinished skins. His own stepfather had worn them, like every man of his generation, and saw it as his right to strike out at any woman who passed him by on the open side of the garment.

Still the man stalked him and still Munyasya kept his distance. The other's naked legs strode strongly and firmly, but still he came no nearer.

So you have not yet remembered me?

The man stopped moving and so did Munyasya.

I will not tell you who I am. A dead man cannot talk about the dead.

And I will not say what it is I want with you until you have remembered and spoken my name.

I am an old man, older than you. I have told you my name. I order you to introduce yourself to me now. You are my junior, so it is not you, but I who have the right to make demands. If you have lived to your age without learning that, then you are a fool, so choose your words carefully.

The man's constant smile broadened again. Was he laughing at Munyasya? Then, bending forward to look at the ground before him, he made a sweeping gesture with his arm, inviting Munyasya to share the sight. The old man's eyes obeyed the unspoken command and, on looking down, he coldly surveyed his own body, prostrate in the dust. The other sucked a sharp intake of breath, thus making his histrionic shivers of fear audible.

It must be very cold there on the ground, Munyasya. Tell me how cold it feels. Why do you not get up and walk home to your fireside? You have a comfortable bed at home. Why do you not get up and go to it?

But I am standing here! I am on my feet looking you in the eye.

The man gestured again towards the earth.

You are not, Munyasya.

His voice was no more than a whisper.

You are here on the ground, too drunk to stand. You fell over some time ago as you crossed the market place on your way home.

He paused again here to stare for some moments in complete silence, a silence that Munyasya now dare not break.

Are you asleep? Or perhaps unconscious from your fall? Or are you dead?

Dead? What a fool you must be! Am I not standing here in front of you?

How can you be sure? Is that not also you, lying there on the ground?

For a long time no more was said. Munyasya stared at his own body before him. He was seeing himself in a way he had never done before. He could see himself in his entirety. He could see his own eyes. They were blank and staring. He could see the side of his face, an angle on himself he had never seen before. Here lay a stranger who was himself.

If you doubt me, my friend, then shout to your friends in the bar for help. Or run to them. Look, they are all still there in the bar, in the same place where you left them so angrily only a few minutes ago. The door is open. The lamp is still lit. There they are. Can you still see them? They could easily hear your call from here. Go on. Call them.

Munyasya turned to look as instructed. No more than fifty yards away, through the narrow doorway, he could see Mbuvu and Mutua still talking as they sat at the bar. Unwittingly he felt himself enact the other's commands.

Mbuvu! Mutua! Come quickly! I need help! Mbuvu! Mutua! I have fallen here in the market place by the tree. I can't get up!

The louder he shouted, the more the other laughed at him. He tried to move but could not, and suddenly he was afraid. He turned to face the other again and found that he was still laughing. Munyasya lunged forward to strike, but the hand that held the stick did not respond. The body on the ground was still there, motionless.

Now, Munyasya, what do you think? You have no voice to shout, no legs to walk and no arm to strike. Over there in the bar they cannot hear you. They think you have gone home. By now in their thoughts you are already asleep in your bed. They have not the slightest suspicion that you might have fallen here. Only I know that. Now look closer and tell me my name. You know me as I know you, make no mistake about that. I am not trying to trick you. If you think that, look down again and see yourself lying on the ground to remind yourself that this is no ordinary meeting.

The other's smile dissolved into an expression of concern. His unblinking eyes followed Munyasya's as they sought every detail of the face, but still found no recognition.

Keep looking, my friend. I am closer to you than you think. Do not be afraid. I have come as a friend, as one who means well and wants to help you. I have never been your enemy and never will be. You would know me in a second had you not drunk too much beer. You never did listen to me, did you? How many times, Kathui, did I tell you that beer was for men and not for boys?

Kathui... Your beer? ...Nzoka!

The other gave out a long triumphant cheer. He laughed and clapped his hands in pure delight.

So you have found me and I you, Kathui.

Nzoka... Nzoka... Nzoka...

So you are my elder, Munyasya? Is that what you think now? You have grown very old, Kathui, but you can never be my elder.

No. You are still playing with me. Nzoka is dead. He was my father's brother. He was old when I was young. You cannot be him. I mourned his death as a child. He was a father to me. He married my mother when my own father died. You cannot be him.

Then why do I call you Kathui, a name you have not heard since you were a boy? Who else could call you that name? Look more closely, old man. I am he.

Kathui...

The man's face confronted Munyasya. It was closer now and unsmiling. It was almost a young man's face. When he himself had been a boy, he had seen that same face as that of an old man, wrinkled, sagged and worn. But now he looked young, though the lines and shadows on his skin were all the same. Slowly Munyasya realised that all the other said was true. It was Nzoka. He knew this face he could no longer remember. Something within him had stirred, something he had forgotten long ago, but which, deep in his sub-conscious mind, had clung to him. Now the past was alive and he, himself, was part of it.

Who else could possibly call you Kathui? Who else could have claimed to be the brewer of the beer you drink? Oh now, my poor old friend, there is no need to be so frightened. I am, after all, only a member of your own family. What need is there to fear your own flesh and blood, especially the kind old uncle you learned to call your father? Now I know that lasted only a short time. I'm afraid that having to look after so young a child as you after some years of relative laziness proved to be too much of a strain for my poor old body. Don't misunderstand me, though. I am not saying that you were the death of me, but when I took your mother into my home, I must admit that I had forgotten how exhausting a new wife and a new baby can be. Anyway, enough of the past for the moment. How are you, my child?

Despite the fear that seemed to make his eyes shake, Munyasya answered on command.

I am very well, thank you.

A little too much beer, perhaps?

Nzoka spoke in the avuncular admonitory manner in which an adopted father speaks to his son, the overt concern not quite backed by real interest, caring without loving.

Yes. Tonight I am very drunk, but you can blame that on Mbuvu, not on me. He has kept me here much longer than usual by saying stupid things designed to make me mad. I am afraid he succeeded and I got so mad I just drank and drank and never noticed how drunk I was becoming. Not until I got up to leave and tried to walk across the market place did I realise, and by then I couldn't even get back to the bar. It would have confirmed everything Mbuvu had been saying.

Could it be that Mbuvu's opinions are true, and that you just don't want to admit it?

Never. Let me tell you what I think. The man is sick with envy. I have money. I have education and I have respect. There are many things to be done, nowadays. Now that the British Governors have been chased away by the Kikuyu swine, now that we have won our 'freedom', behold we have suddenly been forced to realise that it is not easy to organise these people, that it is not easy to administer this land. People like me are in great demand to arbitrate, to sit on councils and committees and the like. My years of experience in the army make me an obvious choice for such work...

Munyasya, you speak of 'these people'. Are you not one of them?

Ah, Nzoka, things are very different now from what you would remember. There are so many people who just do not understand how things should be done. I never used to believe what Major Cunningham...

Ah yes, Cunningham. That was the man who owned you when you were a slave?

Slave? I was never anyone's slave and certainly not his. He was...

I know, Munyasya. I know what Cunningham was and I know what you became. I was with you all the time. Hyenas always stay with their friends.

Munyasya's confusion was immediate and obvious.

But surely you know, my child, that I have been with you all your life, as I have been with all other members of my family? I have never left your side, not for a moment. I know everything there is to know about Major Cunningham, and all the others you have served. I have seen the world as you have seen it, through your eyes. But I have also seen it, at the same time, from my advantageous position. I have also seen your place in it, something you have never known. You will understand before too long, my child. You will remember that the one who makes the spell cannot be the one who breaks it and then you will understand my words. But don't let me interrupt. Continue with your story.

Munyasya fixed his gaze upon the other's face for a moment. Why should he trust this man? How could he know he was telling the truth? He began to scold himself for being so drunk, thinking again that this conversation, this entire meeting must be some kind of illusion, simply a drunken hallucination. A hint of a smile from the other convinced him.

Ah, you are playing with me again. I don't believe you are whom you claim to be. If I could think more clearly, I could end this dream. Nzoka is dead. He died when I was still a child. You cannot be him. Anyway, if you have seen my life already, you should know everything that happened in that bar without being told. Why should I have to repeat it?

The other's expression hardened immediately. Again the hand gestured towards the ground. Munyasya's gaze followed and the body, his own body, still lay there in front of him, eyes staring at the dust.

This is no dream, my friend. This is no ordinary meeting. And I am not asking you to tell me: I am ordering you. Now an old military man like yourself surely does not need me to explain the difference between 'asking' and 'ordering'. It is still an old man's duty to keep the young out of mischief. I do already know all of what happened in there, but I want to hear it from your own mouth.

Involuntarily, Munyasya continued. He now seemed to have no control over the words that flowed from the very depths of his mind. The other seemed to be reading him.

Mbuvu is envious. He was saying that I have no right to the respect that I receive in this community.

And the reasons?

They are not reasons, they are excuses; excuses for himself. Anyway there are too many to list...

The reasons?

He says that, because I helped the British and spent most of my life working for them, I am a traitor to my own people and that rather than receiving respect, I should be vilified and punished.

And why should he be respected rather than you?

Because he is a trader and a father. He believes he demands respect because he has a large family and much wealth, because he has never accepted the Europeans' teaching, values, religions or culture, and because he is now, as a trader, actively trying to construct the modern Kenya which we all desire.

So you have no family, Munyasya?

No.

No one? No one to watch over after you are dead?

No one at all. They are all dead.

And you never married?

No.

Why not? Only a woman can preserve a man's memory. Why did you never marry, Munyasya?

There are many reasons...

Why, Munyasya? An unmarried man's words are worth no more than a boy's. Why did you choose that path, my child?

I was rejected.

Ah! You were rejected once, Munyasya, because you couldn't pay the dowry and then you never tried again? Does one empty trap mean there is nothing to catch? Why did your white friends not offer to lend you the dowry? They could have easily afforded it.

They did not approve of the custom.

I know, but tell me why.

I was baptised a Christian. A Christian should not pay dowries to buy a wife, because it is merely a pagan custom. I could not ask a fellow Christian to help me to do such a thing. I would be leading him into sin.

So the way in which your father married and his father married before him and all of your people marry is wrong, is sinful?

Yes.

Why?

Because the Christian religion says so. It demands better behaviour than that which applies to pagans.

Because you were taught to look upon your own customs as evil and wrong.

It is the same thing.

It is not, Munyasya. There are many people here who are Christians now, but all of them still pay a dowry whenever they take a wife. But enough of this. Why does Mbuvu not respect you because you have no family? Surely he ought rather to pity you?

He pities me, but he also despises me.

Why?

It is not important.

Why, Munyasya? Does he say that a man should look for a wife in his

363

own village before he goes elsewhere? But it is not marriage that concerns him, is it, Munyasya? Come, my child, you must say it!

The command forced Munyasya to speak, but no words would come this time. It was all too complicated. When he remained silent, the other urged him yet more strongly, but still the old man could offer no explanation. There were simply no words to explain the problem. It was all too complicated. And then things might have worked out differently if we had been luckier.

Say it, Munyasya! Say it!

I cannot.

Say it!

Whether it was his assailant's words or the vice-like grip that suddenly seemed to squash his eyes, he did not remember. His only memory was one of pain, an intense pain, stabbing in his head and down the length of his back. It was dark, deathly dark, and he was alone again. Where was Nzoka? He called out the name, but there was no answer. He felt a sudden panic that he might have let from his grasp some great privilege that he alone had been offered. But he could see nothing, nothing at all. He called again, but still there was no answer. The pain grew harsher, causing him to move his hand towards his head in search of the comfort of touch, but any movement only made the pain worse. He tried to call out, to scream for help, but his mouth seemed to fill with dust as he breathed ever harder and he merely coughed and retched as a result. As he gasped for air, the dust stuck in his throat and dried his mouth. He tried to call again, but no sound came and his tongue seemed to stick to his gums. Only curdling vomit swelled in his throat and, suddenly he sat bolt upright, instinct moving the body with ease where consciousness had utterly failed, and threw up the contents of his stomach onto the ground at his side. As nausea began to subside, the pain returned, harsher and deeper than before. A hand touched his shoulder, causing him to cower with both fear and pain.

Nzoka, he cried. Help me! Nzoka, is that you? Come back! I will tell you everything you want to hear...

His words dissolved into silence, the sound falling like a stone to earth.

***

When Munyasya awoke, his vision was blurred. The pain behind his eyes, which caused him to squint, confirmed only that he was in a very brightly lit room, but little else. Certainly this was not his own house. Was he still living his dream? His sightless eyes sought confirmation of a solid world around him, but all they saw was a blinding light that hurt. He tried to move, but he could not. He tried to shout, but the sound stuck in his throat, now parched and swollen, infected by his mouthfuls of dust. His limbs seemed lifeless meat, useless to him, unable to respond to his commands to move. His entire body felt like iron, stiff, cold, too heavy to lift. Still dazzled by the light, his eyes closed again, but they still saw the same brilliant dancing blur behind their lids. Squares of light flashed behind his eyes. Red to green to yellow to blue, constantly moving, floating like reflections on water, darting randomly like a hunted antelope. The images taunted him, inviting him to look and then moving whenever his closed eyes sought them. Slowly they began to fade, overcome by an all-pervading but flashing red, a redness that covered everything, a constant colour of all sensation.

Then a hand gently encircled his wrist and began to lift his arm. Nzoka, he screamed at the top of his voice, but no sound or movement came. Where have you brought me? And then the pain of this movement came to the fore and he groaned and stiffened against it.

And when his eyes opened again, they could see. Four people stood by him, staring, their faces showing concern. Concern for him? Again he tried to move, fighting against himself to raise his head and chest, but his back was solid and stiff, like stone. The four still watched. Three women, two dressed in blue and one, a white woman, dressed in white, and one man, a white man with a red face, stared down at him in silence. The white woman was holding his wrist. When they spoke, he was surprised to find that he could hear.

"Well, Father, he's alive," said the white woman, laying down his arm, "but I think he must have suffered a stroke when he fell." The man nodded. The two black girls remained silent, but nodded their agreement. The white woman bent low over his face and spoke loudly, mouthing each syllable as if it needed chewing. "Can you hear me? Try to move your arm if you can hear me." But Munyasya could not move. "What's his name?" she said, turning to the priest at her side.

"Munyasya," said the white man.

"Munyasya, try to move your arm. Can you hear me? Can you move your arm?" She bent forward as she spoke so that her face filled the entirety of his fixed vision, presenting a dark shadow, devoid of detail, back-lit by a brilliant halo of sunlight from the open window behind her. The breath was heavy and hot, and bore the sickly smell of rotting food. Instinctively, he threw his head on one side away from her mouth.

"Well that's something at least," she said with satisfaction, as she again stood upright. "Have you any pain?" she asked. She was shouting without knowing it.

He managed to nod this time. His head moved just noticeably, but inside he felt as if he had contorted his entire frame.

The Sister's voice was quicker this time, as she addressed the nurse, on her left. "We'd better give him another pain killer. Fetch me a hypodermic and the same dose as we gave him last time." The nurse went silently away, and again Sister Doctor spoke to the priest. "You say he was out all night?"

"As far as I know," replied the man, without averting his gaze from old Munyasya as he lay in his hospital bed. He stood in a direct line between the bed and the window in the opposite wall through which flooded the direct brilliant sunlight of early morning. From Munyasya's viewpoint, the man's entire frame was dark and haloed with golden yellow light. "They told me he left the bar at about 2 a.m. He was on his way home, but he certainly didn't get very far. I found him in the market place just before dawn, so he must have been there for four hours or so."

"Had he bled much?"

"No. There were a few drops around, and a smear on a stone. He must have gone over and hit his head on it as he fell."

"The wound isn't actually all that bad." Again she looked down at him, pensively, biting her lip as she thought. "I still think he's had a stroke as well. I know he was horribly drunk, but he seems to be paralysed to me. And he seems to have lost his speech... Can you move your arm? Your head? Anything?" she shouted at the old man.

He obeyed. He strained to move like he had never strained his muscles before, but his limbs were inert and iron-heavy. But the effort hurt and he gave out a deep groan.

"You see, Father. He is trying."

"Sister." The nurse had returned with a small white tray.

"I'll give him something to make him sleep for a while and then we'll see how he is when he has sobered up. We'll give him a drip as well, which should help." The white woman assembled the hypodermic and filled it from a small brown bottle. Munyasya watched her lean over his body and push the needle firmly into the top of his leg. He felt nothing. He saw her push the piston up the tube and the liquid therein disappear as if by magic.

"There you are," she said as she withdrew the needle. "Cup of tea, Father?" The white man nodded eagerly and moved away with her. Again blinded by the sunlight that streamed through the open window opposite, Munyasya closed his eyes and the dancing lights in his head began to fade.

A moment later he was awake again. The room was in total darkness, but he could see clearly now that it was a hospital ward. Two rows of beds faced each other across the floor, but they were all empty; all empty, that is, except for one, the one closest to him. He was standing next to it, and was thus able to look down and see himself lying in the bed, alone in the room. His left arm was protruding from beneath the sheet and he had to look closely to see exactly what had been done to him. A long tube, attached at one end to a bottle of liquid, snaked its way down and into his arm. Fascinated, he traced its path with an invisible finger and then stared closely at the bottle that hung upside down on a metal stand. He felt afraid. What are they doing to me? He decided to disconnect it, to pull the tube away from the bottle, but with what? I cannot touch because my arms are down there in the bed. My body is there and my mind is here.

The door catch clicked. He looked across the room but saw nothing.

You were always slow, my child. Even a little stupid, but a stupid man's cows can still buy a wise bride.

He looked back at the bed. Nzoka was bending over the body but looking directly into the eyes that saw him.

Where am I?

Nzoka gave a cynical laugh. Are you trying to tell me that you don't know?

The last thing I can remember is you touching me. I fell. You knew I was hurt, but you still touched me. The pain was too much.

It was not I who touched you, my child. It was one of your white friends. He drove me away. There is great evil in that man. Did you not feel it? And who is he, Munyasya? Do you know him?

Where am I now?

He brought you here. Left you in the care of that bull of a woman. She carries more meat than any cow. This is what they have done to you. He gestured with his hand, leading Munyasya's eyes over his own body. It looked dead, this body. They have pricked you with needles, put pipes in your arm. I don't understand what it all means. Lie down with dogs, get up with fleas.

I don't remember undressing!

Nzoka laughed at him again. Ah but I can remember that, Munyasya. It was very funny indeed.

Why?

I watched it all, Munyasya. It was very funny, quite the funniest thing I have seen in years. You have not entertained me very much in your life, but you certainly made up for it this morning. There were three of them, Munyasya. Three of them! Women! Now I have heard of a man having three wives, but not all at once! Nzoka's words were broken by laughter. Was this man serious? Two young girls undid your clothes and removed them one by one. He mimed the actions. And the big white cow stood back and watched, mooing. And then, when they pulled down your trousers and your limp little penis fell out, she completely ignored it! She ignored it on the outside, at least. But I can see more than that Munyasya. Inside she went as hard as stone. They covered you up, of course. They didn't leave you there to discuss your manhood. Anyway they probably knew that its life deserted you some time ago...

Don't mock me, Nzoka. Stop it! Why have you come here? To torment me?

Nzoka's laughter switched off and he remained silent for a while, his piercing eyes once more questioning Munyasya. My child you have not yet understood and it is high time that you did. You should have realised by now that I own you. I am you. Last night I came to claim you and you escaped... Or should I say that you were stolen from me by your friends, just like last time.

What do you mean, to claim me? And when on earth was this last time?

Ah, you cannot be so stupid. He strode forward from the bedside towards the eyes that watched him. You were dead last night, my friend. I came to say goodbye to you and to give you the instructions that everyone must receive. That which is not confirmed is not yet decided, and the task of confirmation fell to me.

Nzoka stood disturbingly close. He didn't breathe. There was no sound whatever, either from him or from Munyasya. He stared with blank, unblinking eyes.

Why should I believe you? Munyasya courageously confronted the other with firmness. Why should he be afraid? If I was dead last night then why do I live now? Is that not me, over there in the bed, breathing, alive, if not well? You are wrong, Nzoka, and you know it. You are trying to trick me.

Oh no, my friend. It is you who are wrong and I will prove it. If it were not for this... this witchcraft... He pointed now to the bed, the drip feed and tube. ...I would now be free of you and you would be relieved of me. You must try to remember our conversation of last night. We had reached a crucial point when that white man interrupted us. Think, Munyasya. Think!

I remember it perfectly, Nzoka, but I am not drunk tonight. It won't be as easy to trick me into the same corner.

Ha ha, my child, you are perhaps not as stupid as you used to be, but only just! You may not be drunk from drinking beer tonight, but you are certainly intoxicated. I have no idea what it is these Europeans put into their little glass tubes, but there is some powerful medicine running in your veins tonight, far more powerful than any beer I ever brewed! I will ask you later to tell me how they brew it. An old man must learn new things from the young. But still, you are correct in the strict sense. You are not drunk tonight, for once; but the truth is unavoidable, even when a man in your position is sober. So think back. Think back to where we were last night. We were about to discuss Mbuvu's argument, the one that sent you fleeing so crest-fallen from the bar.

Ah, Mbuvu again. Why bring him up? He is no more than a fool!

You dismiss him too quickly, Munyasya. He paused for a moment waiting for Munyasya to offer a beginning. When none came, he continued. Now you are acting like a boy who has been caught stealing, and what you have stolen now tastes bad. As your elder, it falls to me to keep you from this mischief. You will have to admit it, Munyasya. He is right. Tell me what you think.

Nzoka was certainly in control. Munyasya spoke and his argument was this. If a man is to command respect in a society, he must command it for very clear reasons. His age is certainly one thing that determines the respect he both deserves and is granted. This has always been so.

But there are other reasons too. The most important consideration for Mbuvu is the man's achievements in life within and on behalf of his community. Here we are agreed. Where we differ is how we measure those achievements.

Now, Munyasya, we are making progress. Continue, please, continue.

My opinion is this. Mbuvu is an uneducated man. He has seen nothing except Migwani and a few other places nearby. He is not yet an old man, himself, and has therefore little experience of life. Yet he desires not only to pass opinions about our pressing needs in the locality, he actually wants to see his wishes carried out to the letter. He believes that, as a trader, he is of vast importance to the life of the town. He argues that because he controls the buying and selling of maize, beans, skins and meat in the town - he is now the only trader with a wholesale licence - he therefore controls the success or failure - and therefore the destiny - of the agriculture and thus all the people. On the other hand, I am old, Mbuvu's senior by many years. I have had an education. Not the best education, but certainly one worth having. I am experienced in the ways of our former rulers and therefore better placed than him to see through the good plans that they made. I have seen many other parts of the world. I have seen other people's successes and failures. The knowledge, the wisdom, I possess is borne of this experience, so my advice is not just desired, it is essential.

Nzoka listened intently, but with growing impatience. Munyasya has not yet reached the point. The raising of his hand stopped the flow of Munyasya's words. Enough. You are not doing as I asked. I know all this, Munyasya. Do think I ask for your opinions? Do I not know them already? A young man might know new things, but he can never educate one wiser than himself. Of course I know what you think. What I command you to repeat are Mbuvu's opinions, not your own.

Then you yourself must also know them. You claimed to have lived my life for me. Why should I have to relive anything for you?

Yes. I do know them. But what I want to ensure is that you know them. That is why I want to hear you repeat what he said about you. True wisdom is always remembered. Have you remembered? Speak what you now know, Munyasya!

Munyasya's involuntary reply caused him much pain. It was as if he had been given a drug, which compelled him to speak, but the revelation of these memories hurt him. He does not argue that he is a man worthy of great respect, but it is his opinion that I am worthy of none. His voice faltered and his gaze drifted down, as if under the weight of guilt.

For what reasons, Munyasya?

Again Nzoka was in view. Munyasya's eyes were lifted up as if by a hand. There are many, Nzoka. First, he brands me as a collaborator who not only aided the oppressors, but also who believed all they told me and so I became one of them. In his eyes, I am infected with a vile disease that must be avoided at all costs. He says that since the people of Kenya have fought and died to rid themselves of the British, then the people of Migwani should also rid themselves of me and should treat me as if I were a traitor.

But it is not this that causes you so much pain.

You are right again, Nzoka. His second argument concerns responsibilities, responsibilities in the community, and responsibilities to others. A man without responsibilities should not be trusted, he says, and, in his eyes, I have none.

Why not? Nzoka began to speak like a man who had just achieved some lifetime's goal, more slowly and with obvious contentedness, savouring every moment of his closeness to victory.

Mbuvu believes that my life has been a betrayal of all the values, which it should have respected, and thus I should not be entrusted with either the people's respect or the power now to arbitrate on important decisions.

And what values are these, Munyasya?

I never married so I have no children. I have no surviving relatives and that worries Mbuvu deeply. If my decisions in life have led directly to the death of my family and the end of my name, would not my advice for the community as a whole result in the same fate for the people of Migwani? He looks upon me as a potential, perhaps real, curse upon the community, intent upon exterminating its life, as I have done my own. He doesn't realise that I am not worried by loneliness. I am a Christian. I am baptised. When I die, God will be my judge, not my descendants.

So that is what you believe, my child? If what you have just said about your God being your only judge, then why am I here with you now? Tell me that?

I don't know. I must be dreaming...

What? Nzoka's body stiffens with rage. His smile dissolves into anger as he strides across the room to confront Munyasya. Without another word he raises his arm and strikes Munyasya a sharp blow. Munyasya feels himself fall. The blow hurts, stings, like the slaps on the leg he had so often received as a child from his stepfather. I am no dream, Munyasya. He almost spits the words. Munyasya looks up to see Nzoka bending over him. Now let me explain, more clearly than Mbuvu ever could, exactly what your responsibilities are. I am not speaking of these responsibilities to the community that seem to occupy your thoughts so much; I am speaking of your duties - yes, duties - to me and your fellow ancestors. I have grown very impatient with you over the years. At first I was even a little proud of you. When I died you were merely a boy, but I followed your life, no less than lived it with you, sometimes helping, sometimes hindering. That was my duty to you. To watch over you; to do as much as I possibly could to ensure that your life followed the right path for both of us, but always giving you the right to choose. If you consider your life a success, then I must at least share the credit, but if, like Mbuvu, you consider your life to be a failure and yourself to be a traitor to something greater than yourself, then also I must share the blame. When a branch bends, the whole tree moves. Unfortunately for you, Munyasya, I believe Mbuvu is right.

Think, for a moment, what I taught you; what every caring father teaches a son. I told you that when I passed away, I would not forget you; that I would live on with you, inside you and with all my relatives and friends; to watch over them; to do my best to protect them from themselves and from others until they themselves were released from life and its ties.

Then we would all be reunited and would prepare ourselves for the next stage. I would then leave you again to begin the final journey toward complete rest, complete fulfilment, and complete happiness. Now a man who knows where he is going does not ask the way, but you have been lost, Munyasya, and so you needed me to help you on your way. That is where you and I stood last night, with you dead on the earth and me in control. And then our mutual friend arrived. And so I was trapped. I was in the wrong place at the wrong time. You and I are now joined in your continued life. You know that I cannot start that journey while ever I live in you. Over the years I am willing to accept that I have gradually lost whatever influence I possessed over you. It seemed that you rejected me, but would not let go of your memory. For years I have waited for you to return and in vain. Time and time again, you have come near to death and I have prepared myself to step forward to claim my prize, made ready for the journey I must begin when my duties to you have been completed. But every time you have faced death, Munyasya, you have cheated it, as you have done again today. I have grown very impatient with you. I cannot begin my journey while you remember me in life. It is my duty to care for your life, but by caring, I prolong my own death, a state that, itself, should be no more than another transition. Munyasya, let me go! I should have started my path long ago. Let me go! I should have left behind this God-forsaken place for a greener land, which only seems to move further away and grow more barren as I watch. All this is your doing, Munyasya. For years you have been the only person to keep my memory, my name alive and I have grown to hate you for it, especially because you have rejected it. What makes it worse is that you are alone. You have no wife and no children. There is no one to share my burden. You live, but your life has ended. You are now useless to anyone, condemned forever. Your death will be mourned by no one. You have no future. Unlike me, you will die with your body's death. There is no living soul within which your memory can grow and mature. Your weak and infant memory will be thus cast out from the protection of mourning, straight into its journey. If the path were straight and even, an infant might survive, but there are many pitfalls and many dangers, so surely you would perish for ever and would thus be doomed never to reach your paradise. So what have you to lose? Why do you cling so fearfully to a life that can now give you nothing? Why do you bind me so tightly to the present and so stand between me and my own destiny? Why do you not think of me? Consider your duty to me and please release my soul! It is you and only you who hinder my progress. Why, you could kill yourself! That would release me and because your state is so lamentable anyway you, yourself, would be no worse off than you are already. Think of your duty, Munyasya. Kill yourself to release me. If you refuse, I can bring great pain upon you. You would live only to regret your decision, if you made the wrong one ...

I could never kill myself. No one ever mourns a suicide.

You have no one to mourn you anyway, so why do you worry?

Munyasya had listened intently. It was as if his own conscience had sprung to life to confront him, to punish his years of disobedience. Inwardly, he knew the truths to be unquestionable, but publicly he dare not admit it. The lie had been lived for so long that even he had begun to believe it, but now a larger truth had caught up with him. It was inescapable. No matter how convincing, no matter how convenient another's truths might be, these revelations were undoubtedly inevitable. They were tried and tested, made indisputable by Nzoka's presence. His guilt was complete, acknowledged with downcast eyes, like those of a child who knows he has done wrong. He had learned all these things before. And he had turned his back on them.

All these truths of life and death had been passed on to him by this same Nzoka during the days of his childhood. The logic was clear then and it was clear now. Death was not an end but a beginning. It brought to a close that period of testing which all souls must suffer. They must pay the price for their expulsion from the paradise at the beginning of time. The evil ones must be punished, but first they must be identified and their guilt proven. Life is but the first judge. Life is the soul's only chance to prove its worth, to confirm its worthiness to return to paradise, to identify its willingness to uphold all things good and shun the bad. The responsibilities are clear: to survive the perils of childhood; to marry and procreate; to die and to be mourned.

But that is just the first step. In death the journey begins. While life's present recedes into one's own past, a soul must retrace the passing of all time to be reunited with its own beginnings in paradise. For a while, death and life stay together and it remains the duty of ancestors to protect the lives of their family. But then, with that accomplished, a person's life task is completed and there remains only a shared journey to retrace time, itself. The journey is long, the path tortuous and full of pitfalls. But those who are left behind eventually follow and offer help. No one, dead or alive can ever make such a journey without help. But then when it is made, time is no more. There the sun shines every day, the rains never fail and the harvest is always good. There is no illness, no hunger, no vice, everlasting labour and complete rest. But there are duties on the way and the first and most important is to ensure that you are mourned. While you are remembered you are tied to present, given time to grow in a new infancy, time to recover the strength that the tribulations of death have sapped. Just as youths undergo seclusion before and after circumcision, which is just another of the necessary changes in the cycle, the dead must live on the memory of present for a while to receive the help and support of their descendants. Without them, without their remembrance, the still youthful soul is doomed. It is too weak, too naive to survive the tortuous path along which it must travel.

But this waiting serves a dual purpose. It is also the duty of the dead to watch over those who survive them, to ensure their worthiness to enter paradise. They must be advised, influenced, cosseted through the difficulties they face. Then, if a direct descendant is shown through life to be unworthy, and to bear part of this, humanity's ultimate guilt, the responsibility is shared. The whole family shares the guilt and all who have not yet found release from the present must suffer. If the offence is shown to be minor, then the handicaps imposed are correspondingly small. The journey will be longer and harder, but it will surely succeed. If, on the other hand, the family is responsible for a major crime, those still mourned by the guilty one suffer his fate. They are locked in the present, destined to wander this land forever, unable to achieve their eternal goal.

But when a name ceases to be spoken by the living, once mourning is over, a freed soul can begin its own journey. It cannot start until it is strengthened by the memory of the living, but thus strengthened, that nurture must be withdrawn, and then, just as a child emerges from a parent's care, the soul can make its own way.

Munyasya had known all this, but had tried to ignore it. Now its obvious truth flooded back to him, reinforced by Nzoka's prompting. In the bar, Mbuvu had spoken of these things and had listed all the reasons why he, Munyasya, had failed the test of life and therefore bore the guilt. There was no judgment in death, only in life. There was no great council, where one's life was arraigned for assessment, no such simplistic arbitration between good and evil. Every man born was both good and evil in life and therefore the same in death. Life's test merely proved the ability to control evil, for it can never be defeated, never be eradicated. Paradise is thus equally open to both the pure and impure in life, if they accept the responsibilities it imposes. If they are unwilling, then they are lost and rejected forever.

In an instant, Munyasya remembered and knew it to be true. He was afraid, and repentant, but powerless. I cannot help you, Nzoka. If I kill myself, you will share the guilt that this very action will bring upon me. That is inescapable. As you say, I am clearly doomed, but you could still survive. You are my stepfather, not part of my immediate family. It is they who are really suffering.

I know, Munyasya. I am here on their behalf. They are fast weakening. They have already waited for you for far too long. Without my help they will be lost. They cannot survive alone. It is you who holds their destiny in your hand, just as you also hold mine. Ending your own life now will release all of us. They are already weak. Any more delay will damn them forever to the present.

For what seemed like hours, they confronted one another in silence. Munyasya frantically thought through his predicament, balancing influences against truths, possibilities against desires. Every fact fit the scheme, and it meant that he was trapped. But there might just be one flaw, one inconsistency that troubled him and rendered Nzoka almost powerless in his eyes.

You should not be here.

Nzoka's confidence drained in an instant. His stern expression dissolved to betray confusion and apprehension. He tried to protect himself. That is not your worry. What I do in my position is my business. It is you who holds the key to all this, not I. I came here to confront you, to advise you. If you reject my advice you are doomed.

You have said that I am doomed anyway.

Munyasya awaited a reaction. None came. For the first time since they were reunited in the market place, Nzoka looked away, vulnerable. He was suddenly defensive and ponderous, conscious of the need to protect his weakness. He retreated towards the bed in which Munyasya's body lay. He stopped and stared and then lifted the limp arm into whose vein the drip-feed passed. On release, it fell like a dry branch, inanimate and useless. You are dead, Nzoka observed in a whisper, half-turning towards the eyes which watched him.

I think not, Nzoka, replied Munyasya slowly. What you are seeing is the effect of the drugs I have been given. They take away all feeling so I have no pain. But neither can I be conscious while they work.

There was another long silence before Munyasya spoke again. You should not be here, Nzoka. If I remember your teaching well, the mourned should follow and influence the living, but they should never intervene directly. They must never be reunited until they can meet on equal terms as spirits. Only then is it my duty to help you prepare for your journey and see you on your way. You have committed a great wrong, Nzoka. You have been caught in your own trap.

Munyasya, I will tell you again, you are dead. When I came to you last night, you were breathing your last breath. Your life was over, so I came as duty demands, in the way it has always demanded. This, he said gesturing vaguely towards the drip feed, is mere trickery, a vile spell cast by enemies, enemies who must therefore be your friends, just as Mbuvu said.

You are making excuses now, Nzoka. You always were an impatient man and it seems you are no different now. You have appeared to me too soon and now this - this spell, as you call it, which prolongs my life, has trapped you. You cannot escape now, can you? Wherever I go, you must follow. You have misused your power, wasted it and now lost it. Now it is I who must carry your spirit. You are mine! My suicide would release you again, but while I live, you are not only tied to the present, but also you are tied to me!

Nzoka began to seethe with rage. The mistake was not mine. I came when you summoned me and you then saw fit to cheat me, to trap me like some hyena. Well now you have me. Mistakes can only be seen after they are made. Now you control me, but beware. It could be that I will control you until we die together.

It was Munyasya's turn to laugh at the irony. You came to re-educate me, but it is not I who has overlooked the truth.

Nzoka was now deep in troubled thought. Listen, my child, before you begin to enjoy your power. Think back to last night. Remember what happened and interpret it. It can surely be seen only in one way. I set my trap for a leopard. Did I catch a hyena? Were Mbuvu's words true? Are you that traitor?

Almost involuntarily, Munyasya did as he was asked. Nzoka's power over him was still total.

You were drunk. You were angry because your drinking friend Mbuvu had spoken the pure truth about you and you had tried to reject it. You fell, hit your head hard against a stone and died.

Munyasya offered a silent question.

Well you were about to die. I came to you to settle what needed to be understood between us. You have stood in my way for years and you could have held me forever because of the disrespectful and irresponsible way you have lived. Whatever happened you were doomed - and still are - to inhabit the present forever. All I wanted from you was an assurance that your misguided ways did not come about as a result of my influence as your stepfather, that my part in your life is beyond reproach, that this hopeless position in which you find yourself is a result of only your own actions, of your wanton rejection of my sound advice and blind acceptance of others' trickery. Eyes that once could see can go blind. You have been used, Munyasya, used to further interests which have been and still are alien to our people. You have been tempted away from the true path by the promise of rewards you were never destined to receive. Thus you have been a traitor to yourself, and I bear no responsibility.

And so you are safe?

Yes.

Munyasya laughed cynically. His words began to shine with a new confidence. And now your plan has backfired on you. Oh, Nzoka, what a mistake you have made; what a dreadful mistake... now you are utterly tied to me and I to you. And I am still alive. Munyasya was laughing hard through the words. If I kill myself, then so do you. You would play a part in my suicide and would be branded with the same iron as myself. And now because of this trickery, we will live on together, to share the same broken old body and the same fate! Our paths are now inextricably joined. My life is now yours! May God preserve us!

Whose God, Munyasya? Our God or your Christian God? Your decision is vital to both of us.

Is there more than one God? Munyasya looked up to stare quizzically at the other, now deadly serious. Nzoka's pathetic look of resignation, the sheer hopelessness of worry, made him laugh so deeply that it hurt, though he was not sure where.

I should cut a switch and beat you, you insolent child! How dare you treat me like this?

Munyasya could only laugh even harder, and then suddenly all was dark.

When he awoke, the white woman stood at the end of the bed, again haloed in sunlight. The white man stood at her side. Both peered down at him wearing expressions of impotent concern on their faces. He could see them clearly this time. The woman was passing her middle age by, but the man was still young. Now that he felt rather better, he recognised them both and realised where he had been taken.

We are in Muthale...

So what is special about Muthale? What does that little hill top have that cannot be found in Migwani?

There have been many changes over the years. One of these changes is that missionaries have come to this area. They have done wonderful things for us. This building is an example of their work. It is a hospital. There is no such place in Migwani. They care for the sick here.

Who are these people? The woman, the white cow...

Yes, if that is what you want to call her. She is Sister Doctor. She is called Kitunduma, thunder and lightening, by people here because she shouts at men - and farts, very loudly. Her words can sting a man's pride.

And the man? Who was he?

He is Father Michael. He is a priest in Migwani. I have come to know him well though he has not lived there very long. He is a truly great man.

But he is very young... how can you describe one so young as 'great'? Surely he cannot possess wisdom at such an age.

Ah, you do not understand Europeans, Nzoka. They become wise at a very youthful age. They can teach us very much if we listen.

Yes, they are fine teachers, but perhaps teachers of trickery if this 'caring' for the sick is an example. How were we brought here? Who brought you here?

It must have been the Father. He sometimes stays out very late at night. Some people call him a bad man because of it. They say that he behaves like some common drunk and frequents places where there are prostitutes and thieves. Well he must have been out late last night. He must have found me lying in the market place and brought me here.

Alone? He could not possibly have carried you all that distance. Muthale is half a day's walk from Migwani!

Nzoka, have I not told you that there have been changes since you were alive? I am surprised that you have not seen these things if you really have been living my life alongside me throughout these years...

There might have been occasions when I was not as attentive as I might have been, my son.

Well, Nzoka, nowadays there are cars, machines that move on wheels very quickly. The Father must have put me in his car and driven me here. In a car the eight miles from Migwani are gone even before one cigarette is finished.

More trickery! So this man is the culprit: the one responsible for my mistake! I should have known it would be one of your European friends. And also one who, it seems, insists that people who are unrelated to him address him as their 'father'. What bigger insult to people's family loyalties could you imagine? Are you sure you didn't plan all this with him to bring about my downfall?

Nzoka, you claim that you have followed my life that you have heard all that I have said, and vetted all the plans I have ever made. There was no such conspiracy.

"Can you make it out?"

"No. It's gibberish to me."

"Sheer mumbo jumbo."

"No. That would be quite normal for him. Even drunk he was always full of words, but never like this."

Sister Mary and Father Michael listened intently to the old man's murmuring, trying in vain to decipher some sense, but finding none.

"I'm sure I've heard him say his own name once or twice."

"Yes, that was clear enough all right. I've managed to make out 'Nzoka', as well, two or three times."

"Nzoka," Sister Mary repeated. "Nzoka... Snake. Nzoka, it means snake! You don't think he was bitten by a snake, do you?"

"Not unless it came out of a bottle."

"I suppose we would have noticed by now if he had been bitten."

Again both listened intently, but found no sense. "I think it's his name, Sister, though he has always been just Munyasya, or Major, as far as I know. I have never heard him use his father's name before, but I have heard some other people use Nzoka as his father's name."

"He has definitely improved since you were last here. He seems to be able to move his arms and legs a little now."

"Can he stand?"

"We haven't tried that yet. Another fall could easily kill him. We'll keep him in bed for a while yet, until he's got some more strength. I doubt if he'd eaten for a week when you brought him in. We emptied his stomach and all he brought up was liquid."

"Again, that's not a surprise. Old Munyasya is a drinker, not an eater."

"And I suppose there's a wife at home doing all the his work while he stays out till all hours in the bar? I don't know. These men. They don't know they're born."

"Not him, Sister. He never married and he has no family. He lives quite alone. An army man, if ever there was one."

Sister looked surprised for once. "An unmarried man of his age is certainly rare hereabouts."

"He is a strange fish altogether. The uniform is real, you know. He never takes it off. He is so proud of it. He has spent his whole life in the army. Been all over the world. Goodness knows what would have happened to his world if someone had ever turned it on its head and made him see that he is a kind of colonial leftover. He's a much-respected man, even though he is quite simply a drunk. He's even on some of my parish committees."

"Well it looks as if he's finished with all that for good, Michael. I'm convinced he's had a stroke, but it's very difficult to tell..."

***

In the bottle is my madness, the spirit that haunts me, exhausts me, taunts me, entraps me. I, the hunter, the warrior, am caged like a monkey. Let me free! Let me free to live my own life and die my own death. You hold the key, not I. I would break the lock but I can't find the door. Another drink. Another drink to bring me closer to you, to hold you near until you let me go. Do you hear? You? Nzoka? Do you hear?

He had been ignored until then. Hundreds of people had passed him by, but even those whom he had befriended in the past offered neither greeting nor any sign of recognition. People had met and stood in conversation less than spitting distance from where he lay without even acknowledging his presence. It was as if he had become a part of the tree beneath which he sat, merely an exposed root to be stepped over and avoided lest one should trip. His constant, almost silent murmuring remained always inaudible amongst the daily bustle of the market place, especially on market day, itself, when this flat triangle of hardened, bare, red earth rang with the noise and commotion of trade and humanity.

These last words that he said, however, this oft-repeated question, habitually delivered with the air of a command, these words were never a whisper. Every muscle in him strained and shook to throw out the sound. His entire skeleton of a body stiffened and convulsed, the words grumbling forth from deep within his squelching chest. Thrown out as if spewed in rejection, the sound bellowed like thunder, chased by its own echo. It demanded attention, and received it, albeit begrudgingly and obliquely. It forced people to react, to look his way and thus acknowledge his presence. At such moments, all conversation, all business stopped for a moment as heads turned towards Munyasya's tree. Those with no direct view craned their necks to see, would jostle for position for just a glimpse, but no one would want to go too close. No one would ever answer. No one would ever intervene.

Everyone had a personal idea of what might be revealed by a glance in Munyasya's direction. The whole town, the entire locality, no less, knew that now he was mad, a child of God, *mwana wa Mungu*, and thus permitted to see that which always ought to be denied to the living. This strange state in which he lived thus enabled him to reveal the forbidden. Any movement he might make, any audible word he spoke was noted, heeded and interpreted in case it proved to be the revelation which his privileged position was believed to be capable of both perceiving and communicating, but no one ever understood what he said, his only clear word being 'Nzoka', a word heard and carefully noted by all whom he encountered.

Do you hear me, Nzoka? The words were clear, addressed to Nzoka, a snake. Is he talking to snakes? Is he calling a name? There were some who knew that the old man's stepfather had been called Nzoka, but surely he could never be speaking a dead man's name? But then Munyasya was mad now, a child of God. It was now almost his duty to do with contempt those things that were forbidden to the living. In another second the silence was broken swiftly and utterly again by the usual daily business of the place. The old man spoke no more and interest faded as fast as it had risen. Business resumed. A few passing comments acted as a postscript to the declaimed outburst, before its complete confusion was forgotten.

I know you hear me. You can deceive me sometimes, but I know you are listening now, like a frightened child about to be beaten by his teacher. You must listen to me, Nzoka. You have no choice because I have you. I have you here in my head. My skull is your prison, your only heaven. Not the paradise you looked for, eh? And you'll be in there forever if you don't loosen your grip on me. Look at me! Look at me, Nzoka! Do you call this life? Do you call this bag of bones a man? I live, Nzoka, only because you shield me from death. You hold the key, not I. You are chained to me and I to you. If you would release me, you would release yourself. You have the power and don't you try to deny it. My next drink could be poison if you so wished. How much easier it would have been for both of us if you had let me alone that night when I fell. But you couldn't stand aside, could you? Impatience was your greatest folly in life and it followed you through your death. You just had to meddle. Ah, don't give me that! I've heard all your arguments a thousand times and they still don't convince me. So you died too soon, left jobs undone and have returned to finish them? But what jobs? You cannot even tell me that. You are still thinking, trying to remember. You are still a fool, Nzoka, and thus we are still here, you and I, still locked together. Another day, another night, another drink, another talk with you and yet we are no further along our road, no nearer this goal you cannot even see. What? What is it you say? You are doing all this for my good? To rescue me from a fate worse than my own death? You make me laugh, Nzoka. Am I not suffering now? Am I not telling you that I would rather be dead? Do I look as though I care whether or not I am condemned never to leave this place either alive or dead? We have argued too much, Nzoka. Oh, how I've tried to tell you that I want to take my chance. You say that my destiny is written, and that I can never escape; but I have different ideas and I believe in them, perhaps as strongly as you believe in those which governed your life and death. All I ask is for you to let me take my chance. I do not fear God. He can do me no harm. He can do no one any harm, even you. God protects people. He has no desire to harm us, so why do you fear Him? I don't fear Him, but I fear you, because you stand between me and my future: you have trapped me. Do I want to join you? Of course, Nzoka. Have I not told you a thousand times? Even since this morning dawned? Don't I see you beckoning me every day? Come on, come on, you say, as if all I had to do was piss. Pass away, I am told, but how can I when you tie my hands and keep me in this prison of life? Ah shut up, shut up, Nzoka. Speak to me no more. I have heard you say that you have tried everything. Well let me tell you that you have tried nothing. You are as lazy now as you always were in life, and also as weak, so weak that you can't even cut down this dry old maize stalk which is all that is left of my life. I am so thin that the wind bends me like grass - and yet you can't even crack my will! You see this string? Look at it. Do you see how its weight does not even bend my thumb? Do you see how I can make it stretch and loop, do anything I wish? Well this string is you, Nzoka, a snake, which has become my constant companion, my tame caged pet.

If you bar my way, the cage will stay locked. You will be tied to me as my prisoner until you release me.

Ever since his accident, it had been clear to all that Munyasya's mind had been affected. It had been easier to accept his physical deterioration; he was after all very old, and for quite some time had threatened to bring serious illness upon himself through heavy drinking. His acquaintances and friends - who had been many - expected to find him weaker after his fall and subsequent illness, so, when he was finally discharged from the hospital in Muthale, and he returned to Migwani but a wizened and broken memory of his former self, they had tried to show no surprise and had greeted him as they would have always greeted the Major Munyasya they knew. They found, though, that this old man knew no one. They were new strangers to him and he would not speak a word to them. The obvious initial response was that he had been seriously affected by his fall, that he had become deaf, or blind, or both, or that he had even lost the power of speech and this indiscernible murmuring was his vain attempt to communicate. All these explanations were soon shown to be wrong, however. Old Munyasya could always see what he wanted to see. And old Munyasya could certainly hear whatever he wanted to hear.

He would always react when a bus passed through the town. Every single one demanded his attention and interest, required his presence at the edge of the market place where people gathered to wait. While ever a bus stood on the town's main road to load and unload, Munyasya would mount guard over it, standing to attention beside it, or sometimes presenting imaginary arms in front. It was as if he regarded this as a duty to the town, an act of guardianship that the community, perhaps, had neither the strength nor the authority to provide for itself. For this essential task, the town paid him in beer. Yes, he could certainly hear, because the very first knocking drone of a Diesel engine in the distance would cause him to stand and begin to make his way to his imaginary guardhouse. By the time the bus arrived, he was always in position, standing respectfully sentry-erect in greeting, sometimes even offering a slow, clumsy salute.

He could also certainly speak when he desired, though, when he did, the voice was surely not his. In the past he had always been such a mild-mannered, even-tempered man, but now, whenever he spoke above an inaudible murmur, his voice was almost as harsh as the words he used. His rasping and phlegm-rolling voice seemed to command his very body and hurt him deeply, as if his mouth were some mere tool manipulated by some other power greater than himself, and whose words not only pained but tortured him. At first his outbursts were seen as merely those of a demented mind, sheer nonsense shouted amid violent convulsions of pain. But, as time passed, it was noticed by some that he spoke consistently of a life which was not his own. He spoke of his own children, of which there had been none, and of the beer he himself brewed. Munyasya's long-standing friends privately realised that here they were hearing of Munyasya's stepfather, Nzoka, and they remained careful never to say the dead man's name.

There were two distinct interpretations of the old man's condition. Either he was a sick, demented and senile old man, or surely he had been possessed by a spirit. Irrespective of which opinion a particular person held, however, the pure fear which the latter explanation engendered guaranteed that everyone dealt with this stick of a wizened old man with cautious respectful distance.

A libation of piss in your memory, Nzoka. How do you like your own beer now? Grit your teeth and drink it, as I do! This is what your descendants have made of your famous brew. No honey, no *muiatine* to make it ferment. They use different things now, Nzoka. Sugar, water and a packet of yeast. And what do you think gives it the colour? The sugar is white, not brown like the honey you used. No, it's the water that colours this beer. They make it with dirty water from the dam. It's brown with silt, and on some days it stinks of the cow shit our herds have added for flavour. How do you like the changes, Nzoka? Drink and see. Do you agree with me? It's piss when it goes in and piss when it comes out, but it keeps me alive. Ah, you know that! I can see you cringing! Well, it's all in your hands. Do you know what happens to an eagle that soars too long? It starves. Pounce now, Nzoka. Do your work and leave me. I am tired, Nzoka, tired of arguing with you, day in, day out, all night, every hour. You never listen to me. I don't know why I bother to speak because my words are useless. You have the power, not I. It is your commands that move my limbs, your words that I speak, your eyes that see. I am too old, too tired. How can I be of use to you? How can I possibly act out your plan? Surely I have no time left. And you still don't even know what it is that you want to do! You don't even know what your plan is! I am too old, too tired to go on much longer. If you stay in this body much longer you will be like a cabbage growing to seed in the sun. Is that what you want? To dry into seed? To be reborn again a thousand more times, carried on the wind so that you can infect new ground, new minds? How can I know? Only you know, Nzoka, what awaits me. Tell me! Tell me while I sleep, because it's too hot today. And my bottle is finished. See that someone drops a coin or two so I can refill it.

The old man drifts back to sleep. His bottle is propped upside down against his hip to show everyone who passes by that it is empty. A few people, on seeing this, throw small coins onto the ground as they pass, if, that is, a cartwheel Kenyan ten-cent piece could ever be described as 'small' change. It is clear that they have done this many times before and, although Munyasya is completely unaware of the accumulating sum which surrounds him, and despite the fact that such a sum would pay a bus fare home for almost anyone in the market place, no one tries to steal even a single coin if it lies near to the bedraggled old man's bent frame. He sleeps for some hours, from midday to mid-afternoon, and, unknown to him, the day changes. The still heat wanes and a wind begins to grow. It is cool, blowing from the east. Clouds grow thicker and heavier. Occasionally they cast chill rainy shadows across the town.

Listen, Munyasya, there is not much time.

Not much time, you say? Then what about the years you have wasted?

If you will listen to me I will tell you, my child. At least now I understand what it is that we must do. It has been clear all along, but we have been blinded to it by your reluctant mind.

What, me? Reluctant? Nzoka, I would have left this place long ago had you not prevented me.

You still don't understand, Munyasya. It was when you said that we would go to seed... You were right. Don't you see?

Nzoka, I thought that you had become my eyes? How then do you expect me to see?

Think back, Munyasya. Think back to the night we met. You were angry with yourself. In the bar, Mbuvu had made you see yourself as a failure, as a traitor to your own beliefs. You hated yourself that night. Your conscience had been awakened.

Nzoka, we have been over this a hundred times. I have agreed with what you have said. I have accepted that Mbuvu was right. I have understood that others see my life as that of a traitor to my people. Why speak of it again? You know it causes me pain.

Pain is yours to bear, Munyasya. It will never release you. I have sympathy for you, but I can do nothing to help. All that is your own doing and so it must stay with you forever. There is no escape, not even through me. But wait. Hear what I have to say. That night, when your mind was lost in thought, when anger clouded your senses more than the beer you had drunk, you tripped and fell. Now I will freely admit that I was impatient. I had waited for too long for you, Munyasya. For years I had waited, through wars and through peace, through danger and safety. There were times when I was sure that your days were finished. I even went as far as bidding goodbye to those waiting there with me, so sure was I that this particular moment would be the time to be summoned. And you still survived. I had waited too long for you, Munyasya, and I was eager to be on my way. I promise you that when I came to see you, you were all but dead. Your last breath was in you.

You are stupid, Nzoka. I am even still alive here and now, years after that night when I fell.

But why? Why, Munyasya? Do you not believe what I say? I have said that I had grown impatient, but I had been that way for half a generation. I chose my moment. I didn't come running at the first sign. I waited. Made sure. Now think back, Munyasya. How is it that you managed to survive and trap me?

I can't remember, Nzoka. Let me sleep. How can you expect me to remember what happened years ago when now I can't seem to remember what I did yesterday? I was ill, unable to move and too drunk to see.

Precisely, Munyasya. You played no part in your own survival. Left to yourself you would surely have died, and died quickly. All my problems would have been solved as I expected they would when I came to you.

But your problems, Nzoka, as you were soon to learn, were only just beginning.

Now I see that, my son, but it is the source of these new problems that gives us the clue that will lead to a solution. What has happened cannot be changed, my son. But I can see now that what is afflicting both of us is not of my doing and neither is it yours. No, we have to look outside of ourselves to see the cause of our predicament.

Tell me, Nzoka, what is today's explanation of why we are being punished like this?

I can answer that now, Munyasya, but only when I have explained all the circumstances. Think back. You had fallen. You were on the ground, incapable of helping yourself and surely dying.

Nzoka, I am still incapable of helping myself.

I am not talking about your bowels, Munyasya. I am just trying to make you see that to survive you needed help from someone else.

But that is obvious, Nzoka. I have known that all along. When I woke up I was in hospital in Muthale. I told you that it must have been Father Michael who helped me. He must have found me there in the market place and then taken me to the hospital in his car.

Exactly, Munyasya. You are now beginning to follow me. Let's see if the path leads you to the same destination. Now it has taken me a long time to get used to this place again. It is not the place I remember. I felt a complete stranger here in my own town when I first saw it again through your eyes. But now I know my way around. You see, until recently, all these people you speak of were no more than names on your lips. Now I can see them and now I can explain what went wrong. This Father Michael is a priest, yes? A white man? A missionary for his Church?

Nzoka, I think you must be getting more stupid as you get older. Are not all priests white men? Without them we would never have known the truth that is Christianity. It came from them.

So there are no African priests?

There are a few, but they are not real priests. They are mere boys among men. Everyone prefers that their home town should have a white priest. They are much more highly respected.

And they are here to persuade people to worship their God?

There is only one God, Nzoka. That is the first thing they teach. The God you know is the same God they know and the same God I know.

But, Munyasya, you have told me that they teach you to worship a man!

That man is God, Nzoka.

So God is a man!

No. God is God and God is man.

So there is more than one God. He cannot be both a man and not a man at the same time.

He is also a spirit, Nzoka. God the Son, God the Father and God the Holy Spirit.

So then there are three Gods!

No. There is but one God. They are the same.

Munyasya, you are confusing me. Just listen to me. These priests, then, are responsible for converting someone like yourself to their religion? It was they who insisted that you ignore the truths that I had taught you?

Not these priests, Nzoka.

Others like them?

Yes.

Do you not see, Munyasya? For many years they had bewitched you, held you in their power, and used you to further their own ends. They controlled you so completely that you forgot even your responsibility to yourself. They worked you so hard for their own ends that you never had time to find even one wife, let alone a household to nurture a family. Your present lamentable state is all their doing. Had you fulfilled your responsibilities in life, you now would have a family and your name would be mourned. Your future would have been secured in their memories. Your death could be mourned and you would not need to cling to life and cause us both so much pain. It is all their doing, Munyasya.

You are lying, Nzoka. If they had bewitched me, then why did the spell break?

Munyasya, truth is more powerful than any lie. It is inescapable. You can hide from it, but it will find you out eventually. That night, truth found you through the voice of your friend Mbuvu. You knew he was right and that is why you were so offended by his words and therefore so angry. That's why you left the bar in such an impatient state and that's why you fell. Truth had finally reclaimed you. When I came to you I was happy. It seemed there and then that all the problems you had caused me over the years had been solved. I came to greet you and thank you.

But I wasn't dead, Nzoka. You should not have come.

Munyasya, please remember that I am still your stepfather. You should not speak to me like that. What I have said is true. What I did not know then, however, is just how powerful these people are. They knew they were in danger of losing you so they had to act immediately. You see, you were still of use to them, Munyasya. Think back. Remember how much you were still helping them to get their own way. You were always having meetings for this and that. Everything you did with your life was planned by them. And yet, they were doing this so that they could preserve you like a piece of dried meat. Then, by displaying you in public, showing you off like some promise of good things to come, they used you to persuade others to do only as they, themselves, wished. They need you, my son.

So they brought me back from the dead?

That's right, Munyasya. After all, who was it that took you to his doctor for medicine? Father Michael. Correct again. And he is still using you in the same way even now.

But Nzoka, how can I be of use to them now? How can you explain that? I have not been near Father Michael or even the church since that night. You have always refused to go.

But you still don't see, Munyasya. The white woman, the doctor, knew that her medicine, her spells were not strong enough to overcome the power of truth. They knew they had lost your mind so they did this to your body to make sure you cannot warn others against them. Do you not remember what they said that night? He will never walk again. And now, are you not walking?

I still cannot see how I can be helping them now.

Oh, they are using you even at this moment, be sure of it. You are setting an example for them, Munyasya. Have you not heard what this Father Michael says to people? Only this morning he was there in the market place, not spitting distance from where we are sitting now, saying what a marvellous man you were, how hard you used to work for his church. More than this he reminds people that since your accident you have not been to his church. It is such a pity, he says, that you have lost your mind. Now many people know the story of that night. They all know you left the bar angry because you had been arguing with Mbuvu. Many people even know what the argument had been about and that Mbuvu had called you a traitor because you had worked all your life for foreigners and had betrayed the values by which we are all taught to live. People know how he goaded you, how he dared you to reject the white man's lies and learn to respect the truth again. Now what this priest wants them to think is that you took Mbuvu's advice that night and pledged yourself to rethinking your ways. Now that priest uses you. First, the fact that you very nearly died when you fell shows people how powerful his God is. Second, this God was capable of bringing you back from the dead.

There is only one God, Nzoka.

Look, Munyasya, when will you stop playing children's games with me? You have already said that there are three! Let me continue. Besides proving the power of his Gods, he also displays how powerful is his medicine.

Then why did he not cure me completely and restore me to my full strength?

Ah, there are three reasons for that, Munyasya. One, he wanted to use you as an example to scare others and two, you had to be punished. The third reason, however, is the most important. Unfortunately for Father Michael and his plans, I intervened. It may well originally have been his intention to restore you to health, but with me here it was impossible. Did I not say to you, Munyasya, that there is no lie that can have power over truth? With me here alongside you representing a truth that is greater than their lies, their medicines failed. It is I who commands you now, not three Gods and the white man. So now he makes you an example and punishes you for apparently rejecting his power. And you said before that your God could do you no harm. Now that is certainly true of the God we both knew, but this priest's god, his three gods are capable of punishing people in life if they reject him or them. Why, the man even admits it openly. Think about it yourself, Munyasya. Does he not use you as an example of one who has been punished in life for the way you have lived? See if I am not right! It has taken me a long time to understand it myself, but I must possess greater wisdom than you. It must be correct. It must be.

Let's suppose you are right, Nzoka. How does that affect us? How can it help us if you are right? You said yourself that we must solve our problem together. How can this knowledge help us?

Think, Munyasya! Think! Do you remember me speaking of an appointed task, some work left undone in life? Well I assumed that it was some task of my own, but I was wrong, wrong from the beginning. It is all so clear now. You see, as your stepfather, I am still responsible for you. I share the credit for your achievements, share the blame for your mistakes. I must absolve myself by helping you to throw off this burden, which presses you to this earth and holds you here. That is it, Munyasya! It is clear.

It is as clear as your cloudy beer, Nzoka. It is still a riddle to me.

You are as slow as a tortoise, Munyasya. Think. This man has been using you as an example to others to prove the truth of his message. While you did as he said, you were a pillar of the community he desired. When you rejected his ways, you grew like this as punishment. Through you, I must use him to do the opposite. We are going to make an example of him, Munyasya, so show everyone that he is wrong and that he is using deception to trick people into following his false ways. He tells people not to ignore his version of the truth as you did. We must convince them that ours is the only real truth. Now I know what I'm doing, my friend. Trust me. We have found the door of our cage. Now we can step through it together.

Munyasya awoke from his drowsing with a start. His body was cold and stiff. The day had changed completely. Wind was howling across the market place lifting whirls of dust into the air. The sun had gone and the sky was laden with darkness. He had to move. There was no time to waste. The bar, already, was too far away for the time he perceived, so with bottle and stick firmly grasped, he shuffled unerringly over the uneven ground to the nearest refuge, a restaurant, one of the line of concrete box shops closest to his tree. He reached its safety only just in time. By the time he had crossed the room and claimed a chair in the corner furthest from the door - a chair which had been vacated unasked by another who had seen him enter - the market place was a flurry of frenzied activity. Rain had already started to fall. People were running for shelter clutching their as yet unsold wares. Women held their skirts up in front of them to hold their potatoes and fruit, before bouncing towards the shops for shelter, howling with laughter and whoops of excitement along the way. It was not often that rain came here, and even less often that it came during the day. It would be a long storm, Munyasya told himself. A cup of tea appeared on the table before him, but he ignored it. He felt suddenly tired again after his exertions, and went quietly to sleep.

Munyasya! Munyasya! Wake up! Oh no, not you again. Go away. Do you never sleep? Can't you see how tired I am? What need have I for sleep, my child? I have no life from which to seek rest. Anyway, there is no time to sleep. Listen! I want you to look over there, by the doorway. Who is that woman, that white woman? I don't know her name. Is she a priest? A woman cannot be a priest, Nzoka. They are all men. Then she is the wife of a priest? No. She cannot be that either. Priests are not allowed to marry. What is that, Munyasya? Priests cannot marry? That cannot be natural! Just another reason why we should not trust them. Unmarried men cannot be wise. Listen, Munyasya, I don't know who this woman is, but I have seen her before with this man Father Michael. She must work with him. I have heard it said just now that she teaches our children in the church. No, Nzoka, you are wrong. I can explain. The people of Migwani wanted a school where their children could be educated. Why? Because with an education you can get a job. For example, nowadays it is not possible for a man to enter the army like I did when I was young. You must attend school first and get qualifications. Yes, Munyasya, I have seen what happens. These whites run the schools and teach people to follow their ways. No, Nzoka, that is not true. They teach many things... I know what they teach, Munyasya. I am not blind. Let us say that I see it differently from you. Tell me, did this Father Michael help to build the school? Yes. Well he helped by providing some of the money. Look, Nzoka, I have known this man and I still cannot believe that he is in any way evil, as you claim. You don't? Munyasya, if it is so obvious to me, why is it that you cannot see it as well? That man must have affected you with his trickery more deeply that I thought. I do hope that we are not going to fight over this. Come over here with me and watch this. I will prove it to you.

Munyasya now almost burst to life, as if fired by some new spring of youthful energy. This sudden movement first surprised and then provoked instant fear in those around him. His stick-like body was erect and stiff and his previously sagging flesh newly alive with tensed muscles. The walking stick, without which he was formerly unable to stand, was now a swinging baton, a means of asserting his newly re-created power, his newly reclaimed strength and superiority. This was the Munyasya that people feared.

He crossed the room, his step still unsure, but now his shuffling displayed a confidence, his gait suddenly stronger than before. He seemed to know he would not fall. On reaching the table where Janet sat with her friends, he stopped and stared directly at her. He seemed pleased when she displayed immediate unease. When he spoke, the mumble was gone. His words were now shouted at the same scream that had momentarily stopped life in the market place earlier that morning. When he behaved this way, he demanded attention and invariably received it. While rain thundered to earth outside, the room had become full of activity and noise. People had packed into the restaurant's single bare room to shelter from the storm which had brought market day to a premature close, and there was a loud buzz of conversation and laughter as trays of tea were distributed over the heads of the crowd and then sipped by drenched customers. But when Munyasya spoke, all conversation, all laughter and all clanking of teacups abruptly stopped, the performer instantly winning his audience. For some moments he said absolutely nothing, preferring to stand, silent and threatening, towering over the diminutive seated group before him. With a broad smile showing brown teeth through his saliva and rain-matted beard, in turn he looked people in the face and, it seemed, offered a silent challenge. Wide eyed, he was noting every reaction.

The white woman was consciously trying to ignore him. An occasional sideways glance in his direction revealed her growing concern. In vain she tried to continue her conversation with her three companions, all younger than herself, mere boys, in fact. Everyone else in the room was watching old Munyasya, however, awaiting the expected tirade of words they knew would soon come. The short, but seemingly endless silence was tense. Only the near whisperings of the white woman to her friends broke it, in spite of the general animation that seemed to pervade that crowded room. When Munyasya finally spoke, it was with the thundering voice of Nzoka, the voice his audience had expected. It was not the light tone of Munyasya, the voice which would murmur its almost inaudible request to have his beer bottle filled at the bar several times a day. No, this was the voice of Nzoka, loud, declamatory and spat forth like a curse. It was clearly a great effort for the old man, to speak like this. His entire body stiffened and heaved, his head jerked back on his neck, as if the words demanded an easier passage from the throat. The strain caused him to spit, and saliva soon began to hang like strands of silk from his mouth, matting to a glistening mass the hair of his beard. Each time he spoke, his words dissolved all the tension that had built during the moment of silence that had preceded them and provoked much of his audience to laughter, hilarity that was clearly born of both expectation of entertainment and the tension of fear. Renewed silence, and with it his renewed unerring stare at his target, retrieved the momentarily lost sense of foreboding. What would he say this time? What would he do? How would she react?

So you can buy tea for all your friends, all these bleating sheep that follow you without question?

The woman quickly grows nervous. Her young friends begin to giggle with embarrassment. Since she cannot understand him, one of the boys offers to translate and he leans across to whisper his words. She listens intently, but still does not seem to understand.

Look around you. Look! This is your flock. These people have been obedient. They have followed your path blindly, led by the empty promises you have made. Now prove to them that you truly want to share the riches you speak of. You have shared your ideas, now share your money! Say yes, it is a word that can do no harm.

The translation provokes her to act. She calls to the owner of the restaurant, a man she knows well by name, and asks that the old man should have a cup of tea. Wails of laughter rise in the room as a waiter theatrically holds out a cup of tea for Munyasya, who shows no interest in the offer, until he turns slightly to the side and spits. More laughter, and this continues until new convulsions in the old frame indicate that he is ready to speak again.

You must use more than one finger to kill fleas in a bed! Buy everyone tea. Buy everyone food. We have heard how rich you people are. Prove that you are willing to share those riches with us as reward for having listened to your teaching. This time the woman clearly dismisses the translation her friend offers. She begins to think that she should leave, but outside the market place is completely awash and the rain is still torrential.

Tell him I have no money.

Before the boy speaks, Munyasya has silently translated for Nzoka.

But you come here ready to travel! How can anyone be ready to travel, be waiting for a bus without money? It is said that you must pay money on the bus. Ah, I see! A beautiful girl never pays her bus fare - especially a white one!

Everyone in the restaurant bursts into laughter at this. A few people even applaud his cheek. No one, except the white woman, appears to be taking him seriously. They are all lucky because he is not accosting them. This old man can obviously do no one any harm. He is too old and too weak to be of any danger, but still people fear him like they fear the night. He is unpredictable, a quantity as unknown as darkness. Janet soon begins to react as Nzoka had hoped. She begins to dismiss him impatiently, becomes scornful of the words. He spits more words at her.

Ah! So now we see the truth behind your ideas. No riches until we are rewarded by your God after death. Stay blind in life so you might see in death? That is what you say in your church?

He looks for a reaction from Janet and the boy who is translating for her. One of the other boys at the table is suddenly afraid that he himself is going to be confronted; the direction of the old man's gaze is ambiguous. In a flash his laughter has gone and he is rushing through the mass of people towards the door. He does not stop until he is outside in the rain. Now the old man joins in with his audience's laughter.

Tell the man he is stupid and a fool!

Janet still does not yet realise how well he understands English. He reacts again, before the translation comes. The boy, anyway, dare not do as he is asked.

Is it not true? Am I stupid if I speak the truth? While your Church becomes richer here and now, you tell your sheep to forget wealth - that it will be theirs when they die - as long as they heed your commands! And then the wealthy ignore the poor.

He now moves closer to the woman to emphasise what he says to her. His intention is to intimidate and he succeeds immediately. She seems reluctant to look his way. When she does not offer an answer immediately, he prods her with his stick. She pushes him away. His expression hardens.

Don't play with me! You are too young to play with me! So, I am stupid because I can see how you teach these children to dismiss the truth I speak. What a boy learns the man remembers.

He moves closer to her again. All the time, with almost mechanical repetition, he is stretching and flicking loose the string tied to his thumb.

I am Nzoka, the snake. I am older, wiser than you.

The string, which is always tied to his thumb, becomes the snake. He pulls it out to its full length and then lets it go, so that it coils and loops as it falls.

I am Nzoka. How dare you push me? Children today must be taught what is right and I will teach you.

He approaches her, now getting uncomfortably close to her, and stretches the string, his signature, out to its full length just in front of her face. He bends low over her and tries to place his hands, still holding the string upon her shoulders. His intentions might be kind. He is playing the role of the father admonishing a wayward daughter.

I am Nzoka. You are my child. I must teach you. I am Nzoka.

He moves too close, much too close. Suddenly her terror that until this moment had rooted her to the spot, now forces her to act. With one heave she throws him to the side. He staggers and then, dropping his stick and therefore unable to correct his balance, he falls. She is gone out into the rain before he can stand. The old man is mumbling again. He is too weak to stand, too weak to lift the body that a moment before had seemed stiff with power. No one helps him, however. No one wants to risk becoming the object of his attention.

Oh my leg... Munyasya, it worked! My head, it hurts... Listen, my son. Listen! What do you want, Nzoka? Why did you make me do that to her? She was frightened. And look what she did to me... She could have killed me. I wish she had, Munyasya. Oh my head... But don't you see? It's true. Everything I have said to you. It's all true. Why do I always have to do your dirty work? You speak and I get punched. Why must it always be me who suffers? Why do you do it to me? Stop whimpering at me, Munyasya, and listen. Didn't you see her reaction? Didn't you hear what she said? Didn't you hear how she set you up as an example to those children? She was telling them that you were stupid, obviously wrong. She was telling them not to grow up like you. I didn't hear anything. You are inventing the things you want to hear, Nzoka. No, Munyasya, it proves what I was saying to you earlier. These white people have used you - and they are still doing so - to benefit themselves. You have been and still are their slave. Am I alone? Am I the only person who has followed their ways, who has worked for them, learned their language? Of course you aren't. That's why we have to act, to make people see. But Nzoka, they were good to me. They educated me, paid me to provide for my needs, fed me. And yet, Munyasya, they always used you to accomplish their own ends. How do you explain the fact that you spent your life fighting for them, risking your life on their behalf? You were so much in their power that for a time you even fought your own people so that they could achieve their own ends. Don't you see? So what do we do? I suppose you have some ideas already, or do we sit around for another few years until you have made your plan? No, Munyasya. At last I know what it is that we should do. We must make an example of these people. Just one of these people... but who? Who, Nzoka? I am still not sure yet, Munyasya. We have to choose our victim with care so that people will see what it is that we are trying to tell them.

Come on, Nzoka, whom do you suggest? The great idea is yours. Tell me. I've said I don't know yet. I need more time to think and you're disturbing me. The best plan is the one that needs the least effort. I must have more time to think. More time? Nzoka, you've already had years and years! How much more time do you want? My son, you are the impatient one. When we act we must act with care. We must not waste this knowledge we have discovered. We must wait so that we can pick our moment and make it tell.

***

A campaign starting in Sudan and then moving into Abyssinia during World War Two left Munyasya with enduring memories of adventure, camaraderie and pride. These places were not home, but relating their differences to the cultural landscapes he knew was not difficult, the contradictions thus providing him with experience, knowledge and expanded wisdom. The active service in Malaya almost a decade later, however, left him stunned, insecure, certainly changed and not a little paranoid, haunted by an expected encounter with a nearby but never seen stalking enemy. First impressions had shocked him with false familiarity. He came from Africa an *askari* and found himself called the same by these people. He was around fifty years old, the same *hamsini* here and there. His beloved fried fish – an enduring favourite of Major Cunningham's, which he had learned to prepare for his employer – remained *samaki*. He could not understand, but when people spoke, he could hear pinpricks of familiarity, known word-islands in an unfamiliar sea of sound. But the occasional word did not begin to bridge the chasm of alienation he felt with every minute in this place.

The forest, above all else, was a foreign place. His short training had helped, but East Africa's fundamental dryness was no preparation for this humid, sweating density of life. In Kenya a thorn bush could be bypassed, skirted without contact, but here hanging *rotans* often barred the path and their fierce spikes had to be pushed aside, often only to spring back with a parting stab once released.

Though most of their work was just guarding facilities, occasionally he was called upon to join a deployment charged with locating an insurgent group, or known individual enemy. But how could you see in this country, where it was always easier to hide? And how could you identify an enemy who might be leading a buffalo one minute and levelling a rifle against you the next? To patrol like this, through the dense thicket between the giant trees, unable to use whatever paths might exist for fear of booby traps and ambushes, was to experience fear. Not the sudden onrush of shock borne of an unexpected event, but a constant aching pressure which rendered the prosaic a potential nightmare.

If only you could trust something here! But the forest never revealed itself, always returning the same vista with each step: more forest, more undergrowth, near darkness under the canopy of the cauliflower-topped trees two hundred feet above. Sometimes there was quiet, sometimes deafening noise from insects and who knows what which were never seen and – contrary to what he thought on arrival – he never saw an animal, not even an insect of any size. Always sure that whatever was there could see him, he found it deeply unsettling that he never saw a sign of life, not even a bird. Surely this enemy who knew this place also knew its ways and could see without ever being seen.

The first time he shared the success of one such patrol, he knew that he was changed forever. On intelligence they had parked their vehicle only a mile or so from the village, though the single building in a small forest clearing to which they eventually laid siege would not have qualified for such an exalted title in Kenya. It was, however, a large house, all of wood, raised on stilts with a thatched palm leaf roof, and had a large open veranda along the long side of its rectangle. Inside, they were told, was the man they wanted. Munyasya and the other King's African Rifles were surely there just as support staff. They were carriers and path clearers for the specially trained combat personnel who were in command of the group. And so they had picked their quiet way through the growth, off-path, carefully avoiding the stumble that might announce their approach, but consequently taking hours to cover a distance they could walk in ten minutes across flat ground. And when the clearing revealed itself, with its single house and apparent lack of activity, they spent another hour, whispering and puppeting sign language to decide what to do next. The marksmen, however, were on station, concentrating their gaze on the raised open terrace of the house. When, after what seemed like an age, the hunted quarry revealed himself, nonchalantly emerging bare-chested from within, still half asleep from his afternoon nap and sauntered to the wooden railing for a breath of air and a smoke, the marksmen of the special forces did their job and holed his body. As expected, others rushed to seek their weapons, but Munyasya and his men did their covering job and shot at anything that did not immediately lie down and surrender.

They killed six in all, mostly men and left no wounded. Another five cowered in fear, apparently clinging to the floor and had to be pushed with rifle butts to raise their hands. They were no threat, these survivors, at least today, and, to ensure they remained so, they were handcuffed and marched back to camp, to be later transported to a more secure place. As for the dead, the safe and easy option was to cremate. The clearing would ensure that the fire did not spread. Munyasya, along with all the others who were alien in this place, had quickly learned that forest fires rarely burnt themselves. Mere embers or ash would not kindle the damp vegetation of a rain forest, so the fire from burning this house would not cause wider consequences and would never be traced, since the growth would show again after a couple of weeks. But they had to prove their mission, to verify success and achievement of task. The experience-hardened members of the patrol went straight to their job as Munyasya and his men kept the prisoners from possible mischief. Six left ears were thus quickly and neatly removed from the dead with bush knives that later might be used to hang toast over a fire. Duly stored in their belt pouches, these proofs of accomplishment and achievement were all that was needed and torches were set against the timbers. This was what Munyasya learned, skills he would later transfer to his own people in his homeland.

The opportunity to do so soon arose when, for the first time as a soldier, he was posted to an assignment in his home district of Kitui. The long-serving and trusted chief of the northern region had been attacked in his house by bandits and his colonial paymasters, who knew the value of the stability that Mulonzya Mwendwa's steady administration had produced, insisted that he accept the military protection he had neither requested nor wanted. And so, in command, Major Edward Munyasya and his dozen comrades took up their station in a speedily-erected brick and corrugated iron building resplendently titled Mwingi Military Base, adjoining the euphorbia-hedged District Officer's compound, with its private house, office block and vehicle servicing sheds, all single storey concrete with grey rendered walls, contrasting starkly with the deep red earth brick of the rest of the town.

From day one of the assignment, Mulonzya Mwendwa treated his *askaris* almost like members of the family. This meant that he rigorously required observance of his seniority and status in all dealings with them, kept the soldiers in their place, demanded their total devotion to him alongside dedication to his interests and expected to hear not a single word of criticism. In return he ensured they were always well fed and kept comfortable. At the start of the soldiers' deployment, he had still been recovering from the vicious attack, which had left him with two messy pink stumps where once the beautiful smooth black skin of his wrists used to glisten in the sunlight. Let us say that he had not quite been himself, uncharacteristically sluggish and often sleepy as a result of his reaction to the various drugs he took to prevent infection and pain. At the time he was also of necessity unusually lacking in industry, spending several hours a day away from his tasks to have the wounds cleaned and dressed. But he was healing quickly and Major Munyasya was more impressed each day by the grit and resilience demonstrated by this old man, who spoke English with an accent as perfect as his own, as taught by his beloved Major Cunningham.

Perhaps because of the soldiers' presence in the town, perhaps not, there was no hint of any further action by Mulonzya Mwendwa's attackers. It may have been a case of mission accomplished and therefore no need to return, or it may have been because the presence of a dozen King's African Rifles under the command of an officer with experience in three campaigns genuinely deterred future assailants. Rumour admitted an alternative to the accepted view of events: that these men had never been anything to do with the Land Army or the struggle for *uhuru*, that they had been paid by Mulonzya Mwendwa's political opponents to render him powerless. But then why did they not kill him? Why just relieve him of his hands? Rumour explained this by the need to hide the identity of the perpetrators, so the attack had used the stock-in-trade anti-collaborator punishment to make it look like something bigger than a local skirmish. But it was also probably true that Mulonzya Mwendwa did not have opponents powerful enough to have done this, so complete had been his domination of local affairs. Certainly Mwendwa's son, James, on his regular visits from his base in Nairobi, never countenanced the idea that the attack had local origins. All this Major Edward Munyasya learned within days of his new posting as commanding officer in the new Mwingi Military Base.

Only a few weeks after the attack, Mulonzya Mwendwa was effectively restored to his old self, his old self minus his hands, of course. He had never entrusted his officially employed secretarial assistants with any task relating to his 'personal' interests, a division of labour which had served him dependably over the years, allowing him to maintain an apparently clear distinction between official business and personal gain. But without hands, he found himself newly and unaccustomedly powerless. Administration progressed without a hitch via dictation to his trusted staff, but when that particular matter of 'personal' import had to be dealt with in timely fashion, how could he now manage? James was often there to help, but he could not stay in Mwingi all of the time. He had his own interests to organise and administer and the journey from Nairobi along the potholed and stone-spotted dusty track they called a main road took several hours. Two days a week was all he could manage, travelling out one day and back the next to manage, therefore, just a few hours of useful work on either side of his overnight stay with his wife and child. And so, Mulonzya Mwendwa turned to Major Edward to carry out occasional 'personal' tasks. The soldier's English was good, he was used to administration and management and he was – it went without saying – utterly dependable, perhaps a little too much so, as things turned out. It only happened once. Such things could only happen once with Mulonzya Mwendwa, whose hawk like perception never missed a detail and whose requirement of total loyalty extended as far as a ban on any form of initiative.

Munyasya had dealt with those letters before. Only a few weeks into his unpaid part-time post as personal assistant to the chief, he had perfunctorily knocked on the office door at the usual time and entered to find all unexpectedly quiet. He had completed his morning command duties, checked the correct deployment of his men to their various stations in the town and then continued, as had become his habit, to offer an hour's assistance to Mulonzya Mwendwa. Later he would learn that the chief had closed the office for the day and sent the staff home having, that morning, received an unexpected letter advising him that, at his convenience, he could visit a hospital in Nairobi where he would be fitted with prostheses to replace his missing hands. Excited beyond reason by the prospect of regaining some of his lost abilities, he could not be persuaded to wait and so he had travelled immediately to the appointment. He would, of course, at first sight be disappointed by the hollow strap-on wooden cups on offer, designed to hide his scars from others' eyes rather than help him regain the ability to grasp, but, as time passed, he would invent ingenious and often creative ways of using these two cumbersome crude tubes, with their slotted hemispherical ends, to accomplish the most delicate of tasks. He would learn, for instance, how to slot a spoon or knife into the hole at the end to feed himself. The same hole, he later found, would admit a pen, allowing him to learn afresh how to write letters in his once delicate hand, but which now, even with the most carefully expert control of his bulbous block of a hand were at best legible. Eventually, he would thus learn to be satisfied with these tools, but his initial shock of disappointment that day was enormous, greater than the original excitement he had felt at the prospect he imagined.

Perhaps that excitement of anticipation was why, that day, he had been uncharacteristically careless. Ever meticulous in his habits, both at work and in his personal life, Mulonzya Mwendwa never left a task half finished. But that day, lying on the always-unmarked blotter pad on his desk was a blue manila folder that Munyasya had grown to recognise. It was newer than most others and bore his full name in the top right hand corner, Major Edward Munyasya, preceded by the three crucial capitals, FAO. For Munyasya, these letters were tantamount to an order. Now he knew the file was usually stored away, that he never saw its contents, that Mulonzya Mwendwa would sit with it open before him, where only he could read its contents. On any particular day, there would never be more than two papers to deal with and the task would never be arduous. The chief would scrutinise his papers and then dictate a suitable letter in response that Munyasya would write, place in an envelope and then take to the post office. Two letters a day and then a fifty-yard walk to the town's miniscule huddle of shops. This surely was not real work, so he never once resented his duties on behalf of the man it was his job to protect.

So it was with an air of practice, familiarity and duty that Munyasya took hold of the folder that was marked for his attention, despite the fact that he had never before touched it. Inside was a single sheet. A scan of the short text revealed a format and content he recognised as matching several letters he had written on the chief's behalf in recent weeks. So apparently predictable was the action required that he decided he was only helping by dealing with the task. Keeping the wheels of his work turning without troubling his superior was how he justified it to himself. The letter in the folder summarised receipts of produce, bought wholesale from local farmers, thus relating to Mulonzya Mwendwa's licensed concessionary trading business. Carefully, double-checking against his own memory, since the previous letters he had written in response to similar reports were all locked in the cabinet, he drafted the seemingly perfunctory confirmatory note that had to be sent to the District Commissioner's office in Kitui. Thus he recreated the short letter he had written several times already and amended the memory to include the latest figures from the report in the file. He would never have dreamt, of course, that the numbers in the note to the District Commissioner, whose office collated such figures for official statistics and taxation, should be significantly different from and lower than the ones reported by the warehouseman. Even if he had access to the locked-away files marked 'Personal', he would not have noticed the discrepancies, since the warehouse reports were never filed here, only the confirmatory letters to Kitui. So he wrote the letter, reported the quantities, addressed the envelope and posted it, aglow with the knowledge that Mulonzya Mwendwa would thank him for completing the task. The following day, when Mulonzya Mwendwa returned from Nairobi, disappointedly sporting a pair of stained-black, heavy willow clubs on the ends of his arms instead of the new hands he had expected, Munyasya respectfully allowed him an hour to himself before entering the office to report the task done. Thus, one of the first things Mulonzya Mwendwa learned to do with his new club hands was to strike someone hard across the face. The blow struck before he had even started the torrent of abuse – all in Kikamba, without a word of English to stain the message – that followed. Major Edward Munyasya was left in no doubt that never again should he do something without the expressed and accurate direction of Mulonzya Mwendwa. From that moment, he would do as he was told, nothing more, nothing less. It was only to be a few weeks later when this modus operandi began to benefit the chief and his son, James, who claimed that he had thought up the plan all by himself.

The colonial authorities had never taken to the idea of pastoralism. It was a problem in both the north and south of the country. The border with Tanganyika, however, presented no real problem. True, it crossed the ancestral homelands of the Masai and some families did drive their herds to and fro, from one country to the other to find grazing.

But the land here was quite good. There was usually enough grass and no one travelled very far, so the requirements of this border could be easily enforced in the future. The north, however, posed an altogether different problem. Arid, semi-desert scrub offered few grazing opportunities, and the general lack of rain accompanied by the unpredictability of what did fall meant that Somalis, in particular, would often drive their herds hundreds of miles to sustain life. Not caring too much about which country they were in today, they would set off to find tomorrow's subsistence, the continued well being of their cattle fundamental to their existence. Borders, and the governments that were defined by them, therefore could not accommodate pastoralists on the move.

James Mulonzya had discussed these issues in Nairobi, a town known for good grazing but few cows, and had reported the conclusions to his father. Opportunity, it seems, is often the product of entirely random and independent factors coexisting in time and space. Opportunity grasped, however, is a sign of genius, and so, later, when the product of the campaign was revealed, most people assumed that it had come from the father's brain and not that of his dull son. A government policy to encourage the settlement of the pastoralists, a respected and trusted administrator's standing, a nascent political presence promising future achievement and, crucially, a devoutly obedient group of armed soldiers, comprising mainly poor recruits eager to earn a little on the side, were the ingredients. History would record the 'Shifter' problem as having taken place over decades, on many fronts and taking many forms. Often described as a 'tribal' conflict over land, grazing rights and ownership, it would record many skirmishes and minor battles resulting in loss of life and occasional stealing of women as trophies. History would make no special record or reference, therefore, to the activities of a particular armed group in the north of Mwingi District. Always at night and always with what some described as 'professional' precision and competence, they attacked nomadic groups who entered an area that could be recognised and delineated only by those who had designated its limits. The surprising and unique characteristic of these often brutal attacks was the victors' habit of removing the left ears from the dead. This was both noticed and recorded, but, in the overall run of things, these occurrences were a relatively small proportion of the large number of incidents, which spread in different manifestations right across northern Kenya. And so it was also unrecorded by history, but certainly not unnoticed either by officialdom or people in general in that area, that Mulonzya Mwendwa and his son, James, established in their joint names, within a newly erected fence where the like had never been seen before, one of the largest cattle ranches in the soon to be independent country on land their faithful detachment of King's African Rifles had vacated on their behalf.

***

All right, Munyasya, you can sit down now.

Thank God for that! I was beginning to think I would have to carry on walking all the way to paradise.

Munyasya, just sit down and be quiet. Have a drink and leave me in peace for a while. I have to think.

Have a drink? A drink of what?

There's a bottle in your coat pocket. Now be quiet. Go to sleep if you want. Let your stepfather think in peace for a while. I'll keep watch.

Look, Nzoka, what is all this about? Keep watch for what? I am tired of being your donkey. Carry me here. Carry me there. Go here. Go there. Carry me this way and that. Lie here. Walk there. Sit here. Sleep. Wake up. Drink. All I hear from you are orders. You are worse than a sergeant major on a parade ground. I wouldn't mind if I had a choice. I try to say no to you, but my body doesn't even listen; it just does whatever you say. And for what? Every idea you have ever had has been nonsense. You seem to come up with a different one every day and none of them ever seem to work. Munyasya, lie down in front of this bus. There might be more stupid things a man could do with his time, but I have certainly never come across them. But off I go, limbs obeying every command you even suggest, let alone deliver. You say it will kill me and then make both of us free. Especially yourself, no doubt. I remain nothing less than sceptical at what it can possibly accomplish from my point of view. My goodness I feel uncomfortably sober. Where did you say that bottle was?

In the inside pocket of your coat. Can't you feel the weight of it?

Where was I? Oh, yes. When this bus runs over me, people will somehow be immediately enlightened so that they will see this white man's invention, and everything else associated with it, including the white man, himself, as equally evil. You will have destroyed me and will have atoned for your mistakes in the past at the same time. Rather convenient from your point of view, if you ask me. And then what happens? They come into the road, pick me up and move me - or the driver goes backwards and then drives on his way as if I was never there in the first place. I am either scraped from the road like squashed lizard or ignored like some cow shit that got in the way of a tyre. And if it did succeed, if the bus did drive over me, what would it prove? People would look at me and say that it's only a stupid fly that gets killed by a falling turd.

But that proves my point, Munyasya. Don't you see?

Nzoka, for years what I have seen is only what you have seen. You are my eyes. And you say this proves your point? Only if your point is nonsense!

Look, Munyasya, people know these things are evil and dangerous. If they were not, then they would ignore you - drive their animals over you - even they themselves know it is evil, but it controls them. It forces them to protect it, to keep its evil hidden. So they move you, or just avoid you.

Then you were wrong in what you thought...

No, Munyasya, not wrong, but not quite right either. A bird does not thatch a nest from a single blade of grass. It has taken time to collect all the facts.

I am growing sick of your excuses, Nzoka. You have dragged me around with you for years now and I am sick of it. Why don't you accept your fate, my fate! And just let me die? You keep trying to convince me that you are trying to bring this pathetic sham called a life to an end, but for years it has been you who has kept it alive. I have certainly done nothing to help! It is clear, Nzoka, that you are dealing with some power which is both stronger and wiser than yourself. If that is the case, then could I offer the judgment, if you would be so good as to pay attention to me for just this once, that you will not be able to beat it, no matter what it is.

Wisdom is something that grows, Munyasya, and I am certainly much wiser now...

Wisdom may grow, Nzoka, that I would not choose to deny, but not all of us start from the same point, do we? In your case, you are still the same failure in death that you always were in life. Why should you have changed, for God's sake? And you are still trapped. There is no way out now. You may be wiser, Nzoka, but you are certainly no nearer your goal.

Ah, but there you are quite wrong, my son. I have made mistakes, it is true, but unlike you, Munyasya, I have learned from those mistakes. And I now have a plan that must succeed.

Oh no, not another of those schemes which...

Wait, Munyasya, and hear what I have to say. This one is perfect - and very simple. We will not fail this time. Once the traveller knows the way he no longer needs to ask for directions. I have a plan and this time we will not fail.

I see. The plan and its perfection are both yours alone, but any failure will be ours? I suppose that is one step better than it being my responsibility alone, but as usual I am going to get the blame when it all goes wrong. I suppose you're going to tell me that the bus is going to come along the road and I am going to lie down in front of it. There wouldn't perhaps be an easier way of making the same point by any chance?

No, of course not. I am not having you deal with any more buses. I have already told you that I have concluded that the tactic is simply no good.

So if no bus, what? Pray?

A small bus. A car.

And that makes a difference?

Yes.

You are more senile than I, Nzoka. Why push me all the way to this place just to try the same trick again? We could have found a car in Migwani. There was no need to come all the way to this place. Even Father Michael has a car.

Exactly. But my plan is better than even you think.

To have more than nothing is not necessarily to have something... Ah, Nzoka, I am truly an old man now, not the child that was your brother's son. Don't beat me. You can't teach an old dog like that!

It's about time I did treat you like a child, if you ask me, you old rascal. I have tried and tried to make you see, but you are always too lazy even to make the smallest effort to think or see for yourself!

Lazy? You call me lazy, you... you layabout? What choice have I in the matter? You command and I follow. It can hardly be my fault if my body is too weak to respond. How can I be expected to do everything you ask? You seem to think that I am still seven years old and that I can jump fences and run to catch a bus...

All right, Munyasya. That's enough for now. Listen first and then make your complaints later. I now command you to listen to me. What I have to say is neither new to you nor difficult to understand. Listen, and my argument will convince you as it has convinced me.

Can I have a drink first?

All right. You can have your body for now, but listen and listen carefully. Now you know as well as I do that this world in which we live is a punishment. It is a desert to which we have been banished to prove ourselves worthy of paradise. We know that is true because our people have lived their lives according to this for generations. I know it is true because I have seen what happens after this world is left behind. Unlike you, Munyasya, I have seen the argument from both sides.

What if it has three sides? Or even more?

Arguments only have two sides, Munyasya. Yes is one side and no the other. There can be no room in people's lives for anything harder to comprehend. That is why there is no language that has an alternative to saying 'yes' or saying 'no'.

Hmmm... maybe...

No, believe me, Munyasya, I have seen the argument from both sides. Life is but a trial, designed to allow us, each and every one of us, to prove that we are worthy of achieving the paradise that is just beyond our temporal life.

Nzoka, it is a long time since my grandfather taught me such things by the evening fireside. I can remember hardly anything of what he said. Anyway the stories weren't true. The Bible explains how the world was created. It's all written there - and it is a different story from the one my grandfather told me.

Munyasya, how many times do I need to tell you that I am not interested in the white man's myths? There are no white men in paradise. There never were any and there never will be, because they are evil and always have been and always will be. What you have to remember from your childhood is the truth. It seems that you still need me to remind you of what that is.

If I remember correctly - if you remember it correctly, that is, because I'm sure that these thoughts are yours - the story - the truth - is that

409

paradise and the world in which we live are the same thing. They are the same size. The land is the same and even the people are the same.

So why are they separate places?

They were not separate in the beginning.

Just in the beginning?

We call it that, but there was no time to measure then. Paradise and life were the same thing. They were held together by a strong rope that would never rot. People lived their lives in an unending paradise. There was neither birth nor death, just an unending humanity. There was always good rain and crops never failed. There was always enough to eat.

So how did it change? Why is it that life now is far from anything that might even be linked with the name 'paradise'? Why is it that time pushes paradise itself ever further from the clutches of the living? Why is it that we must now all undergo the torture of standing here and watching our life's only goal receding ever further from us?

It is because of the hyena.

Correct, Munyasya! Correct! Go on, tell me what happened and even you will begin to understand.

Well the hyena gnawed at the rope that bound life and paradise together. That was the first evil act committed since the start of all creation, and through it evil triumphed. The rope broke and thus cut the path that joined the two worlds. Life was then forever severed from paradise.

Why was the rope not joined? Why did we not just tie the ends together and repair the path?

It was not possible. Paradise began to drift away from us. While we stood still and watched, paradise drifted away from us like a cloud.

Ah yes, the beginning of time. With every new day, our life's goal drifts further from us...

And still we sit here in the present doing nothing!

Munyasya, the very fact that we are here shows that we are doing as much as we can.

As much as we can? You are surely more of a fool than I am, Nzoka. What in heaven is the difference between sitting under a tree in Migwani waiting for the next bus and sitting in the shade of Kitui's Post Office waiting for the next car?

Impatient, as ever, my son.

I am not your son and never was...

But you were - and still are - my ward.

And I have grown old to become your prison.

You will soon see that I have served my time. But we are forgetting our lesson in history! Come on, Munyasya, tell me the rest of the story.

There's no more to tell. The hyena cut the rope and here we are. Imprisoned by the lives we lead, without a hope and unable to recognise one if it hit us in the face.

No more to tell? You are not as wise as you think, my son. Do you think the hyena alone bears the sin?

Of course not.

Why?

Because it is said that men stood and watched as it chewed. They knew what it was doing. It was a conspiracy by those in paradise to keep it all for themselves. They believed that if they gave the hyena a juicy joint of meat, it would cut the rope for them and they would be the sole inhabitants of the comfortable place they had made for themselves.

A good plan?

No. A very poor one.

Why?

Because God sees all.

And what did God make of what He saw?

Obviously He blamed everyone who took part in the scheme. All living things shared the blame as He saw it. He banished them all to this world and invented time as their trial. Every living thing was granted its own time to prove its individual innocence, to show God that it took no part in the original sin, or on the other hand to admit what it did and then to atone for that sin and thereby to show itself worthy of paradise.

You have remembered well, my son, but that is still not the full story. Life is not simply one test. It is a series of trials that must be lived through. Each separate step must be attempted before the next may be approached, each in its own place and time; never the next without the last completed. With each step the path grows steeper until the final leap to the top of the hill. There a man can rest, proud of his success and achievement. While he takes a breath he watches over his still striving kin, lends a helping hand or word of advice whenever he sees fit. It is his duty to help them, for if he does not, and one of them should fall by the wayside, the failure will hinder even himself. He will then have to drag the dead weight of shared evil along with him forever because the bonds that tie his family together are made of the same rope that once bound worlds. Only hyenas, lying and cheating people, can break these bonds and can be disowned by a family. But let us not pass final judgment before we have heard your case, Munyasya. Speak. Speak now.

You cannot be my judge, Nzoka. Only life can judge me. You should beware of misusing what you think is your power. You should not judge others, lest they judge you.

Then let us see what your life has to say. If it has been the witness, then let us hear it. Now don't try to avoid any of my questions, my son. That would only make your case worse.

Nzoka, if I tell lies then it is merely you who are lying to yourself.

I have warned you not to play with me, my son. Now, let's make a start. Step one. Birth.

I had no problem crossing that bridge.

I should hope not. Those who fail here are clearly not even worthy of trial. Only the totally evil spirit is denied even a chance to show itself in life. So we can both be thankful that you passed that first test.

You mean that you are thankful, Nzoka. What you are admitting is that you would be too lazy to carry such a burden of responsibility. It would have been a handicap for you to bear and you never were one to be the first to volunteer when there was a job to be done.

If you go on like this, I'll not even give you a last chance to redeem yourself!

And what would you do, my wise old Nzoka? Kill me? Remember that if you should do that you will also be killing yourself and then you would share my fate, my guilt.

We are discussing you, Munyasya, not me. Let us both recall how you took life's second step and made the transition into manhood.

I stepped proudly forward as do all young men.

But I think you went no further... You never married, Munyasya, my son, did you?

I was rejected!

My son, every man is rejected at least once, but not every man refuses to walk because he falls down at the first attempt...

I wanted to marry. Dearly I longed for a wife. But the opportunity never came my way again.

So you sat under a tree at a crossroads waiting for women, but none came? Opportunities do not come your way in life, my son. They must be sought out. If a man wants a wife, he goes out looking for one. And when he finds a woman who can keep him happy and bear his children, he makes her father an offer. Then, if it is accepted, he has his wife, but if not he looks elsewhere. He doesn't just give up! Now you have always had money. You have always been rich enough to afford a fine dowry. You could almost have taken your pick from all the women in Migwani, even the prettiest, most voluptuous young girls. But you were never seen here. Why did you not come home to your own village, Munyasya, and talk to the fathers of these girls? I know they were there. Throughout my years, I have always enjoyed spending the early part of the morning sitting by the old town dam where the young girls go to wash. Even when you get to my age, Munyasya, the curve of a buttock, the shake of a breast and that oh so sweet shape of the thigh, all of these still taste very sweet indeed... But not, it seems for you in your life, my son? Why did you never come home to marry?

If I had met a woman I loved I would certainly have married her...

Loved? How do you expect to know whether or not you love the woman before you have married her? Love is about caring for one another, about families and progress through life. The joys of such things can only be felt after marriage, never before.

But paying dowries, treating women like goats or cattle being sold at market, it is wrong. I would never have stooped to those depths.

Wrong? Who says it is wrong?

I do.

No, not you, my son. It is the white man who says these things. It is he who is speaking through your mouth. It is the lies of the white God that you are speaking. A man who tries to remember two things forgets one, and you have forgotten the truths you were taught as a child. Are you trying to say that what was correct for your father and his father before him is not good enough for you? In denying your own culture, Munyasya, your very identity, you are denying respect to those who reared you. And do you not see that what you have done has not only condemned you, but has also hindered your ancestors? They share your sins now. Your father was never a strong man and the added burden of your mistakes means that even after you are dead, he will find his journey very difficult, and made even more difficult by your mistakes. You will still be holding him back all the time. But anyway, spilt water can't be picked up.

Nothing I have done was ever meant to hurt him, or anyone else, for that matter.

But you have hurt him, and continue to do so.

I did only what was right.

You did what someone else told you to do, not what was right. What is right is what you know to be right and what was good enough for your father was surely good enough for you. Don't you see? You are now an old man and close - very close indeed - to your own death. Ever since you met these Europeans, you have thought only of yourself and never of your responsibilities to others. You have always known that it was your duty in life to marry and have children to preserve your name and with it the family line, itself. Think of all the poor souls waiting to be given their chance to prove themselves in life! By your actions, five, ten, maybe twenty of them will never get that chance. By your actions, your very kin, such as your own father, mother and even myself are still punished in death. There will be no family ties to steady you as you approach your own death to ensure that you arrive at the top of life's climb with the promise of support from below should you fall or stumble. There will be no one to mourn your death, to hold you at the top while you rest and regain your strength. For people like you the top of the hill may as well be the bottom, for even if you should get there, you will surely fall back whence you came. And I have told you already that the way is steep, and that once you have started to fall, only the bottom of the climb will stop you if you have no help. You need strength to ride the crest of the hill and that can only come from sleep and rest. For you there will be none.

I'm tired. I'm tired of all this, Nzoka. Every day, every night, you never stop...

You're always tired, especially when you are made to see the fate you surely cannot escape. For once, today, I will not allow you to sleep.

Why? So that you can just go on mocking me for longer than usual? Slap me like a naughty child, the way you always used to do?

No, Munyasya, just to teach you, like the stupid one you were. So the first two steps in your life were well taken, but the next two, your marriage and then the rebirth of your line are completely missing. What I can tell you, however, is that without those two, the final step is now so large that you have no chance at all of reaching the top of the hill. It would be too far, even for a giant's stride, let alone the poor shuffling of old decrepit Munyasya.

Then why should either of us worry about my trial, if I am so clearly guilty even before it starts?

Because your position may be difficult, my son, but it is surely not yet lost.

But you have said all along that for me death will be an end and not a new beginning...

It is not what I say which will determine your fate, Munyasya, but life, itself, when it finally releases you. And your life is not yet over. While there is life there is always a chance.

So I am to take a wife and have a family here today? If anything would kill me in my present state... A stick might bend when it's young, but when old it merely snaps.

Don't play with me, child! At your age you would need a donkey to do the work for you!

So what is it that I can do which will so help such a lost cause as mine?

My plan is not simple, but when you have heard it, I am sure you will agree that it will work. It makes good sense, and so I am confident that it can achieve for your name enough respect of the right kind to replace that which would have come from your family, if there had ever been one. There is hope for you yet, my son.

Without a wife? Without a family tree branching from my body?

You cannot undo any of the wrongs of your life, Munyasya. You will have to cope with those forever. But with one final, momentous achievement, you might just possibly be able to atone for them.

But what is it that a bag of bones like me can do?

You can save others from the same fate as yourself, my son. Ah, I can see now that you are really confused. Think, Munyasya, if you yourself can turn others from evil and set them on the right path, you could restore a chance in life for more souls than you could ever have released through the labour of your pathetic little penis.

So I am to become a preacher in my old age? And I suppose that while Munyasya's mouth moves, Nzoka will speak?

I cannot help you, my son. What must be done must be your doing and your doing alone.

Then why are you trying to help me?

Advice is all I offer. I can make no promises, but at least listen to what I have to say and then you can judge for yourself whether the plan makes sense.

Even if I were to say no, you would still make me listen...

My plan cannot work without your cooperation and agreement, Munyasya...

Tell me to stand and I will stand. Tell me to walk and I will walk. Tell me to say yes and I will say yes, Nzoka. Just tell me what you want me to do.

First of all let me explain. Think of the beginning of our world. Try to imagine yourself witnessing that very moment when our world broke away from paradise. Before you is a great rope, binding together our two worlds, but the hyena has already been at work and his crime is almost done. You can see the vile creature gnawing at the rope and there remain only a few strands to continue to bind you to everything you could ever wish for in your immortality. You know that if those strands break you will lose everything and that you will be punished for your part in the crime.

But I would have had no part in it!

Oh yes you would, my son. Men are not stupid and they can only harvest what they plant. If they stand idly by while so great a crime is committed, they are as guilty as the animal, itself. They are all responsible, because each and every one of them is capable of guarding the bond to ensure its safety against attack. Thus everyone shares the guilt because no one tried to prevent the crime from happening in the first place. So Munyasya, you, the hunter...

Hunter? I am a soldier.

Hunter, soldier - there is no difference. You the hunter are there. You know what is happening, you can see it clearly, but the job is not yet complete. Can you do anything to stop it, or are you totally powerless?

I could shoot the animal.

Exactly! You are learning well, my son. You could raise your bow and shoot...

Bow? A gun would be better.

It makes no difference. But tell me, would you shoot at the head to stop the teeth from gnawing, at the body to stand the best chance of a hit, or at the legs to make the beast fall, or where?

You clearly were never a hunter, Nzoka. Despite all your claims to be the upholder of tradition, you really seem to know very little of the life you claim to defend. You would miss the head and one leg broken leaves three with which to stand.

So where do you shoot, Munyasya?

At the body! It is the biggest target. You might even hit the heart if you are lucky.

And if not?

The beast would be wounded. It would be able to move only very slowly, if at all. I could then rush forward and finish it off with another shot through the head from close range.

Exactly! This is working perfectly.

But it's not helping me.

It is, my son. Now listen carefully. Have I not told you that the loose strands, which were once twisted to form that rope, are now used in life as a family's guide rope on the climb through life?

So the ties within a family between its members can only be broken by evil acts.

Exactly. But now suppose that there are hyenas prowling here also and that they are gnawing at these family ties trying to break them. If you could shoot the animals, would you try?

Of course. Calm down, Nzoka! You're jumping around so much you're making my stomach rumble!

You should have another drink. All my talking is making you thirsty.

When do we start shooting the hyenas?

It seems I may have made you see, but not yet think.

What has all of this got to do with me, Nzoka?

It is your last chance, my son. Nothing more than your last chance. But don't judge it until you have heard everything. Now I have drawn a picture for you to see. Look at that picture and think while I explain what it means.

We are agreed that our only path to heaven is along the family line?

Yes.

We are agreed that our family line is all but broken, that no more threads bind us together?

Yes, but I have not seen hyenas in this area for over twenty years.

But you have, Munyasya, you have indeed seen them. What above all else has persuaded you to turn against the truths both I and your own father taught you?

You have answered that for me many times already - the white man's teaching.

All of his teaching? Did learning how to fight in his army contradict your father's words?

No. It was the teaching of the white man's God.

Precisely. And have you ever spoken with this God?

Of course not. How can a man possibly speak to God?

Then how did you learn?

I was taught by priests.

And what they taught you has gnawed at the strands of the rope that binds you to your family. Over the years it has been weakened until today there remains but a single weak and fraying fibre to be broken. These are our hyenas. The priests.

Nzoka, you are senile. Priests are men, not hyenas. There is only one God and his advice is always for our own good. He is the God of love.

My son, this is where you must think a little if you want to see my plan. In paradise there were only men, but some of them were evil. It was they who bribed the hyena to do their dirty work. They knew all along they were doing evil and hoped that the stupid hyena would take the blame. The animal could equally have been a man, bribed to commit great evil as many men are, so that some other person might benefit. In life good and evil are often the same thing. While you starve, I can happily eat a feast. For me it is good, but for you it is certainly evil, for there is enough on my plate to feed two, and feed them both well. If I also know that, and I still ignore your need then I am evil. It is no more than your father's teaching, my son.

But there is still only one God!

In paradise there were only men, but they managed to produce evil in a place where previously there was none. Look, Munyasya, at what these priests and their church have done to you. They have all but cut through your family line. There will be no descendants following on behind you to offer help if you should fall on your way. They have caused you to forget your ancestors and your duties to them. And now for all time they will be burdened with their continued responsibilities toward you. But have we rejected you? Have we tried to cut the bonds that bind us to you? Have we tried to be rid of you? No. We have done the opposite. I am here to try to make you see the wrong things you have done. I am here to try to redirect your thoughts back to the path that can lead you away from this place. Through this I am trying to remake the bond that has been almost broken. We know you will always remain a burden for us, but to lose one of our own kind would be a tragedy none of us would want to bear. In the end that would prove to be the greater burden. The truth is clear. These priests and their teachings are the hyenas gnawing to break the bonds which themselves can only be good. In your case, Munyasya, they succeeded not only in claiming your poor old self for themselves, but also through sheer evil, they tricked Nzoka, your poor and long-suffering stepfather back into life where they have imprisoned him. Surely a hand that can reclaim the dead from their journey can be nothing other than purest evil!

But Nzoka, in paradise the evil ones stood to gain from their crime. They thought they would win everything for themselves and banish all other men but themselves from paradise forever. If the priests have convinced me with their words, and even if they have caused me also to convince others, they themselves have gained nothing. They themselves are neither richer nor poorer.

Ah, Munyasya, you must now again think of the poor hyena. When he cut the rope, he himself was also lost to his own paradise forever. Even when he accepted the bribe he was offered to carry out the evil act, he knew that would be the case, and he also knew that if he succeeded then paradise would always be for men and only for men. He did the only possible thing and hoped that he could rule life just as men would rule heaven.

But he was wrong!

They were all wrong!

But what can the priests gain from this conspiracy you describe? They are not rich and they never will be. Compared to what I have seen, not only elsewhere in the world, but also here in our own land, the Church is itself poor.

Remember, Munyasya, that those who pay the bribe win most of the profit. You have seen white men who are not priests. You have seen their fine riches and their fine countries where there is always plenty of food and plenty of rain. You have seen how they can stuff themselves with more and more of the fruit that even our poor land can grow and be happy to watch others grovel in the dust for the skins they drop.

And their priests? What do they, these people's hyenas, what do they get? A share of the skins?

Look around you, Munyasya. Look over there at the size and the obvious power of the great building before you. I have heard it said that your priests have built this place to be the heart of the lands they have won. This, and the lands that go with it, are their bribe. From Kyuso in the north, through Mwingi and Migwani to here; from here to Mutito in the east; to Yatta in the west and Ikutha in the south, all people like yourself, tricked into ignoring the still obvious truth, now look upon this place as the heart of the Church, as the manifestation of the power the Church embodies. It is a church, but a grand church, a parent to each and every other church, great or small, throughout our land. It is the new heart of the power.

The hyena's heart?

Indeed, the hyena's heart.

So we are going to shoot the church?

You are a stupid child sometimes, Munyasya. Can you still not see what it is that my words have shown?

Oh yes, I can see that, my friend. I can see everything, but perhaps only through your eyes. It is certainly very convincing, but I still cannot see how any of this can help me to rid myself of you! And I will not believe anything that you tell me until you can give me complete proof. If you can show me without doubt that this new knowledge can help me and can give me a chance of redeeming my life, then I would believe you. Indeed then I must believe you.

Now that I have explained everything to you, the plan is not difficult to describe, Munyasya. The heart continues to beat because its body protects it. Its body consists of all those people who have been tricked by its promises. Like you yourself have done, they have nurtured it, found joy in seeing it grow, believing that they will receive the benefits it has promised. You were promised those same things, Munyasya, but through me you now have learned that they were lies. What we must try to do...

We?

Yes, Munyasya, we: what we must do is to make that protected heart miss a beat, and then another beat, as many beats as possible. There are many people here who are under its spell. If we can lessen its power over them, then they can be released by the vision of their own thoughts in the same way that you have been reformed by my influence, my son.

They can be made to see the evil of which they are a part. I have seen the evil. Now you have seen it. We have seen this great church built here with labour that could surely have helped our poor people. Together we have seen your Father Michael, the Migwani priest-man-father, forget all the work that he says is so important to him as soon as his fine house burns down. And does he replace it with a house that would be fit for the likes of you, Munyasya, or even I, myself? Or does he rebuild his palace in the face of all the poverty that surrounds him? Of course he does, because he exists merely to bribe people like yourself, so he must show his wealth as a way of saying how able he remains to promise wealth to others. It is a share of these riches that he offers everyone who assists his trickery. You, Munyasya, shared some of those riches until such time that you could no longer be of any help. Then, when you were a poor and wretched and confused old man, they not only forgot all you did for them, but insulted you in public and then held you up as an example to the young so that they would be warned away from the misguided ways you had come to represent. If only we could have told these youngsters that the reason you had grown sick was because of these priests and their church and its lies!

If only... But my body does not allow it. Nzoka, I am a weak old man. Do you expect this frame to stand, to gather a crowd and convert them to your ideas with a rousing speech they cannot deny?

You are tired, Munyasya, my son. You can never do that, but for some time, while you have slept in the shade of your acacia tree in the market place, I have been keeping your eyes and ears open and I have been learning all those things that I have needed to understand life today in its own terms. I have learned that this priest...

Father Michael.

...I can never remember that strange name. The title 'Father' is very difficult to say... Anyway, this priest comes to Kitui from Migwani every week to visit this place before us. And here we are in Kitui. There are always people everywhere, many people coming and going. There is the great new cathedral and Kitui town's priests' house before us, and the post office behind, where people come for their money and their letters. And Kitui is the main town of the District. Whatever happens here is known within an hour throughout the whole area. Now we know that this priest thinks only of himself. We have seen it with your own eyes. Here, Munyasya, he will not be protected by the iron bars that guard the windows of his house. Here we shall meet on equal terms and he will show everyone that he cares not a thought for our people, not even for poor old Munyasya, who has devoted his life to the white man's work and a good part of it to his Church and its God. He is not here yet, but I know he is coming sooner rather than later. All we have to do is wait for him and be ready when he arrives.

But Nzoka, it is a strange place for me here. Nobody knows me. Who will feed me here? Who will give me my beer? There is no shade here and when a car or a bus goes past it sprays us with dust and stones from the road. I will not survive for long here. I need someone to help me. You can help me in spirit from inside this bag of bones, but I need food and drink to keep myself together.

You need not worry, Munyasya. It will not be long now. Will you carry out my plan? If you do, you will surely die, but it will give you one last chance to atone for your wrongs, but it will be a good chance. What will be seen here will be learned by many. When your heart ceases its beat, neither of us will know how many people will see through the evil conspiracy which tricks them into feeding and supporting their enemy. But, for every person who sees a new truth and whose own heart changes, one step along the road which we must travel together will be made easier for you, Munyasya. It is your chance to save the spirits of those still alive, and every success you have will help. Will you carry out my plan, my son?

If I say no, Nzoka, you can easily command me to act out whatever plan you have devised...

But then you cannot benefit from the results yourself, Munyasya.

I know that. Also if I were to hinder you, your plan would be more likely to fail. I fear that I have done that to you many times already. I have never really supported the things you have attempted and that has been why they have never quite succeeded. But if I help you and you are wrong, I am totally lost forever. I am putting my trust in you, Nzoka, because you are of my family. I am still not sure that you are right, but I can remember what you taught me as a child and you are speaking the same truths even now. Command and I will follow.

You are indeed brave, my son. I can be proud of you again. You and

I are both hunters now. All we can do is wait until the trap we have prepared is sprung. Enjoy one last sleep in life, Munyasya. Enjoy it now while I keep a watch for our prey.

***

Wake up! Wake up, boy! It's time. Come on. Get on your feet and walk. Quickly! Get those sticks of legs moving. It's not far. Only a few steps...
I'm still asleep.

Come on. It's not far. And I thought you would be fresher if you had a quick sleep! Come on. Wake up, Munyasya! If this priest of yours had not decided to stop again, we would have missed him already. My plan must be correct, because someone with a greater power than mine has helped us to carry it out. He came along the road and I prodded you, but did you wake up? He went up to that great church of his and I was still prodding you, but did you wake up?

I am getting too much like you in my old age, Nzoka. It was always you who was the lazy member of the family, as far as I can remember... And anyway I have had nothing to eat or drink since I came here. I am weak.

Well at least we have been lucky. I don't know why he decided to stop again at the side of the road, but at least it proves that God is on our side. We must be right. Everything is working in our favour. Now be careful not to let him see you. Be quiet and be careful. Move quickly, but quietly. It looks to me as if he is not even interested in what is going on around him. Careful, Munyasya, he will see you. If he recognises you we are finished... Now slowly, my son. Be careful. Lie down here. Be careful. Don't touch that machine of his. It may not be alive, but he can feel it when you touch.

It's only a piece of iron, Nzoka!

I don't care what it is. All I want is that you should take no chances. We're almost there. Lie down here, Munyasya... No! The other way! He will be able to see you if you lie there. Now lie down... Munyasya, that's it! We have done it! We have done it!

How many times have I heard you say that before? How many plans have you hatched since you came back from the dead to haunt me?

Don't move, Munyasya. Stay where you are! Be patient!

Move? How can I move with you sitting on me, Nzoka? I can't even lift my own legs these days, never mind set off in my own direction...

At last, Munyasya, this is it!

You sound very happy and very proud of yourself.

I've waited generations for this, my child, many many many more years than I ever should have.

Impatient as ever.

No, Munyasya, I know I am in control this time. It is not impatience you can hear this time, but confidence. I know I am right. And I know others will see it and that their attention will be fixed forever on what we both want them to see. Look! Over there! There are people coming down the hill... We'll even have an audience!

I hope you're right this time. You made me bang my head last time... And today I have not even had any beer. If that happens again, I will feel it this time. I hate to think what I will have to go through today if it turns out that you are wrong...

More audience, Munyasya! Look! There are a dozen people, no, even more than that! They are all coming this way. I hope they are not too busy driving their cows to see what will happen. It's going to work this time, Munyasya. And at last we have chosen the right place.

Father Michael does not seem ready to set off. Perhaps he is going to leave his car here all day and go down to the bar... It will be very hot lying here in the road all day waiting for him to come back. I'll get very thirsty.

You're always trying to prove me wrong, Munyasya. Look! Behind us! Another of these metal cows has come to watch. Munyasya, look there! It's stopped just behind the priest's machine and it's mooing.

It's in gear, Nzoka! You are right!

Calm down, Munyasya. Calm down, now. Didn't I tell you it would work? Are you all right?

All right? I'm dead!

I'm free.

But every bone in my body is broken! How did you ever expect me to walk the path like this?

Munyasya, look at all these people. Look at their faces. Look at your priest. He doesn't know what to do! We have done it, Munyasya. We have done it!

Nzoka, how did you ever expect me to be able to journey forward through the past with every bone in my body broken? How can I ever get back to paradise like this? You've tricked me again!

Be quiet, boy! Listen to what they say. It's important for both of us. If my plan works, they will turn on your priest. Maybe they will kill him and then they will have seen through all like him.

But, Nzoka, my bones...

Shh! Oh, Munyasya, my son, thank you for what you have done. You could not have been luckier than this. Look who has come from that other machine. It's Mulonzya, one of our great chiefs. Surely he will give you all the help you need. If anyone will uphold the values we both need to be strengthened, it is him.

Nzoka, everything is broken. My legs, arms, ribs, back, neck... I can't even stand up. I could do without a stomach. I don't need to eat any more. I could do without a head, for I have nothing to think about. But to walk a path as long as time itself without any legs...

Munyasya, we have won! Listen to what Mulonzya is saying! Listen to what he is saying about you, yourself, and these priests. He is praising you, demanding that everyone recognises your achievements in life. You are to be mourned, my son! It has worked perfectly.

But I need crutches, not words!

It will take time, Munyasya. No one is ever very well fitted to start their own journey. Death, after all, does not leave a man whole. Over time, acts of mourning, which these people here will carry out on your behalf, will strengthen your spirit and eventually rebuild it. When enough time has passed, they will then forget you. By then you will have been made strong enough to make your journey and, by letting your memory fade, helped by carefully never speaking your name, the living will release you so that you may start.

And you, Nzoka, for you are still tied to me.

That is still true, Munyasya. But at last the beginning of the end is in sight. Listen! He is now turning against your priest! It's worked! Mulonzya is saying that this priest does not live his own life by the rules he teaches to others.

Nzoka, I don't really care any more what he is saying. I want a beer.

Don't care? This man is saving you through these words. What men do is forgotten, but what they say is remembered. Can't you feel the strength he is giving to you? Can't you feel it beginning to grow? He will soon give you the final push you need to start you on your way.

But it hurts, Nzoka.

Of course it hurts, you idiot boy! You're dying! Everything has worked perfectly for both of us. I couldn't have asked for more. But listen, Munyasya, because what this man says can make things very much easier for us and, if we are still lucky, he will say everything that we will need.

Yes, Nzoka. It seems that everything you have asked for, I have received...

Well I think I can say that this is my part in the process finished, my son. Do you want me to help with your last breath? Or will you be able to manage it yourself?

Don't do anything more, Nzoka. It hurts.

There's no more I can do now. I am beginning to feel myself become free of you, my son. Your priests are condemned. You will be forgiven because you have surely saved hundreds of people from their deception and treachery, from the same fate that you yourself suffered and has caused you such problems in life and death. Through the example I have helped you set here today, you will be mourned and made strong and then you will be ready to start your own journey. People will remember the teaching, but forget the teacher as the knowledge becomes common.

Are you sure, Nzoka?

Completely. My plan cannot fail now. Everything has worked perfectly. And having a great chief here to witness the event and then to interpret it is surely proof that God wanted this to happen. We could not have been luckier, Munyasya, for now we are assured that our message will flow from the mouth of a great advocate. I think, now, my son, it is time I was on my way. How I have waited for this moment.

Impatient as ever, Nzoka. You should not leave me until we have met as equals.

But you have already taken your last breath.

That may be true, but my ribs cannot push it out...

My son. I have waited for you too long already. It's time I went. Until we meet again in paradise...

Don't shake my hand! It's broken and it hurts like hell. Ah! Ah! You had to beat me one last time! To hurt me again as you did when I was a child! Nzoka! Wait! Are you still listening to your great chief? Come back and listen! Come back! Ha, ha ha...

What is it now my boy? I was already on my way and you have breathed again. If you delay me for nothing, I will take a stick to you! What is so funny?

Listen to your friend Mulonzya! Listen to what he is saying! Ha, ha, ha...

What's he saying? Munyasya, tell me what he is saying. I can't hear! You've got another breath in your body. Will you never die? Tell me what's he saying?

Oh no, my friend. It was your idea. You had better learn to live with the results.

But you are not Munyasya Nzoka! What fool told him that was your name? He is called Munyasya. I am Nzoka. We are two people, different people. And I am now free of this half of a man who calls himself Munyasya. He is the one you want and his name is Munyasya Maluki. I am Nzoka. I have nothing to do with him any more. Munyasya, say something while you still have a breath in your body! Say something, man! Tell him he has spoken your name wrongly!

Listen, Nzoka. This is just what you always wanted to hear. Munyasya Nzoka they call me. I am you. I have become you and you have become me. Over these years when you have lived again inside this body, you have taken the power of life into yourself and made it your own. You have acted in this world and become a part of it. And now they will remember your deeds, not mine, for they never were mine, and they will remember your name alongside mine, for we are joined in their memory. Your plan did work in one way, but...

Munyasya, what are you saying? It has worked. People have seen this priest exposed for what he is.

But he is not the hyena you stalked, Nzoka. You left a trap for a hyena and caught a gazelle. It is the hyena who is speaking now and he has condemned both of us, both you and I, to eternal death by demanding that we will live forever in the memory of this place. There, he said it again. Munyasya Nzoka, your name will live forever here. It is your great chief who is the hyena. It is he, Mulonzya, who is destroying the values you came back to rediscover. Hear what he has said of Munyasya Nzoka, you and I. We are to be honoured forever by a monument for what we have shown today.

But this is not what I wanted, Munyasya!

Ha, ha. Nzoka, but wait a moment. Listen again to what your great chief, for whom you show such respect, has said. He has also said that the people of this place will remember what has happened forever. And again, they will place a plaque here by the road to mourn the tragic death of Munyasya Nzoka so that everyone will remember our name and the circumstances of this death forever. His jaws have closed on us, Nzoka. You chose the wrong target. We are now companions in this place, where people will forever speak the names of the dead. And so we will be tied to this place, imprisoned here for all time.

Munyasya, one last breath! Say something to the man. He is wrong! Tell him he is wrong!

Ha, ha, ha, ha, ha...

Printed in the United Kingdom
by Lightning Source UK Ltd.
132855UK00001B/7/A